His Power Over Me

By

Tracey Haynick

Copyright © 2017 by Tracey Haynick

Published in the United States by Tracey Haynick

Cover design and art direction: Tracey Haynick

Editor: Michelle E Zieske

All Rights Reserved. No part of this book may be reproduced in any form without written consent of the publisher, except brief quotes used in reviews.

His Power Over Me is a work of fiction. Any references or similarities to actual events, real people, living or dead, or to real locals are intended to give the novel a sense of reality. Any similarity in other names, characters, places and incidents are entirely coincidental.

I want to dedicate this book to my family. To my daughter, my first true love. You taught me how to love unselfishly from the moment our eyes met. You are my "person". To my husband, my only real love. Thank you for loving me and supporting me through this and encouraging me to keep going when I felt I couldn't do it. To my son, my surprise blessing made from real love. What an amazing little bundle of joy, I never saw coming. To my parents for their never-ending love and support. I am truly blessed to have parents like you to set the example of how real love truly looks. To my siblings... Life's first set of best friends... Words can never say the love I feel for you. To my best friends... My tribe, Missy, Megan, Hannah, Betty and Denise, for telling me to dream as big as the sky. I love you girls. Finally, to the rest of my friends and family. Thank you for all your love and support.

I have a very special dedication to one of my many angels in heaven... Patty. We bonded at times, sadly over the commonness of abuse from our past... yet our love for each other grew, more, from sharing the commonness of something better... Love. Love, for the same wonderful man... your son. I will always, take care of him for you, and share your life and story with your grandchildren.

I love my family... Always and forever.

Chapter 1

"Margo, it's time to get up." I hear my mom calling to me. I wish I could just keep sleeping, but I know I must get up and get my chores done.

"Okay." I say, really wanting to say something more flippant, but I bite my tongue. I don't want to do anything to get myself in trouble so that I get grounded and miss the big party tonight. Getting dressed quickly, I hurry out to the barn to go feed the horses. Hoping the fact that I hurry up, will give me first dibs in the shower. Having a big family means not always getting hot water when you try to shower.

Lauren is already out in the barn doing some stuff when I get out there, but I don't have to worry about her wanting to shower. In fact, I'm surprised she is here because she technically moved out on her own already.

"Hey why are you here? If I didn't have to be, I wouldn't be here." I say in a pissy mood, I'm not a morning person.

"Dad asked if I could stop by this morning and help because he had to go into work early." she says.

"Well of course because God forbid mom comes out and helps." I bitch, and I am about to say more when she cuts me off.

"Margo stop, it's too early for your attitude. Cut mom some slack, besides I thought you said you have plans tonight?"

Staring at me in her bossy, I'm older than you are way, I just roll my eyes and answer. "I'm just going to Shelby's, it's not exactly earth shattering."

"What about Megan? Are those two friends now?" Good grief she is being nosy.

"No, they aren't, but I'm still hoping they will eventually be friends." I hate talking about those two not getting along. I want us to all live together in New York City after graduation. I want out of West Seneca so bad and this boring small-town lifestyle. I know I'll need roommates to make it work financially, so I'm hoping they can learn to like each other.

"That's never going to happen, you do know that? Right? Those two are like oil and water, they just don't mix." she says. I know she's right, but Megan is my best friend, and I've known Shelby since I was eight. I so badly want this to happen for us.

"You never know, if we all head to the city together they could learn to like each other."

"Let me know how that turns out. I hope it works out for you." Lauren smiles and finishes up with watering the horses. I smile back to her and start walking back towards the house. I know she means well, but sometimes I think she forgets she's only a year older than me. Maybe it's being the oldest child, that makes her feel like it's her responsibility to always set the standard for good behavior. I know she doesn't mean to do it, but sometimes it's a hard standard to live up to.

When I get back in the house, I rush into the shower so thankful I beat Brittany to it this morning. While I'm showering my mind drifts off to my conversation with Shelby yesterday.

"You have to figure out how to get to the party my cousin's friend is having tomorrow night." she said when she rushed up to me after our last period.

"You know my mom will never let me go to a party and you know if I say I'm staying over, your mom won't lie to her for us." I said.

"Okay, but Justin is going..." She trails off and waits for it to register.

"Are you sure? He is actually going?" I instantly get a faraway dreamy look in my eyes. I have liked Justin since seventh grade. If he is going to this party too, he will see I can be cool and maybe he will want to go out with me.

"I'm almost positive he is going, Kevin said he is. I can double check, but do you want to risk it if he does and you don't go?" she smiles then says "Who knows, this could be the party that makes him like you. Margo, you just have to come." She knows how much I like him and I'm so grateful she is trying to help me impress him.

"Okay. I'll figure it out, can I invite Megan? I think it would be fun for all of us to do something together." I hold my breath hoping she will say yes.

"Oh sure, what the hell. If you think you can get her to come party with the big kids, go for it." I think she's being flip, but I'm just happy she didn't say no.

"Okay." I laugh in case she's being funny. "I'll ask her, and I'll call you later to figure it all out. I have to go, you know if I get home late my mom will flip out and be worried." I run to my car, so I can hurry home.

Someone knocking on the bathroom door breaks into my thoughts. I realize it's Brittany and I know if I don't hurry she will somehow manage to get me in trouble. "Okay, I'm almost done, I'll be out in a minute." I yell. I hurry up and finish my shower, so I can get ready to head to work.

I get to work so hyped up and ready to go to the party that the day is flying by. I almost forget I still need to call Megan. I talked to her earlier, but I couldn't mention the party. I ask on my break if I can use the phone in the office and my boss says sure.

"Hello?" I hear Megan's voice.

"Hey Megan, it's me, I'm so sorry I haven't been able to call back until now." I'm so happy I can't stop smiling.

"Oh, that's okay. What's going on? You said something about getting together later? Maybe?"

"Yes, I'm going to spend the night at Shelby's. We are going to a party and I wanted to know if you wanted to go?" I realize I'm holding my breath hoping she will say yes.

"Oh, um, who's party?" I can tell by her tone she isn't going to go, I know her better than anyone. If I even have a shot, I need to try fast to change her mind.

"No one we know but Megan, Justin is going. Shelby said he's going to be there and I really want you to go with me. You know I need you there, so I don't embarrass myself. Please..." I trail off.

"How did you get your mom to let you go?" I knew she would ask that.

"I lied. I told her we are hanging out at Shelby's and watching movies. You know she won't let me go to a party." I feel my heart sink because I know she won't go now.

"Look, I hope you have fun I honestly do, and I hope Justin can see you are an amazing girl. Margo, I'm not covering for you though. Tell your mom I'm not going to Shelby's. If she calls here and asks, I'm not lying and saying I am."

"Damn it, Megan." I feel my voice shaking and I know I'm going to cry. "Can't you just this one time not be so good? Shelby's mom isn't going to answer the phone, you won't have to lie. My mom isn't going to know. If you aren't home to answer her call you won't have to lie." I feel like a jerk getting mad, but my mom trusts Megan and I also want her to go.

"I'm sorry I can't. Besides I already have plans tonight." she says.

"With who? Doing what? Can't you change them? Do you even care I'm your best friend and I need you?" I know I'm making her feel bad, but I don't care.

"I have plans with Darby and no I can't change them." she says a little firmer.

"Fine." I say in my most fuck you tone. "Have fun with your new best friend. I won't forget this, I don't need you for anything anyways." I slam the phone down on her. I can't believe she won't lie to my mom for me. I know it's because of Darby. I can't stand that girl and I don't see how Megan can even be friends with a girl like her. I go back to work and try to forget all about Megan, and just think about Justin and the party later.

Finally, I get to Shelby's and I'm so excited for this party I can hardly contain my excitement. We tell her mom that my mom wants her to go to church with her, so maybe she should just ignore her calls for a few days. I think it's a brilliant plan to avoid them talking to each other. Shelby's mom hates anything to do with church and religion stuff.

Shelby and I disappear to her bedroom to get ready, we have the music blasting, and no one is yelling at us to turn it down. It's something I could never do in my house. She is so lucky to be able to do whatever she wants. No one tells her what to do and they just trust her to do the right thing. I can't hardly have music on at all or I get yelled at. Plus, there is no way I could listen to rap music either, especially not the kind we are listening to tonight. It feels so good to feel so free for a change.

Shelby tells me for sure Justin will be there, that she heard this from Kevin, he's her new boyfriend. I have met him a couple times, he's older than us and seems nice. He hangs out with a group of kids I don't really know but everyone thinks they are cool. Leave it to Shelby to have an older boyfriend and he's cool too.

I wish I was more like her. "Thank you for letting me borrow an outfit and jewelry." I say to her. She is so lucky to be pretty and have nice things and mostly, she has freedom. Her mom lets her do whatever she wants, and it kills me because I'm older.

"I hope this party plays good music, I feel like dancing" Shelby says over the music. She gets up and starts to dance a little as she's looking for an outfit for herself. She can dance good and of course she has a great singing voice too.

"I wish I could dance like you," and be cool, I think. "Thank you for inviting me, I'm so excited to party." I yell. I'm glad she wants to be my friend and invites me to cool parties like tonight.

"No problem, guess what?" she doesn't wait for me to answer, "Kevin and I had sex." She says so matter of fact. I try to act like it's not a big deal and as if I know all the stuff she's talking about. "He likes the way I go down on him, and he told me I'm the best ass he's ever had." she says smiling then adds, "But I'm going to get on the pill or something because he hates condoms."

"Wow, that's great, but will your mom let you?" I say, trying to think of something else to add, when her sister comes in and they start talking. I'm thankful for the distraction, so I can think a little. What would it be like for a guy to love me enough to want to have sex with me? I wonder if I will ever fall in love, or if any guy will ever be able to fall in love with me? I wish I had a killer body, or I was pretty. I so badly want to fall in love and be like Shelby.

I think about Brittany and how she always says I'm ugly and no guys will ever like me. The other day I picked her up from work and it was a disaster from the moment I walked in.

"Hey fat ass," is how she loudly greets me from across the store. "Look Tom, it's my older nasty sister, she can't bother to fix her hair or try to look nice because she knows it won't matter. I mean look at her, she's so gross." She says this to her boss, who she is standing too close to, hanging on his am. She knows exactly how to push my buttons, and I instantly get pissed. Why does she do this shit all the time? So instead of taking the high road like I know I should and ignoring her, I take her bait.

"Well let's see bitch, I actually work at my job instead of flirting with my old ugly boss to try and get ahead." I say all of this not caring how mean I sound, and not caring that her boss's mouth is gaping open and his jaw just hit the floor.

"You're just jealous someone hot like him likes me over you." she says back.

This is what she wanted to happen in front of her boss and coworkers. To point out once again how no guy likes me, and I'm not cute enough and she can get any guy she wants. Well once again I fall for her shit and I'm responding the way she wants.

"Let's go or you can walk, by the way Tom," I add sweetly, "My dad has a twelve gage and he's willing to use it on old married men trying to fuck his fifteen-year-old." I look him up and down and turn and walk away. It wasn't my best moment in life, and not something Lauren would have done but it felt good.

Shelby's sister leaves and I snap back to reality when she says to me, "My mom won't know anything, I'm going to go to Planned Parenthood and I can get them there." Referring to the pill. I have no idea where or what that is, so I start putting on lipstick, so I can just mmmhmmm her and not talk. Sometimes I wish I knew more about life. We finish getting ready and finally head out to the party.

Oh my gosh I think. We are here, finally at the party. We just pulled into a driveway and I'm so excited I can hardly sit still. I pull out a cigarette because, well it looks cool and it will give me something to focus on in case I'm nervous. I've played this scene over and over in my head for weeks. Walking into a beautiful house, seeing everyone dancing and drinking and just having the best time ever. I guess I wasn't prepared for the reality of what It really is.

We walk into a mostly unfurnished, beat up little house full of blue smoke. It is so dark my eyes can't adjust at first, all the lights are on, but the shades are just so dirty it seems gloomy and dark. There is music blaring, but it is heavy metal, and no one is dancing. People are all sitting around the house in random places, like on folding chairs, a dirty loveseat and milk crates. We take a few moments to say hi to some people, mostly people I don't know. There is so much smoke, my eyes are already burning but I don't want to complain, after all I am smoking too.

I follow Shelby in to the next room, which is a tiny outdated kitchen. She grabs me a beer and I happily take it, thinking holy shit my first beer. I crack it open and take a big swig, and it is the worst tasting thing I've ever put in my mouth. It is this warm bitter grossness I can barely swallow. All I can think is, why do people drink this and why did I want to so badly?

I smile though and act as if I'm enjoying it and finally look around the kitchen better. I see a pile of what looks like dead dried up plants or something on the kitchen table. I ask Shelby what is that and she laughs at me.

"Oh my God, you're so sheltered, its pot." She says.

I laugh and say "Oh my god I couldn't really see, my eyes are bad. I've seen pot, I've actually tried it with Megan." I am totally lying, and seriously trying to cover my ass for not knowing. I know she will never ask Megan so, I doubt she will ever know the truth.

I somehow finish that first nasty warm beer and someone thrusts a second warm beer into my hands. I start sipping on it to keep from talking, with a fake ass smile plastered across my face. Looking around the room I realize it's a crowd of people I never talk to. People I would never hang out with. I really don't want to be here now, but what can I do? I'm hoping this is a first stop to another party and this isn't "the" party for the night. Maybe Shelby promised to swing by this one too. I just feel so out of place.

After about an hour I realize this is, indeed "the" party. The one I've been waiting for, what a disappointment. At this point I need to pee, so I find the bathroom and lock myself in there for a minute, thinking I can collect myself. I once again look around in horror and realize I'm not sure how I can even pee in here.

It is so gross, I can see urine all over the seat and all around the floor. I can't believe I'm thinking this right now, but I see why my mom is a freak about keeping the bathroom clean. I finally decide to just squat over the bowl. It's not going to matter anyways if I drip piss on the seat, because from the brown ugly stains in and around the toilet, I don't think anyone cares. I feel so disgusting afterwards, even though I didn't touch anything.

I walk out of the bathroom thinking why the hell did I think a party would be so cool? Too much TV that's for sure. I've watched one too many high school teen movies I think, laughing to myself. I look towards the living room and I see a whole bunch of people standing around someone. I notice a small crowd is forming so I go check it out.

Oh my God it's him, Justin. The kid I've liked since sixth grade. The boy that just embarrassed me and said he wouldn't go with me to homecoming. The guy I can't even be mad at because I have liked him for seven years. Oh my God, he's here. He will see now I'm cool and maybe, just maybe decide to finally ask me out.

He pulls this bag out of his pocket, and says "So who's ready to do some lines?"

I completely freeze. All I can think is, I'll drink some warm nasty beer, I'll even throw back a shot of whatever, but I'm never ever doing drugs. I feel like crying. I look at Shelby to catch her eye, hoping she can see I want to leave.

Shelby jumps up instead and says, "Finally Justin, I didn't think you were going to show."

In what feels like slow motion, I watch her snatch the bag from him, lay it on the table and do some weird shit with her driver's license and use a tiny straw to snort it up. I want to run, yet my feet won't move.

Finally, my brain starts working, and I quietly shrink back into the dirty living room, trying to blend into the wall. I have so many thoughts going through my head. At this point, I just want to leave. When did Shelby start doing drugs? How did I not know? I feel stupid when I realize I wish my mom caught my lie and never let me come.

I know drugs are something I want no part of. I want to get out of this town and I'm realizing this is the typical trailer trash shit you read about. Girl goes to party, girl gets stoned, girl gets raped, or has sex with a random guy, has baby, gets stuck raising that baby alone and lives on welfare for the rest of her life. I have big dreams and being stuck in a shitty trailer park for the rest of my life raising some brat I don't want, isn't that dream.

I stand there for what feels like an hour, when a voice breaks into my thoughts.

"Holy shit is that Margo?" I look up and it's him, Justin, speaking to me.

I say a timid hi to him, not really wanting to have a conversation with him now.

"Well shit had I known you were here I would have saved you some of the good shit." he says.

Still trying to be cool though, I say "Oh no, are you serious, it's all gone?" To which he says yes, and he apologizes and says he might get more later. I say something lame like cool let me know, the whole time I'm terrified somehow my dad is going to bust through the door and drag me out by my hair. I also realize right then, even though I still want to look cool, I lost any crush I had on him in that moment. I don't find drug dealers or users appealing.

I finally get Shelby alone and tell her I don't want to stay much longer, trying to play it off that I drank more than I did, and I'm drunk. She says that's fine she's getting shitfaced, and we would leave soon. A few minutes later though her boyfriend finally shows up and before I can stop her, they disappear upstairs. So instead I grab another beer, and at some point, someone hands me a shot or two. The next thing I know I'm back in that nasty bathroom, vomiting. I'm trying to keep my cool, I never really drank before, and this isn't at all what I thought it would feel like. Eventually I find Shelby again, so I get her attention and say we need to go.

Shelby agrees, and we say our goodbyes. We get in her car and after driving around for what feels like hours, we somehow drunkenly make it back to her house. I silently thank God, we didn't kill anyone or ourselves on the way. There is a short period of time, where I am silently praying for my life when I notice she can't keep the car straight. Once again though trying to be cool, I am too afraid to speak up. All I want to do is go to sleep and forget this night ever happened.

Chapter 2

Oh my god, the morning light is killing me. What the hell? My head is pounding, and I feel like throwing up again. I spent half the night sprawled out on Shelby's bathroom floor because I couldn't stop throwing up. I know I should hurry and get home soon, my mom expects us kids home early when we stay over at a friend's house. God forbid she lifts a finger and does anything herself around the house. I know I have a shit ton of chores to do and I feel awful. I think maybe I'm getting the flu.

I nudge Shelby and tell her I'm going to take off. She hardly stirs and kind of lifts her arm in an okay, go away I'm sleeping kind of way. I get up and head out to leave when I feel this terrible pounding in my head and I'm overcome by the need to vomit. I run into the bathroom and I get sick again. Yes, I think, that must be it. I must have the flu. I clean off my face and do my best to tie my hair back, and I see I now have gross vomit in it.

I go out to my car and the cold November air burns my nostrils, but it feels so nice, I just let it engulf me for a minute. I finally feel a little better and I head home. I know my mom is going to be pissy for not getting a phone call. I need to try and think about what my story is, so I can say it as convincing as I can. She can smell a lie a mile away and I feel down right awful, I don't need her shit today.

I just make it home, when I feel the need to vomit again. I fling open my car door and fly out of my car to the grass on the side of the house and throw up yet again. I'm on my hands and knees in the mud, filthy, with vomit in my hair and on my clothes. I'm a mess and I feel like I have been run over by a truck.

By the time I have strength and I walk into the house I look as bad as I feel. There is no sign of my mom, so I hurry up and jump in the shower. It feels good to wash my hair and get the vomit and smoke smell off me. The mixture of it in my hair sends waves of nausea over my body again, but I'm able to control it this time. I just sit on the floor of the shower and let the water run over me.

Finally, after sitting there forever, I know I should get out and start my chores, but I just feel so awful. I try to go get some toast thinking that might help, but I just can't do it. My hands are shaking, and I can barely stay standing up, so I quickly slide into the breakfast nook before my legs give out. Right at this time my mom comes out and sees me and I'm prepared for the lecture and grounding, but instead I hear "Are you sick? You look sick."

She already has her hand on my head and tells me I'm clammy to go lay down. I'm thinking holy shit, she's being nice. She surprises me even more, a few minutes later when she brings me soup broth, toast and some hot tea. Wow, it's been awhile since my mom has been this nice to me. She didn't even yell at me. I start to think maybe she isn't that bad, and maybe she does still love me.

I eat and drink a little and curl up in my bed and sleep almost all day. My mom lovingly comes in to check on me throughout the day. I love that she is being so nice and really showering me with love. We almost feel close like we used to be, before my brother got sick. At this moment right now, I love and need my mom so very much.

I don't blame my brother for getting sick, he's just a kid. I seriously love that little brat too. The problem is, when he almost died a year ago, a few things happened to my family. My mom got clingy to him understandably, but also to all of us. She wants us to live in a safe little bubble, and it's just not realistic.

Another thing that happened, was Brittany. She got jealous of the attention Tony started getting and she started any drama she could to pull attention to herself, even lying. My mom is so busy worrying and fixating on our health, she can't see Brittany's lies. Lauren is pretty much always gone now that she doesn't live here, so I get the brunt of Brittany's bullshit. Every time my mother believes her over me, it puts a bigger strain on our relationship too. I just don't know why my mom thinks I'm so bad? It makes me count down the days to moving out on my own.

By evening I start feeling better, and I can get up and move around. In the meantime, Brittany comes into our room and starts primping. To be polite I ask her what she is getting all dolled up for and trying to be nice. I tell her she looks pretty.

"My new boyfriend Steve is coming by and bringing some friends to meet mom and dad."

Oh of course, a new boyfriend again. How is it I get told I'm not allowed to date, yet this girl can? My parents make a big deal about me going anywhere, and who I'm with and call and check on me. Brittany though, does what she wants, when she wants, with whomever she wants. It really makes no sense to me at all.

I decide maybe I should try to look nice too, I just hate when people come over and I look like shit. I start fixing my hair and putting makeup on when Brittany looks over at me and says, "You know God loved me more, right?"

I'm a little confused so I say, "Oh really?" laughing, "How would you know that?" thinking she's so weird.

Her response to me is, "Well look at me and look at you, it's obvious, I'm pretty and you aren't. It's obvious then, he loved me more." She hops off her stool and gives me a huge fuck you smile and takes off before I can even react.

Tears well up in my eyes and I focus hard to keep them at bay. I just finished my makeup and I don't want smears all over my face, especially not because of her. I don't know why she always says mean things to me, but it really hurts. I know I'm not the prettiest girl in the world, but I don't need to hear it all the time. I don't know why she points it out all the time that she's so much prettier. I have eyes and I can see it, I know she is.

I head upstairs just in time for her new boyfriend to make an entrance, and his friends to pile into the kitchen. They look like an interesting group of guys. My mom tells them to go in the living room, she is going to head downstairs to grab snacks to make from the basement freezer.

I decide to head into the living room and see how it goes. Hoping just once my sister will be nice. Right on cue she pops up from the chair she's in and gives me the biggest hug. Then while still holding me in a side hug like she loves me, she says "Hey guys, this is my sister."

I smile thinking wow she's being nice, feeling grateful. My thought isn't even fully finished when I hear her say, "Before you ask no I'm not adopted, but apparently every family needs a pretty one, and well, that's me" she laughs, then they all laugh, and I stand there red faced and fuming.

I look at the boys and fire back at her, "And every family has that slut willing to fuck anything, and well, that's you too." I shove her away from me, and I take off to go outside. I can hear her calling my mom, but I don't care. She has no reason to act that way, yet she does.

Even though it is freezing outside I don't care, I enjoy the cold. I just want to go out and feel the cold air and get away from her. I just wish my parents weren't here, so I could smoke. Why does she hate me so much? What did I ever do to her? I just don't get it.

A few minutes later, I'm startled to hear "Hey, ignore her, she's just jealous of you." I turn around and one of her boyfriend's friends came outside. I could die, I'm embarrassed because I'm crying, and he caught me.

I laugh a little and say, "You must need glasses, there's no way she's jealous of me, I promise."

He walks right up to me looks me straight in the eyes and says, "She is, and it's because she knows you are the better sister, so she tries to make you feel like less. Don't let her do that to you."

For a second, I honestly think I am making this whole thing up in my head. "My name is Christopher, well call me Chris."

He shakes my hand and won't let go, I don't know what to do so I say. "I'm Margo."

He says, "I know, and next weekend I'll be back, and we'll go to dinner."

I cocked my head to the side and say, "Will we now?" kind of laughing.

He locks eyes with me and says, "Don't laugh at me it's not nice, I'll pick you up Friday."

I answer, "Well, I can't, I work Friday till close which is midnight and I have a curfew."

He smirks and says, "Okay fine I'll see you Saturday at six." He steps closer to me, pulls me to him, and kisses me. A real kiss. I feel like I just stepped into the twilight zone. I have never had something like this happen to me, and I'm not sure it's even real. He lets go of me and just walks back into the house.

I eventually go back inside and try to engage in what was happening in the living room, but I can't wrap my head around what just happened outside. Who is this guy, and why the hell would he be interested in me? Maybe he thinks I'm fun and crazy like my sister? I need to let him know I'm not like her, but then if I do, he may not like me or want to go out. I find his bold almost bossy way attractive, and something about it makes me want to get to know him more.

"Hey earth to Margo." I hear Brittany say and everyone is looking at me.

"Oh, I'm sorry what?" I blush.

"Oh, I was just wondering since you're a fat ass and love food and work at a pizza place, do you eat a large pizza every night to stay looking like that or just every other night? Really, what's your secret?" I seriously hate this girl.

"Fuck you." I say just as my mom walks in and hears me.

"Margo, you can go to your room. You don't talk like that to your sister." I glance over, and Chris is just shaking his head no, I think he's mad.

I try to tell her what happened "Mom she..." but Britany cuts me off louder.

"Mom all I did was ask her if she could give me a ride to work tomorrow." Fake tears glistening in her eyes and all. That lying bitch. I hear my mom telling her yes, I'll give her a ride and if I don't watch my mouth I won't be doing anything the next weekend. I just glare at my sister, but I go to my room.

All I can think is how much I hate living here and I can't wait to move out and never come back. Well the truce didn't last long; my mom is back to her mean self now. I wish just once she would listen, really listen to me.

Being sent to my room though, gives me time to think about what happened outside. That was the strangest thing on the planet. What if he just said that and he is planning to stand me up to be mean? Why though, would a guy do that? Maybe because I was crying, and he felt bad. Maybe he is serious. He didn't even give me his phone number, so I can't call to be sure. How will I know for sure he plans to still come? I can't risk going back upstairs to ask though, because my mom will probably ground me and then I wouldn't be able to go anyways. I guess I will just have to wait and see.

The whole week is a drag, school is awful, work is boring and I'm fighting at home with everyone. I swear they have all lost their minds. I can't wait to see if Chris will come back, and if we go out on a real date. I am incredibly nervous but excited too. I never had a real "boyfriend" so what if he is the one? Someone to hold hands with, or even fall in love with.

 I fantasize all week that we will hold hands and kiss and watch movies together snuggled up by a fireplace. I keep thinking of all the ways it's going to be so romantic. I know I am letting my mind run wild, but I just have a feeling it is going to be wonderful. I know, I just know in my heart I will finally have love. This is the guy that sees me for who I am. He wants me, not someone like Brittany. Me. I can't wait until Saturday.

 Saturday Is finally here and I'm so excited. I bought a new outfit, and I got some new makeup to try out too. I don't care what my mom says about it either. I painted my nails this morning, so they would look nice and I showered earlier too. My makeup is already done, all I have left to do is my hair, and get dressed.

Brittany comes bursting through the door, all fired up and in a mood. "Why the hell did you have to throw yourself at Steve's friend?" she yells at me.

I'm a little dumbfounded and I reply "I didn't, he asked me out. I didn't do anything."

She looks me up and down and says, "No sweetheart he feels bad for you and is doing his good deed for the year." with that she stomps out of the room, throwing over her shoulder on the way out. "Trust me. Steve told me, he's so embarrassed about it. I'll bet you anything, he will probably take you to McDonalds and make you eat in the car to hide you."

I'm trying not to cry. Why did I agree to this, why do I set myself up for this shit? I'm just going to tell him I'm sick and can't go. I take a few minutes to collect myself, I fix my hair and finish getting dressed and head upstairs. I know I'll be telling him I can't go, but I still want to look the best I can when doing it.

I'm preparing what I'll say to him when he gets here, when I turn the corner and there he is. He is standing in the kitchen talking about cars with my father. I can feel my legs trembling as I force them to move forward to him. I can't believe I have to do this face to face.

Blushing I walk up to him, and right before I can say anything he says, "You.Are.Beautiful." That's it. Three words that make me change my mind, three words I've wanted to hear from a boy for so long. Three words I've never thought I'd ever hear, at that moment I was gone. I was his, and his smile says he knows it.

I look at my sister and I just beam, she does her little fuck you look and walks away. No, she stomps away, and we hear the door slam downstairs in our bedroom. I tell my mom I'll be home by one a.m., she then counters with midnight. I don't even argue. A boy likes me, and he thinks I'm beautiful.

We head out for our date and I'm so excited. I can't wait to go to a romantic restaurant and be "wined and dined". I know my dad still takes my mom out on dates and they have been married for centuries. Oh my gosh, what if we get married one day and have a family? I could be a cool mom, one that understands life. All previous thoughts of never having children go right out the window. I realize it's our first date, but I seriously feel like he hangs the moon.

"So, I'm thinking we just grab a quick bite at Wendy's before we go to my uncle's house, I really want you to meet him." Chris says I'm still flying high on him saying I'm beautiful, so I happily agree. I'm not sure what we will do at his uncle's and I don't care. I just want to be with him, and right now being in his car listening to music is exactly where I want to be.

He interrupts my thoughts a little bit later asking, "What do you want?" I didn't even realize we are already at the drive through window. I need to pay attention and stop daydreaming.

"I'll just have a Jr bacon cheeseburger please." I say, my favorite at Wendy's.

He kind of gives me a funny look and says, "Are you sure you don't want a salad?"

I say "Oh, no thank you, I love the Jr bacon cheeseburgers."

He looks at me for a minute, then orders a salad. I'm a little disappointed, and he says, "I don't want a fat girlfriend, you can have a salad."

I blush, but laugh and say, "I'm hardly even close to fat"

I'm confused by the comment because I'm five feet nine inches tall, at only one hundred and twenty-five pounds, with a solid athletic build that I work very hard at keeping. I work out daily and lift weights to keep my body lean, yet strong. I have never had a weight problem in fact, I used to get made fun of for being too thin.

"For now, you'll do," he interrupts my thoughts, then adds "but if you get fat you're out. I won't date a fat chick."

I laugh and say okay, I honestly think he's kidding and just prefers to eat healthy which is fine. I love salads. I let it go, I don't want to make a big deal out of nothing on our first date.

He pulls forward and grabs our food, then we start eating, in his car. My sister's words come back to me and suddenly I'm feeling very insecure. Maybe he doesn't want to be seen with me.

I decide to ask, "Chris, is there a reason you don't want to go eat at an actual restaurant?"

He looks at me, glares, then says "Oh I had you all wrong, I see this date was about me spending money on you? If that's what you want, go find someone else."

I'm completely at a loss, and fumble to say, "No, no that's not it, I'm sorry." as tears well up in my eyes. I need to fix this, "My sister said you were embarrassed to be seen with me that's all."

He looks over at me and replies "Your sister is a whore and doesn't know anything." He won me back in that instant.

"I'm so sorry, I never should have listened to her." I look up at him and smile shyly.

He smiles again, then grabs my hand and says, "It's okay, she's the type of girl a guy likes to fuck, but you're the type of girl a guy wants to marry." with that he puts the car in reverse and we start heading to his uncle's.

He just said marry. I completely ignore the part about her being the one guys are sexually attracted to. Instead, I think about how one day he would want to marry me. Could a guy really like me enough to see a future with me? I realize we are just starting to date, but he is completely filling my heart up with so much hope already. I never imagined I could ever find real love.

Someone loving me has always been an unimaginable dream for me, especially after every mean comment Brittany has said about my looks and body. Those mean remarks have made me wonder, over and over if a guy could ever like me. Yet here I am, on a date with a guy that said I'm the type of girl a man will want to marry. In my head I'm telling Brittany to fuck off. I can't stop smiling now.

We arrive at his uncle's house about ten minutes later. I only go to Buffalo to shop at the mall or if my parents take us kids to something special. My little town is so small it doesn't even have a Wal-mart. It is exciting going to a bigger city without my parents, although they probably won't approve. I don't know what to expect at his uncle's or understand why he would want to hang out there. All I can compare it to is my own family and well while great, my uncles are well, just uncles.

I am in no way prepared for the over the top, beer drinking uncle he has. He is younger and cooler, and a bit intimidating. He has a nice, beautiful wife and three cute little kids. He right away offers me a beer, and I have the terrible taste still left in my mouth from that terrible party I went to, so I say no thank you.

He immediately turns to Chris and says, "Why did you bring this uptight chick here? Dude, you guys can leave."

I almost die. Chris looks at me and glares as if I just castrated him in front of someone. I want the floor to swallow me up. I quickly recover, laugh and say, "Oh my God I'll take a beer, I thought being his uncle and all I should be proper and say no."

I go grab the beer crack it open and take a swig, It's not that bad. It's cold and has a better not so bitter taste. We all sit down around the table, and I see his uncle and aunt smoke, so I reach into my purse and grab one of my cigarettes. I'm just about to light it when Chris yanks it out of my mouth and says, "No."

I just look at him, and he says, "I'm not going to have a girlfriend that smokes." I know I should be mad at him, but he just called me his girlfriend.

His uncle butts in and says, "Whoa dude you going to let him tell you what to do?"

I know I should stand up for myself, but I hear myself defending him "No, he's not, I want to quit. He's been helping me." Chris smiles, and thankfully his uncle moves on from it, but I can't help feeling little shocked by it. The rest of the visit goes okay, but I find myself getting bored quickly.

We finally leave and are heading back to my house which takes about twenty minutes or so, and I get up the nerve to say something. "What was the whole cigarette thing? You knew I smoked when you asked me out."

He responds with "If you want to be with me you're done."

I try to stand my ground a little, "Chris, I have a father I don't need another one."

His next words cut deep, "Brittany doesn't smoke huh? Maybe she wants to go out."

I want to cry, that was a low blow but all I say instead is, "I'm just kidding, I want to quit anyways." I know now, if I want to date him I must stop smoking.

The rest of the drive is quiet, we have music on, so I just sing quietly. When we get back to my house he tells me he had the best time ever. He says he is so happy and asks if I want to go out again, of course I answer with yes. He kisses me and tells me he knows; really knows in his heart he is falling in love with me. He adds between kisses, if I behave and let him love me, our life will be so good together. It is such heady stuff. I know it was the best early birthday gift anyone could ever give me. Love. It's all I ever wanted and here I am with this guy telling me, he loves me.

Chapter 3

The next few days fly by and I am so happy to see him again for my birthday. This time he takes me to a restaurant and we have a nice dinner. He wants to go to the mall after dinner and walk around so I say sure why not, I love the mall. While we are there, we stop in at one of my favorite stores to window shop. Instead spontaneously I sign up to get a credit card and buy a leather jacket.

It is a beautiful long, just past my butt, yet form fitting through the waist, hunter green leather jacket. I instantly fall in love and buy it. It accents the shape of my body. Chris tells me I look sexy and he can't wait to see me in only that. He says it in such a way I instantly feel sexy, and attractive, I feel so beautiful and grown up, and wanted. I've been wanting a leather jacket forever, but it's not something my mom would buy. When we leave the store, I am floating on cloud nine. I am completely blown away by his words, that I look sexy.

Out of nowhere, he says, "Fuck." it startles me and then he adds, "my ex is here."

I ask "Where?" looking around because I want to see her. I have a bit of curiosity as to who she is, and what she looks like. I start to walk in the direction he was looking. I figure he could introduce us or something and this way I can get a good look at her.

The next thing I know I feel my head being yanked backward by my hair. I'm tripping and stumbling backwards not knowing what the hell is happening. I realize quickly it's Chris, pulling me back by my hair. "Oh my God stop. Chris, you're hurting me!" I yell at him.

It all happens so fast, and less than a minute later, I am back steady on my feet and I'm rubbing my head when the tears start coming. "Get away from me." I say and quickly walk away from him trying to just get away.

He catches up to me and asks, "What's your fucking problem?"

I yell at him, "You fucking pulled me by my hair. That's not okay." Before I can process what is happening I am in his arms, he's hugging me and he's apologizing up and down about it. He swears he didn't mean to, he was just too upset from seeing his ex that he grabbed my shirt not realizing he had my hair too.

I start to feel bad and stupid. "Oh, it's okay." I hear myself saying. Then he's kissing me and being so sweet I realize there's no way he could have known he did that. I feel silly, and stupid. "It's okay." I whisper.

"I'm so sorry I over reacted, should we get going?" he asks, and I agree we should just go.

The next few weeks go even faster, and we see each other as much as we can. He has a job and I still work at my job after school, but we figure it out and spend a lot of time together. I know I want him to meet Megan, I cooled things with Shelby once I realized she was choosing a scene I didn't want to be a part of.

Megan and I talked, and she forgave me for being shitty. She knew the shit Shelby was doing and she was afraid I wouldn't listen to her about it. She's most likely right because I have a terrible blind eye when it comes to Shelby. I've known her since third grade and it's hard to let that go. I know I need to though at some point. Megan was right if she would have said something, I would have assumed she was jealous. Friday night though she's going to hang out with us on a double date. I'm so excited for her and Chris to meet, I hope they like each other.

Friday night Chris picks me up and he doesn't look to happy to see me. He's kind of cool towards me and he doesn't say anything for about ten minutes. Finally, he says "So were you purposely dressing like a slut tonight or are you just too dumb to realize it?"

I'm a little thrown back by this, and I respond slowly with "I thought I was looking nice for you."

He answers back with "You look like a hooker and it's embarrassing, but hey... if you want to be a slut then you can be a slut with someone else."

I hear myself telling him I'm so sorry It will never happen again. I just wanted tonight to be perfect, and I didn't mean to mess it up. My mind is whirling, and I just don't understand where this is coming from. Eventually he reaches over and takes my hand and tells me he forgives me, and it's okay. He adds just don't do it again, with a smile. I feel myself smiling back and nodding yes and saying okay. I'm happy he's happy again, and I don't get to dwell on it long, because we are here.

We go into the bowling alley and go to a back area where they have the pool tables. Megan Is there with a guy, she introduces him as her friend, Jay. He seems nice and they are cute together, but they both insist they are just good friends. I introduce them to Chris, and he's all smiles and charm. Thank God, I was afraid he would be moody now.

Megan and Jay play pool against us, and it is a pretty good game. Jay is witty and fun, and I find myself laughing a lot and enjoying myself. We are tied up, and it is my turn and right before I take my shot Chris says, "Blow this and I'll make you blow me." I am incredibly embarrassed by his comment, but I just laugh it off. I steady myself then leaned in to take my shot and sure enough miss.

The next thing he says is "You stupid bitch you had one job." I silently stand there shocked, staring at him not sure I heard him right.

I finally register voices and I hear Megan tell him "You're a real piece of shit, don't you dare talk to her like that."

He comes back at her with "Hey skank, when I want your opinion I'll ask, until then take your ugly face and small tits back to your car and leave."

I know she's about to explode, I know Megan so well, she is feisty and always ready to say it like it is. I see her friend is about to step up to Chris and frankly Chris out muscles him by a whole person. I need to put this fire out, and fast. I must stop this from becoming bad.

I jump into the middle and start laughing and say "Oh my God Megan he was kidding, lighten up. He would never say that and be serious, we joke like that all the time with each other."

She just stares at me and I see the doubt in her eyes, but she just says, "Fine, but I'm leaving I'll talk to you tomorrow" and she storms out before I can say anything else.

I honestly don't know what to say but I get my stuff and start walking to the car. I am full on bawling my eyes out by the time we got to the car.

Chris says "Stop it, you're embarrassing. Christ this is ridiculous I'm taking you home and I never want to see you again."

At this point I can't even answer. I just cry. "What the hell Chris?' I say, "That was so rude to say to Megan, and Jay was nothing but nice to you too."

"Nice?" he says, "Nice? That guy wanted to fuck you, and you dressing like a slut didn't help."

I'm so upset, I want to reach over and take his hand, or fix it but I also know he is being mean. I whisper instead "Chris, please don't think that."

I have such mixed-up feelings about his behavior and no one to talk to. It's not like I can talk to my sister, Lauren and for sure not my mom. They will tell me to break up with him, and I don't want to. But then again, he just broke up with me, so it doesn't matter. By the time we get to my house I'm so upset I can't breathe. Chris turns off the car and looks at me, he grabs my face and starts kissing me. I'm so happy and sad all at the same time, but I find myself responding back. My body is craving his love and attention, yet my brain is screaming this isn't right.

"If you ever let someone talk to me like that again I will be done with you." he says.

I'm so confused with all my feelings, all I can say is "I'm sorry, I don't know what happened." Then I hear myself whisper "It won't happen again I promise."

He sits there thinking for a minute. "If I stay with you, you owe me. I have waited, and I have been patient. It's time you show me how much you love me."

I know exactly what he wants but I'm not ready, I start to tell him that "I don't know if I'm..."

But he cuts me off "I have a girl that wants to date me, and she would fuck me tomorrow." He pauses and looks me right in my eyes "But I'm waiting for you, I want to make love to the girl I love not just fuck some whore," he shrugs his shoulders and says "but I'm human. I'm a guy and I have needs, if you won't do it I will get it from someone that will. You can tell me tomorrow when I take you to meet my mom."

He leans over and kisses me, and I find myself saying "Okay Chris I will." and I get out of the car.

He rolls the window down and says, "Oh, If I ever see that bitch again, were done:" He rolls up the window and leaves.

Great I must choose between the guy I love, and my best friend. I go in the house and go to bed. I lay awake most the night thinking and crying. I don't know what to do, Megan has been my best friend for years. We have done just about everything together since sixth grade. I know lately things have been tense, but am I ready to end the friendship completely?

I think of all our fun times riding horses, riding at the County Fair, even the state fair. I think of all our sleepovers, and our pretend adventures to look cool. Our trips to amusement parks, skiing together, being in track together, all the time in the weight room, weight lifting and all the High School football games we've gone to together. Our first home coming, and so many more memories flash through my head. I mourn not being together for our senior prom. We always said we would be in each other's weddings. We have been best friends forever, we are like twins and I assumed we would be for the rest of our lives. How can I do that to her?

Then again, she just couldn't leave shit alone. Why does she always have to start shit? She didn't have to say anything, she could have laughed it off and talked to me tomorrow. Why did she have to make such a big deal out of it?

The more I think about it the more I convince myself she did it on purpose to ruin my happiness, and she's jealous. She doesn't have a boyfriend, so she doesn't want me to have one either. It's exactly like how she always tries to out lift me in the weight room, or out ride me with the horses or out run me during track. We both have a very competitive nature and for once I'm thinking it doesn't work anymore as friends. It used to drive us to do better but now I'm rethinking it all.

That's the conclusion I come to, it's all about jealousy and competition. Well forget her, I'll show her. No way she will come between Chris and I. Tomorrow I'm going to give her a piece of my mind once and for all. I made my decision. It's Chris. I need him. He makes me feel so loved, and all I need to do is listen to him. He knows what's best for me, for us.

The next day, Chris picks me up and I go meet his family. His sisters are nice, but the one is weird and kind of hangs on him like a girlfriend, and he hangs on her back. It's almost an uncomfortable feeling the way they are together. She hangs all over him in a weird possessive kind of way. I choose to just ignore it and tell myself I'm nervous.

His mom is fake and pretending to like me, but I can tell she doesn't. She has short almost rude answers to everything I say, and a few times just point blank rude. I try to ask him about it, but he brushes it off as if it's me. I let it go because, I don't want to upset him today.

I follow him through the house as he gives me a tour, and lastly, he leads us to his room. I'm a bit surprised when he closes the door.

I say, "Wow my mom would kill me if I closed the door."

He just laughs and says "I'm twenty-one years old, my mom doesn't care. So? Did you make a decision?"

Wow, not what I expected but I say breathlessly "Yes, I want to be with you." In what feels like a second, he crosses his room and is passionately kissing me and starting to undress me all at the same time.

"Wait I didn't know you meant today" I'm trying to get him to slow down, but he isn't listening… the next thing I know we are making love. I feel so confused when we are done, I'm trying not to cry, all I can think to ask him is, "Was that okay?"

I am floored by his response. "No, I've had better, you need to learn to be better at that, or I'm gone."

I am so embarrassed by it I say, "I'm not experienced, but I will try to be better."

He cuts me off "No shit, I think I can tell you have no idea what you are doing, get your shit together if you want to be with me. Watch a porno or read a playboy and figure it out."

I can't help it and I start to cry because I'm humiliated, and the next thing I know he's on top of me, sitting on my hips pinning my arms down at my sides.

Bending down inches from my face, looking me right in the eye, he says "I own you, don't forget that." I try to wiggle and buck him off me, and he pushes me down harder laughing. "You're never going to be as strong as I am so stop." he gets up and tells me to get dressed, fix my face, and stop crying.

I get up to do that while he leaves the room and I'm mad, thinking I don't think I can date him. I regret my decision to sleep with him, and wish I would have said no. When he comes back he hands me a glass of water, then kisses me and says he loves me. I sadly pull away, about to tell him to take me home when he adds, "Hey for real, no worries I was just kidding you were fine, lighten up and don't be so uptight. Don't be mad, you know I love you right?" He stands there with a pouty look on his face basically asking me to forgive him.

I smile and relax thinking okay, I still need to learn his personality. Maybe I'm being too emotional, after all that was a very emotional thing we just did. He holds my hand and takes me back to the living room where we watch tv.

.   Now he's being sweet and charming again and I know this, is why I love him. He can be so nice at times. Maybe it's his home life, maybe that's why he gets moody. I promise to try harder to be nice and understanding and not create problems that don't need to be there. I cuddle up to him and he whispers, "You do know I only say things to you because I love you and I want you to be the best you can be." I feel it in my heart and know, really know, this is the truth. He is just trying to make sure I have a good life and he's trying to help me be a better person.

On Sunday, I'm waiting to hear from Chris, and the phone rings. I run to grab it, before anyone else assuming it is Chris, but it's Megan. "Is Margo there?"

I answer, "Hey it's me."

She doesn't even mince words, "That guy's an asshole, and he treats you like shit."

I'm instantly on the defense. I knew it. I knew she was going to be a bitch about it. "No, he isn't you're so uptight and you don't know how to take a joke," I say to her then go in for the dig "If you ever had a real boyfriend you would know this."

I know I hurt her but at this moment I don't care. Chris said I can't have both. He wants what's best for me and I know he loves me. Megan is just jealous.

"Wow, that was mean. I guess you two are made for each other." she says "Have a great life together, but I want you to know something. When he hurts you, which he will, I'll always be here." and she hangs up. I can tell she was crying, which makes me cry. I don't understand why she is so mean. Somehow in my mind this all became her fault. Somewhere In the back of my mind I know this is wrong, but I can't lose Chris.

By four o'clock I still haven't heard from him, and I am thinking maybe I heard wrong and I was supposed to call him, not the other way around. Not wanting to upset him, I call his house and his sister answers, the weird younger one.

"Hello is Chris there?" I ask.

"Yeah hold on Sheri, he's been waiting for your call." I freeze, maybe she forgot my name? Who Is Sheri? Then I think, wait isn't that his ex's name? I'm trying not to cry when he gets on the phone.

"Sheri what the fuck? You were supposed to be here an hour ago." I'm completely speechless. I'm not sure what to say and I want to hang up, but I'm pissed.

"Who the fuck is Sheri?" I say.

He stammers "Uh, wait who is this?"

I say, "It's MARGO!" there's silence, but I can still hear him yell at his sister while covering the phone mouthpiece with his hand.

He says to her. "Hey shithead wrong girl. Thanks." I'm so pissed I want to reach in the phone and slap him, instead I wait, and when he says "Margo..."

I cut him off and yell, "Screw you!" and I hang up.

That asshole. I'm so pissed, but I'm crying because I wholeheartedly thought he loved me. I thought he meant it when he said he wanted to spend his life with me. What a fool I am, and what's worse is Megan was right. How can I face her at school Monday? I know she's right, but how can I admit that? The more I think about it the angrier I get.

He embarrassed me in front of my friend. He made me believe he loved me... enough to sleep with him and give up my best friend. What a jerk. He has no clue how bad he broke my heart, and probably doesn't care. I'm so glad right now nobody is home. I don't have to deal with any nosy "what's wrong?" questions. It's a rare day in this house when no one is here and I'm thankful I can be alone to cry. After a good twenty or so minutes of crying my heart out, I think screw this. I'm not going to lay in bed crying over a boy all day.

I decide to go upstairs and make my favorite feel good snack, cream cheese on crackers and read a book. I love reading and it will take my mind off things. Reading has a way of helping me escape reality, it's something I do a lot to relax.

Wonderful, all I want is to be alone and read, yet there's a knock at the door. Assuming it's Brittany forgetting her key again and not wanting to deal with her, I fling the door open ready to bite her head off "you always..." I stop mid-sentence, it's Chris.

I want to slam the door in his face, but I'm also blown away he drove here to see me. This is not something I would ever expect from him. "Um, no one is home, so you can't be here." I say, knowing the rules are no boys when my parents aren't home.

"We need to talk he says as he shoves his way past me and comes in anyways. I try to tell him again, "Look I'm going to get in trouble..."

He cuts me off "I'm not afraid of your parents, I can handle them, but I am more afraid you got the wrong idea." I'm a little thrown by his face, and the way he sounds like he's trying not to cry. His voice is shaky, and his eyes look like he may have been crying. The least I can do is hear him out, it can't hurt anything.

"Okay you have five minutes, so start talking." I demand.

He glares at me and walks up to me, so we are face to face inches apart and he says "I will today understand you are upset, but never ever tell me what to do. Do.you.hear.me?"

I'm a bit intimidated by his tone and stance. I sigh, my shoulders sag, and I say "Okay, please can you tell me why you are here?" His body relaxes a little and his face looks a little nicer, less harsh and rigid. He sits down, and I sit across from him.

"Sheri is my ex, that's it. I was waiting for her to come get stuff she left at my house and she was fucking with the time all day." Oh, crap I'm an idiot. "My sister knew I was pissed and waiting for her, so she assumed you were her." He continues, and I feel like a total jerk. "I'm not with Sheri we broke up months ago, but she hasn't gotten her stuff and I didn't want you to find anything and get the wrong idea. You did anyways." He says looking sad he whispers, "I love you."

I feel two inches tall. I'm so taken over by emotion, I lunge myself into his arms and I'm apologizing and telling him it will never happen again. I feel so terrible. I can't help but cry, and this time he wipes my tears and he's so sweet my heart feels like it's going to explode.

"I promise I'll never act like that again." I say, and he kisses me, nice at first then before I know it he has me on the floor, pinning me down again but he's more sitting on my chest and his knees on my arms. It's kind of a surreal moment that I can't wrap my head or heart around.

"If you ever treat me like that again I will give you a reason to think I'm cheating. I will fuck your sister." He says this to me and before I can respond he is pushing his tongue down my throat and he's lying on me, grinding on me, wanting more. I feel like I'm in a daze, and I'm trying to wrap my head around what's going on when the dogs start barking and he stops.

He gets up and says, "Your parents are back, get up." he walks into the kitchen and says, "Act like you're making us a snack." I'm still collecting myself and he says, "Oh my god, you stupid bitch. Hurry up." I don't want to piss him off, so I grab the cream cheese and crackers and start to make us a snack.

My parents come in and I can tell they are a little pissed, but I quickly say, "Hey mom, I'm sorry Chris was out this way and stopped in on an impulse to see if we could hang out. I told him you guys weren't here, but should be home any minute and I had to ask first." I try hard to look calm and like we were all about respecting the rules.

"It's a school night, and you know you can't be out late on a school night." my mom says, I want to roll my eyes and say I can do whatever I want, I'm eighteen.

Before I get a chance to respond though, Chris says "If it's Okay with you guys I was thinking we could hang out here and maybe watch a movie or tv. I won't stay late I just wanted to see her."

He smiles at my mom and I can see she's pissed but she says, "Sure that's fine, just clean up your mess when you're done Margo." Oh my God she acts like I'm three. I say Okay and continue to make us a snack. It gives me time to think anyways, while Chris goes in the living room with my parents.

He sends such mixed feelings sometimes. I feel he is so angry at me but I'm not sure why. I also know he loves me. He drove all the way here to be sure I knew the truth. I must give him credit for that. Maybe he really is trying to help me be the best person I can be. I've never had someone care about my well-being before. It's always about Britney in this house and how she can be the best. It's nice someone wants me to be the best. Maybe I need to learn how to behave better, after all my mom tells me all the time I like to push her buttons. I need to learn not to push Chris's buttons, so he will always love me.

After about an hour Chris gets up and says he's going to get going, so I walk him to the door. "Did you ditch that girl yet?" he asks, referring to Megan.

I tell him "Yes, you were right, she tried to call and tell me you weren't good for me. What a bitch." He likes that, and I'm rewarded with a kiss.

"I'm always right, just listen to me and you will go far in life. I'll see you Tuesday night, I'm off."

"I can't I have to work."

"Switch with someone or call off, I'll be here by five." He says as he walks to his car and leaves.

About thirty minutes later I get told I have a phone call. My mom isn't too happy, and she makes sure to tell me "You know it's late."

I glare at her and ask "Who is it? And how can I control someone else calling me when I don't know who it is or that they were going to call?"

Jesus, she is such a bitch. "Watch your tone." she tells me.

Oh, for god sakes it's always a fight with her, but I smile and say." Okay, I'm sorry." and keep my tone light, and not bitchy.

"Hello?" I ask since I still have no idea who it is.

"I miss you already." I hear Chris say.

I smile and turn away from my mom, "I miss you already too."

"Margo…" my mom says.

I roll my eyes and say to Chris, "Hey I can't talk long, my mom's mad it's so late.

"That's fine I just wanted to call and say goodnight and you need to quit your job." I try to tell him I need money, but he cuts me off and says, "I'll support you, call and quit, I want to spend my days off with you and not worry when I can." Oh, my goodness he really loves me that much. I hear myself telling him okay I will, and he says "Good, I'll see you Tuesday. and Margo," I wait, thinking he will say I love you. "Don't ever question me again" and he hangs up.

Chapter 4

Thanksgiving came and went with no major issues. We had dinner at my family's house, then later went to his mom's house. We spend most of our weekends at his uncles and while at first it was fun to sneak and drink, after a while it's so boring. I notice Chris is drinking a lot more every time we go and it's starting to bother me. I'm thinking with Christmas around the corner I shouldn't say anything and rock the boat, but his driving is starting to scare me when we leave. If I can, I'll wait until after Christmas, so I don't ruin the holiday, but we do need to talk about it.

The only other issue I have had is Megan. While we aren't fighting, we aren't talking either. I notice she's hanging out with Darby all the time and all her little friends. It kills me to watch. I miss Megan, but I know Chris hates her and I love him enough to walk away.

"Margo? Are you listening to me at all?"

My thoughts are interrupted by Chris "Oh, no I'm sorry I was just thinking." I answer.

"About what?" he asks.

Not thinking I say, "Megan and our friendship or our not so much friendship anymore."

The next thing I know he slams on the brakes and my head smashes into the dashboard of his car.

"Oh my God Chris!" I yell at him, "What the hell is your problem? That freaking hurt." I instinctively reach up and touch my forehead and I can feel a goose egg forming.

"If you had your seatbelt on that wouldn't have happened and why would you ignore me, to think about that little cunt?"

Right now, I'm pissed, and my head is pounding, so I snap back at him "I can think anything I want, it's my brain."

He shoots back at me, "You have no brain. You're an idiot and you show it every day."

This is getting out of hand, and I don't know how to stop it. I start crying and decide to open the door to get out and walk to a payphone. I don't want to be in the car anymore with him, but he puts the car in drive and starts driving. I quickly pull my one leg back into the car and I close the door.

"Chris pullover." I say.

He glares over at me and keeps driving. I can see he has no intentions of pulling over.

"Whatever," I sigh "As soon as we get to your uncle's I'm calling Lauren to come get me." While I know she will be pissed, I also know she will come get me. She is always there if I need her. Always. I cross my arms across my chest and stare out the front window.

A few minutes later, Chris whips into this little dirt entranceway off the main road and drives into a wooded area. I have no idea where we are, I wasn't paying attention. I'm kind of getting scared that he will leave me in the middle of nowhere in the cold. My mom's voice is coming into my head, she is always telling me I need to wear a jacket and have gloves and a hat with me. Damn it, why don't I ever listen to her? I hate being hot and I enjoy the cold, so I never wear a jacket. I realize though if he were to drop me off, I'd probably freeze to death.

He finally stops the car in this little secluded opening and turns to look at me. "Get out." he orders me.

I start to cry again and plead, "I'm sorry. Don't leave me here. I don't know why I'm so crabby please forgive me." Right now, I will beg if need be, not to be left alone in the woods. I know it will be dark soon and that thought terrifies me, I still sleep with a nightlight on at home.

He gets out of the car and comes to my side and physically pulls me out. I'm expecting him to turn around and get back in the car and leave me when he pulls me close and starts kissing me. I'm completely taken by surprise after his anger outburst and there is so much passion in the kiss, that I find myself responding to him. He is gentle at first then he starts getting rougher and he shoves my body up against the car, hard. Now I'm scared again, and I try to tell him to stop, but he isn't listening. Somehow though I end up on the cold ground, and my pants are down, and he is pushing himself inside of me. He isn't even trying to be nice. I beg him to stop but the more I beg the rougher he is. I have rocks and sticks digging into my back, and tears are pouring down my face, but nothing comes out of my mouth anymore.

Finally, he finishes and pushes himself half off me, he looks at me and says, "See that's how a good fuck is supposed to be." he gets up and goes back inside the car. I'm completely shocked and unable to talk as I stand up and collect myself. I pull leaves and twigs out of my hair the best I can, I try to rub the dirt off my clothes too.

I get back in the car, shaken, and he leans over the center console and pulls my face to him. "That right there was the best I've ever had, so thank you." I'm still in a daze when he says, "I have never loved someone like I love you." He kisses me so sweet now and starts the car and we leave.

I am more confused tonight then I have ever been in my life. I know he loves me. He tells me all the time. Maybe that was what my mom used to warn us girls about. She'd say "Be very careful the situations you put yourselves in. The heat of passion can make guys do things they normally wouldn't." She would also say "Don't wear short skirts or shorts, sit like a lady and don't wear too revealing of a shirt." She never wanted us to wear bikinis and warned us about teasing boys and not leading them on.

That's when It hits me. Passion. This was his form of passion and being in the heat of the moment. That was his truest deepest passion coming out for me. He had no control, because he loves me so deeply he can't help it. I have every emotion imaginable going through me right now. I feel scared, I feel love, I feel happiness, I look over to him and he looks back at me. I now have the biggest smile on my face.

He says, "What are you smiling about?"

I say, "Because I'm the luckiest girl in the world, and I love you."

He shakes his head and smiles then replies with "Don't ever forget that."

In this moment I feel everything will be okay, this man loves me so much he can't control himself.

Christmas day is the most fantastic day. My parents are in a good mood and for once I'm not fighting with Brittany, and Chris is over. I can't wait to give him his presents. I still had some money left from working, so I didn't have to ask him for money. I don't like that part of not working, but it has been nice seeing him whenever he is off. I made sure to look as cute as I can. I have on his favorite jeans, and a super cute sweater I got a month ago that matches my eyes. When he gets to my house I can see he is in a great mood, so today should be perfect.

After dinner he opens my gifts. Both are nice long sleeve shirts that I got at a local clothing store. He honestly seems to love them. I'm so happy because with clothes, you never know if a person will like the same thing as you. He tells me he didn't have time to get me anything. Although I'm a little disappointed, I'm not too upset.

"Chris, I'm not the type of girl that needs gifts, I only need your love and that's it. Besides, I love watching other people open gifts more than I like getting them." I add to help him feel better and that's truly how I feel.

"You passed my test" he's all smiles, "Hold on I have to go to my car." He runs out to his car and brings in a box. He's so happy and giddy, it's contagious and I can't stop smiling. "Be careful, it's fragile." he tells me and sets it down. I look in the box and there is a ton of newspaper covering something, so I carefully start to pull the papers out of the box. Inside the box is a beautiful ceramic black horse rearing up on its hind legs. It's beautiful.

With tears in my eyes I thank him, and give him a hug, "This is the sweetest gift I've ever gotten." I whisper.

"You better be worth it." he whispers back in my ear as he hugs me tighter.

I smile through my tears and tell him "I promise I will be."

Right at that moment, Brittany walks in "Get a room." she is being flippant.

I laugh instead of getting mad, I give my own flippant answer back "Been there done that." I'm trying to keep the mood light and fun, but her face turns to complete disgust and shock.

"You fucked her?" she rudely directs towards Chris.

Before I can say oh my god I was just being sarcastic back to her, Chris says "Don't be jealous we both know you wanted my cock and since I didn't give it to you, you're mad."

I don't want this turning into something bad, not on Christmas day.

"Brittany stop it." I say trying to put out the flames.

There's no use, she fires back at him instead saying. "Trust me if I wanted your cock I'd have it and when you get bored with little miss goody and want to know how a real pussy can fuck, call me." she turns and walks away.

I'm so stunned, who says that? And who says that to their own sister's boyfriend? I'm so sick of that little bitch trying to ruin my life. I'm so upset, because I don't want Christmas ruined I tell Chris I just want to leave. He agrees with me, so I tell my mom we are going to run out for a bit. I say it's, so I can give his mom a Christmas gift and we will be home in a few hours.

I don't have a gift for his mom, but it was the only thing I can think of, so she wouldn't argue about me leaving. Even though I'm eighteen she treats me like a child, yet Brittany does whatever she wants. I honestly don't get it. How do they not see through her lies and manipulative bullshit? When I have kids, I'll never be blind to that crap.

Chris and I leave and while I have no idea where we will go, I also don't care. We make small talk as he drives, not talking about anything specific. I just want to have the rest of my Christmas be as wonderful as it started out.

Chris pulls into a car dealership and parks the car off to the side. "What are we doing here?" I ask.

"I like coming here to look at cars. I'm going to get a new car in a few months and I like to see what's new." he says.

So, we walk around the dealership, even though it's closed. I'm a little nervous we could get into trouble, but he reassures me we won't. I dream about having a new car myself someday, and how fun it would be to get a faster one.

"You're smiling, what are you thinking" he asks me.

"I keep thinking one day I want a new car, a really fast car." I reply shyly.

He chuckles at me and says, "Keep dreaming I'll be the one with the fast car, you will be the one driving the family car."

All I hear him say is family car, he wants a family with me. This man loves me and wants to be a family. I love him so much. This has been the best Christmas ever.

January is going by so fast, and I don't get to see Chris very often. He got a job at night now too, and I'm sad I don't get to see him that much. He insists I don't need to work but, I wish he would understand I want to help. Every time it comes up I say I hate how he is working so much, but he says he wants to take care of me. So, I patiently wait for him to have days off, and focus in the meantime on my school stuff.

Megan and I still aren't talking, but occasionally, we try. It almost always ends up in a fight and it's doesn't seem worth it at this point. I finally see Chris in the middle of the month and it has felt like forever.

He picks me up and takes me to his house, because we could have the place to ourselves. I try to broach the subject of Megan with him again, "Chris, Megan feels terrible," I Lie, hoping he can't hear it. "she didn't understand you were kidding, what if we try to all go out again?" I'm crossing my fingers hoping he will say yes.

"What part of don't talk to her don't you understand?" he asks me.

"I have classes with her, so I have to a little bit, and I miss her. She's my best friend." I say.

"Oh, you miss her?" I can see his jaw clenching. "Well let's invite her over, I've been wanting a threesome. You can watch me fuck her then suck my dick" He responds angrily.

I'm once again blown away by his crude remarks, "You're a pig, and that's not what I meant."

The next thing I know he picks me up by my neck and pushes me up against the wall and as he's choking me he says, "Keep pushing me. I told you, you won't talk to her and I mean it." He lets go of my neck and I start crying.

"I want to go home, you need to take me home." I demand, but he only laughs at me.

He repositions himself in front of me laughing and says "No." I stand there crying, what else can I do? He comes over and holds my face between his hands and tells me, "If you would listen to what I say, I wouldn't have to do that. You never listen, and you make me act like this. I don't like having to be this strict with you."

I'm still crying trying to wrap my head around what just happened, when he starts kissing me. I want to pull away, but he still has my face between his hands, so I don't want to piss him off. Instead I kiss him back. He is now being gentle and nice, telling me he loves me and I'm beautiful and he will always protect me.

My mind is screaming to tell him stop, it feels so wrong, but then again, he is trying to be nice. I realize I let things go too far when he is breathing heavy, panting, and he is trying to pull my pants down.

"No Chris," I'm trying to stop him "I don't want to, not now, not after fighting."

I think he agrees because he stops kissing me. Faster than I can blink, he has me by my hair, and yanks my head back a little and twists my body so now I'm face down bent over the bed. He is pushing my face into the bed and I'm struggling to breath. I try to wiggle out from him, but it's no use he is way stronger than me.

The next thing I feel is him tugging my pants down. I try to fight against him, but I'm no match to his strength. Once again without wanting him to, I feel him forcing himself into me and he doesn't even care it hurts me. I cry out and he gets rougher shoving my face into the bed harder hurting my neck as he laughs and says, "Scream all you want we're here alone." I stop asking him to stop, instead forcing my mind to shut down, and I just cry, while he finish what he's doing. I lay there thinking over and over, I hate this man so much.

Once he is done, he tells me to get dressed, and that he will be right back. I assume he is going to the bathroom, so I take a minute to collect myself. Again, I'm asking what the hell that was? I'm so shook up I feel like I'm going to throw up. I can't stop shaking and crying so I climb up onto his bed, I pull my knees to my chest and close my eyes.

I wake up some time later and it's dark in his room. He is lying next to me with his arms wrapped around me. I try to get up and he tightens his arms, so I try and wiggle out and he says "Again? I'm glad you see things my way." I know now even if I say no, he won't listen. I accept my fate and just let him do it again, but this time he at least tries to be nicer.

This time though when he is done, he tells me he loves me so much. So, I say "If you loved me you wouldn't have done that earlier when I said no."

He responds with "Be happy I love you so much and want you so much I can't control myself, the day I can... you're gone."

I ask, "What the heck does that mean?"

He bluntly says "The day I don't lust for you, is the day I'll start fucking someone else. Someone like maybe your sister, so you better keep me interested"

I'm so confused by that terrible response, I softly say "Okay."

Chris finally takes me home and I know it might be a while before I see him again, and that's okay with me. I need time to think. I know I don't like when he acts like that, but I can't figure out how to be better, so he doesn't do it. I figure I need to ask someone, but I don't know who. I don't have any friends, and my parents aren't an option. I guess the only thing I can do is believe he loves me and figure out a way to keep him happy. No man would deal with someone like me if he didn't love me that much. I need to learn how to be a better girlfriend.

As the days go by we talk a lot on the phone since we can't see each other. We have deep conversations about life, and I realize he's right. He just loves me so much and needs me so bad he can't control himself. At eighteen it's heady stuff. This must be how grown men with adult passion love woman, not how little teen crushes are. How real relationships are with real lust and desire.

I realize my dad doesn't act that way with my mom though. Then it hits me, oh my God maybe he doesn't really love her. Maybe he is with her because he married her and feels stuck. I need to pay better attention to what's going on in my own house. I vow to start watching the dynamics between my parents on a more adult level.

I take the next few weeks to overly watch my parents. My dad seems to do anything my mom asks, and he never says no. They don't argue much, they bicker, but not fight. He kind of bows down to her. I don't get it, If I even try to say something Chris doesn't like he gets mad. Maybe for my dad he does it because he doesn't care, and it's easier. Maybe if the chance comes up and my mom isn't around, I'll ask him.

That chance finally came up when my dad was out in the garage working on his car. It's an old muscle car that he's restoring. "Hey Margo, I need a hand" my father calls to me. I go out to the garage, and he tells me he needs me to lay under the car and hold his headers up, so he can get them on. I love working on this car with him, so I happily slide under the car.

While I'm helping I ask, "Hey dad, why do you do whatever mom tells you to do?"

He says, "I don't know what you mean, but if you're asking why I help her around the house and stuff it's because that's what married people do."

I say "Yes, but you always do everything, and never get mad about it. For example, even if it's in front of people. Don't you worry your friends or other people will make fun of you?"

He laughs and says, "If someone wants to make fun of me for loving my wife, I don't need them in my life."

So that didn't fully answer my questions, but I couldn't say, hey do you ever get too rough with mom? I don't know how I'm supposed to figure this all out. Maybe Chris handles his feelings differently than my dad. After all, it's not like I've ever seen the intimate side of my parents. Gross! What they do and how they act in private could be so different then how they are in front of us kids.

The rest of January flies by, and before I know it, it's almost Valentine's Day. My first one with a boyfriend. I'm so excited and not seeing him, has made me miss him. I hope we will do something romantic, but if not that's okay too. I always hear about people eating dinners by candle light, drinking wine and guys buying girls roses and such. My dad still gets my mom a dozen roses all these years later for Valentine's day. I know I want to get Chris something sweet, so he will always remember our first one together.

Chris finally calls me on the ninth to tell me he'll be working on the fourteenth. Although I'm sad I understand. He said he gets off at ten, so it would be too late to come get me and have me home by midnight. Although I'm heartbroken, I understand he is working for us. I find myself sulking and pouting when I have an epiphany. A romantic Valentine's day can happen after all.

I know my parents will go out. My dad takes my mom out all the time especially for Valentine's day. I'm going to surprise him and see Chris after all. I carefully think out my plan, before taking any actual steps to have it happen. I know I need to have my story perfect before I bring it to my mom, or she will know I'm lying.

"Hey mom on the fourteenth do you care if I go to Megan's for the night?" I ask ready to put into action everything I practiced.

My mom answers with "I thought you girls weren't talking and don't you want to see Chris?"

I act sad, I knew she would bring that up. "He has to work so there's no way I can see him, and Megan and I are trying to fix things. We've been talking, and we want to do movies and pizza like old times."

I cross my fingers praying she can't tell I'm lying, "Sure," she says "I think that's a great idea, it will give you some time away from Chris. You know I think you guys spend too much time together."

Of course, she has to say that, I hardly see him now. I sometimes feel she doesn't want me to be happy. I don't know what it is, but nothing I say changes the fact she can't stand him. It doesn't help Chris feels he can act rude to her and not even try.

I ignore her response and say "Thanks."

As I'm walking away she says "Why don't you see if she wants to come here? We miss her too."

Shit, not what I expected, I think quick "She can't. She has to watch her sister and her sisters friend; her parents are going out to dinner with friends."

"Oh okay," my mom says, "Tell her hi and maybe next time."

Oh my God I did it. That was way easier than I thought it would be. I'm going to get to see Chris. I'm so excited. I know I want it to be such a romantic night. I need to go to the mall, so I need to lie again, because my mom doesn't let me go to Buffalo by myself. Even at eighteen she is ridiculous. I'm on a roll I might as well see if I can get this past her too.

"Hey mom after school tomorrow I have a meeting about maybe trying out for basketball again." I lie.

"Oh good, I'm happy to hear you might play again." she says, and I know I'm being a terrible person, but I want to make Chris happy. I want him to know I hear him and I want him to want me.

The next day I cut my last class. It's a study hall so it's no big deal and I know this will give me more time to run to Buffalo and back. I easily handed my teacher a forged "leave early" pass and I know there is no way I can get in trouble now. Being able to sign the secretary's signature along with the passes I stole comes in handy, that's for sure.

Thank God it isn't snowing. We get terrible lake effect snow here In West Seneca, sometimes we will get twelve inches around the Buffalo area and the rest of the state will still have grass. My car isn't the best in the snow and if it was bad out I'd have to rethink my plan. Thankfully luck is on my side today.

I make it to the mall fine, and I know what I want but honestly, I have no idea where to get it. So, I walk around for a little bit, and finally I see what I need. A Lingerie store. I want to buy something sexy to wear and make him see I want him to love me. I'm willing to do anything that will keep him from leaving me.

I walk in the store praying my face isn't red. I mean after all I'm eighteen, I'm an adult, and I can do this if I want to. There's nothing wrong with two people loving each other. I look around and I find a cute little outfit to wear. I go try it on and I think I look great. I take the leap and buy it. I'm so excited to see what he thinks.

I go next, to another store to buy him a card, and I want to buy him some chocolate at a local candy store near home. It's a family owned business and they have the best chocolates around. This is going to be the best Valentine's Day ever. After all, it's about love, and he loves me so much.

I hurry up and get back to my car because I need to get home, so no one asks any questions. I put the bags in my backpack which I purposely brought empty today knowing I will need it to sneak my stuff in the house. I know once I get home I can hide it all up in my ceiling rafters. It's the only place I know no one will look. I have a drop ceiling in my room and I can push the tiles up and hide stuff up there.

I also need to figure out what I'll do with my car. I can't take it to Chris's house, because what if my parents decide to drive by and check. I don't think they will, but you never know. Somehow my mom has a knack for knowing when we lie to her and an even better knack for finding us. I wonder if I can somehow leave it at his work? I guess it wouldn't hurt. His work parking lot is far enough off the road, and I don't think my parents even know where he works. So, all that's left to do is surprise Chris.

Thank God, my parents are leaving early tonight, or I'd have a hard time explaining why I'm getting all dressed up to go spend the night at Megan's and watch movies. Another lucky little miracle, is Brittany is already gone too. So, there is no need to worry about her and her mouth.

I go upstairs and wait for my parents to leave. While I'm waiting I decide to paint my nails. At least that, I can at least explain off as boredom. I paint my nails enough that it won't draw unwanted attention to myself.

Finally, my dad comes out from their bedroom, and I know that means it's only a few minutes before my mom comes out too. Trying to sound casual, I ask "So, where are you taking mom for dinner?"

"I think to Buffalo, to the Olive Garden." he answers.

Oh good, nowhere near Cheektowaga and where I'll be headed. "That sounds good. I know mom loves that place." I say hoping to not sound happy or excited for them to leave.

Before he can answer my mom comes out, and I whistle "Wow you look nice." I say.

"Nice?" My dad says, grabbing my mom and pulling her close to him. "You look beautiful, I don't know if I'll be able to behave tonight and keep my hands to myself." he releases my mom, so she can put her shoes on and when she bends over, he swats her butt and says, "Or we could just stay here."

Oh my gosh... Maybe he is like Chris. I guess guys do have those moments, even my dad.

"Stop it" my mom laughs and swats his hand away, that found its way back to her butt. Even though I find this behavior gross, I also find it insightful.

"Okay, you two have fun. I'll see you guys tomorrow, drive safe." I say. It's hard not to sound too excited, after all, I'm supposed to be watching movies tonight. I try to be interested in how my nails are drying, as they head out to the car. I wait to hear them heading down the driveway before I get up. I feel like any moment they will figure it out and come back and catch me, they have this sixth sense about these things. I'm hoping they were distracted enough by each other, that I wasn't really a thought.

I run down to my room, crank up the music and start getting ready. I want my hair to look perfect, so I spend a lot of time curling it. I put makeup on, and make sure it's dark enough that it won't fade by the time I leave. I step back and look at myself in the mirror. I think wow, for once I feel beautiful. I don't know if it's because I'm doing something so adult, or if it's because I'm feeling so loved. Either way I'm beyond excited to head out and surprise Chris.

I grab my stuff from my ceiling, and head out to leave. As I'm getting in my car all I can think is I hope he's surprised, and he sees how much I love him. As I'm driving to his work I realize I really want this night to be perfect. I think if I can show him tonight I'm more mature and sexy, he will stop saying he's going to be with other girls. I think he says that stuff to make me behave better and listen to him. I just feel in my heart he loves me and doesn't want that.

I'm so nervous, but I'm so excited too. I truly feel this will give us the little boost we need to take it to the next level. After all, he is the one that has brought up having a family and getting married. I don't think men say that stuff unless they mean it. I think back to how sweet he was after he told me he loved me, and I think of when he thought he lost me because of Sheri. There is no way this man doesn't care deeply for me and do these things to make me a better person. I need to figure out a better way to show him I'm listening to him and show him how much I love him.

I think about the many ways I can be better to him and I realize, I need to make him feel more important. I think men need women to make them feel strong, and important. Chris is always telling me my dad is "pussy whipped" and he will never be that way. So, I think he needs to feel he is in charge. I need to let him have some power, and that will make him happy.

He likes to decide where we go and honestly even though I'm so tired of going to his uncles, I'll leave it alone. I'll let him make that choice. He also likes to tell me what to or not to eat. That one is harder for me, but I can learn to listen to that, at least when we are together. The hardest is him telling me who can be my friends. So far, he doesn't like any of them. He only met Megan, but when I talk about any of them he shuts it down. So, for now I'll let it go, we can always work on that later.

I finally pull into his work and I'm so nervous I feel light headed. I'm a little early so pull in to the back-parking area and park near his car and sit there a few minutes, I figure I can calm my nerves down first. After about five minutes of closing my eyes, breathing and listening to music, I prepare to go in. I want to quickly touch up my makeup and fix my lipstick first.

I see a group of people come around the building and my heart stops. Chris is with them and has his arm around some girl. He not only has his arm around her but is laughing and acting like he does with me. They walk to his car and he opens the passenger side door. I see him look in his car, then give her a hug. She says something to him all smiles, and then bounces back into the restaurant.

I'm beyond upset at this point. I feel I have nothing to lose so I get out and walk towards him. I know he doesn't know it's me because he closes his door and starts walking back into work. I say his name loud enough for him to hear me, and he turns around. I can see him good from the light above his car, and he is surprised to see me, but I also see him quickly push that surprise aside.

He comes towards me and finally says, "Hey, what's up?"

I'm trying not to cry, I don't want him seeing me shed tears over him. I say "Nothing... What's up with you?"

He kind of stares, yet glares at me, his eyes getting darker, and mean and his jaw clenching. "What are you doing here? I told you I had to work." he says.

I say "I know, I was trying to surprise you. I gave my parents a bullshit story, so I could spend the night with you. Obviously, you have other plans. Have fun with that bitch." I can see he's stunned by my outburst, but I don't stick around. I turn on my heels and start going back to my car.

I just get to my car and I'm about to open the car door when he slams into me, pushing me up against the car. "Who the fuck do you think you're talking to?" He's pissed, well damn it so am I. "If you would ever listen to me, you wouldn't have seen that." he tells me.

I'm so hurt and angry, how dare he blame this on me. I don't hold back "Well I did see you with your little friend and she can have you." I try to push him away from me "Go away Chris, I'm going home."

He smirks at me and says, "No you're not." he yanks the car keys out of my hand and says, "Stay here I'll be right back."

I have no choice but to wait, so I can get my car keys back. He comes out about five minutes later, grabs me by the arm and tells me I'm coming with him. I tell him no and I try to stop him, but he squeezes tighter on my arm and it feels like he's about to break my arm pulling me to his car. He opens the car and moves some stuff around, and I see there are balloons in the car.

Well I know they aren't for me, being we weren't supposed to see each other. I don't even care at this point. I only want him to let me go so I can go home. He holds my arm tight while he's moving stuff then starts shoving me in his car.

"I'm not going with you." I tell him.

He laughs and says "Yes. You are. Get in now or I'll force you in." I know he means it and will follow through with his threat, so I finally give up and get in.

He heads out of the parking lot and once again I'm nervous as to where he is taking me. In a minute I see we are heading towards his house, so I relax, knowing at least someone is there and I can also use a phone and call my parents. I realize though I'll need to call them to come get me and I'm not thrilled about that. I do know I'm not staying with him. I don't want to be with someone that cheats. It's not the kind of relationship I want.

He pulls into his driveway and we get out of the car. He takes me in and tells me to go to his room and wait for him. I head to his room and realize there aren't many lights on in the house. Great, I think we are here alone.

He walks into his room a few minutes later and says come with me. Not wanting to argue or antagonize him, I follow him to the bathroom. He surprises me and tells me he's going to shower, and he wants me to shower with him. I'm put off by this, I want nothing to do with him. Pissed off I turn to leave the bathroom and he grabs me, turns me around and pushes me up against the wall holding me there by his forearm against my chest.

I am terrified at what is going to happen when he leans in, I think to kiss, but instead he starts licking my face. He is licking it over and over like a dog, I can't even wrap my head around it. He is soaking my face with spit, and it's so incredibly disgusting. I try to turn my head away, but he's way too strong for me. He finally stops, then looks at me and says, "Do you want to wash your face?" I shake my head yes because I don't trust myself to speak. He says, "Then get undressed and get in the fucking shower." I quickly do as I'm told.

In the shower he is all sweet again. He washes my hair and tells me I'm beautiful, and he loves me. I feel he thinks he means it, but I don't want to hear it.

"Why were you with another girl?" I ask, "And why did she put balloons in your car like she's your girlfriend?" He keeps kissing my body as he is washing me with soap and washing himself with soap.

"Stop it." I tell him, but he doesn't listen to me. I push him back a little, I can't really move him much, but he gets the hint.

"What?" he snaps.

"Who was the girl you had hanging all over you?" I demand, and he can see now I'm not going to let it go.

"Well if you must know," he says through gritted teeth "That was my cousin. My mom's sister's daughter and the balloons, she ran and grabbed for me to give to you."

I stand there staring at him in shock. I shiver, and I'm not sure if it's from the water getting cooler or a little bit of excitement knowing he got those for me.

I finally say, "But we weren't doing anything tonight and last I knew you work tomorrow too."

He smirks at me and says, "Well for your information I was able to take off tomorrow and I was going to bring those over to you tonight and tell you."

Well I stand there feeling like a complete idiot. I'm so mad at myself for doubting him I go ahead and tell him I'm so sorry.

"You better be." he answers to it, then starts kissing me again. I feel so silly, and I allow him to go ahead and have sex with me. He isn't as rough as he has been in the past so now I'm worried he's losing his feelings for me. He did tell me the day he can't just lose control he will be with someone else. I don't know how to fix this. I want to be a better girlfriend, but I can't seem to behave right. I'm going to make him leave me if I don't get it together soon. I'm so grateful the shower water hides the tears running down my face.

We spend the whole evening in his room, we talk about my insecurities and I figure out it's because I don't like myself. He tells me that If I learn to like myself, I will be more trusting and happier. We conclude I should lose some more weight and maybe get my breast done. I need to improve my looks to make myself feel better. I never realized how much I don't like myself until he helps me figure it all out. I'm so happy and grateful that he loves me enough to help me be the best me I can be.

"Next month I want to go on a trip with you." Chris says out of the blue. "I'm thinking Florida."

I'm surprised, because other than with my parents, I've never gone on a trip anywhere.

"I don't think my parents will let me go." I say to him.

He laughs at me. "You're eighteen, they can't stop you." he says, and I realize he's right. "I'm planning to go on your spring break, so you don't miss school." He can see the look of worry on my face, so he adds, "If you truly love me you will figure it out."

I turn over and try to go to sleep. I have a lot to think about, like how I have never spent the night at a boy's house and slept in the same bed as if we live together. It feels a little weird, but it feels nice too. I feel so loved, having someone there to hold me and make me feel safe. I also must think of how I'm going to broach the subject with my parents that I am going to go on a trip to Florida. I know he says they can't stop me, but what if they can? Could I if need be go up against them and go? I really want to go on this trip. I think it would be such a fun thing for us to do together.

Chapter 5

As it turned out, no my parents couldn't stop me from going, but instead they decided to join us. I have no idea how that happened but we all went to Florida together. Supposedly my parents were planning a trip down anyways, and what better time than spring break? I call bullshit, but I have no way to prove it. At least Chris was nice about it all. We had a fun car trip because we drove separate from the rest of them.

The trip itself was fun and we had a nice time. No one got in our way, so we even had some alone time to sneak off and be intimate together. All in all, I'm glad we went. The trip seemed to have brought us closer together.

I'm sad to be back home, the week we were gone went by so fast. Chris is back to working a lot of hours at both of his jobs. I don't get to see him that much and It's starting to get to me. I feel myself wondering if he is seeing any other girls. I feel myself becoming more and more insecure.

"I think I should get a job, so you can get rid of your second job." I tell him one night when he is over.

"No." is all he says. So, I try again, hoping I can get through to him.

"Honestly, I don't mind, and it would give me a reason to get out of this house."

Instead of considering it, he glares at me and says, "I told you no, so stop pushing it."

I'm a little annoyed but I let it go for now, I'm trying the "let him feel like the man in charge" route. I change the subject instead, "Okay. So, I know you said, I won't see you until Friday evening, but I wanted to tell you I'm off school, so we can get together earlier than normal. Maybe I can come over and we can have the whole day together."

"No, I have plans." he says.

I'm a little sad so I ask, "What are you doing?"

All he says is, "It's none of your business."

I'm getting annoyed with him today, so once again, I push back a little more. "How is it none of my business when you do something, but everything I do you have to know about or approve?"

"That's different and you know it." he says, and he moves to get ready to leave and now I'm pissed at the double standard.

"Fine, you go do whatever you're doing, and I'll make my own plans during the day. I'll let you know if I can see you Friday night, but I might be busy." I say feeling feisty. I start getting up to go to my room. He can find his own way out.

He gets up and pushes me back down at on the couch and sits on me, facing me, pinning me down in my spot on the couch and says, "Do not get smart with me."

A little scared, I say "If I yell my dad will come out here and get you off me."

"Do it and I'll be done with you." he says then continues with, "I have court tomorrow and it has nothing to do with you, but If you need to know I have a son. I'm trying to get custody of him."

I instantly feel like I got punched in the gut. I don't really know what to say. "Oh." I whisper, I feel like I can't breathe in any air. Why didn't he tell me this sooner?

I think that is all he's going to say, but he once again he turns mean. "I'm about done with you being such a bitch, I'm ten seconds away from walking out that door and never coming back."

I'm crying now because I have so many thoughts going through my head and I have no idea what I'm supposed to think about all of this. He has a kid and I had no idea. He didn't think it was something I should know about and that bothers me. I'm also seconds away from losing him, and I don't want that either. This emotional roller coaster I'm always on is starting to make me feel so overwhelmed. I have this terrible ache and heaviness in my chest that I can't even explain if I was asked to do so. It's nothing I have ever felt before.

"Chris I'm sorry but I wish you would have told me rather than be so secretive." I finally say to him, "I think I should have known this stuff. How old is he and why are you having to go to court? Why aren't you with his mom then? Is It Sheri?" I have so many questions to ask.

"Don't push it anymore" he says so I agree to drop it for now, but I tell him I need to have answers to my questions. "I'm not sure this is going to work if you can't tell me important things" I say still crying, wrapping my now free hands around myself.

He grabs my face with his hands and gently wiped my tears away and kisses me. I cling to him out of fear that this is it. I'm so afraid right now he is going to leave and never come back. He surprises me and says "I love you, I was scared to tell you until I knew what happened in court. I don't want to lose you because I have a child."

I'm so happy that he confesses his fears to me. I tell him I love him too and I'd never leave him for being a dad. I promise to be there for him if he needs me to help him raise his son. Finally, he knows he should go, so he gets up and I walk him to the door.

"Good luck Friday I'll see you after court and I'll have my fingers crossed everything works out for you." I kiss him one more time and watch him leave. All I can think as I go to bed is I could end up having a stepchild. I know it would be weird, but I would do anything he needs me to do to make this little boy happy. Who would have thought, I'd be talking about kids?

Friday is finally here, and I am so worried about what is happening at court with Chris. I try to drown myself in a book, but it isn't happening. Usually I can get completely lost in a book and forget there is a world around me. I go out to the barn, and mess with my horse for a little bit, but even that isn't helping. I'm so stressed I even smoke a little, I bummed a few from Lauren when she stopped by. I quit mostly, but here and there I still have a cigarette and today was a day I needed that. Thank goodness Chris doesn't know or he'd be pissed.

Finally, I figure he should be done with court soon, so I hurry up and get ready in case he decides to come right over without calling first. He's been known to do that, so I want to be ready for whatever he needs. In the middle of me drying my hair, I hear a knock on my bedroom door. "Come in" I yell assuming it's my brother. In walks Chris, and he doesn't look happy.

"Are you okay?" I ask as I go to him to hug him.

"No." he says then adds, "Are you almost ready I want to leave and not be around here or deal with anyone, especially your parents."

"Sure, let's go, I don't need to fix my hair tonight." I say and try to hurry to get the rest of my stuff together.

We head out and I'm trying to be respectful and quiet. I honestly want to bombard him with questions, but I know it will piss him off. So instead I wait for him to say something. Finally, he says "The adoption is going to happen." I'm a little surprised because I knew nothing about an adoption, so I wait to see if he offers more.

Eventually, I say, "Can you tell me what adoption? I truly want to help you right now, but I can't if I don't know what is going on. I love you and I'm sorry you are hurting." He decides to pull off the road, and we park in a parking lot at some medical building.

"My ex got pregnant, and her parents made her put the baby up for adoption." He pauses then says "I didn't know what was going on till it was too late. By the time I saved the money to get a lawyer, the process was far along. Her family has a lot of money and pull. They are threatening if I continue to pursue this being she wasn't eighteen yet and I was, they will press charges on me for rape." He looks so crushed, and he finishes with, "So today at court I had to sign off on him and let the adoption happen."

My heart is breaking for him. I don't think I've ever seen a man look so sad before. I can't believe someone would do that to their child's father. To take his kid away is the most hurtful, hateful thing anyone could ever do. I reach over and take his hand and tell him "I'm so sorry, I don't know how anyone could ever do that to you. Right this moment I hate her and her family."

"She will have contact with him through an open adoption," he tells me, "I might be able to see him from time to time, but it will depend on the new parents and how much they will allow."

"Well, that is something at least." I say then add, "If you can stay in touch, at least you can see if he is safe and being raised right. You can also one day explain everything to him and he will see you were always around." I hope I am saying all the right things. I don't want to upset him, not today.

"Thank you." he says then, "Let's head to my uncles for a bit" I'm not even going to complain about going tonight. I'm so bored going there but it's okay for tonight. He might need to be around his family, and I want to be supportive for him.

We get to his uncles and of course first thing Chris does is go for a beer. I'm a little annoyed, but I figure after the day he's had he deserves to be able to relax a little. I also grab one, so they don't all get on my case for it. I could care less if I drink. I thought drinking would be more fun, but it really isn't that great. I don't like the buzz feeling you get when your head starts feeling dizzy. I'll sip on this enough to keep people off my back. Worst case scenario I'll do what I do a lot... I pretend to go pee and dump it down the drain.

Tonight, I notice Chris is drinking a lot. I don't think I've ever seen him drink this much, this fast. His words are slurring, and I realize there's no way he can take me home. I don't think he can keep his eyes open much longer. I know I should let my parents know I'm not coming home, but they are going to flip out.

I finally get up the courage to call my parents and I'm ready for them to yell at me. The only thing I think will save me is that it has started to snow heavily in the last hour. We are getting our typical last burst of winter; our end of the season lake effect snow and it's coming down fast.

My dad answers "Hey dad it's me, Margo," I say then quickly add, "So Chris and I stopped out at his uncle's here in Buffalo, and the roads are a sheet of ice. I'm not too sure it is safe to be driving. His aunt said if we were her kids she wouldn't let us leave. Should we stay here tonight?" I word it more, so it will be his decision, not me asking to stay. I feel terrible playing the safety card with my parents. I know safety for us kids are one of their biggest concerns.

"No, no. Stay there, his aunt is right." I feel relieved because honestly, I am doing what they told us to do. If we were ever with someone that was drinking to call for a ride. I'm just staying in, not asking for a ride.

"Okay thanks and I'll head home tomorrow when the roads are clear." I'm grateful for no argument and I feel bad, but I know if I let Chris try to drive me home I'd end up dead.

I get off the phone with my dad and realize I have another problem. Chris is in a weird mood and I'm not sure how to deal with him. I walk over to him expecting him to still be distant when he grabs me and starts trying to dance with me to the music that's on. It's kind of a drunken I'm more holding him up dance, but he's laughing so I relax and try to keep us on our feet.

"If you ever try to control me I'll kick your ass." Chris says to me as we are dancing.

"I wouldn't do that to you." I answer, and he spins me around and around.

"If you ever cheat on me, I'll kick your ass too. If you talk back to me I will too." he is saying the strangest stuff tonight. "If you talk bad about me or try to leave me I'll make you wish you were never born." he starts singing off tune to me at this point the Doors song "Light My Fire".

I'm assuming it's the alcohol making him say this stuff and he has no idea what he's saying. He keeps trying to sing and dance and he's completely drunk by this point. I want to go to sleep but I have a feeling he isn't going to go to bed any time soon. I'm getting super dizzy and I almost feel like throwing up, when his uncle comes over and tells him he needs to go lay down. Chris puts up a little bit of an argument, but he's in no real state of mind to do much other than listen and go to bed.

He follows his uncle to a bedroom and a few minutes later his uncle comes back out alone.

"He's passed out like a little bitch." he says and laughs. I'm debating what I should do when his aunt asks me if I want a glass of wine. I figure I might as well have one, in fact I've been wanting to try it. I didn't want to say I've never had any, so I say sure.

"What kind do you like? Red or white" she asks, and I truthfully have no idea.

I say, "I like either, so whatever you're going to have is fine." I'm silently praying I like it.

"I have white Zinfandel if that's okay with you?"

"Sure." I smile trying to look like I knew what the hell that was. She hands me a glass and I take a sip. Thank God, I like it. It has a nice taste. This is way better then beer that's for sure.

"Thank you this is good." I say, and I look at her cigarette wishing so bad I could have one right now.

"Here." she hands me hers and says, "I can see you want one just have one."

"No thank you if Chris found out he'd be so mad at me" I say.

"That little prick isn't your boss." she says then adds "Oh my God he's passed out, I won't say anything jeez, go ahead."

"Okay." I smile, I like her and I'm so happy to have a cigarette right now. It's hard not to smoke and especially when my nerves are all over the place when I'm with Chris.

"So why was he drinking his ass into a stupor tonight? You guys have a fight?"

"No, he had court today." I say praying they knew about it, because if they didn't I'm going to be in big trouble.

"Oh, that's right, his kid. I take it that didn't go to well?"

"No, they are letting the other family adopt him." I'm glad I have someone to talk to about this.

"Well it's probably for the better. He said he didn't think it was his anyways. After all his mom is why he was fighting this, now she can't say anything at least he tried."

Oh, a little piece of the story I didn't know about. I wonder if she can tell me more.

"I know the breakup was hard for him." I lie, I assume it must have been because he doesn't want to ever talk about it.

"Yes, that girl cheated on him, and then said she was pregnant. He didn't believe her that the baby is his, but his mom forced him to go to court and fight for it." she said, then surprising me with, "She had all these crazy accusations about him hitting her and forcing her to do sex things she didn't want to do."

"That's crazy." I find myself saying, yet I hear little bells going off in my head. That is how I feel, and he just told me he would have no problem kicking my ass.

"What's wrong? Was it something I said?" she asks. I realize I have tears in my eyes.

"No, not at all, I feel bad for him." I lie, then finish my cigarette and tell her I'm tired and going to head off to sleep.

I climb into the bed next to him and realize I need to break up with him. I don't want to, but I know now, I must. All the things his aunt just said to me, hit me hard. Chris has done some of that stuff to me and he always claims it's because he loves me. I don't think that is how love is. In fact, now I'm sure of it. I watch my parents all the time and as annoying as they are to me, they don't do that. I can see my dad wholeheartedly loves my mom, and she loves him. I see how they always put each other and the other one's feelings first.

I also know if I stay with Chris, he will always come first. Not just by me, but by himself. I know I will always have to be careful and behave how he expects me to. I'm not the best at behaving or listening to what people tell me to do either. I tend to speak my mind, and he doesn't like that. I don't know how I can tell him right now when he is already so upset. Maybe I can wait a few weeks. I know it' not going to matter, I won't see much of him. He already told me he will be working a lot since he took time off for vacation. I guess I'll have to wait until he gets through this a little bit, then I'll tell him how I feel.

I watch him sleep a little and I feel tears falling down my cheeks. I know I have big dreams for my life and I don't think he will let me chase them. I'm going to miss the funny him, and the sweet him. I won't miss the angry Chris though, that thought makes me shudder a little and it's just enough movement to jar him a bit. He rolls over and puts his arms around me and pulls me tight against him. This is when it's hard to see the bad stuff, when I feel loved and safe in his sleeping arms.

We get up and hang out for a little bit at his uncle's house, but I tell him I need to go home soon, so I don't get into trouble. I can tell by his face I'm pissing him off, but he decides to thankfully let it go. I hug his aunt and tell his uncle goodbye and thank them for letting us stay the night. I'm almost sad to know that most likely I won't be coming back here.

We drive back to my house and I try having small talk with Chris, but my heart and head aren't in it. Thank goodness, he is completely wrapped up in his own thoughts, so he doesn't notice. He lets me know the next month or, so he will be working a lot, and we will see each other when we can. I tell him okay and try to look happy as he kisses me then leaves.

I feel kind as if a weight lifted off me, as I watch him pull out of my driveway. I haven't yet figured out how I'm going to break up with him, but I do know I need to do it. I'm relieved to know I have a bit of time away from him to think about it all.

One of the things I'm looking forward to in the meantime is going to my family's Memorial Day party in a few weeks. I think I need to be around my family and have some relaxing by myself to think. My aunt and uncle always have such good food at their parties, and I'm looking forward to eating it without Chris's judgment. I originally thought I was going to see if Chris wanted to go, but now he works and I'm glad he does.

Chapter 6

The next week is nice being alone, I haven't seen Chris much. I realized in school today prom is coming up. I never got a dress, and I never asked him to go. I did already by the tickets though, I didn't want them to sell out and now I don't know what to do. Maybe I can still go to prom, and then after I graduate break up with him. I know It sounds mean, but I also don't want to miss my senior prom or explain to people like Megan and Darby why I'm not going.

Chris called me on Tuesday and said he was coming by on Thursday, which is tonight. I guess I can bring that up to him and see what he says. I know I might need to ask him for money for a dress, although I think I'm going to ask my parents first. I'd rather borrow it from them, because Chris likes to make me feel bad for asking for things.

I go upstairs to wait for Chris and my mom is up there for a change by herself reading.

"Hey mom, can I ask you something?" I ask.

"Hold on a sec," she finishes her paragraph then says "Okay, I wanted to finish that paragraph." I laugh because I do that, and I knew that's what she was doing.

"So, prom is coming up and I already paid for the tickets, would you be willing to help me buy a dress if I pay you back?" I hold my breath hoping she will say yes.

"I would love to go prom dress shopping with you, I wasn't sure if you were going." she says, and I think that's not really what I asked, but it could be fun to go together. We never do anything just us anymore, so it sounds like a fun idea.

"I promise I will pay you back when I get a job again." I say, then ask "When would you want to go?"

"Actually, we can go tomorrow after school if you want." she says.

"Okay." I go give her a hug and I'm so excited to ask Chris now. "Thanks mom. Oh, good Chris is here." I yell as I skip into the kitchen to greet him at the door.

I'm so happy to see him that I forget all about the issues I have with him, and the fact that I've been planning how to breakup with him. He looks happy to see me too, so I think our time apart has somehow changed everything. "So, I have a question" I say to him, "And I'm hoping you will say yes."

"Okay" he says, and because I'm smiling he is smiling too. "What is this question that has you smiling like a goofball?"

"I already have the tickets and my mom will loan me money for a dress, will you please go to my prom with me?" I ask, and I'm so afraid he will say no, I almost miss his "yes."

"Did you just say yes?" I ask so happy I'm jumping up and down like a kid on Christmas morning.

"Yes. I said yes." he is laughing, and I'm so happy he came here. I can't believe I even thought about breaking up with him. I must be crazy to think I could ever have a better boyfriend, than him. I feel like such a terrible person, but I vow right then and there to be a better girlfriend. I will treat him better and I won't let my thoughts run away and think badly about him either. I feel my brain is my worst enemy sometimes.

The rest of the day we hang out and watch a movie. I know he can't stay late, he works early and It's a school night. I don't want to give my parents any reason to not let me go to prom now. So around ten o'clock I say it's time for him to go and I know he doesn't want to, but I whisper "I want you to stay so bad, but I don't want to mess up my chance to go to prom. I will see you in a few days, I love you."

He agrees, and goes to the door, "If anything changes for Sunday I'll let you know, otherwise I should be here around noon and we can hang out all day."

"Okay I can't wait to spend the day with you." I say, and I kiss him goodbye.

The next day after school, my mom and I head out to Buffalo to shop for a dress. We head to some exclusive dress shops, in a ritzy area. I'm hoping to find a dress that looks good on me. The hardest part about being five feet nine inches as a teen girl is finding clothes to fit my height. Most dresses look to short on me, as do most of my jeans. If I happen to find something long enough for me they are way too big around. I think my mom realizes this, and it's why she is taking me to more exclusive dress shops. I'm so grateful.

The first store is so incredibly beautiful. You can tell everyone that shops there has so much money. I try not to feel too out of place, but I know I am. We go to a few stores and of course I run into the problem that nothing fits right. If it is long enough it's too big around and if it fits around, it's way too short. I'm starting to feel deflated as we walk into one last store, but it has a lot of dresses, so fingers crossed.

I pull some dresses off the racks and my mom grabs some too. The sales lady is kind of looking at us as if we shouldn't be there and I can tell my mom is annoyed. We aren't rich, but we aren't poor either. I think it's rude to assume by looking at us we don't belong there.

Finally, we ask for a dressing room and the lady gives my mom another look without hiding it, she looks her up and down. I see my mom stand tall, square her shoulders and look right back at the lady straight in her eyes. Next my mom says in her most authoritative snobby voice, "Lady my money is as good here as the next person, stop looking me up and down and open the damn door before I call your corporate office." Never once wavering her eyes from the sales lady's eyes.

"Oh, um, I'm sorry ma'am." The lady quickly says stumbling over her words, as she lets my mom and I in a dressing room. As soon as the door closes we quietly started laughing, covering our mouths like little school girls.

"What a Bitch" my mom says, and I am surprised because she never talks like that.

"I know, but you sure put her in her place," I say still laughing, but I stop when I look at the price tag of the dresses. "Mom these are way too expensive." I say.

"Oh well, I still want you to try them on. I'm not letting that lady know that." she says.

So, I go ahead and try the dresses on. The first few are awful. They either make me look like I'm a hooker, or they are super long and baggy. I'm almost in tears by now, and my mom hands me another one. "Try this one on and if it doesn't fit, I think I can sew the blue one that we did like that was too loose. I think I can pull in the waist and the bust and make it look nice." She says trying to make me feel good.

I put the last one on and I can't believe the girl in the mirror. It, no... I, look so pretty. The dress is black, incredibly long, where it has the smallest amount of fabric touching the ground behind me. It is form fitting and fits my entire body in all the right places. It has no shoulders, so the arms are attached just under the underarm area, and it goes all the way up my neck in a very elegant manner. The longs sleeves fit my long arms, and its very form fitting to my slender arms. The best part is even though it's floor length it has a slit just off center, almost to the top of my thigh so it still has a sexy feel to it although I'm completely covered. I.love.it.

I step out of the dressing room to use the floor to ceiling mirrors and the little pedestal area to stand on, so I can see every angle. I can't stop twirling and looking at myself. My mom is smiling, and I see she has tears in her eyes. I know I want this dress and I'm afraid to look at the price tag. I go back in the dressing room to change out of it and ask my mom to come unzip me.

Once she gets in the dressing room I take the dress off and look at the price. $300.00, there is no way I can get this dress. I'm about to tell my mom I understand, when she says, "I will pay for this dress, but you have to pay me back half." Then she adds, "Don't tell your sisters, because I don't want to hear any crap about it." Before I can argue, she walks out while I finish getting dressed and pays for the dress.

I'm so incredibly grateful and happy. I'm going to feel and look like a princess for my prom. I hope Chris likes the dress on me. I think he will, it is beautiful. I turn to my mom and say "Thank you so much. As soon as I get the money together I will pay you back, I feel bad you had to pay it up front but thank you."

"There was no way I was telling that sales lady I didn't have the money for it. I would have spent $500 to wipe that smug look off her face."

I couldn't help but laugh and silently thank the snooty bitch for being that way, because it made my mom mad. I learned today when someone tries to make my mom feel like she is less than them, she will be sure to reverse it on you. Good for her. I will remember this day for the rest of my life.

Finally, it's prom night. I'm so excited to get all dressed up in my new dress. I talked to Chris the night before and we decided we will go to prom and after prom, but not anything else. A lot of kids go to parties or some go to amusement parks, but we both think we will be tired and we should just save the money.

I fix my hair and makeup and I can honestly say I feel so tonight. I never feel pretty, but this dress makes me feel so grown up and elegant. Even if Brittany gets shitty, I know I look good. Nothing is going to ruin my night. I hear the dogs barking upstairs, so I assume that means Chris is here. I try to calm myself down so when I go upstairs I won't turn red and be embarrassed. There is nothing worse than getting that beet red look I get when embarrassed.

I walk upstairs feeling like I'm floating on a cloud. I still can't help blushing when I see him, and he tells me I look beautiful. He looks very handsome in his suit and we make a nice-looking couple tonight. As I expected Brittany is here and I can tell she wants to say something, but I think for once in her life she is speechless. We go outside to take pictures and my mom fusses over me and it feels nice. I can see she is so proud of how I look, and she is happy she got me the dress. I hug her and thank her again and we head out for our evening.

The prom dinner is very good. I have never had such a fancy dinner and it feels extra special being in such a beautiful dress. I know one problem I may run into is if Megan and Chris see each other. So far, we are almost through dinner and I haven't seen her. I wish things were different because I miss her so much, and that confuses me on what I should do about Chris. On one hand if I break up with him I can see if I can mend my friendship with Megan, who I miss so much. On the other hand, if I stay with him, I will still have someone to go out on dates with and to get me out of my house. It's such a confusing time for me and I wish I had someone to talk to.

They start playing music and I want to dance because I love dancing. I convince Chris to come dance with me and we are having a nice time until I hear, "Oh look Megan, it's Margo and her asshole boyfriend." I don't even have to see who it is. I'd know her voice blindfolded in the middle of a Mardi Gras. It's Darby.

I know Chris hears her too and before I can say anything or move away, he uses my body to ram into her almost knocking her down. I'm not too worried about her doing anything back, she's four feet eight inches and maybe ninety pounds soaking wet and has the strength of a child. I am worried she will create a problem I don't want with Chris, not tonight. I have looked forward to tonight too much to let that little bitch ruin my night.

While she's regaining her balance and pride, I grab Chris's arm and tell him I'm ready to leave. I want to stop and grab something to snack on later before we head to after prom and all the stores close. I'm glad he doesn't argue or make a scene and agrees to take off. He goes out to get the car and I go over to get our stuff from our table. The last thing on my mind was running in to Megan, but there she is right in front of me.

"You look so pretty." she says and smiles at me. I can see it's a genuine smile, but I don't care because what just happened with Darby is way too fresh in my mind.

"I know I do." I snap "I don't need someone like you to tell me that. Go find your new best friend Darby and kiss her ass." then I add, "The next time you talk shit about me or Chris to someone, then want to be nice to my face, make sure they aren't going to let me know." And I storm out of my prom. The look on her face was pure hurt and shock.

We stop and get some stuff to snack on later and we almost don't go to the after prom. I decide though I'm not letting a bitch like Darby stop me from having this last high school experience. I walk in with my head held high and refuse to look in her or Megan's direction.

We end up having a nice time, but after about an hour it is boring, so we decide to head back to my house. I am so tired I can hardly keep my eyes open. In fact, by the time we pull into my driveway I am sound asleep. Chris wakes me up and helps me walk into the house, he tells me he will call me sometime tomorrow. This is the first time ever, I have a three-a.m. curfew and here I am, home by one.

I watch Chris pull out of my driveway, and I am silently grateful he didn't mind coming home so early. I am so exhausted, I take my dress off and crawl into my bed just in my underclothes. I don't even wash off my makeup, or find something to sleep in. I think I am out before Chris even gets to the end of my street.

The next few days go by drama free, and it is finally Memorial Day. I wake up not feeling too well, but I get up and moving and get ready to go. I love our family Memorial Day picnics so much, because my aunt and uncle always have the best food. I can't wait to go eat it and see my older cousins that I don't get to see as much as I wish I could. Now that I'm eighteen, I think they will be more willing to hang out and socialize with me. They used to only talk mostly to each other and sometimes Lauren, but I noticed more and more they treat me like an equal now.

I get to the picnic around the same time as my one older cousin Angel. We are catching up, and getting our food together when I look at her funny and she says, "Are you okay?"

"Yeah," I mumble, "But I feel super shaky and sick." I take a bite of my food thinking that I just need to eat when suddenly, I feel like I'm going to throw up. I run to the bathroom, but nothing comes up. I am sitting there for a minute on the floor before I realize Angel is there too.

"Oh my god, are you sick?" she says, "Or do you think you could be pregnant?" I stare at her for a second.

"I don't know, I don't think so... But I guess it could be possible..."

"When was your last period?" she asks me, and I honestly have no idea.

"I'm not sure, I never know because it's never the same every month." I reply, feeling very stupid.

"Okay, look I'm going to think of something to say to people and we will go buy you a test and see." she says then runs off to find my mom.

Angel comes back a few minutes later and says, "Okay your mom said you can go with me, let's go."

I don't even ask her what she says, I keep thinking I might be pregnant... I might be pregnant. I don't know how, or if I want to be a mom. As soon as she pulls out of the driveway she lights up a cigarette and I ask for one. In my head I know if I'm pregnant I shouldn't be smoking but I tell myself it's just today. If I am, then no more after today. I am so scared I can't think of what else to do to calm my nerves.

We are stuck having to drive to the next town. Nothing is open nearby being it's a holiday, so I try to distract myself and tell Angel about prom. I kind of want to ask her about Chris's behavior, but I realize he has been nicer to me now that I keep quiet and don't rock the boat. I decide it's not that big of a deal, and it must have been me. I also don't want to risk her saying anything to my parents, after all we aren't that close.

We finally get to a drugstore, and I realize I have smoked two more cigarettes. There's no way I'll keep doing that if I'm pregnant, but I keep telling myself I'm just getting the flu. I'm too embarrassed and nervous to even go into the store so Angel runs in for me. She comes out a few minutes later and tells me we will go down the street to McDonalds, so I can use the bathroom there.

I run in with the test, knowing what I need to do because Angel explained everything to me. I hurry up and pee on the little stick and lay it flat in my purse and run back out to the car. I get it out and hand it to Angel and she sets it up on the dash of her car and we time it by the car clock. I'm so incredibly scared and nervous, I realize I'm holding my breath. I take a few deep breaths and when it's time I ask her to look for me. I don't want to be the one to look.

She picks it up and says, "Holy crap, Margo you're pregnant." I can hardly register what she is saying as she hands the test to me to look at myself.

"Oh my God, I'm pregnant." I don't know what to say and I start to cry. It's not something I was expecting, but I realize now I'm going to be a mom and I need to figure it out. Fast. Abortion isn't something I'll even think about so, it's never an option for me. I try very hard to respect and not judge someone that chooses that route, but for me it's not an option. So, all I can do is wipe my eyes, and I ask my cousin to drive me over to Chris's work. Thankfully he works right down the street from where we are, or I'd probably chicken out from telling him.

I ask Angel to wait in the car and she is okay with that, so I head in to see if I can talk to Chris. I ask the girl in the front of the restaurant if she could please go get him, after she asks who I am, she does. I wait outside for about five minutes then he strolls out not to happy to have me there.

"What the hell are you doing here Margo? I'm working, and since you made a big deal about advertising you're my girlfriend, they are going to give me shit about it," he says mad.

"Look I didn't 'advertise it'. I asked for you and she asked who I was, so I told her. I didn't know I was some big secret." I say trying not to cry. I don't want to argue with him and now I'm wishing I never came. "Just forget I came, I don't even care right now to tell you why." I start to stomp off, but he grabs my arm and pulls me back roughly.

"Well you're here now," he loosens his grip and his voice is nicer, "Being I'll probably get in trouble, you might as well tell me what's up? Do you need money?" At least he is trying to be nice, I think. Oh well here goes.

"No, I don't, and I don't really know how to tell you this so I'm just going to tell you. I'm pregnant." There I said it, it's out.

He stares at me, then says "I had a feeling you were going to tell me this." I'm a little surprised by his reaction, so I ask him why?

"Well you have been extra moody, and your boobs are bigger and firmer." I'm stunned. I would think I would have known this being it's my body. I can't help but think he knew because he has gone through this already. It kind of makes me upset, but I know better than to say anything.

"What are you going to do?" he asks me.

"There is nothing to do." I say then add, "I'm going to have a baby and you're going to be a dad, again." I'm worried he is going to be mad or break up with me, but he instead surprises me and hugs me.

"Okay." he says, "I have to get back into work, I'll come over tomorrow and we can talk." He gives me a kiss, smiles at me and heads back into work. That went a lot better than I thought, all things considering.

Chapter 7

The next day Chris comes over to my house. We have a lot to figure out, but I know we can do it. I'm not sure yet how I'm going to tell my parents, and I'm pretty sure his mom is going to flip. My parents will support me, even if they are unhappy about it. I know I'll never be homeless or thrown out on my ass, but I'm still scared to tell them. I'm mostly scared to see the disappointment on their faces. I know I act rough and tough, but I want them to be proud of me and I fear this will ruin that.

We are sitting in my room talking about it when my mom comes in. She sees us in my room sitting on my bed and she says, "Hey you two what are you doing? You know the rules Margo, you're not supposed to be in here" She actually says it nicely and not in her mom voice.

"I know, but we are just talking about stuff and it's the only place to do it in private." I respond.

"What's so private you need to hide down here?" she asks. She must have seen something in my face, that sixth sense or something because she asks, "Is there something I need to know?"

Before I can stop myself, I say, "Well, there is, I'm pregnant." I can't believe I just said it.

My mom looks at me and I think for sure she is going to yell or something, but she asks instead, "I'm going to be a grandma?" Then she surprises me further and happily shouts, "I'm going to be a grandma?!"

I am speechless when she grabs me and hugs me and happily swings me around and says, "Okay. So, we have a baby on the way, did you go to a doctor? How far along are you? Have you started prenatal vitamins?"

"Whoa slow down, no. I just found out and honestly I have no idea what I'm supposed to do now."

"Thank goodness for moms." she laughs, "I will help you set everything up and we can get the ball rolling so we know everything will be okay." then she says, "I will tell your dad tonight."

Chris chimes in at that "No I'll tell him."

"No, you won't." My mom says and I'm afraid we will have our first "baby speed bump", but my mom continues, "Trust me when I say if you tell him we will have problems that nobody wants. If I tell him and show him it's going to be okay, then it will be okay."

I step in before Chris can say anything. "Chris, I agree with my mom, I want her to be the one to tell him."

I can tell he isn't happy, but he finally says through a clenched jaw "Fine."

My mom ignores him and directs to me," Don't tell your sisters or your brother until I tell dad." Which I wouldn't have, but I get why she says it.

Holy crap I'm going to be a mom. I still can't wrap my head around all of it, and I'm glad I can share it with my mom. I have so many questions and I'm kind of excited. I know I should be more scared, but I guess knowing my mom will teach me things, I'm not.

I'm glad now I didn't jump the gun and break up with Chris. I think it would have been hard for him to find this out if we broke up. I know that is what happened before, and that child got taken away from him. I also know I would never do that, if he wants to be a part of this child's life he can be.

My father comes home about forty-five minutes later and my mom says she wants to take a drive with him. He is a little surprised, but he doesn't argue. He hurries up and changes out of his work clothes and they leave.

As soon as they leave, Chris turns to me and says, "If your mom ever tries to tell me what to do again, especially with my kid, I'll make you leave and never let her see it."

I honestly can't believe he just said that to me. Here we go again, his attitude is coming out. This time though I'm not putting up with it, I'm a mom now and I will stand up for what is right. "Stop acting like you're my boss, I will not tell my mom anything. I need my mom to help me through this and I need you to be nice." I start to walk away, when he grabs me from behind in a bear hug pinning my arms down to my sides and carries me into the living room.

"You will never tell me what to do. I'm not your father, some pussy whipped guy." he says as he tosses me onto the couch and before I can get up he is sitting on me once again pinning me down where I can't move. I'm terrified he will hurt the baby and I start crying.

"Please get off me, you will hurt the baby." I plead.

"No, I won't but if I did, it would be your fault for talking to me like a piece of shit." he is livid.

I try to wiggle, but I realize quickly just like any other time it's not worth my energy to try.

So, I try to ask again. "Okay, I understand, please will you get up?" At this point I'm trying not to panic about the baby, but I can see he knows I am. His eyes get darker, meaner, he's the boss.

He laughs at me and says "no" and continues to sit there. He finally moves slightly, barely enough to take some of the weight off my stomach but I'm grateful, so I don't try to move. I lay there and wait for him to talk.

"I will not be some pussy whipped guy like your dad," he says again. "This is my kid you have in there not your moms, not your dads. I will be the one to decide what is best. Got it?"

"Yes, of course." I say. "I wasn't trying to tell you what was best for the baby. I was saying what is best for me and telling my dad." I'm racking my brain trying to think of a way to switch subjects and calm him down. "Speaking of our baby" I hope this works. "When I go to the doctor, will you be able to go? Or should I go with my mom?" He shifts more, I think it's working.

He finally gets up, so I can sit up and he sits next to me but facing me. He says, "If I can go I'll be there but there is no way I can miss work. If you can, try to go either Thursday this week or Tuesday next week.

I'm not sure how all this works. I don't know anything about those kind of doctors, I'll have to ask my mom. Although to pacify him, I tell him, "I'll do the best I can, I think it would be nice if you could come too. I really want you to be able to experience this whole thing right along beside me." I smile at him and he finally thaws and smiles back. I can see he is back to being the nice Chris, so I lean in and give him a kiss. Pulling away I shout out laughing, "Holy shit we have a baby on the way!"

He laughs too, and says "You better be a good mom, or you will be out the door." A typical Chris response. I ignore it, not wanting anything to start again.

I'm feeling tired, so I say, "I'm going to go lay down for a while if you want though you can stay."

"No, I'll head home, I have to work in the morning." he says.

I'm relieved, because I want to see what my dad has to say without Chris around. I feel if Chris gets shitty with my dad it could make this next nine months or so incredibly long. I also want to talk to my mom about things I will start expecting, and I feel Chris may make me feel stupid. I have no idea what the doctor will be like and how they do all that stuff. I kind of want to be alone with my parents, thankfully he wants to leave. Chris walks me downstairs to my room, and I climb into bed. He kisses my cheek and tells me he will call tomorrow night. Last thing I remember he turns out the lights.

I wake up and It is dark out. I know my parents must be home by now, so I head upstairs to see if they want to talk. I'm a little nervous to see my dad. I know he won't be happy, but I am not at all ready for his reaction. He sees me coming and gets up and walks right up to me and pulls me into the biggest hug I've ever gotten.

"We love you and we will be right here to help support you through this." My dad is saying as I stand there and bawl my eyes out.

"I'm so sorry dad, and I can't seem to ever stop crying. I don't know why, but right now everything makes me cry."

"That would be your hormones, there will be lots of crying and I'm betting some mood swings too." he laughs and walks with me to sit down. I sit next to my mom on the couch and my dad goes back to his chair. I realize I'm lucky to have parents like mine. I know a girl that got pregnant in high school and her parents made her put the baby up for adoption. I also know a girl that decided it was best to get an abortion, rather than even tell her parents. Yes, I'd say I'm lucky.

"Mom, how do I make a doctor appointment for this? I don't have a baby doctor or even know where one would be. How do I even find one?"

"Well first, you need to call and make an appointment with an OB GYN doctor. I can help you with that tomorrow. Since you are still on dad's insurance we need to see if they will cover this and if so, how much." she says.

Wow, there's so much to figure out. I don't know If we will live here, or move in together, or live separate. I still have a few more days until my graduation, but thankfully I'll have my high school diploma. It also dawns on me, I won't be going off to college. I won't be living in the big city either. Once again, I find myself crying as I mourn the life I thought I was going to have. I make a vow though right then and there; no tears will be shed after today. I will not raise my child to think he or she was a mistake and unwanted, or that my life was ruined. None of that is true, this baby surprisingly changed the course a little and that's okay. I firmly believe in life what is meant to be, will be. Everything happens for a reason, even if we don't see that reason right away.

    I wipe my eyes and tell my parents I love them, but I'm going to head back to bed. I can't help feeling so tired. My mom explains that too, is all part of being pregnant. She also warns me the morning sickness can be a little rough. Luckily, I've been able to somewhat control that. I hope that means It won't be as bad as I heard it was for my mom.

A few days later I have my first doctor appointment. Chris can't go, I wasn't able to get the appointment on his day off. I didn't go out of my way to try though. I just wanted the first one they could give me, and I told him that's all they had available. My mom can come and I'm so glad. I feel it's better to have her here anyways, after all she went through this, four times.

I realize when we walk into the doctor's office and people are staring at me, this is how it's going to be the whole pregnancy. People are going to prejudge me and being I look younger than eighteen, it makes it worse. I look like a fifteen-year-old girl and while not yet showing, they hear me say I am here because I'm pregnant. For the first time since finding out, I'm embarrassed and feel I should explain I'm older or something.

One lady keeps staring at me and I can tell it is pissing my mom off too. She has her daughter with her and I know not for the same reason I'm here, but I asked. "What are you here for?" Even though I heard when they checked in I am just trying to be nice.

The girl blushes and says, she has an UTI and maybe a yeast infection. Her mom is acting as if she can catch my pregnancy, turning her nose up at me like I'm scum. It is so embarrassing, but thankfully they call my name. I smile at the young girl and say, "Good luck," and I feel an overwhelming need to be a bitch to the mom, so I add in a twang "Hopefully I can find out who the babies daddy is, it could be anyone since I get paid for my pussy" I know it's vulgar, but I won't ever forget her look of shock. I laugh so hard and I'm about to apologize to my mom when I see she's laughing too. We needed that laugh, we are both so nervous.

The appointment itself goes well. The doctor says I'm six weeks pregnant and the baby is due very early February. She also says the baby has a great heartbeat, and everything looks great so far. She explains the tiredness, the queasy feeling, and tells me it could get worse but it's all to be expected. She also says she wants me to try to keep my weight gain to around thirty to thirty-five pounds total. I know I will have many more questions, but I can ask my mom those when they come up. I say goodbye to the doctor and schedule my next appointment for in two months.

Mom and I leave and head back to our house. I know I should ask what's going to happen with Chris and I and our living arrangements, but it feels weird. I figure now is better than never, so I bite the bullet and ask. "Hey mom, where are Chris and I going to live?"

"I don't know what you're asking." she says then, "Nothing will change. You will live with dad and I and he will come visit."

"What about when the baby comes? I think we should live together."

"Margo, let's give this some time to talk over, don't make any sudden decisions please."

"I won't" I say, but I know Chris is going to want to be together. I can't see him letting me stay at my parents. Not without him there and I don't see them allowing him to stay with us. I'm so nervous to even talk to him about it all. I just don't want to fight with him. I try to push it out of my mind, and ask "Do you think I can have a baby shower? I don't have anything for a baby." then I say, "I also don't have any friends that will throw me one."

"Yes honey, I will make sure you have a baby shower. It will help get you a lot of the stuff you need, but you guys will still have to buy some stuff yourselves."

That has me scared because Chris is already working two jobs, and I don't have a job. Maybe tomorrow I'll have to start looking. I can do something that isn't physical, maybe work in an office or something. These are all things Chris and I need to sit down and talk about. For now, though, I'm going to worry about eating right and taking care of this little baby inside my belly.

Chapter 8

    Saturday morning is finally here and it's my graduation day. I can't believe I'm graduating high school. I never thought this day would come. I get up and go upstairs to get something to eat. I take about ten bites of my cereal and within seconds my stomach turns bad. I jump up, run to the bathroom and throw up, I'm so sick, I can't even stand up. I sit on the floor for a long time before I get the strength to get up and get in the shower. That was probably the worst vomiting experience of my life. I pray I don't do that again, especially today.

    I let the water run on me for as long as I can, but I know I need to finish up because without a doubt someone will start complaining. Once I'm done in the shower, I dry off quickly and head downstairs. I need to get dressed, fix my hair and do my makeup, yet I feel awful. I know Chris will probably be here soon, but I can't seem to move any faster. Midway through drying my hair, I feel the need to lay down for a few minutes. The room is spinning, I'm shaky and I feel like I'm going to get sick again.

As if on cue, my mom comes in my room with toast and a glass of water. "Drink the water but nibble on the toast." she says then, "You need to drink a lot more water now and more frequent little snacks. It won't completely stop it, but it will help a lot." How does she do that? She always appears at the right time. Usually it's when I'm doing something I shouldn't be doing. Today I am grateful for her uncanny ability to do this.

"Thank you, I'm not sure how I will get through today if I feel like this:" I feel like I'm going to cry again, as my mom comes over and hugs me.

"You will." She says, "It might be hard at times, but you will because you are a strong young lady."

That does it, now I am crying, and she says, "It's okay, but if you keep crying your graduation pictures will have a red puffy face in them." I smile at this because she knows I hate my picture taken, let alone if I look bad.

"Okay, I'm done crying." I say smiling as I get up to finish getting ready.

I am so happy that I get to walk for my diploma. I look forward to seeing all my friends get theirs too. I'm sad that my friends and I have drifted away over the last five or six months. I hate how things have changed so much since middle school. I thought we all had way more time to fix all of it. I guess time slows for no one.

Right when I'm about to finish my makeup, I hear a knock on my bedroom door.

"Come in!" I yell, and in walks Chris looking nice as usual. I smile and walk over to give him a kiss.

He jerks his face away and says, "No. Not with that crap on your lips."

I can't help but laugh and say, "Oh my goodness it's lipstick, it won't hurt you."

"I won't be kissing you with that on, so you might as well wipe it off." He says, and I can tell he's in a bad mood. I don't feel well enough to do this today. I like wearing lipstick, and I feel pretty with it on. "Chris, today is my graduation, I only want to look nice." but as I'm saying it he hands me a tissue and tells me to take it off.

I hurry and do it, I honestly don't want to fight. I know if I don't take it off, I will eventually cry, and ruin all my makeup. I'll add it back on when I get to my graduation, so I look nice to go across the stage.

"Good girl, was that so hard?" he asks. "I've told you before if you would just listen to me, things would be easier for you." I look over at him and try to smile. I feel so nauseous, I honestly don't have it in me to fight today.

"Are you going to be moody now?" he is getting mad, I see the change in his stance.

"No, I have been sick all morning with morning sickness, and I feel awful."

"That's all in your head." he says, "Stop looking for attention, it won't work on me."

"It's not, I have been throwing up all morning." I say trying again not to cry, I seem to cry over everything these days.

"Yes, it is all in your head. Stop thinking about it and you will be fine."

I nod my head okay, and say, "We need to go soon, and I need to see if everyone is ready." I want to head upstairs before this becomes a major issue.

We go upstairs, and my parents are waiting for my sister to get out of the other bathroom. Thankfully Brittany got ready upstairs, so there was no fighting today. I think that was because my mom knows I feel like crap, and she probably told her to. While we wait, I drink a little more water and my mom brings me some saltine crackers to nibble on.

"Here put some of these in your purse so if you feel sick later."

Chris interrupts her with "She's fine."

My mom looks at him with a look of disgust. "Excuse me?"

Before they can get into it, I speak up "He's right I'm okay now, but thank you."

I can see Chris wants to say more, but before he can Brittany comes out and says she's ready to go finally. She is of course dressed in a micro mini skirt and a shirt where her boobs are almost completely showing. She starts strutting around the kitchen pretending to be busy, but just looking to get attention. This is my day and that about kills her. She can't stand it when anyone else gets any kind of attention. She realizes she's caught Chris's eye, so she walks over to put her shoes on right in front of him and seductively bends over and points her ass right at him. I glance over at Chris and he's blatantly staring at her ass. I'm so pissed and hurt, he could at least pretend to respect me and look away.

"Good grief, is there a reason you have to hang your tits and ass out in front of us?" I speak up, and my mom finally looks over.

She says "Brittany go change right now. You are not leaving the house with that on."

"Thanks a lot bitch." Brittany whispers to me so my mom can't hear, but she stomps off to change.

"Mom, Chris and I are going to leave, I can't be late because Brittany is being like this." I say, and we head out the door.

After we are in the car driving for a while Chris finally speaks to me, "What the hell is your mother's problem?"

"I don't know what you mean." I say knowing damn well he is pissed about the crackers.

"Yes, you do, and stop playing dumb. Do you live on another planet? I know your head is in outer space all the time, but are you really that stupid?"

"That's not nice. I have no idea what is wrong with my mom, but feel free to ask her. I'm not a mind reader." I'm so hurt he is starting crap today of all days. I also feel so sick; my stomach starts turning and I know I'm going to throw up. "Pullover...seriously I'm going to throw up pull over fast." I yell at him. He listens, probably because he loves his car and doesn't want me getting puke in it. I thankfully get my head out of the car in time and vomit all over the pavement.

"Oh, for Christ's sake, you're ridiculous." he is glaring at me, "I can't believe you are acting like this today." he says.

"I'm not acting, I have morning sickness, and the doctor said it can get bad."

"Bullshit, it's all in your head to get attention, you need to stop it."

"I swear it's not, I need something to drink, maybe ginger ale will help."

"No, we don't have time." He was about to put the car in reverse when I hurry up and hop out.

"I don't care if I miss it, there's a little store right here I'm going to go in and get a drink."

"I'm not giving you money to waste on that." Now he is being mean, as usual.

"Fine I have money; my dad gave me money the other day for milk and bread and he never got his change back." I shout at him.

I go into the store pretty much expecting him to leave me behind. I don't even care at this moment If I make my graduation or not. He surprises me though right as I'm about to check out and wraps his arms around me from behind and pulls my backside close to his front. He starts kissing my neck all sweet, and whispering he loves me and I'm the best girlfriend in the world. I'm a little surprised by his public display of affection, but I don't care, I'm happy he's being nice. I go to pay for it and he says "Babe, you know I want to take care of you I got this." Once again, I'm surprised. Then he adds "I will always take care of the girl I love," He hands me the keys and says, "Head out to the car I'll pay and bring this to you."

I go sit in the car and I'm confused by why he started being so nice to me. I love when he's sweet, I wish he was like that all the time. He finally walks out, and hands me the ginger ale. I open it and take a few sips, while he backs the car up and we head out.

"Just so you know that girl at the register, that was Sheri." I'm completely stunned, I honestly didn't look at her, so I have no idea who he means.

"Why didn't you introduce me then?" I realize now that's why he was being nice to me. It had nothing to do with me. He was rubbing it in her face that he has a new girlfriend. I'm a little hurt, but I don't want to fight again.

"I would have been nice, I'm not a mean person." I pout.

"Don't worry about it, she's a bitch. I didn't want to introduce you, but I wanted her to see I have someone better."

I'm not sure If I should be flattered or mad so I take the high road. I stop pouting to smile and say thank you. I figure rather than fight again, I'll focus on the half ass compliment he gave me. I would have liked to get a good look at her though. I have no idea what kind of girl he was attracted to before me. It's a weird curiosity that I have, to see what his type was before me. Maybe one day I can go back when I'm by myself and see her. I guess I know he loved her and according to him, she hurt him bad. I'd like to be able to have a face to go with that pain.

We finally get to where my graduation is being held and thank goodness, I'm feeling better. That ginger ale makes a huge difference. Chris finds a parking spot and I grab my cap and gown, purse and other shoes I want to wear. Chris looks at the shoes and says, "Why do you have those?"

"I'm changing into these for when I walk across the stage." I know he hates heels.

"They better be off you when we meet back up, I won't have you towering over me like some huge amazon."

Okay is all I say, and I get embarrassed that I'm so tall. Being five feet nine inches is such a pain as a girl. Especially when your boyfriend is only five feet ten inches. If I wore these heels by him I'd be at least two inches taller than him. I knew when I saw them though that these shoes with my gown, will look so pretty. I will have to make sure to get them off before anyone sees me by him.

I see a lot of people I know already chatting in groups waiting to go inside. I find Megan immediately and in perfect unison, our eyes meet, and we smile at each other. I quickly look away and thank goodness Chris doesn't notice. I'm so afraid she is going to come over here, I grab Chris's hand and try to get lost in the crowd pretending to look for my parents.

Eventually I do see my parents and we get to them right as the principal is telling us we need to go in and get in the back room behind the stage, to get ready. I say goodbye to Chris and my family and tell them I'll meet them back out here right where we are after it ends. Chris grabs my arm, pulls me into him and kisses me, and whispers "You better not be talking to any guys back there, I'll be watching."

I kind of laugh and say "Oh really? How's that?"

"Don't worry about it, I have my ways." when he catches my frown before I can stop it he squeezes my arm that he is still holding and asks "Why did you frown? What are you hiding?"

"I'm not hiding anything, and you're hurting my arm."

"You're making me hurt you, you are hiding something. Is there some guy you talk to that I don't know about?"

"No, I promise, you can watch all you want. I probably made a face because I don't feel well." I hope my lie is convincing. There is no guy, I wanted to talk to Megan, and now I'm not sure if I can.

"Fine, but I swear if you're lying to me I will leave your ass. I'll take my kid and leave you."

"I'm not, I promise. I love you, I'll see you when I'm done. I have to go so I'm not late." I quickly kiss him and head off to the back rooms with the rest of my class.

Every day with Chris is up and down. I feel like just when I think things are going well, Bam! He gets mad at me. I can't seem to stop it from happening. The more I try to behave and listen to him, the more he seems to want more from me. Maybe this is normal though. I mean, we are about to have a baby and I'm sure all families go through this. I need to try even harder now to keep my family together.

I scan the room hoping to find Megan. I see Shelby, but Megan is nowhere to be seen. I'm about to give up when I hear, "Hey Margo," from right behind me. I turn around and Megan is right there. We hug each other, as natural as if we just hung out the night before. I don't know if it's from the hormones, all the fighting, all the memories, or me hugging my best friend, but I start to cry.

"Hey, stop you're going to mess your makeup up." Megan says and we both kind of laugh at it. I tower over her five-foot four-inch height, but she hugs me as if I'm a child and she's a grown adult. I can feel her love, and it breaks my heart that we aren't friends anymore.

"We can't have that, I can't go on stage with smeared makeup." I laugh and try to stop but the tears just keep falling.

"Let's run to the bathroom and we can fix it," she says, and I notice she had tears running down her cheeks too. She's always so strong, so to see her vulnerable is almost my complete undoing.

I try to think of something else, so I say. "I have to tell you something, and it's big."

"Okay, let's go over here." she says, and we duck around the corner to an empty room.

"I'm pregnant" there I said it fast. I think she is in shock, she stares at me for a minute without speaking.

"Oh, my God. Do your parents know?" I knew that would be her first question.

"Yes, they do. Right now, my siblings don't and neither does his family but I'm due the beginning of February. I had to tell you. I couldn't have you hear from someone else, and I know we don't talk much, but I wanted to tell you myself." I'm trying not to cry again.

"I'm glad you did. I miss you and maybe over the summer we can try to hang out again, and fix things."

"I'd love to, right now Chris is still not happy about what happened, but I'll talk to him and fix it." I know that may not go well, but for sure I'll try. I miss Megan so much. It's like missing my arm or a leg. We have been best friends since middle school and I'll try anything I can to fix it.

"Well I still think he was a jerk, but for you I will try to be nice to him. And especially for the baby, after all I should be its aunt." This is so the Megan I know and love, willing to set aside her feelings for me.

"Okay, and you better be this baby's aunt." I laugh and then they tell us we need to line up to go take our seats. I hug Megan one last time and I feel so happy I could burst. I think everything will be okay now. I hide my ginger ale in my gown and head out to take my seat.

Everything went smooth at the graduation. I don't remember much of it. I couldn't stop thinking about Megan, and Chris and all of us getting along. I thought about the baby, and I kept seeing myself dressing up a little girl in cute doll like clothes. While I know the baby isn't going to be like a doll, I can't help picturing cute dresses with adorable little shoes and accessories. It's silly, but I really want a little girl to be my little friend one day. I know I want to have a close bond and be there for her. I would be happy with a boy too, the most important part being the baby is ok.

I find my family after and I'm happy to see Chris is with them. I wasn't sure if he could sneak in the back and if he did if he saw me with Megan. I hate this feeling, thinking everything will be a fight. I want everything to be okay today. I go up to Chris, hug him and say, "See I told you there's no guy... obviously if you were watching you know this now." then I kiss his cheek.

He smiles and says "Yes, today you were good. I'm proud of you for getting your diploma". He hugs me back, and I breathe a sigh of relief, he didn't get backstage. I'm super tired from all the excitement of the day, and the fighting. My family wants to go out to eat, and I agree, although I'd rather just go home and sleep.

Dinner ends up being good. We go get my favorite food, Mexican. For a change, I can eat it too, and not feel sick. My aunts and uncles and cousins, meet us there and we have a really nice time. Angel is there, and we run to the bathroom together and she asks if anyone knows yet. I tell her my parents do but not the others. She hugs me and tells me she is so happy for me.

Her boyfriend is here tonight, and I don't like him much, but I am nice to him because I know how it feels to have someone start shit. I feel like he can be a dick though. A couple of times he reminded me of Chris, it was subtle stuff that no one else saw, but I did. I don't focus too much on it though, I figure she knows what she's doing.

Finally, I stand up and tell everyone thanks for coming, but I am going to head out. I'm so tired, I fall asleep on the ride home. When Chris stops the car and shuts it off I wake up thinking we are at my house. We are at his uncle's house instead. I'm a little annoyed, but Instead of saying something and us fighting, I follow him inside.

Everyone is already drinking and having fun. I don't feel good and I want to go lay down. I tell Chris, and he says hold on he will be right back. He comes back and says his aunt said I can sleep in her daughter's room because she is at a sleepover tonight. I go up to her room and climb into her bed. I have no care at all what Chris is doing or if he is drinking. I know I should call my parents, but truthfully, I just don't care. I can feel myself drifting and finally I let myself fall asleep.

I'm out cold when I feel Chris trying to have sex with me. I shift my body trying to move away from him and I try to tell him no, I'm tired. He tightens his hold on me and this time grabs a pillow and puts it across my face, so no one can hear me. I know I should try harder, but the pillow on my face is making it hard to breath and now I'm worried it will affect the baby. I feel myself try to relax so it won't hurt as bad. After a few minutes he gets up and I know he is done. I pull the pillow off my face and quickly get up and run to the bathroom. I make it just in time to reach the toilet before I start vomiting. I honestly don't know if I'm throwing up because of the baby, or the pillow over my face or the fear of him when he is like that.

  I am in the bathroom for about a half hour before I can get myself together enough to go back to bed. I sneak back to the bedroom and I thank God, that he is passed out. I climb into the bed as quietly as I can and try to go back to sleep. I have a hard time doing that though, because I keep thinking he will wake up and want more. As I'm lying there I keep thinking this isn't what I want. This life, with this man, isn't what I want. I have no idea what I can do about it, but I want out. I think I'll talk to my parents and see what they think I should do.

The next morning, I get up before Chris and head out to the kitchen. I know someone has been up because there is fresh coffee. I pour a little cup of it. I don't want a lot, half a cup, but Chris walks in. He marches over to me and takes the cup and says "No."

"Chris the doctor said a little bit isn't bad, just not a lot." I try to explain.

"I said no." He responds and stares at me. I figure he can't do much here, so I feel a little braver and push back.

"I don't care what you said, give me my coffee back." I say with more spunk.

That was a mistake, the next thing I know he tosses the hot coffee at me. It hits me in the neck, and on my chest area. It's still hot enough that it burns me through my clothes.

"What the fuck?" I say, "Oh my God that is hot, you asshole." I go to pass him, so I can get the hot wet clothes off when he grabs my arm and stops me.

"Don't fuck with me or once my kid comes out I'll take him, and you'll never see him again."

I know I should be focused on his temper right now, but I can't help but snap "Him? It could be a girl you know."

He smirks in my face and says, "I don't doubt you will probably get that wrong too." He lets go of my arm and says, "If you do fuck that up and it is a girl, I'll take that brat too."

I'm standing there wondering how true that is, if he could take my baby from me, when his aunt walks in

"Oh, my goodness what happened?" she directs to me but before I can answer, Chris does.

"She's clumsy and spilled her coffee," he looks at me laughing and adds "Hey klutz, go clean yourself up so we can go." I walk out of the room, knowing there's no point correcting him, especially in front of someone.

I remember his actions last night, so I pull the sheets off the bed disgusted he would do that on someone else's bed, especially a kid's bed. I would be livid if that was my child's bed and someone acted that way. I assume his aunt would change them but just in case, I decide to at least strip the bed. Then I change into something his aunt let me borrow, and I thank her, and we head out. I want to hurry up get home and talk to my parents. I want this nightmare of him taking sex when he wants it to end.

Chapter 9

I decide to try to talk to my parents that night. I don't know how I can afford a baby on my own, with no job, but I'll do whatever it takes. I know I can't keep doing this with Chris. I know he knows I'm upset, but he isn't saying anything. That worries me, but I try not to think about that. I need to get through the day until he leaves and hopefully not set him off at all.

I was nowhere near prepared though for my parents pissed off attitude when I get home. I completely forgot I never called them to tell them I wouldn't be home last night. It wasn't intentional, but I messed up.

"Well well well, look who decides to show up." My mom says to my dad. "Apparently graduating makes her think she doesn't have to come home at night."

"I'm sorry I..." I can't even finish because she cuts me off.

"The phone where you were at was broke? You got a flat tire and slept in your car all night? Oh, I know, you were lost in the jungle and couldn't find your way home?" she says sarcastically.

"No, I wasn't feeling well, and I went to lay down and I never woke up." I try to explain but she's on a roll today.

"Oh, I see, and Chris is pregnant too, and he had to sleep huh? Or is he not familiar with how to use the phone?" she is super pissed and overreacting.

"Maybe he can act this way with his mom, but you can't. You are grounded for the next two weeks Margo. Then she looks at Chris and says, "That means you don't come here or call here." I'm so completely stunned. I'm eighteen, I graduated high school, and I'm having my own child. How the hell does she think she can ground me?

"I have news for you," I say, "I'm not grounded I'm eighteen, I don't have to listen to you and I refuse to let you treat me like this." I'm so angry I hear myself saying, "You no longer have the right to talk to me like a child. News flash, I'm having a child, I'm going to be a mom and I promise, I will never be a mom like you."

"Listen here young lady." My dad jumps in, I can see he's pissed and I don't care. "You will not talk like that to your mother. You live in my house and if you do, you will listen and respect my rules. Or you can leave." Of course, I think... he takes her side.

I'm about to say I'm sorry when Chris speaks up. "You may let your wife boss you around, but she won't boss me around. And she won't talk to Margo like that when my kids inside her." I can't believe he is saying this to my dad, I'm afraid they will come to blows soon. Chris looks at me and says, "Go pack your shit you're moving out."

My dad and Chris are staring each other down, neither one looking away. I'm afraid my dad is going to sock him one, when my mom steps in and tells my dad to go cool off.

"No one is going to move anywhere, Margo, you need to have respect for the people that live here." I can tell my mom is trying to calm things down. Chris on the other hand, stares down my mom, with an angry glare.

"I told you to go pack your shit. Go do it." He says to me.

"Chris it's fine, it's not a big deal." I say. "I'm not ready to move out, not right now."

"Can't you hear? Are you deaf too? Go pack your shit. I will not have you living here alone when people act this way towards you, not when you are carrying my child. Go.Pack.Your.Stuff. He says each word, slowly with anger. He is so mad, I scurry out of the room and go try to pack my stuff.

By the time I get down to my bedroom, I'm hysterical. I can't stop crying and I don't know what I'm going to do. I try to get my clothes together, but I have nothing to put them in. I go back upstairs to get some garbage bags when my dad comes back into the room.

I feel like if he starts yelling again, I won't be able to keep things from getting worse. I don't want him and Chris to come to blows. I know Chris is strong, but I think my dad would kick his ass and then Chris will hate me for it.

My dad surprises me when he says "Okay, I've had some time to cool off and think. Maybe we did approach you guys the wrong way, can we talk?" I see my mom also came back out with him and her eyes look like she was crying. It's almost my undoing again.

"Yes dad, we can talk." I answer before Chris can have a chance to. "Can we go in the living room though?" I ask, I feel so awful I'm not sure I can stand too long. He says sure and heads that way, so I grab Chris's hand and we head into the living room together.

"Look I don't want you to move out. I do think for the sake of your younger brother and sister, we need to keep rules in the house." He looks at both of us and says, "I know you don't have to 'listen'. I'm asking you out of respect, so we don't worry from now on, can you let us know if you aren't coming home? You're not asking permission but being courteous to this household. You will see one day, that just because your child turns eighteen it doesn't mean you stop worrying."

I feel like this is a good compromise, but I can see Chris is still pissed off. He finally says, "The fact that you thought you could keep her or my kid away from me isn't going to fly." then he adds, "We should be living together as a family so no, she needs to move in with me."

We haven't even talked about living together. I don't even have a job, so how can I help pay for anything? I don't want to go live with him, not yet and not alone. I never get a chance to say anything, my dad responds first with "Then you guys can stay here, you can move in here and save your money. You will need to buy stuff for the baby and we can help you out by letting you stay here." I never expected today's fight to turn into Chris moving in to my parent's house with me. I'm not too sure how I feel about it all, but it's better than us moving out on our own.

"That's fine." Chris answers with an attitude, then says he can move his stuff here this week on Wednesday. It's his only day off for two weeks.

"We can't share a room with Brittany, or Tony." I say trying to figure out where we will sleep.

"Don't worry about that," my mom answers "We will have everything figured out by Wednesday."

Chris says "Fine, Margo is going to come stay at my mom's house a few days" Then he adds with a smirk and sarcastic tone, "So you know where she is." I secretly don't want to go with him, but I know I can't make a big deal about it tonight.

"Okay thank you for letting us know." My dad says, and I can see he is trying his best to ignore Chris's flip remark. "We will see you on Wednesday" They go to their bedroom and leave us alone; my guess is to talk alone.

"Um, well I guess we should go, let me grab some clothes." I say and once again head down to my room.

I grab enough clothes for a few days and wish I didn't have to go with him. I hate the feelings I have, but I know I don't want to be with someone that is so... well...Mean. I never know how he is going to act, and I'm afraid, he will treat our childlike that too. There seems to be nothing I can do now, but go with him, and hope it will be okay once we move in here. Maybe moving in with my parents together, is a good thing. Most of the time my mom is home, and I can't see him acting that way in front of her. By the time we leave, I am convinced this will be exactly what we need to mend things. I will try to get through the next few days with no arguments. I will be on my best behavior, so he has no reason to be angry at me.

That night Chris doesn't talk to me very much. I can tell he's mad about everything, but him not talking gives me no idea about which part. I have been nauseous all day and by evening it's terrible. I can't sip water without it coming right back up. I finally ask him if he could go to the store and grab ginger ale.

He doesn't even look up from his magazine he's reading, and he says "No, this shit is for attention and it's not going to work with me." I start to cry and tell him, "It's not. I swear I can't help it, I don't know what to do." But he isn't budging. He won't stop reading and he won't go. I get up and go get water and try once again to drink that instead. It comes back up less than ten minutes later. It's going on 8:30 in the evening and I haven't had food since lunch. I finally say "Do you think food will help? Maybe some soup? Do you think your mom has any here?"

"No, she doesn't and if she did, it's for her, not you." He finally gets up and says he will run out and grab food, but he adds, "I probably shouldn't get you anything this is your bodies way of telling you, you eat too much and you're going to get fat if you keep it up."

I have no energy to even fight with him, so I say, "If you don't mind a garden salad sounds delicious." I figure I can't go wrong with a salad, and I really have the taste for one.

All he says as he leaves is "We'll see." and he closes the door.

In the meantime, I keep trying to sip on the water praying it will stay down. About every ten minutes though it comes right back up. After a while I realize Chris has been gone for over an hour now. I'm so hungry I start to cry, I don't know why it's taking so long. After another 45 minutes, he finally comes in with a salad from McDonalds.

"Where have you been and why did it take you so long?" I ask, my face is all puffy from crying.

"I ran to my work and I got busy there, they asked if I could help for a little bit, so I said yes." he answers with an attitude.

I start to eat my food and I finally say, "Were you there drinking?" And before he can respond or deny it, I add "I can smell it and I don't understand why you even stopped there if you got our food from McDonald's."

"Yes, I had a few beers and I'm not explaining myself to you. If you didn't nag me all day I wouldn't want to go there and drink." He always has a way to make me feel like things are my fault. He adds, "If you're not careful you will make me do more than just drink." and he storms out of the room. I have no idea what that even means, but I don't want to find out.

Once again, this is all my fault. I really don't care at this point though. All I'm praying for this minute, is to be able to finish my dinner and keep it down. I don't want to over eat, but It tastes so good I eat the whole salad. I finally feel a little better, but I'm so tired I lay down to try to sleep. Silently I'm praying, he doesn't want to have sex. I don't think there is any way I can get through it tonight.

I must have fallen to sleep, because I'm jolted awake and I feel horrible. I know I'm going to once again throw up, so I leap off the bed and grab the plastic bag the food came in. I just make it in time and I throw up my entire dinner. I feel so horrible and I know Chris is going to be mad, because he wasted money on my food. I have no way to hide it and I realize thankfully he isn't even in the room. I look at the clock and it's only a little past midnight. I thought it was morning. I sneak out of his room, to see if he is in the living room. He isn't there either. I know they keep the big garbage cans in the garage, so I hurry up and throw the bag in one.

Once I get rid of the bag I go look to see if I can find Chris. I can't find him anywhere, so I finally go look out the window and his car is gone. He must have left after our fight, I'm guessing he went to a bar. I want to go back to sleep and I hope I'm done being sick. I realize I should grab a few more bags to bring with me in case I'm sick again and can't make it to the bathroom. I look around the kitchen and I find some small grocery bags to have on hand.

When I get back to Chris's room, I line his garbage can with a bag and lay back down to try and get more sleep. After about twenty minutes of tossing and turning, I hear him open the door. He's falling down drunk and thankfully falls onto the bed and passes out. I curl up into ball and cry. I never wanted this kind of life. I had huge dreams and I am laying here realizing those dreams are long gone. All I can do now is live the life I have made for myself. It's the most depressing feeling I have ever felt. I eventually fall asleep and surprisingly enough stay asleep the rest of the night.

I wake up late and see it's almost noon already and Chris is still asleep. I quietly slide off the bed to make sure not to wake him. I'm hungry, but I know I'm not welcome to eat his mom's food. I see Chris's keys on the counter and think I should run out and grab food. I know I should ask, but I'm thinking if I surprise him with something good he won't mind. I think about it a second, then I grab the keys and decide to go ahead and go.

I unlock the car and realize I need to move the seat and I have no idea how to do it. I start to fumble around looking for the lever when I feel something fuzzy. I pull it out from under his seat and it's a brown teddy bear that is holding a red heart that says kiss me on it. I think how sweet he either got this for me or the baby, then I see a card on the floor that has his name on it. I can't stop myself and I open it. It reads, "Chris, Happy Valentine's Day. I hope you like balloons and chocolate... and here's a little kiss too. Till next time, love Misty".

I freeze. I have no idea how long I sit there but eventually I feel the tears pouring down my face. I believed him when he said that was his cousin. Come to think of it, I'm still waiting to meet this cousin. I feel myself about to get sick, so I hurry up and get out of the car. I just make it before I start throwing up all over the grass. I grab the teddy bear and the card, and I march my ass back into the house.

I storm into his room and fling the teddy bear at his face. I have a good aim and hit him square in the nose. I know it didn't hurt him, but it woke him up. "What the Fuck Margo?" he sits up and is about to say something else, when I cut him off "Misty? Seriously is that her actual name?"

I see he knows exactly who I'm talking about, but he's confused on how I know. So, I read the card and glare at him. I'm honestly expecting him to feel bad and maybe even apologize. I'm not at all prepared for him to jump off the bed and grab me by my neck and push me up against the wall. I'm instantly regretting confronting him before I can get a scream out he has his other hand over my mouth.

"Why the fuck are you snooping through my shit?" I try to answer but I can't because he is squeezing my mouth so tight. "You stupid bitch. Who do you think you are? You can't fucking leave anything alone." Once again, I'm crying, and I feel nauseous. I'm afraid I'm going to throw up and I won't be able to breath because he is covering my mouth. I start blinking my eyes. Super-fast blinking hoping he will let go of my mouth. He finally gets so annoyed with my eyes blinking he lets go of my mouth.

"I'm going to throw up" I say, and he lets go of me in time for me to get to the trash can and be sick. I'm not sure if I'm sick because of the baby or because I know, in my heart he cheated on me. "I want to go home, I really don't feel good." I try begging him "Please can you take me home? Please? We can talk more there but I need to eat, and I'm so dizzy I need to go home" He doesn't move from in front of the door. It's his way to keep me in here, and I know unless he wants me to leave this room, I'm stuck here.

"No, I'm not taking you home. You need to settle down and quit being so dramatic. It's not a big deal. This girl at work got those for me and I didn't want to hurt your feelings. I don't like her, and she doesn't work there anymore. It's really not a big deal." he says.

"Fine, I don't even care. Right now, I just don't feel good and I need to eat something. It can hurt the baby if I don't eat." I'm praying he finally lets me go so I can eat.

"Fine I'll get you something to eat, but remember this, if you get fat... you're out. I won't be with a fat girl."

"I'm not going to get fat, I'm pregnant, so yes I will get bigger, but that's because there's a baby inside of me."

"Well I'll let you know if you're getting too fat. I'll be the judge of that." and finally, he leaves the room.

I need to get myself composed. I need to be on my best behavior, so he will take me home. I honestly don't care if he is seeing this girl or not, at this point I just want to break up with him and be done. My biggest worry is if he can take my baby from me. I don't see how he could, but he is certain he can do it. I need to talk to a lawyer or someone and see if it's true.

Chris comes back with some toast, and I'm so happy I gobble it down. That was a big mistake, because not even five minutes after my first bite, I'm throwing it all up again. I break down bawling my eyes out. I'm so thirsty and hungry and tired. I don't know why I'm feeling like this, but I think it's the morning sickness mixed with stress of us fighting. "Jesus Christ" Chris is upset again "You can stop with the getting sick. It isn't working, I'm not going to baby you and cater to you."

"I'm not doing it on purpose, I keep telling you something is wrong. If you don't want to help me, please take me home." I beg.

He shakes his head and tells me "No, you can go back to bed and rest. I have to go to work I don't have time for this shit. I'll bring you home some dinner, what do you want?"

I have no idea what to ask for, so I say, "Chicken noodle soup sounds good." I'm guessing it will help because it does when you have the flu.

"Fine. I have to go, try to rest." He walks over, grabs the bear and the card, and kisses me goodbye. It takes everything in me not to shudder, and I manage to say, "Bye I'll see you later."

"I'll be home around 930 or so, I love you." I can't believe he even said I love you.

He is looking at me expectantly, so I finally say, "I love you too." then roll over on the bed so my back is to him and he can't see my tears. I hear him close the front door, so I peek through the blinds to be sure he leaves. I want to call my parents, but I'm so embarrassed I can't do it. I feel I put myself in this position I will get myself out. A big part of me also doesn't want to admit my mother was right about him, so I get back in bed and curl up and cry myself to sleep.

Chris comes home like he said, right at 930. I know this because I just took a shower and I looked at the clock when I got out, wondering if he was ever going to bring dinner. He strolls into the bedroom as if nothing even happened earlier. At least he's in a good mood, so I cheer up and start eating the food he brought me. Thankfully tonight he got me a sandwich and a salad. I feel he is trying, so I start talking about the baby and what we need, trying to keep the mood light. I'm not even halfway through my sandwich, and I feel I'm going to get sick. I run out of the room and just make to the bathroom in time.

When I come back in the room, Chris rips into me. "You need to stop doing that. I'm not going to keep throwing my money away like this." He seriously thinks I like throwing up?

"Chris, it's not my fault, I can't help it. I don't love this, it's not something I want to do."

"Stop acting like a baby I won't put up with it, I'm not your dad and I'm telling you now, I won't cater to you."

"I understand that and I'm not asking you to cater to me. I am asking you to understand this isn't my fault. Go to my next appointment with me and my doctor will tell you all about it. I know she can explain it much better than I can."

"Sure, she's a woman so I'm sure she will." He is obviously not going to understand at all what I'm going through. He is such a jerk about women in general, what kind of father will he be to a daughter? I shudder at the thought of that.

"Okay, well go find a guy doctor, I'm sure a man will tell you the same thing. Or better yet, pick up a book and read about it." I realize too late I should have kept my mouth shut.

Chris yanks me up off the floor by my hair. I feel like he is pulling it out by the roots. "Stop it that hurts, I'm getting up." I yell at him, but he keeps my hair wrapped around his hand, and turns me at the same time to face him.

"You need to stop talking to me like that or I swear to God as soon as that brat comes out, I'm taking it and I'm leaving you. Test me. I'm not fucking kidding." he is inches from my face and I can now smell the alcohol on his breath. I want to bitch him out for it, but wisely I keep my mouth shut this time.

"Okay, I wasn't trying to be mean. I swear it must be my hormones, I'm sorry." I feel like shit for having to apologize to him, but I'm hoping it will settle him down.

"Fine, you can make it up to me now." He starts kissing me and he is still pulling my hair, so I have no choice but to let him." he slowly inches towards the bed, and I know what I have to do now, and I'm so disgusted. He starts undressing me, then tells me to get on the bed. I do what he says, and he undresses himself and gets on the bed next to me.

"I'm going to fuck you now, but the whole time I'm doing it… He pauses for dramatic effect. "I'm going to pretend you are someone else." I can't believe he is saying that to me.

"You're a jerk, I would never say something like that to you, get off me." I try to push him away, but of course he is stronger than me and I'm wasting my energy. He shoves me back harder and holds me down on the bed by my forearms. "Well I was going to pretend it was a random stranger but now…" once again he pauses, and with a wicked grin he sneers "Now, I'll pretend I'm fucking your sister."

Now I'm beyond upset, and I try harder to move away from him, but he has a tight grip on me. I finally give up and go limp and let him do what he's going to do, because I have no fight left in me. The whole time he keeps calling me her name and saying things like you fuck better then Margo and I like fucking you Brittany. It's like a slap in the face and a disgusting way to punish me. I have no idea why he would think that is okay, because it isn't.

More than anything I want to go home and have my parents tell him he can't move in. If I can just get back home things will be better. I think I can get through a few more days. When he is done he rolls over and goes to sleep, or passes out, I'm not sure which. I get up and go back to the bathroom and take another shower. I feel so gross, and to top it off I get sick again. I finally make it back to the bedroom and climb into bed and fall asleep.

I'm so sick the next morning I can't even get out of bed. He stands by the door glaring at me before he leaves for work. The whole day I sleep, I can't eat or drink anything and by midday I give up trying. I climb back in bed and I'm guessing I was sound asleep because I sleep through the night into the next day.

Again, I am so sick I can't get up. Chris decides to go ahead and go meet some friends to hang out, he thinks I'm doing this to stop him. He likes to tell me he won't be pussy whipped and sit home taking care of me. He works tonight so he wants to go have some fun for a bit, and my needing attention isn't going to stop him. I could care less, what he does or where he goes if it keeps him away from me and from bitching at me.

After he leaves, I try to eat some toast, but it comes back up. I'm not able to even keep water down anymore. I feel so awful, and wish my mom was here to help me. Again, I think I should call home, but I'm so exhausted I can only think to sleep instead.

Chris comes home and brings me a late lunch. As soon as I smell the food I run to the bathroom and throw up. I start to cry because I'm so hungry and he's going to think I'm doing this on purpose again. More than anything I wish I could eat. I would give someone my last dollar to be able to eat and keep it down.

I finally go back to the bedroom, and I see he's pissed but he doesn't bitch. Instead he says, "Maybe you need to see a doctor, you don't look so good." He is being nice to me. I feel like death, and I'm so grateful he's being nice I burst into tears and hug him.

"If I'm not better tomorrow maybe I should, thank you for caring." He helps me get back in bed and says he needs to go, but hopes I feel better later.

I don't even try to eat I just go back to sleep. I hear him come home, but I pretend to be asleep. For a change he leaves me alone except he snuggles up to me and holds me. I'm so confused about how I feel right now. When he's like this, I love being with him. But when he's angry, or drinking... not so much. I want to be loved and held so much, as I'm drifting back to sleep all I can think is how nice this feels and everything else once again for the moment gets forgotten.

The next morning, I feel so awful I can't walk. I try to get up and everything starts spinning on me. Chris helps me walk to his car, and we are finally heading to my house. "I'm going to drop you off then come back here and get my stuff."

I feel somehow, I have made this move a disaster, so I say, "I'm so sorry maybe I have the flu too, I think this is more than morning sickness."

He agrees with me finally and says, "I think it is too." then with genuine sympathy says, "If you aren't better by tomorrow make a doctor's appointment so they can check." I just nod my head because I have the seat laying back and I fall asleep again.

We get to my house, and there is a note from my parents telling me they moved my grandma in with my aunt and Chris and I will be in her old room now. I'm totally shocked. I can't believe they did that for me. I feel terrible because my grandmother loves living here and my mom loves having her here. I know what a huge sacrifice this is for me, and I'm incredibly thankful. I can't overly focus on it right now because I just make it to the room and I collapsed on the bed. I'm so incredibly week, and dizzy I can't even stand for very long.

Chris leaves quickly so I can completely relax and go to sleep. I wake up to a lot of noise a bit later and my mom knocking on the bedroom door. "Come in" I say barely loud enough for her to hear me, but she does.

"What's wrong, what's going on with you?" she asks. I can see she's worried.

"I think I have the flu, I can't keep food down or even water." I say.

"How long has this been going on? Chris said he didn't know."

"I haven't kept food down all week, and the last two days nothing, not even water."

"Okay," she says, "That's it you're going to the hospital." She gets up and walks out of the room. I can't even argue with her because I have no energy to even try.

She comes back a few minutes later with Chris and my dad and I try to get up, but I can't, everything is spinning.

"Get up, if it's that big of a deal you need to get up and put your shoes on." Chris is pissed but I don't care. I'm secretly grateful my parents stepped out into the hall and can't hear him.

"I can't get up, the whole room is spinning, and I don't know what way is up, my legs are cramping too now." I finally, frustrated say this loudly trying to make him understand. I then collapse back onto the bed.

The next thing I know my dad is right there and swoops down and picks me up like a baby. "Let's go Norma" he says to my mom.

"Ed wait, I can carry her." I can't believe Chris trying to have a pissing contest with my dad. But my dad says, "I already have her go unlock the car, let's go."

I don't remember anything after that. I wake up in the hospital with an I.V in my arm and my parents sitting by my bed. "What happened?" I ask thinking man I'm thirsty, so I add "Can I have a drink please?" My mom jumps up and goes to grab a nurse and see if I'm allowed to drink anything. While she is gone I ask my dad, "Where's Chris?"

"He's at work." my dad answers.

"Did they call him in? He was supposed to be off, so he could move today." I say so confused.

"No, that was yesterday... He works today... Today is Thursday." I can't believe I slept another day away. This is crazy, and I still feel tired like I could sleep hours more. My mom comes in with the nurse. She checks me out, then says I can have a drink and she goes to get the doctor.

I take a few sips of my drink and it feels so good, but I'm terrified I'm going to start throwing up again. The doctor comes in and I finally ask him "What was wrong with me? Did I have the flu? Is my baby okay?"

"Yes, the baby is fine, and no, you did not have the flu. I explained this to your husband, but I see he isn't here, so I will happily explain it to you too."

He thinks Chris is my husband. I don't correct him, instead I say, "I'm sorry, he had to go into work today."

"That's understandable and with this bundle of joy coming, he can't lose his job I'm sure." the doctor smiles.

"What happened was you were severely dehydrated. The morning sickness you have, is a little more than regular morning sickness." Oh my god, he's scaring me.

I ask "What does that mean? Am I going to be okay? Will I lose the baby?"

"You have what is called Hyperemesis gravidarum, symptoms can include extreme nausea and vomiting, as well as rapid weight loss, dehydration, electrolyte imbalance, dizziness and excessive saliva… sound familiar?" he responds.

"Yes, that's everything I was feeling. What does this mean for me?" I ask.

"It means you need to be very careful and try to keep hydrated. Miscarriage can happen from this, so we need you to eat, if you throw up, eat again, same with drinking. Something will eventually stay in you. If you feel like this again, come right back here for fluids." he adds. "I'm not trying to scare you, but it can get very serious, quickly. Just come back, don't be embarrassed or put it off. Okay?" he says.

"Okay I promise I will do my best," I answer, then ask "Do I get to go home now?"

"Not today, I want to keep fluids running until tomorrow, but you should be just fine to head home in the morning." he smiles, shakes my hand and leaves.

I thank my parents for coming and tell them I'm okay if they want to leave and head home. They try to fight me on it, but I can tell they need sleep so, finally they go ahead and go. I know Chris will be back tomorrow, so for now I just want to sleep. I'm so glad I got here in time. I hold my hand on my belly and I tell my little baby I will try to take care of her better.

I don't know what I'm having, but for some reason I feel strongly it's a girl. I can't say that to Chris, because he wants a boy so badly. There is just something in me saying it's a girl, and I feel so happy about that. I want a little girl more than anything, someone to talk to one day and be best friends with. I'll always be her mom first, but I know in my heart we will be friends too. I drift to sleep dreaming about my baby girl.

The next morning, I feel a million times better. Chris comes in to take me home, and thankfully the doctor says I can leave. I'm looking forward to getting home and settling Chris into our house. It's going to be so weird living together. I hope it works out, because through all this hospital stuff, I decide once again not to say anything to my parents. I figure this is my mess to resolve on my own.

Chapter 10

The next few months fly by, with no major problems, I had to go back one more time to get I.V fluids, but I'm finally starting to feel better. I have an appetite and I'm kind of starting to get a belly. I'm now seven months pregnant and If I wear a big sweatshirt, you still can't tell. No one other than his mom, in his family knows still. His friends don't know, and It bothers me that the baby and I are his dirty little secret

I don't push the issue because things have been pretty good, and I don't want to rock the boat. We go to his uncle's a lot, like tonight and it's sad they have no idea I'm pregnant. I feel weird not saying anything, but I'm leaving that up to Chris. I feel guilty though every time his aunt and I sit around talking. I wish I could tell her, so I can ask her questions. She has three kids of her own, so I'm sure she has good advice.

The thing I don't like about going there is, Chris still drinks so much. It's not even that he drinks, it's how pissy he gets when he has too much. Most of the time he ends up forcing me to have sex, and I don't know how to stop it. He feels I should give him sex whenever he wants, like he owns me now. I try to avoid it as much as possible and I have figured out if he gets too inebriated, he blacks out and forgets about me. So, I do have mixed feelings about him drinking.

Now that I can eat a little, I love coming because they cook such delicious food. Tonight, they are going to deep fry some food, and I'm excited to eat. I guess the saying is true about cravings. I am craving greasy food tonight, so I tell Chris, "Hey when you go to the store can you grab some tater tots?" I know he will buy beer, so I figured he could grab a bag of those too.

"No, you don't need those." he says back to me. I'm a little upset, because I have the taste for them, so I try to ask again.

"Please? I can't stop it, I have a taste for them and I really would like them, I'm kind of craving them." I throw in trying to hint that it's a pregnancy want. Cravings are something else he doesn't believe in. He tells me that's all in my head too.

"No. Can't you hear, I said no. You don't need them, those make people fat." I seriously can't believe he is saying no. His aunt chimes in next.

"Buy the girl some damn tater tots for god sakes, it's one night it won't make her fat one damn night."

"Stay out of it." he says to her. "I told her no and she needs to listen." he says to her.

"You think you're her boss? Well, you might tell her what to do but you won't me, I'll buy the damn things." At this point I know it's not about the money, it's about him telling me no and I'm not listening.

His aunt walks away to tell his uncle to grab tater tots and he comes at me. I know he's going to hurt me, I can see it in his face, it's bright red. I know the ugly red blotchy color is a mix of too much beer and anger. I also know he already drank six beers and quickly, which is why he is going to go get more.

I react faster than he expects, and I'm able to almost get away from him. He grabs my shirt and pulls me back to him. I know I need to do something, so he doesn't hurt me so when he turns me towards him, I bring my knee up to his groin. I have never done that before so, he is surprised. Unfortunately, he is quick enough to move back but, he lets go of me to do it. Without thinking too much about what to do next I kick at him to keep him away.

This pisses him off even more "You fucking bitch. I swear to God..." he says and at the same time he lunges towards me and picks me up and throws me on top of the kitchen sink full of dishes. The dishes go flying and right as he is about to grab me by my throat, someone grabs him off me. I realize once he is away from me, it was his uncle. I have never in my life been more grateful to someone than I was his uncle right then. I'm also grateful his uncle is one of the only people I know that is stronger than him and can physically restrain him.

I hear his uncle bitching him out "Dude, what the fuck was that? You never put your hands on a girl. Didn't your mother teach you anything? If your dad was here, he'd kick your ass right now, and you're lucky I'm not doing it for him."

Chris yells at him" That bitch freaked out over nothing then tried to knee me in the balls..."

His uncle cut him off "I don't give a fuck if she actually connected with your tiny ass balls." He steps closer to him chest to chest and says loudly, "You walk the fuck away, and never put your hands on her again."

I walked outside to get away from him, I didn't know where else to go. I'm crying and I'm bending over holding my stomach and his aunt is trying to calm me down with kind words.

"I wasn't your fault, don't worry it will be okay, I'm sure he didn't mean to do that. Right? He's never done that before has he?"

But I can't talk, and I can't calm down, finally I look at her and say, "I'm not sure it will be okay, I don't think I am okay, I have terrible pains in my stomach."

"It will be okay..." she starts to say, but this time I cut her off.

"NO! It's not, I'm pregnant. I'm seven months pregnant and I'm having terrible cramps right now."

I see the look on her face that reflects an oh my God look, then I hear walking away to get her husband "Justin she needs to go to the hospital right now." I'm trying to follow her back inside.

"Alright, alright Chill out, I'm sure it's not that big of a deal we can..." But she doesn't let him finish.

"She's pregnant. She's fucking seven months pregnant and he just did this to her. Your asshole nephew probably just killed his own damn kid."

Now I'm crying harder, thinking my baby died. I have no idea what to do so I listen to her and get in the car and she drives me to the hospital. Chris insists on coming so Justin comes too. The whole way they keep telling me to tell them I just started cramping and that nothing happened. I honestly don't know what I'm going to say, when Chris starts crying and says "I'm sorry, it had to have been the beer. Please be okay, I'll never do that again I promise. It won't ever happen again, I need you and the baby to be okay and love me."

I feel so bad for him by the time we got to the hospital, that I agree to keep my mouth shut. His aunt and uncle think this is a one-time thing. I don't have the nerve to tell them it isn't. I think though maybe this time, he truly means he is sorry and he won't do it again. I think this is scaring him so badly he will change. I'm not in the right state of mind to make these decisions, but I think what can I do right now?

We get to the hospital and his aunt and uncle help me out of the car and grab a wheelchair for me. I get to the desk and Chris is already in the middle of explaining what happened. The nurse comes over to me and says "So I hear you aren't feeling well? Your husband said you guys were just sitting around the house tonight and you started having cramps. You didn't do anything strenuous?"

"Boyfriend, he's my boyfriend, we aren't married." I snap at her, I'm not sure why but it bothers me to call this guy my husband. It doesn't feel right, and I don't want to lie about that too. I soften my tone a little, "I'm sorry and no I didn't do anything." I feel bad snapping at her about us not being married but I don't want her thinking he's my husband.

"It's okay honey, we will get you back in a room shortly and check things out for you." She is still so nice to me even though I bit her head off.

"Thank you." I say trying to be nicer. We go out to the waiting room, and luckily, we don't have to wait very long. The nurse comes over and says they are going to take me up to labor and delivery to check things out. "Don't worry" she says when she sees the worry on my face "They take anyone over twenty weeks up there when they come in, good or bad."

I feel a little better about that, but I wish these cramps would stop. I'm not very sure at this point if I have the baby if it would survive. I feel so afraid, and I want to call my mom but I'm pretty sure it will piss Chris off. I know I shouldn't care, especially after tonight, but he says he's going to change. If he does, then making him uncomfortable doesn't make any sense right now. Once again, I find myself more worried about him, and his feelings and not so much myself.

I get situated in a bed and they come in and start asking questions like what I was doing beforehand, when did I start feeling the cramps, and If I was bleeding or leaking any fluids. I fumble my way through these questions, but I think I'm able to cover it up pretty good. They hook me up to a monitor, it checks the baby's heart rate, which is one sixty-five and they say that is good. This will also measure if I have any contractions happening. The doctor comes in with a nurse and asks everyone to leave the room, so she can examine me. Chris says he wants to stay, but the doctor says she can't allow that. I know he is pissed, but he doesn't say anything, he looks long and hard at me then storms out.

"Okay, honey now that it's just us, I need to ask a few more questions before we get started." she smiles at me then asks, "Do you feel safe at home?"

I flinch as if I was smacked, but I answer in an offended voice. "Yes, I feel safe at home."

I'm not sure if she believes me or not but then she asks, "If you didn't feel safe, do you know there is help out there?" I don't know why I'm so offended. I'm not safe at home, but I can't admit that to them.

"I didn't know that and that's a nice service, but since I am safe I wouldn't need to know that." I answer.

She writes something down and then says, "Okay, let's get started with the exam." She checks me by doing an internal exam and says I'm not losing fluid, or bleeding which is good. She measures my belly and is surprised at how small I am compared to how far along I am. I explain to her how sick I have been and that I have Hyperemesis gravidarum. She says that would make sense then and asks the ultrasound tech to come in. Chris asks if he can come back in too, and she says yes.

It is neat for us to see the baby this far along with the ultra sound. The doctor does a lot of checking and a lot of measuring. She is almost done and asks if we know the gender of the baby, and if not do we want to know. I say no, and Chris agrees we want to be surprised. I truthfully don't want to be told it's a girl and him punish me for the rest of the pregnancy. I'm praying, once the baby is here if it's a girl, he will love her and forget his obsession with having a boy.

The doctor finishes up and says, as far as she can tell everything looks okay, and I am most likely having Braxton Hicks contractions. She then explains what that means and how most women have them at some point towards the end. She also says due to my lack of weight gain, which at this point is only eight pounds, I will most likely have a very small baby, around five to six pounds. I am scared to hear this is slightly smaller than the average seven-pound baby. She reassures me if I eat healthy and continue to take care of myself, the baby will be okay.

They decide to keep me overnight, they want to monitor me in case anything changes. I'll keep the thing on my stomach that is hooked up to the monitor, on all night. It isn't terribly uncomfortable, and I enjoy listening to the baby's heartbeat, it has such a wonderful soothing sound.

I convince Chris to leave and go back to his uncle's house for the night. I tell him I'm so tired and that I am most likely going to fall asleep soon. He finally agrees to leave but says he will be back early in the morning. He walks over to me and gives me a kiss and tells me, "I love you so much. I'm so sorry this happened, and I promise it will never happen again." For some reason, the hurt look on his face is so raw, I know in my heart he is truly sorry. I also know something changed in him tonight to make him realize, he was wrong.

"I love you too and I'll see you in the morning." I say, then add "Try and get some sleep, we are okay, and things will be different now, for both of us." I can see the tears in eyes as he leaves which makes me cry.

I am laying there crying when the nurse comes back in and asks me if I'm okay? I answer honestly this time "Yes, I'm relieved everything is okay with the baby and I'm going to miss my boyfriend tonight."

She smiles at me then says, "Try to get some rest, morning will come before you know it and he will be back." Then she quietly leaves the room, so I can rest.

I sleep well and wake up feeling pretty good in the morning. I am startled to look over and see Chris is already here, sitting in a chair reading a magazine. I peek up at him through my lashes, "Good morning" I say not sure why I'm feeling so shy with him.

Maybe it's because I feel like we are starting fresh. I feel myself blush and he chuckles softly and says, "I love when you look at me all flirty." I try to hide my smile, but it gets bigger and bigger.

"I love that you look so happy, and I love flirting with you." I say back. "I'm glad you are here I missed you." I truly in this moment, mean it.

"I missed you too. I can't wait to get you out of here and home. Did they say when by chance?" he asks

"No, but I'm hoping the doctor will come in this morning, not later in the day."

As if on cue, in walks my doctor and she has a big smile on her face. "I'm sure you already know this," she looks at me smiling, then continues. "Your contractions have stopped, and everything looks okay. What do you say to busting out of this place sooner rather than later?"

"Where do I sign and what do I need to do, who do I need to bribe?" I ask while laughing.

"You can cut a deal with me," she says, "the deal is, I don't see you again in a hospital until the end of January or beginning of February for your due date."

"Deal!" I shout, laughing and she says she will be back with the papers and a nurse will be in shortly to unhook me. I'm so happy I can't stop grinning, I turn to Chris and ask, "Do you think we could stop and get breakfast before we go home?"

For a change he smiles and says "Sure, you can get whatever you want." For me that answer seals the deal that he has changed. Before this, my asking that would have had him saying something shitty and mean.

The nurse comes in and takes the monitors off me and takes out my Iv. She says it will be at least a half hour before the paperwork is all done and asks if I'd like to shower. I happily say yes, even knowing I'll have to put my dirty clothes back on. I don't care though; a nice hot shower sounds great right about now.

I go into the bathroom and enjoy a long shower for a change and not getting asked to get out. It is almost better than the thought of eating soon. When I finally do come out, Chris is gone. I figure maybe he went for a walk or to the bathroom. I was about to put my dirty clothes back on when he comes in and says, "Here I got this for you, I hope they fit," He ran down the street to Wal-mart and bought me a cozy sweat outfit.

I am so touched, this is something he normally would never have done. I go back into the bathroom and they fit perfect. Right now, today, I'm feeling so lucky and so loved. This is exactly what I want in life, to be loved and have a family. I guess dreams can come true after all.

We finally leave the hospital and go grab breakfast. For once he has no comments about the food I eat. I do try to be conscious and order healthy food. I want to do my best to also give him what he needs so he can be happy too. I know a happy relationship isn't going to be me always getting what I want the way I want. It's about compromise and I'm okay with that, I don't mind compromising.

Once we finish eating, we head back to my parent's house, so we can relax. "Did you call and tell my parents I was in the hospital?" I ask.

"No, why would I? It's not their kid, it's mine." Chris says, and I can see a glimpse of the old Chris coming back, he is clenching and unclenching his jaw.

"Oh, I know that." I try to keep my tone soft, "But after all I am their kid." I say hoping he gets the light way I'm trying to keep this going.

I see him relax a little and he says, "No I didn't think to call them."

"That's okay, I'll explain it wasn't that big of a deal, so don't worry about it. I just didn't know." I say, and he is back to smiling and looking relaxed.

At least that didn't blow up into something big. It looks like things have changed with him, and I think it helps that I'll be working on it too. We pull into my driveway and I already know my mom will probably freak out, but I plan to keep the heat off Chris. I don't want anything bursting our happy little bubble.

My mom is in the kitchen looking at some crafting magazine. She is always doing something to change the way the house looks. She has a very unique way of decorating, and there are things she does that are considered "in" before it is popular. Somehow, she can decorate and three months later it's all the rage. I often wonder if she should have been an interior decorator, she has a keen eye for design.

"Good morning mom, what are you doing now?" I laugh as I try to see what she is looking at.

"Nothing yet, but I think I want to change up the living room. I think I want to go rustic or something." I shake my head smiling because I have no decorating skills. In fact, I don't have a single artistic bone in my body.

"Well I wanted to let you know I was in the hospital last night, and hold on..." I say when she is about to say something. "The reason I didn't call and asked Chris not to, was because we saw it wasn't serious. Had it been serious, I would have called right away. But I didn't want to worry you for nothing."

"What happened? Why did you go to begin with?" she asks.

"I started feeling like cramping, so we went to see what it was. They said most likely Braxton Hicks contractions and round ligament pain, all of which are normal."

"Oh, yes." my mom says with a smile "I think I went in at least twice with all four of you thinking I was in labor." Then she adds laughing, "After my first baby you would think I'd know better. I'm glad you went to get checked and I'm glad that's all it was." I'm so glad she isn't mad about not calling or worse directing her anger at Chris. The last thing I want is for anything to upset our balance.

I was about to go to my room for a little bit when Brittany comes in the room all in a panic. "Mom I have to go to Buffalo tonight, I need to get stuff for my photo shoot." She looks around and realizes she has an audience and says, "After all I am the pretty one in this family I need something pretty to wear to match my beauty." I turn my head slightly and roll my eyes knowing she can't see me.

"I can't take you tonight." my mom is saying "Dad and I made plans tonight and there is no way I'm canceling to run you around shopping, you should have done this sooner." Wow, my mom is saying no to her, did I step into the twilight zone?

In a blink of an eye, she comes slithering up to me as if we are best friends. "Hey sister that I love so much, could you please, please run me to Buffalo? I really love you."

I shake my head no and say, "Brittany I just spent the whole night in the hospital, I need to stay home and rest."

She flips out like I knew she would, no one can tell her "no". Ever.

"You are such a jerk! You know I can't drive myself. I wouldn't ask if it wasn't so important, but why would you help me? You're jealous I'm pretty and you're not. You hate yourself because you are fat and gross." she is just getting started I can see her brewing for an explosion. When she is like this nothing but venomous word vomit rambles out of her mouth.

"Brittany I'm pregnant. I'm not fat, I have a baby growing inside of me. That baby, your niece or nephew was not feeling good yesterday, so I had to go to the hospital." I try to calm her down, but it isn't working.

"This has nothing to do with the baby. You don't want to help me because I'm pretty. I can't help that you are ugly, and no one likes you."

"Brittany!" my mom yells at her. "Stop that right now! Your sister can not have stress right now, she said no and that's that. Stop it or you will not go to your photo shoot at all."

She is standing there glaring at me, then in true Brittany fashion, she is smiling sweetly again. She turns to Chris, and says "Could you run me to Buffalo? I'd really appreciate it if you would. I mean, Margo is sick so, I'm sure she will be boring and in bed all night and she won't mind." I am shaking my head no, to Chris trying to get him see I don't want him to do it.

"Sure, I can do that" Chris says, and I am instantly pissed. I do not want him driving her anywhere. I don't trust her as far as I can throw her, and I certainly don't trust him either.

I speak up "Chris, I don't think that's a good idea, what if I need you or I start cramping again?"

He gives me this "Shut up" glare that stops me in my tracks. "You will be fine, the doctor said it wasn't anything serious." I cannot believe he is that set on going with her. I want to stop him from taking her, but by his look I know it will start a huge fight. Brittany Looks over at me and gives me the nastiest fuck you grin she has. I feel it in my gut this is not a good idea. I get up and go to my room knowing Chris will come too.

Sure, enough he follows me and as soon as he closes the door I start to cry. "Please don't go, you don't understand, I don't want you to go." He comes over and surprises me and hugs me "Please, I want you to stay here, she can find someone else to take her."

"Look I'm trying to show your parents I can help out around here and this is my way to help. Trust me, I don't want to lug that brat all over but if it helps your parents then maybe they will like me. Don't you want them to like me? Or do you like that they don't?"

"They do like you. I don't like the idea of you guys going off by yourselves. Look I'm not trying to tell you what to do, but I'm incredibly uncomfortable with this." I try one last time.

He pulls away, and then says "Are you saying you don't trust me? I think that's bullshit. That's your insecurity, don't take it out on me." Then he says, "If you're going to treat me like that maybe I should think about not being with you. That's not the kind of wife I want some day." He walks out of the room and leaves me there to cry alone.

I finally lay down, and eventually fall asleep. Chris has no idea why I'm upset. He doesn't understand what it's like having a sister that is always putting you down. Not only that, she is always trying to take what is mine, or ruin anything good that happens for me. I have no choice but to push aside my discomfort and not create an issue with him doing this. Chris and I have been in a good place, so it's up to me to keep us there.

Chris wakes me a few hours later and lets me know they are getting ready to leave. I try once more to see if he will stay home. "Are you sure you can't tell her no now?" I ask. I know at this point I look desperate and insecure, but I can't help how I feel.

"No, I said I'd take her so I'm going to do that. Try to rest and not worry, I have no idea how long all her running is going to take so it might be late when I get back."

Great, that doesn't make me feel any better. I have no choice but to trust that he won't do anything stupid. Trust, all those times of him telling me he was going to fuck my sister, were him speaking out of anger. No choice but believe deep down that Brittany would never actually do that to me, not with the father of my child. I know she has her issues with me, but I must believe somewhere in that girl's heart, she loves me.

They leave, and I lay in my bed and cry. I eventually stop, and go in the living room by myself, and watch a movie. I try not to think about them being together, and finally tell myself I'm being silly. These are the times I miss Megan so much. I know I could call her, but I also know if I do that and Chris finds out it will start a terrible fight. I know I could tell her all about it and she would be my voice of reason. I miss having her in my life so much it hurts. I never thought I would have a baby and us not be talking.

I realize the movie is almost over, and I'm bored, and I don't care to finish it. I turn off the tv and decide to go take a shower. After my shower I go to bed, I'm still tired from us fighting and being in the hospital. I also know the sooner I go to sleep the sooner my brain will stop wondering what they are doing and where they are.

Chapter 11

I wake up and it's morning. I look next to me and Chris is sleeping still. I never even heard him come home. I must have been more tired than I realized. I get up and go make myself breakfast. I decide since I'm feeling good, while I'm at it to make Chris breakfast too. I scramble some eggs, make some pancakes and toast. My dad already made coffee, so I get Chris some coffee too, and take it into our room for him.

I decide not to bring up yesterday and display my insecure feelings again. I don't think it's a healthy thing to do. I don't want to worry, and I don't want to fight either. Breakfast is my way of offering a peace offering. I hope Chris accepts it and moves on too.

I push open the door and go set the food down on the dresser, so I can wake him up.

"Hey, you," I gently shake his shoulders to wake him "I made you some breakfast."

After a minute he finally opens his eyes. "Wow, looks good," he says, "Not something I was expecting at all today, after yesterday..." He trails off.

I say, "Nothing happened yesterday except you were being nice, and I am thankful for you." I can tell he is surprised and he smiles and eats his breakfast.

"So, what do you feel like doing today?" I ask. "I'm feeling better so anything you want to do is fine with me." I add.

"I think I want to stay here with you and maybe watch a movie and hang out." he says.

"That sounds perfect to me." I add "Maybe we can order a pizza too?"

He surprises me with a real big smile and says, "That sounds perfect to me." I will go get some movies at the video store and grab a pizza too." I think all the crap surrounding Brittany and yesterday is forgotten, and I'm glad.

A week later is my baby shower. I'm so excited and I can't wait to see all the cute baby stuff. I feel the baby now all the time, and it all feels real now. Chris and I have been getting along well. The only two major issues we have are how much I eat, and if the baby is a boy.

I don't know what to do about either issue. I'm hungry all the time now. I can eat a good-sized meal, and twenty-five minutes later I feel like I'm starving again. I try not to eat too much in front of him, but if I don't eat my stomach hurts bad. I know I want to eat before we go, but I don't want him to call me piggy, or cow, at the shower if I eat again, especially in front of my friends.

Once again, this will be something Megan isn't invited to. I try not to think about it, so it doesn't make me cry and ruin the day. I push it aside like I have been doing for months. Chris absolutely won't let me talk to her, and honestly, I can't even bring up her name. He told me if I bring her up again, he is going to leave me.

I also don't know what to do about the baby being a boy issue either. I have no control over it, and he keeps telling me all the time "It better be a boy, or I'm gone." I honestly wonder what he will do if the baby is a girl? Could he be that mean and leave me? I don't think he's too serious, but he sure does like to make me stress about it.

We have had may fights over whether I have control over it or not. When he drinks especially, he will say mean things like, "You're so stupid you will probably have a girl." or in front of his so-called friends. "This dumb ass probably fucked up and has a girl in there." The worst one was "If we lived in a different time and different country if you had a girl they would get rid of it."

That last one made me cry, and of course he said I was overreacting and acting dramatic. I didn't like the way he said it. It hurt me, because no matter what gender I have, this is my child and I already love it so much. All I can do is try my best to ignore his comments and get through the last few months of this.

I decide to wait until the shower to eat, and I pray it's not a mistake. I don't want to be sick feeling, but I don't want to hear mean things... more. I know my mom is making all my favorite foods, and what she can't make, my aunts are helping with. I'm excited to get there, so I can see everyone and I'm thankful it's only a few minutes away.

Once we get there I go straight to where the food is and grab some cheese and crackers. I also pile a tiny plate full of fresh raw veggies, knowing Chris shouldn't complain about that. Thankfully he is helping my dad set up a few more tables. This gives me some time to talk to people without him right by me, and it feels great to relax a moment.

There are quite a few people arriving, and I'm so happy to see some of my high school friends. I'm happy so many of them came to show me their support, but truthfully, I want Megan there more. That thought makes me feel like a terrible and ungrateful person. I stop thinking about Megan because if I don't I'm going to cry. I try to plug into the conversation and I think after a while I'm hiding it well.

Chris comes up while I'm laughing and talking with them and says "So Ladies, what do you think she's cooking in there? A boy, or a girl?" Oh, shit. I was hoping this wouldn't come up.

"Chris and I think I'm having a boy," I say then add lying, "I have this feeling it's a boy."

"It's a girl." a few of my friends say together, and a few say, "No way it's a boy."

We are all laughing when Chris says, "It better be a boy if she knows what's good for her." and he walks away. The table is silent, and they are all staring at me.

I'm so embarrassed but I laugh it off and say, "Oh my god, he's such a jerk, men always want boys. He will be okay with either and he knows it." Everyone laughs too, and I can keep them from realizing he is being completely honest.

We are just about to start playing some shower games when Brittany comes bursting through the door loudly. "Hi sorry I'm late. Oh my gosh look how many people are here. Guess what everyone?" she shouts even louder, "I got my photos from my photoshoot back." The next thing I know she has everyone surrounding her to see her pictures.

At first, I don't care I'm used to her, but after a half an hour I start getting upset. Once again, as always Brittany needs to make sure the attention is on her. Today cannot be about me, and the baby. I should have known she would find a way to bring the attention to her. I finally go over to my mom and say, "Hey people are going to need to leave soon, and we haven't played games and I have gifts to open."

My mom tries to get everyone's attention, but they aren't listening, so I finally stand up and say, "Hey guys I hate to interrupt, but since this is my shower, could you pretend to pay attention?!" I laugh to make it light and not angry, but of course Brittany needs to make a scene.

"Oh my God, Margo. You are so rude to the very people that came here to support you. Guys I'm so sorry she is being rude." she says loudly "It's not you. Margo is jealous I have these photos and I'm pretty, so she is taking it out on you guys." I seriously at this moment hate that girl so much.

"No, Brittany, that's not even remotely true." I smile at everyone "I know some of you need to go soon, so I thought we could get this party moving along, that's all." I say and try not to cry as I go sit over where the gifts are and start opening them. I have a huge fake smile plastered on my face, but the day has been ruined. It never fails that she goes out of her way to hurt me and make me miserable.

I finally get through all the gifts and I really can't enjoy looking at them. I keep telling myself to smile, say thank you and don't cry. Once everything is open, most of the people start leaving, and I know I can go soon too. I know some people are going to stay longer than I want to. I go make my rounds to say thank you again and tell everyone I'm super tired and I'm going to head home to rest.

Chris buys my story that I'm exhausted and he agrees to take me home. I make small talk and tell him I had a nice time, but all I want to do is go home and go to sleep. He sees some girl walking and he is creepily staring at her. I can see she's cute, it doesn't help I'm already feeling gross and fat right now. What makes it even worse is Chris says "God damn look at that. I'd fuck her."

I'm completely shocked, and I look over at him and I say, "Excuse me? What did you just say?"

"I said I'd fuck her." he can see I'm upset, so he says, "I don't mean now obviously I'm with you, but if I wasn't I'd hit that." I honestly can't believe he is saying this right now to me. I am about to say what a jerk he is when he continues with "Look I'm human, I keep telling you, you better not get fat or I'm out. I will not be with a fat girl. I already overlooked the fact that you have no tits, but if you get fat I'm out."

"Chris I'm pregnant I'm not fat. I will gain weight, in fact I need to gain weight. There is nothing I can do about that." I sigh, and add "Besides because of it, my boobs are much bigger now." thinking that should at least make him happy.

"I know that," he says "But if you get gross stretch marks and gain extra weight, I'm not dealing with that, it's disgusting. I won't be with a girl like that, fair warning."

I'm not sure what to even say, so I don't say anything. I just want to go home and sleep. Chris tells me he is going to go see his mom for a little bit, and I tell him that's fine with me, I can rest while he is gone. I notice he doesn't invite me, and I'm glad. I think it's rude, but truthfully for a change I'm glad he has no manners, because I don't want to go this time.

He drops me off and I go right in and go to bed. I think I fall right to sleep because I wake up about an hour later to my mom asking where they should put my stuff. I tell her to hold on and I get up and show her where I want everything. I make sure to thank her again and ask if I can go take a shower. I want to be polite and make sure she wasn't needing to shower first. She says that's fine and lets me know Brittany is having some friends over later.

Great I think, every time that girl has friends over she acts like a bitch to me. After earlier with her pictures and her attitude, I can imagine she's going to be full of herself more so than normal. I don't care anymore what she says, I only want to look nice for when Chris gets home. I want to try to look pretty for him. It really bothered me what he said about that girl. I need to take better care of how I look, so I want to fix my hair and makeup and have a nice outfit on. Maybe we can go grab ice cream somewhere or do something fun.

I know if I ask Brittany to borrow her jeans she will say no, but if I already have them on... maybe she won't be a bitch. I sneak off downstairs and grab a nice pair of her jeans out of the dryer and hurry back up to shower. I want to be dressed and back in my room before she gets home and hopefully when Chris gets here we can sneak off without her noticing.

I hurry up and shower and quickly get my hair dried, thankfully I can curl my hair and do my makeup in my room. I listen to see if I can hear her mouth and so far, so good, I'm in the clear. I feel so sneaky, but it kind of feels fun too. I make a quick dash to my room and I make it without her seeing me. I find myself laughing as I collapse on the bed for a second. I feel so free for a second that I almost forget to finish getting ready. It's been a very long time since I have had this carefree frisky feeling and I miss it so much.

Finally, I drag myself off the bed, and finish getting ready. When I'm done my hair looks so pretty and I know it's from my prenatal vitamins. It's super long and thick, so it curls nicely and falls in a beautiful blonde cascade of curls. The curls are in long thick ringlets that will eventually loosen a little and look like gorgeous surfer girl wavy hair. My makeup goes on perfectly. Another thing to give credit to being pregnant, I have flawless skin and that "glow" everyone talks about. I stand back and look in the mirror. I feel pretty for a change and I hope it makes Chris think the same thing.

I just finish touching up my lipstick when I hear him coming down the hall. I have butterflies in my tummy and a smile on my face, when he comes in. Instead of a positive reaction, he glares at me and says, "Why do you have that shit on your lips, and your tits hanging out?"

I specifically picked this shirt out because being pregnant, I finally have bigger boobs and this shirt accents them yet hides my belly. After his earlier remarks about that girl, I'm taken back by his words. I know he likes and wishes I had bigger boobs all the time plus, he just told me so this afternoon. All I wanted to do is look sexy for him, and instead I feel silly. "Go wipe that shit off your face and I don't know why you're dressed up, we aren't going anywhere so you might as well change." he says obviously in a terrible mood.

I'm so disappointed, and honestly not sure why he is in such a bad mood. I leave our room and head out to go wipe the lipstick off when my mom sees me and says, "Margo come here for a minute please." So, I head out to the living room and my sister is out there with all her friends. They of course happen to be guys, four of them to be exact. "I was wondering if you guys are going to be home later for dinner or if you were leaving? If you are leaving, are you're coming back tonight or staying out?" she says

"No, as far as I know I'm staying in now." I answer.

One of Brittany's friends says to me. "That's a shame you look great, such a waste to sit in the house all night looking like that. Why don't you come join us? There is plenty of room in the car, and it will be fun."

I smile at him, but before I can even answer Brittany answers, in her whiny bitchy voice. "Oh my god. She is so gross how could you say that? Look how fat she is. Why would you want her to go with us? I don't hang out with fat people how embarrassing. She cannot go with us."

"She looks cool and it might be fun to have another girl to hang out with for the night, someone to give you a little competition." I have no idea this guy's name, but he is really digging at her and it's pissing her off.

I know I have to say something because she is about to explode. Right when I go to open my mouth she says, "You're so gross, obviously you like fat girls and you are a chubby chaser. If you want to hang out with fat girls, you can't hang out with us."

Finally, I speak up, because I looked around for my mom to say something and she's gone. I realize she probably went out to the garage to talk to my dad, while he's working on his car. Which explains why Brittany is acting this way and getting away with it.

"Brittany stop it. Stop calling me fat, you are being rude and it's not necessary." I look over to her friend and say, "Thank you for the invite but I will have to pass. I hope you guys have a great time though." I am walking out of the room and Brittany throws just one more dig at me.

"Go hide in your room and eat, you cow." She starts laughing as if she's the funniest person on the planet. I turn around and march right back into the living room ready to sock her one, when I realize I have a better way to not only shut her up, but also pay her back.

"Hey guys," I smile and I'm all sweet and nice taking a page out of her book. "Can I ask you all a question?" I start slowly turning around and sashaying my hips all dramatically. "Do I look fat to you? Honestly if you saw me, would you think I look fat? Please be honest." I can see they are loving the floor show I'm giving them, and they all are unanimously saying no not at all.

Before Brittany can say anything, I say, "Oh good I didn't think so, especially being I'm seven months pregnant." I hear them all at the same time saying no way, and wow, and holy cow, when I go in for the kill. "Poor Brittany she's mad, because I'm seven months pregnant and she's not. Oh, and these are her pants my "fat" ass is fitting in. So, I guess if she thinks I'm fat when I'm pregnant, then I can only imagine what she thinks of herself, being she isn't" I turn and walk out of the room but not before I see Brittany's mouth gaping open in shock and embarrassment.

I run into Chris in the hallway and I can see he is mad, so I know he saw what I did. He turns and goes right back to our room and I follow him, so I can explain why I did that. "Chris," I sigh as I walk into the room and he turns around and closes the door. "Let me tell you why I said that to Brittany..." I can't even finish my sentence and he has me by my arm dragging me over to where the bed is and pushes me down on it. I sit hard on the edge of the bed and halfway fall back and before I can sit back up he is sitting on my thighs and pinning me down to the bed.

I'm instantly scared and feel shocked that he is right back to this behavior. I have no idea why he is this upset about me putting her in her place. "So, you want to strut your body around in front of other guys for attention?" he says.

Oh no! Now I know why he is pissed, and it wasn't like that at all. "Chris, please, that's not what that was about. Brittany kept calling me fat and saying mean things to embarrass me and I guess I got mad. All I was trying to do was get her to stop, and for once I had a way to shut her up. I promise that is all that was, I don't care what any of those guys think."

I can see he is beyond mad and I know for sure he isn't listening when he says, "If you think for one second I'm going to let you act that way you have another thing coming."

I try again to tell him "Chris I don't care about those guys or what they think."

He just laughs at me and brings his face closer to me and asks "So, if that's true, why are you dressed up looking like a slut?" I'm so upset I start to cry and that only pisses him off more "Stop fucking crying" He is so pissed he is squeezing my arms tighter and tighter as he shakes me a little when doing it "You did this, not me, you went out there acting like a slut. You got all dressed up with your tits hanging out and decided you wanted to prance around for other guys." He gets up, walks over to his dresser and grabs a tissue off it and is right back on top of me before I can even register it and get up.

"Wipe that shit off your mouth." I slowly start wiping it off and I guess I'm not doing it good enough, because he grabs the tissue and starts wiping it for me. He is pressing so hard and being so rough it feels like the skin is coming right off my lips. I don't say anything, I lay there and let him do it. Inside I feel sick to my stomach, but I know if I say anything he will get meaner. He starts licking the tissue and wiping with his spit, and I feel so grossed out from it I want to throw up. I try to squirm away from him, but he is too strong and too heavy and I'm afraid he will hurt the baby.

Once all the lipstick is off he starts kissing me really rough and pawing at my chest through my shirt. I want him to stop but I know if I say anything, it could get worse, so to protect the baby, I let him do what he's doing. He tells me to scoot up higher on the bed. It's at this point I tell him I'm not feeling well and don't want to do this. He gets mad like I thought he would and doesn't wait for me to even scoot up on the bed. Instead he uses his one hand to hold both my wrists down above my head and uses the other to yank my pants and underwear down a little. Somehow during all of this he undoes his own pants too. I know what he is going to do, and I know it's going to hurt. I'm not at all in the mood so I know I'm not at all ready down there for this. Sure enough, he forces his way into me, even though I'm begging him not to, he does it anyways.

I unthinkingly let out a yell and he quickly cover's up my mouth with the blankets on the bed. I can't breathe well, and I feel like I'm suffocating under the blankets. I focus on breathing over the pain and pray he will be done soon. By the time he is done my hair is matted down to my face and drenched in sweat and tears. My makeup is smeared, and my hair now looks like a rat's nest. I know I shouldn't be thinking about that, but all I can think is how quickly I went from feeling beautiful, to feeling like used up garbage.

He gets off me and tells me "If I even think you are fucking someone else, I will beat the shit out of you, then go fuck some whore." He walks out of the room leaving me there feeling so alone, and unloved. I slowly get up and open a pack of baby wipes and start wiping my face up and cleaning myself up down there. There is a little bit of blood, and all I can do is pray he didn't hurt the baby. I keep thinking about what he just did and feel myself about to get sick. I run to the bathroom and once again thankfully make it to the toilet in time to throw up. I sit on the floor for about a half hour, when my mom comes in and says, "Oh no not this again?" she is assuming I'm sick from the morning sickness. I don't say anything, but I let her help me to my bed.

Chris comes in about ten minutes later, and I see no love in his eyes, just hate. He is so good at putting on a show in front of people, he acts like he is concerned and asks if I need anything. I say no I want to go sleep, I turn away from him, so I don't have to see his face.

He waits a minute then says he is going to go out with some friends for a while. I don't care so I say okay have fun, and I close my eyes to try and go to sleep. I lay there thinking once again this is not how I saw my life going. I have no idea what to do, but I don't want to live like this. Eventually I fall asleep and once again I never hear Chris come home.

Chapter 12

    The next few months, Chris is working a lot and I got a job babysitting. I can finally make a little money of my own, and it feels nice to get out of the house every day. At first Chris was pissy about it, but after a while he got used to it, and finally agreed it helps. We both want to be able to support the baby once it comes without asking either of our parents for help. He also keeps talking about getting our own place.

    I'm not sure how I feel about that, but I know eventually we need to broach that subject. The hardest thing will be making sure we have the money to do it. I know I want to nurse the baby and that will save us a lot of money. I know if I keep babysitting I can take the baby with me, so that will save money on daycare cost too. Things are okay, nothing great and nothing terrible. I am getting big now in my belly and when you look at me it's obvious I'm pregnant.

Chris makes comments all the time, about my weight even though the doctor is saying I haven't gained a lot at all. He loves to call me a cow, or moose, and chubby. He especially likes to do this in front of his friends, now that they know I'm pregnant. He loves to "moo" like a cow when I eat too and tell me everything is bad for me. I feel like I eat healthy. I don't have standard ice cream and pickles cravings, more like fresh raw veggies, and salads. I'm not sure how he thinks that will make me fat, but he likes to say it will. Most the time I laugh it off and ignore him, but I'm truly scared he will leave me if I don't get the weight off right away after the baby is born.

Part of me truly doesn't care if he left me. I think I would be happier and I think deep down I wish he would. I know I can't leave him, he makes that very clear every time I don't listen to him and he gets mad. He has told me over and over, being he makes more money he will get custody of our baby. I have thought about asking a lawyer, but I don't have the money for one. I can't risk him taking me to court and taking my child from me.

I have a plan to try and get the weight off right away. I know I'm supposed to wait a minimum of eight weeks after I have the baby to work out. I already asked about that and I am going to be ready to do it as soon as I am allowed. The hardest part will be not doing other things, like vacuuming, and carrying laundry up and down the steps. I'm secretly praying my mom will help, because there is no way Chris will do it.

Christmas was nice, we decided not to do anything for each other and only get a few things we still need for the baby. My parents surprised me though and got me an electronic typewriter. I was so excited I started to cry. Maybe my hopes of writing one day aren't completely lost. I know Chris was pissed they got it for me, but what could he do? It's not like he can tell them what to do, especially not my mom.

Thinking back, I think all in all we had a great holiday. I'm a about a week away from my due date and It is getting harder and harder to sleep at night. I feel like I swallowed a basketball. I make it to work today and I'm thankful because it's snowing bad. The roads are so snow covered, that the little kid I watch doesn't have school. We are watching a movie and relaxing, but no matter how I sit I can't get comfy.

I decide to get up and walk around and see if that will stop my back from hurting. It kind of relieves it a little and I notice the whole front walk is snow covered. I put on the coat and gloves my dad insisted on getting me and head out to shovel the snow. I never wear coats and he insisted today I bring it, and I'm glad he did. It's crazy how fast and thick it is coming down.

I know I shouldn't be shoveling, but I won't be able to get to my car later if I don't do it now. I'm hoping it doesn't make my back start hurting again, but It needs to get done. I get the front porch all cleaned up and a walkway to my car and head back in to make hot cocoa and marshmallows.

Luckily, I don't have to do much for the child I watch so I'm able to relax and watch another movie with him. I'm super grateful he is okay with that because I am at the point I can hardly get around now. I know his mom will probably be home late now because of the snow so I better think of something to make him for dinner. I don't usually make dinner for him, so I should go see what they have. I just get into the kitchen and the phone rings, I answer assuming it will be his mom, but it's Chris.

"Hey, so I think I'm going to pick you up tonight, the roads are getting pretty bad and I don't want you driving." Wow, that is thoughtful of him. I was feeling a little nervous being I'm so big and having the steering wheel right there could be dangerous if I got hit.

"Okay thank you." I say he says he can't talk long so we say goodbye and I get off the phone to figure out dinner.

I just started to boil water and figured out what to make for dinner when I hear a car pull in the driveway. It's Brandy, the lady I babysit for, she is already home. I hurry and go unlock the door, so she doesn't have to stand in the blizzard hitting us. "Hi" I say as she gets inside as fast as she can, but snow still ends up all over the floor.

"Who shoveled the porch and walkway?" she asks as she is getting her boots off.

"Um, that would be me." I say smiling.

"Why did you do that? What if you went into labor? Next time don't do that. I have a kid across the street that does that, I should have told you." She gets her coat off, and says, "I'm a little worried about you driving home in this mess."

"Oh, Chris is getting dropped off, so he is going to drive us home. He was worried too." I say, and I see the look on her face. She doesn't like Chris. She has never out right said so, but I can tell. She went through a bad divorce and I think Chris reminds her of her ex-husband or something.

"Well, that's thoughtful of him." is all she says.

"I was going to make some spaghetti for dinner, I already have the water started, do you want me to keep making it?" I ask, and she notices I'm rubbing my back, and she asked "Are you okay? Did you overdo it or are you having contractions?"

"No, I don't think contractions. From everything everyone says, I would know right?" I laugh "My back is achy, probably from shoveling, but I will be okay."

"I'll make us dinner, you go sit down and wait for Chris to get here." I'm super grateful she got home early because I feel exhausted today.

I didn't realize I dozed off in the chair while waiting, until she comes over and wakes me up, "Dinner's ready please come join us, with the roads this bad, Chris could be pretty late."

"Oh, thank you." I say and when I get up I have a terrible shooting pain in my stomach and it goes around to my back. "Holy crap", I say, I bend over and a few minutes later it goes away.

"That looked like a contraction to me," Brandy says, "I have a feeling you won't be coming in tomorrow."

"Oh, but I'm not due for another week yet, so this is probably those Braxton Hicks contractions again. I've had them before." I say.

"Well, we will see, but for now come eat, you must be pretty hungry. I remember at the end of my pregnancy, I could only eat a little at a time, so I felt hungry all the time."

"Yes, that's exactly how I feel. Chris makes fun of me because I have food in front of me all the time, but I can't eat a lot in one sitting." I laugh and happily put some food on my plate. The spaghetti is so good, of course I couldn't eat that much, but the little bit I do have is delicious. "Thank you, that hit the spot." I add, "Well for now." and we both laugh.

I am helping her clean up when I see headlights and I know Chris is here. I go grab the door and once again the snow comes flying in the door. "Geez oh man, it's getting so bad out." I say and try to help get snow off him.

"Where are the keys?" he says, "I want to go start the car and let it warm up."

I go grab the keys and he turns to me and says "You better not have eaten. I'm hungry and want to eat and I'd rather not do it alone."

I was about to answer when Brandy speaks up "Oh, no, she said she was waiting for you to eat so she took a little nap while we ate." I could kiss her right now.

"Okay, good girl." Chris says smiling, I see Brandy cringe at his comment as he heads out to clean off the car and warm it up.

"Thank you." I say to Brandy, "He gets grumpy at the end of the day, and this whole me eating all the time drives him nuts." I laugh and try to play it off.

"Well you have a baby in there and I think he is mean and condescending to you. I know I shouldn't say that, but you do know if he is treating you badly there are places that can help. There are even places that will take you and the baby in if you need it. I know you live with your parents for now. Just know there are shelters that specialize in helping woman with children, get away and stay away from not so nice men."

I'm so embarrassed, but I'm thankful she cares. She has no idea that if I tried to leave him he would take my baby from me. He has made it crystal clear, I won't see my child ever again if I do that. I say, "Thank you, I'm okay, he's just grumpy." I can tell she wants to say more, but Chris comes in, so she doesn't.

"Let's go, the roads are getting worse." Chris says.

I get my shoes and my coat on and I'm surprised, when Brandy hugs me and says, "You take care kiddo, I hope to see you tomorrow." Chris looks beyond pissed and I'm not sure why but suspicious. I can see Brandy sees it too, and I'm terrified she might say something to him about these shelters.

She doesn't she says instead, "Take care of her daddy, she has been having contractions tonight. Pretty big ones, so I have a feeling that little baby is coming soon." she smiles, and I see Chris relax.

"Oh, interesting, we will keep you posted." he says, and we shuffle out of the door into the crazy snow storm. It takes all my strength to walk through the snow and get to the car. I am so relieved Chris is here to drive. Normally snow doesn't scare me, but I would be a little scared to drive tonight.

The drive home is long and slow, and I'm so thankful I ate that spaghetti before I left. We finally make it home, and by that time the cramps are getting stronger and more often. I finally tell Chris I think I should call my doctor and see what she thinks about them. As soon as I get in the house I have a big one, and my mom is right there so she helps me breath through it. Chris didn't think I needed Lamaze classes, and I'm regretting listening to him right now.

I get through to my doctors answering service and let them know what is going on. My doctor calls me back fast. After a few minutes of timing things and seeing how long the contractions are, she decides it would be best if I come in. She says she feels better about that, being the roads are so bad and the hospital is forty minutes away, in good weather.

I get ready to go and pack some stuff to take to the hospital and my mom says she is going to get a bag together for herself too. As soon as I get in my room, Chris closes the door and says, "Your mom is not going in the room with us. I don't need her running her mouth making me look stupid and being a know it all."

I'm pretty taken back, we never even talked about this, but another contraction makes me focus on that for a minute. When it's finally over, I say "Chris, It's her first grandchild, and she's my mom. I want her in there in case I need her."

"I'm not arguing about it. Just me and you. No one else, either you tell her, or I tell her I don't care who, but she isn't coming in the room."

"Well she can come in for a while, right? Then step out when it's time for the baby to come?" I'm hoping by then it will be too late to have her leave, but he is adamant.

"No, not at all. You better figure it out, or we are going to have issues." He leaves me standing there having another contraction. I start crying, and my mom comes to find me and thankfully thinks my tears are from the contractions.

"It's okay, cry if you need to, but breathing helps the best. Find something specific to focus on, like a spot on the wall and try hard to keep that in your mind and breath through them."

"Okay I'll try." I say then add "Mom, I think I only want Chris and I in the room. If anything changes I'll let you know, but as of now I kind of want to be alone." I can see her face fall, but she politely smiles through it.

"That's okay, you get situated and when you are ready I will come in. It will be a long night and whatever you need, you get." She has no idea Chris will never let her in my room, not even for a visit. This is not at all how I saw this happening and right now I can't even think about it.

I slowly make my way out to the car and I see Chris has put garbage bags all over the seat and floor of the car. "What is that for?" I ask thinking it's because of the snow.

"In case your water breaks I don't want a mess in my car, so it better not break in here." He says this as if I would have any control over it. I don't even respond, because between the contractions and being scared, I don't want to talk to him. We back out of the driveway and start heading to the hospital. I can't believe it, but the roads are worse than they were earlier.

"Did you say something to your mom? I hope so because I don't want to deal with that bitch right now." he says and he's being so mean about it.

"Yes." I say, and I'm rocked with another batch of contractions, so I stare out the window and try to breathe through them.

"What the fuck is your problem? Are you seriously going to be a bitch right now?" He asks.

"Chris, I'm having contractions, I'm focusing on that right now. I don't fucking care about anything else right now."

"Suck it up, you have a lot more to come so you might as well stop acting like a baby and just deal with it."

I can't even respond to him. He has no idea how painful these are and I'm not even going to try to explain it. I shift in the seat and try to lay back a little, trying to get more comfortable when he notices and tells me to sit up straight. I don't want to argue so I sit back up again. He reaches over and grips my seat belt and yanks it super tight under my stomach. "Oh" I say, "Chris that's too tight."

"Deal with it, the roads are bad, so you need to sit up and have your seatbelt on right." He is being such a prick right now. All I can do is breath and pray it doesn't hurt the baby.

Thank god, we finally get to the hospital, and I undo the seat belt. It was so tight I felt like I had super tight jeans on and I just unbuttoned them to make room. Chris goes in to get a wheelchair and I say a small prayer asking God to keep me and my baby safe. I then pray I can get through this without my mom, because I know he won't let her in.

A nurse comes out with Chris to help me and we head into the hospital. My doctor already called so we don't have to wait, they take us right up to Labor and Delivery. They have me change into a gown, they hook me up to a monitor and start an Iv. A nurse comes in to take my vitals and ask me all about the contractions, then she asks, "Do you want an epidural?"

I never even thought that far ahead, but before I could answer, Chris says "No, she's going natural."

The nurse looked at me and says "Is that your plan? Go natural?"

"I said no epidural." Chris says to her and he is glaring at her.

"Well, I have to hear it from her, not you. She is the patient, not you. We are here for mom and baby, so I'll tell you right now, if you give us any problems at all, we can and will remove you from this room." She stands there and stares right back at him. Finally, he stops glaring and goes over to the corner and sits in a chair like a child in time out. If I wasn't in so much pain, I would think it was funny. No one ever gets away with talking to Chris like that and this nurse just did. She is now my favorite person on the planet.

"Now, Margo, do you want an epidural? If you even think you will change your mind, I'm required to put "yes" so they can have an anesthesiologist on call. Since this is your first child, I highly recommend saying yes, even if you don't need it or chose not to use it."

I know I should say no but having her there with me gives me a silent strength, so I say, "Okay, I will say yes, even though I plan to go natural." I don't even look at Chris. I focus on the nurse and what she is doing. Another nurse comes in and says my mom and dad are here asking if they can come back to my room.

Once again, Chris answers for me. "No, we only want us in here, so tell them they can come in after the baby comes." Then he gets up and says, "I'll tell them." He walks out with the nurse that came in to ask us. I know this is his way of punishing me and paying me back for the nurse standing up to him and my agreeing to the epidural. As soon as he leaves the nurse walks to the door, looks out, then comes back and says, "Do you feel safe with him?"

Once again, I'm faced with the embarrassing question of my safety with Chris.

"I'm okay, he's just nervous so he is being a jerk." I say and laugh a little.

"Well I want you to know if at any point you want him out of the room, even for a little bit we can make him leave. Better yet, why don't you say, 'I'd kill for a Pizza right now'. That will be our code and trust me, most moms use these code words to get a break." I know she is trying to be helpful, but all it's doing is making me depressed. I never saw my life going in this direction. I pray I can get through this labor and the baby is okay.

Chris comes back in a few minutes later and now the contractions are coming steady. I can tell he's irritated with me, so I lay there silently crying. I know if I make any noise or complaint, he will have a smart-ass comment and I can't deal with that right now.

After about an hour, the nurse comes back in and says she would like to check my progress. I have no idea what that means but I soon find out. She sticks her fingers in down there, and measures to see how far I am dilated. It is the most awkward, uncomfortable thing to have to have done so far. She says I am only three centimeters, then adds I must reach ten centimeters to start pushing. She says this is going to take a very long time. At this point she suggests to Chris, that he may want to go for a walk or something and stretch his legs or update our family.

"They are fine, they don't need a play by play." he says, but he gets up and goes for a walk anyways. As soon as he leaves the nurse asks "How are you doing? Really doing?"

I cry a little and say I'm okay, but the contractions are getting stronger and they are really hurting right now. She then says, "I have medicine I can give you, it's nothing that will knock you out, but it will give you a little relief if you want it?"

"Yes, please, and please don't tell Chris. He wants me to go natural and I don't think I can do it." I say. She smiles this I feel bad for you smile and gets the medicine ready. I hurry up and take it before Chris gets back to the room. I just get it down and he comes back in. I hope the medicine works, because these contractions hurt bad already and I have hours to go.

The medicine dulls the pain a little... not totally, but enough that I can close my eyes a little and rest. I wake up later though, to them getting intense and closer together. I think at this point there's no way I'm not closer to being done when the nurse comes in to check me again. "Well it's been a few hours, let's see how you are now." she checks me out down there again, and once again it's super uncomfortable. "Well honey you are only at about a four, so go ahead and try to rest in between these because we are in for a very long night.

At this point I have no idea how I can rest through these. I ask the nurse "Is this as bad as it will get? Or does it get worse?"

She looks at the monitor and says let me see your next contraction. She waits a minute or so and sure enough another one starts. I can barely breath through it.

"Well honey that looked strong, but I'll be honest they will be stronger and come more frequently. At the rate you are going, you have hours of this ahead of you." I want to ask about pain meds, but with Chris sitting there, I can't.

The nurse is so wonderful, she instantly picks up on this and says, "Hey dad? While I finish checking her vitals, would you be so kind and go down the hall and grab some ice for her? Oh, and someone brought some free food for the fathers too, so help yourself. The only thing is, you'll need to eat it there. We can't allow food to be brought down here." laughing she says, "Too many moms try to sneak it, and too many dads let them." She smiles at him.

I'm not sure he is going to go at first, but then he says, "I'm pretty hungry so that sounds good, can I bring the ice after I eat?"

"Sure, she has enough to tide her over for a bit." then she continues to check my vitals while he gets himself together to leave. As soon as he walks out of the room, she turns to me "Okay, I am guessing you want more pain meds?"

"Yes, if I can?" I ask, what about that epidural thing? How does that work, and can I get that too?

"I can give you some Demerol right now, it's a pain medicine, and as far as the epidural, you aren't yet at the point where we can give it to you. You are close though, but not yet. The Demerol should work long enough to hold you over until we can get the epidural in." She then explains how it works and what they do to put it in me.

I wish even more now, I had my mom in here to tell me what I should do. I know if I ask for her though, Chris will be such a jerk and I can't handle anything like that right now. I take the medicine the nurse hands me and I pray I can figure out a way to get that epidural in. I think of something and say to the nurse, "If I say I'd kill for a pizza, that means to get him out of the room, right?"

"Yes, do you need us to keep him out?" she asks.

"No, but he is absolutely adamant I don't get an epidural. I think I might want one, so If I say I'd kill for a pizza with pepperoni…" I trail off.

"Yes." she says, "With pepperoni means you want the epidural, just cheese… will mean, natural" She is beaming.

"Thank you." I say and now I'm smiling, "Once it's in, he can't actually do anything at that point but bitch." I say laughing. I feel much better now, well until the next contraction rocks my body.

Chris comes back about thirty minutes later, and the medicine has kicked in and I'm half sleeping, so he leaves me alone. I can hear him turn the tv on, but that's all I remember because I finally fall asleep.

Once again when I do wake, I am jolted awake by intense contractions. This time they are so bad I can barely catch my breath in between them. I notice Chris is sleeping in the chair in the room and I don't want to disturb him. I try to deal with the pain, as long as I can.

Finally, after about forty-five minutes I can't take it anymore, so I press my nurses button. The nurse come in and says, "Hey honey, let me check and see how things are progressing."

Once again, she checks down there and I'm in so much pain I don't even care. "Well you are at about five and a half centimeters so about halfway there."

At this I just cry. I honestly thought I would be closer than I am. I finally say, "Oh man I'd kill for a pizza with some pepperoni. I wish it was time for that for sure."

Chris is awake now and snickers and says "Well you can't but I might go grab some pizza. Why should we both suffer and be hungry." The guy has no class. I lay there crying and hope the nurse can get it for me soon.

After a few minutes, I say to Chris, "Honestly, I'm going to try to sleep for a little bit if you want to go grab food that's okay. I don't think I'm having this baby anytime soon." I try to pretend like I'm not in that much pain, hoping he will take the bait and go.

"That sounds good to me. I think I'm going to go eat and get out of here for a bit." he says. Thank god. I hope he is gone long enough for them to do the epidural. Of course, he feels the need to be a jerk first, "And if you even try to bring your mom in here when I'm gone you will have serious problems when we leave here. Don't defy me." With that threat hanging in the air, he leaves the room. No kiss, no I love you, no I hope you're not in too much pain... Nothing, just a threat.

About five minutes after Chris leaves, my nurse comes back in and says she saw him in the hall and he said he was going to get some food. She called, and the anesthesiologist will be coming up shortly to do the epidural. She also let me know that she told everyone that before they buzz anyone back to my room, check with her first. I can almost, if it weren't for the contractions, start to relax.

The anesthesiologist comes up about ten minutes later, and they prepare me for everything they will be doing. Before I even get a chance to change my mind or chicken out, the nurse tells me to sit on the edge of the bed and bend over my belly. I laugh at this because my stomach is like a huge round basketball. I scooch to the side of the bed and do my best to bend over my belly. The nurse holds me in place and I feel them put some wet stuff on my back. The next thing I feel is a contraction starting then a pinch in my back, some pressure then something cold. The nurse tells me I'm all done and helps me move back on the bed the right way.

When it fully kicks in, I cannot believe how much better I feel. I can't feel any of the contractions now, and I'm so tired I fall asleep right away. I have no idea how long it's been, but I eventually wake up, and Chris is sitting there with my sister Lauren. I can't believe she got him to let her come back to see me. "Hey, I'm glad to see you." I say, and I feel the tears stinging my eyes.

"How are you feeling, looks like the pain isn't too bad." She says to me and I quickly shoot a look at Chris, and I can see he's pissed.

"Apparently she decided to get an epidural while I was gone." He says.

"Yes, I did, I couldn't take the pain any more Chris, it was too much, and I know I need to rest up to be able to push." I feel braver with Lauren here, so I speak up for a change. I can see he isn't happy, but there isn't much he can do to me right now.

"I should have known you'd be too weak to go natural." He says to me, and I see instantly when Lauren registers what he says.

Eyes blazing, she turns to him, "Fuck you dude, you have no idea and never will know the pain a woman goes through giving birth. Imagine being kicked in the balls over and over with no reprieve. Now imagine that for hours upon hours." Thank God for Lauren. "So... keep your mouth shut. Unless you want me to try to see how many times you can actually handle it to the balls?" She is not the type of girl to mess with when she is mad, and Chris knows this and backs right down. I can see he regrets letting her back here but no way he is getting her out of here now. I can't help but to almost feel sorry for him. Almost.

Chris says he is going to go for a walk and as soon as he leaves I say to Lauren "How the hell did you get him to let you back here? He won't let anyone in, not even mom."

"I took him to grab a beer then when we got back here I followed him to the door. He turned to say something, and I said fuck with me dude, I'm going to see my sister." I break down crying at this point. I love how Lauren is so strong, I wish so badly I could be like her too. One day, I will learn to be strong and brave too.

"How are you really doing?" she asks.

"I'm okay now, he wasn't going to let me get the epidural, but as soon as he left I asked for it. I figured once it's in he can't do anything about it."

"What do you mean 'let you'?" she asks, and I realize I shouldn't have said that, so I quickly covered it up.

"Not let me you know what I mean, he was adamantly against it, for the baby." Oh man, Chris will flip if my sister makes a big deal out of this I continue with "He read some stuff about how it's not as safe for the baby, he's trying to be a good dad already." I lie like it's my job anymore.

She looks a little less fired up and says "Okay, for a second there I thought you meant that fucker was telling you what you can and can't do."

I shake my head no and say, "No not at all, it came out wrong." She relaxes and lets me know everyone is out there waiting to see what I have, and they are super excited. She tells me even my middle school friend Denise is here. She moved away when we were in middle school, yet she always stays in touch somehow. I can't believe she made that hour trip in the snow storm to be here for me.

Chris comes back, and Lauren surprises me and says she is going to go out to update everyone, but she will come back later. I know Chris won't make that mistake again, so I hug her tight and tell her I love her and as soon as she leaves I roll to my side and cry.

The nurse comes in a few seconds later and sees me crying and asks if I'm in any pain. I tell her no, I'm just super tired, so she turns the lights down and tells me to rest again. I'm happy to do that so I don't have to talk to Chris or hear him bitch about the epidural.

I fall asleep for hours when I'm suddenly awaken by so much pain, I can't catch my breath. The contractions are back, and they are so much worse than they were before. I press the call button and I'm bawling by the time the nurse comes in. She says my epidural must have ran out and she needs to check me. She says once she does that, then she can put in a request for more meds.

She checks me quickly while I'm having these contractions and she says "Honey you are at ten centimeters. It's time to start pushing, we can't give you any more of the medicine." I feel sheer panic setting in. I start hyperventilating and she calmly comes up to my head to help me breath.

Once she helps calm me down, she starts setting some things up around the room. I keep breathing like she taught me, but I feel so much pain I'm not sure how I can live through it. I have never had a baby, but this can't be normal. There is no way woman will have more than one child if this is how it is every time.

"Is this much pain normal?" I finally ask, and she assures me it is. All I can think is I'll never do this again and my mom is nuts for doing this four times. Chris is no help, he snickers at me, or says things like "This is karma for the epidural, now it's a shock to your body instead of it working up to it." or "You should have listened to me." He's such a jerk. I do my best to ignore him, I'm in too much pain to even talk.

The nurses have me push on and off forever. I have completely lost track of time, all I know is I'm completely exhausted and I don't know how much more I can do it. They let me rest a little and get me right back to pushing. There comes a point where I don't feel like this baby will ever come out. I lay back completely exhausted and they tell me I need to keep pushing.

The doctor finally comes in and says she sees the head, my baby has a lot of hair, and asks Chris if he wants to see. He goes more towards the end of the bed and says how much hair he sees and at this point I hear myself saying "Then grab it by the damn hair and help pull it out!" I don't really mean it, but it feels so good to get mad and yell.

They all gather around my vagina like it's some wonderful place to be and I start getting madder. Before I have a chance to say anything I have another terrible contraction and they are yelling to me to push again. I keep pushing and pushing and nothing is happening. The doctor on call is not my doctor. She asks what they have charted as the estimated weight. The nurse comes back from looking and says five to six pounds, so the doctor has me continue to push.

After what seems like forever, the doctor asks the nurse how long I have been pushing "A little over three hours." she says. Oh my gosh so, it has been a long time. The doctor says we will give it fifteen more minutes, and if nothing happens they will take me back for an emergency C-section.

Hearing that I'm more scared then I was before. I don't want to be cut open or be put to sleep. I think I need to push harder than I have ever pushed in my life. They tell me to start pushing again and I pretend I'm in a competition. I draw all my strength from my competitive nature and push harder than I've ever pushed.

Finally, after about fifteen more pushes they say the head is out. I hear the doctor say I'm tearing from the episiotomy, and its bad. I have no idea what that means. I push a few more times and the baby finally comes out.

"It's a girl." I hear the nurse say. I try to look, and I'm so confused I have no idea what they are saying. Finally, I hear the baby start crying and I say, "Is he okay? I want to see him." she holds the baby up.

The nurse says, "Honey you have a girl, she's a baby girl and she's big, over nine pounds." So much for a small baby I think.

Once it fully registers, I look over at Chris, and he is smiling and has tears in his eyes, so I know it will be okay. I finally let out the breath I've been holding in and I cry. I'm so happy. I'm not crying sad tears, they are tears of joy. I wanted a daughter so much and I wasn't allowed to ever say it. Now I can show my joy and love her with all my heart. Today has just become the happiest day of my life.

Chapter 13

I'd love to say after Elizabeth came into our lives, everything was perfect, but it was far from. The first few months were okay. I was busy sleeping when she slept and learning to nurse, and care for her when she was awake. Having my mom around for me, was priceless. For Chris on the other hand, he hated her advice, and her.

I am slowly feeling human again. I'm starting to finally get into the swing of being a mom when Chris blindsides me with moving out. He comes home from work and tells me he needs some work clothes washed, then says. "Oh, and next month we are moving out." and he goes to take a shower. Just drops a huge bomb on me and walks away.

When he finally gets out of the shower I am able to ask him "Move out? To where? And how? How do we have money to live on our own and support a baby?"

In typical Chris fashion his response is shitty "Don't worry about it. Make sure you have your stuff ready this isn't up for discussion."

"Okay I understand that but how are we going to do this? I'm not even back to work yet." I try again to ask.

"I said don't worry about it and make sure your shit is packed and leave it alone. You'll see it will be fine.'" That's all I get out of him. The discussion is closed. I think the hardest thing for me will be telling my parents I'm moving out. I know they can't stop me, but I'm sure they won't be happy. Things are tense between them and Chris, so I guess I shouldn't be surprised he wants to leave.

One thing I know about my mom is, if she doesn't like someone, she won't change her mind. She calls it intuition. I used to call it being a bitch, now... I have no idea what I think. She has pegged Chris right about many things. I don't even think she realizes how right she is and I'd rather stay in a shitty relationship than admit it to her. That's a hard pill to swallow, but I hate admitting she was right about him and at this point there really is no point. I'll stay with him, to protect Lizzie or else he will take her from me. I guess, I just need to make the best of all this.

The next morning after I eat breakfast my mom offers to give Elizabeth a bath. I say okay, I know she loves doing it and I also know she's going to miss it when we are gone. I figure this is the best time to tell her, before the day can get ruined by something else.

"Hey mom, so I wanted to let you know, Chris and I are planning to move out next month." I brace myself.

"Well, we figured you would eventually. Are you sure you are ready to do that?" she asks.

"Chris thinks we are, I don't know much about the details yet, we haven't had a chance to talk about it." Like normal for me lately, I lie.

"Well dad and I want you to know you and Lizzie," she uses Elizabeth's nickname, "always have a place here, but..." of course, here we go there is a but... "Chris will not be welcome back here." she says, then adds, "We do think however it's time for you guys to go and figure things out on your own." I am completely flabbergasted by this entire conversation.

I was all prepared for an argument, but instead she is basically saying they don't want me here. I feel my eyes fill up with tears, and I don't want to cry so I say, "I'll be right back I'm going to grab Lizzies clothes."

I hurry out of the bathroom and think to myself, screw them then. I'm going to move out and have a better life then all of them. I'm so pissed, and I don't even know why. I want to move out now, I want to get away from here and be on my own. Yet, I think I wanted her to put up fight too. I get the baby her clothes and pull myself together. They will all eat their words; my life is going to be so much better once I leave here. Chris is right, they all try to hold me back.

I go back into the bathroom and get Elizabeth from my mom to get her dried off and dressed. I decide from that moment forward, I'm going to do whatever it takes to make my relationship successful and succeed in life. I will be sure to never ask for anything from them again.

Chris comes home, and I tell him my parents agree it's time to move out. This time he is a better mood, so I feel I can get some answers from him. "So, I'm super excited to move out and get a place." I try this route, "Where do you think we will look? Are you thinking near here, or closer to one of our jobs?"

"No," He smirks. At first, I think that's all he is going to say, then he surprises me with, "We are going to move in with my friend Mark, and his girlfriend." This was not at all what I had in mind as our first place together. I don't even know who these people are and now I have my daughter to think about.

I know if I make a big deal out of it, it will turn into something big. So, I smile and say "Oh, okay that sounds interesting, when can we go see the apartment? I'll need to know the sizes of our rooms." I am hoping I sound excited, and not weary.

"There are only two bedrooms, so she will sleep in our room still for a while." he says which secretly makes me happy. I'm not too sure how comfortable I'd be if she had her own room with strangers living there. For all I know these people could hate kids. "I'm thinking we can go there and hang out Saturday, we can eat dinner there and you can get to know them." Chris says cutting into my thoughts.

"Okay that sounds fun. I hope they like us, especially Lizzie. I'm excited to move out and make a home together as a family." I say and even though I'm nervous, I am getting excited now. I never thought I'd be moving out and having my own place. I know we will be sharing it with someone else, but it will still be so much fun.

Saturday night we go to his friend Mark's house and meet him and his girlfriend Sharon. They are nice and seemed to absolutely love Lizzie. By the time we left and we're heading home I feel like I'm floating on cloud nine. I think everything is going to change once we move. I feel Chris will be happier away from my mom, and I finally see he was right about her. She is way too bossy and tries to still be my "mom" when I don't need that anymore.

The next few weeks go by fast. I spend most the time nursing, cleaning and packing. I never realized how much stuff we had, until I needed to pack it all up. My mom is being helpful, and I feel sad she isn't more upset about us leaving.

Brittany is being a major bitch. Not only is she acting that way towards me, but she is being downright nasty to Chris. He seems to not care, but it is making me so mad the way she talks to him. I know if I ever did that he'd be so pissed. I guess I find comfort knowing that's because he loves me.

I bring up Brittany and her mouth to Chris the day before we are supposed to move out. "I am so surprised you let her talk to you like that."

"Why make a big deal out of it? Once we leave here I don't have to see that bitch again." he says.

"Well, not really." I say, "We will still come back here to visit and stuff, like for holidays and cookouts." I try making him see he will still have to deal with her.

"We'll see about that." he says and smirks his smirk at me.

"Okay well you don't have to, but I'll have to deal with her when I come over." I say thinking he means he isn't coming back.

"Like I said, we'll see about that." he says again.

"What's that supposed to mean? You know I'll be coming back here, you can't keep me from visiting my parents." I don't know why I said that and regretted it as soon as it came out of my mouth. I have no chance to fix it or get away. Chris reacts quicker than my own brain can realize what I said.

He has my hair wrapped in his hand and my face two inches away from his before I could even register what is happening. I think he is going to say something, but he just stands there holding my head still, so I'm forced to look him in the face. Then he starts laughing. Not the kind of laugh that someone does when they find something funny. More like an evil, something bad is going to happen, doesn't reach his eyes with joy, kind of laugh. He shakes his head back and forth slowly, laughing.

When he finally speaks, he says, "Little girl, you have no idea how many ways I can fuck your life up. I promise if you keep misbehaving I will make your life a living hell and if you even think of not coming, I'll take Lizzie from you too." I am racking my brain trying to figure out what to say to get myself away from him when I hear my mom calling my name. Chris lets go of me and says, "Open your mouth and I swear Lizzie and I will be gone in five minutes." he leaves me standing there crying.

My mom finds me there crying and I feed her a lame ass story about being sad because I have so many memories here. She hugs me and says again; Lizzie and I always have a room there if we need it. I know I should be grateful especially after what just happened, but it pisses me off instead. I feel like I'm being forced out of my home to live with this jerk.

I shrug away from my mom and say, "Well thanks but no thanks. Just because I'm feeling sad doesn't mean I want to stay here, especially if my whole family isn't welcome." At that I walk away to try to pull myself together and gather my thoughts.

I know I hurt my mom's feelings and I know I'm taking my anger at Chris out on her. I feel so alone, and I know I can't say anything to anyone. Chris has made that incredibly clear. If I tell anyone I don't want to be with him, he will take my daughter away from me and I'd rather die than have that happen. I have no choice but to go and try my best to make him happy and try to listen more.

The next day, we load all our stuff into a moving truck and head to our new home. At first, I'm a little sad, but the closer we get to it I can't help but to start feeling more excited. It will be so fun to not have rules to follow and be the adult in my home. For a change I get to decide what is best for me. I get to decide how to do things or when to do things. I know I'll need to behave and listen to Chris, but while he is at work, I will have freedom to do whatever I want. I finally get to be free and do whatever I want, anytime I want. I did, choose to quit my job because it was too far away to travel every day. I'm a little sad about that, but I'm happy I still get to stay home with Lizzie.

We finally get here, and Mark and Sharon are waiting for us. They let us know our room is all ready for us. It is a nice sized bedroom, so we have space for our bed and Lizzies crib. We also have a nice size area for a dresser and the closets are large too.

The four of us quickly get everything in the house. They surprise us and say they are making us a welcome home dinner. The excitement is catchy, and I find myself laughing and smiling more than I have in a very long time. All my fears and doubts are starting to disappear. I have a feeling this move will end up being the best thing to happen for our little family

The first few weeks are amazing, I finally get Lizzie into a great routine and things with Chris are going great. The problem is, Mark and Sharon. The last few nights they have really been fighting. Screaming and yelling and I swear a few times I heard someone hit someone. I have no idea who was doing what though, because it is in their room and they have the door closed.

One morning I am sitting in the living room and I thought they all left for work already, when I hear them start fighting. I pick Lizzie up to take her up to our room when Sharon comes running down the steps. She reaches the door and right as she is opening it, Mark slams into the door and closes it. He grabs her and is dragging her back up the stairs when she notices me, and she starts screaming at me to stop him. She keeps screaming that he is beating her.

I think I freeze from shock, but also fear and it gives him the time he needs to cover her mouth. He says, "She's crazy, I'm kicking her out and she's flipping out about it. Don't worry I'm not hurting her, she's lying." he drags her up the steps and I sit there stunned.

I didn't know what to do. I know if I interfere, Mark is huge and could really hurt me. He is one of the few guys I know that is bigger and stronger than Chris. I know if I sit here I'll go crazy not knowing if he is hurting her. It feels like hours passing when I finally decide I should go knock on the door to see if she is okay.

I creep up the stairs and right when I'm about to reach the door, Sharon comes out. Her face is all blotchy red and I think she has a black eye starting. She looks away fast and goes into the bathroom. I say "Oh. Excuse me, I'm sorry Lizzie needs a change of clothes." and I go in my room and close the door.

I stay in my room the rest of the day. I use some of Lizzie's diapers to pee in. Thank God, I nurse her because I don't have to go warm up bottles. I am terrified if I come out, something bad will happen to me or Lizzie.

Finally, Chris comes home, and I hear him downstairs, talking to Mark. I know eventually I need to go down there and by now I am hungry. I slowly make my way down the stairs and as soon as Mark sees me he says, "I'm so sorry you had to see that, she is nuts, and she won't be back."

"Oh, it's okay. I had such a bad headache, I napped with Lizzie today. I never heard her leave." I lie, there is no way I want him to know I heard everything that happened. I ask if they want me to make dinner and Mark says he already ordered pizza for us all. I say thank you, trying to act casual as I take Lizzie to play in the living room.

Later that night I try to tell Chris about everything that I heard and saw, but he cuts me off. "Well if she would have just shut up and listened to him, she'd still be here." Then he says, "Maybe you should remember that too and mind your own business, don't fuck this up for us."

I instinctively know, that I need keep my mouth shut and play nice. The last thing I want is for both guys to treat me like Chris does. My biggest concern is for Lizzie. If I do anything to overly piss Chris off, he is going to take her from me. I wish I had a job again, because then I don't think he could take her from me. Right now, he could kick me out and keep her and there is nothing I can do. I close my mouth and leave it alone.

Things seem to calm down for a while, the guys like to lift weights and workout every day. I'm okay with that because it keeps them busy and Chris out of my hair. I try to just stay in the background and not aggravate anyone. Lizzie is so cute and crawling all over the place. My cousin Angel had her baby, a little boy and he is so cute. I want our kids to grow up as close as siblings, but Chris is still being a jerk about seeing my family. I keep thinking in time things will change, but right now he still won't let me go see them.

I lie and tell my mom I'm busy a lot and I think thankfully she's busy with Brittany, so she doesn't notice. I figure eventually she will want to come here instead though, and I'm not sure how I'll handle that.

My aunt and uncle are once again planning their yearly Memorial Day party and I want to go but can't. I can't believe it was almost a year ago that I found out I was pregnant. That year went so fast, and my life has changed so much. I was thinking how different everything is and how much I still miss Megan when Chris surprises me and comes home early.

Being I'm not expecting him, I still have clothes out that I need to fold, and my breakfast dishes are still in the sink, He comes barging through the door in a terrible mood. He looks around and sees me sitting on the couch and says, "I always wondered what you do all day now I know, not a Goddamn thing. What the hell makes you think it's okay to sit on your ass all day while I bust mine at work?"

I look up at him and I realize too late that I was crying when I was thinking about Megan, and he sees the tears. I try to turn my head away and wipe them fast, but he is already towering in front of me glaring down at me. "What the fuck is your problem?" I know if I try to lie he will know, yet if I tell the truth he will be pissed. I have no Idea what to say, when he must feel the time for answering him is up. He gets on top of my body, straddling me on the couch and pins me down sitting on me so he is face to face with me. In this position he is still taller than me and it forces me to look up to him when he talks.

I regret instantly not coming up with a quick lie. The way he has me pinned also has my arms pinned at my sides, I am officially trapped here. I glance over in the swing and see Lizzie is thankfully out like a light. "I asked you what your problem is. You need to fucking answer me."

I still don't want to tell him, yet the longer I sit there quiet the madder he gets. "Talk to me." I know he wants me to say something, but my mouth is just frozen. These are the moments I was dreading about living together, especially right now. We are home alone and there isn't anyone here to help me. I remain quiet, not out of defiance, but fear and it makes him mad.

"I fucking said to talk to me. Are you too stupid to understand that?" He grabs my mouth with his one hand and starts squeezing my jaw. The way you would force a dog's mouth open to feed it pills.

"Owe," I try to say then try "That's hurting me." even though it comes out muffled he understands what I'm saying.

"Oh, look here she can speak. So, what the hell are you moping around here about?" He lets go of my mouth, so I can speak but remains sitting on me.

"Nothing." I say, "I'm not moping about anything." In the time he was acting crazy, I had time to think up a good excuse. "Right before you got here I saw on Tv a family divided because a family member molested a little girl. Some of the family members thought they should forgive him and move on." I add "It touched home for me being we have a daughter, I would kill someone that did that." This was somewhat true, it was what was on the talk show, just not what had me so upset.

"Well it would depend on the age. If the "kid" is old enough to say okay, then you can't really blame the guy." I am a bit pissed off and stunned by his response. There is no way in my mind that it would ever be okay.

"The little girl was molested from twelve through sixteen before she finally spoke up, she was still a baby." I say.

"Baby my ass she is probably a slut that asked for it and then got caught and turned the cards on him." he says getting more heated.

"It was her god damn uncle, and that's disgusting. There is no way what so ever that's okay." My voice is raising, and I feel myself shaking with anger.

"Uncle or not she probably flaunted her shit in front of him and he's human. He's a guy, so he reacted, maybe now she will learn not to be a prick tease." I can't believe this shit is coming out of his mouth. What kind of man says that? What kind of father says that?

"So, if my brother decided when Lizzie is twelve, to molest her you would be okay with that?" I'm so fired up I don't realize I'm walking right across that fine line he draws for me. "I'm telling you right now, I don't care who it is. If someone did that to my kid, I will kill them... my brother, my father, a friend, even you... I will kill anyone that touches my kid wrong."

"You think you could kill me? You think you could even try?" Now he has his hands around my neck choking me. I can't get away, so I try to lift myself up and I am somehow able to move him enough to start getting up on a knee on the couch. This infuriates him more and he starts hitting my head on the back of the couch. My head is not hitting the cushions, it is hitting the wood at the very top of the back of the couch.

I start screaming, knowing he will have to release my neck to cover my mouth. As soon as he does it gives me just enough time to shift so my head isn't being hit on the wood anymore. Unfortunately, now he is squeezing my mouth hard a gain and Lizzie is awake. Now she is crying and watching the whole thing from her swing.

"Kill me?" he repeats, "You can't even kill a fucking fly, you weak ass bitch!"

"Please stop. Lizzie is up, she will be scared." I try to see if that will make him stop. Instead he lifts me up from the couch by my neck and pushes me into the hall, so we are behind her and she can't see us anymore. He is holding me against the wall with one hand. I debate if I should try kicking him in the balls. I must have glanced down because he turns his body slightly so now that option is gone.

"Right now, all I want to do is slam my fucking fist into your stupid ugly face." he shouts at me and he starts punching. I thought for sure he was going to punch me, but he is hitting the wall behind me over and over and over. I stay as still as I can because he is out of control and busting hole after hole into the wall.

I am so terrified, and Lizzie is screaming so loudly now that neither of us hear Mark come home. All I know is he pulls Chris off me and shoves him into the kitchen. I run over and grab Lizzie out of her swing to calm her down. Mark says, "What the hell is happening here?" I don't even dare speak, I know if I so much as say a word, Chris will freak out again.

"This fucking bitch is nuts. I swear to God she is fucking nuts." Chris speaks up "I'll fix the wall I'm sorry it was that or her stupid fucking face. I'm leaving I can't be around this bitch another minute." And he storms out.

I feel so awkward now being left by myself with Mark. I can't stop shaking and crying. Lizzie is finally a little calmer, but I can't get her to latch on and nurse. I think she feels me shaking and she can't relax. I don't know what to say so I say, "I'm sorry you had to see that."

"Couples fight, I get it." is all he says, and he goes to make himself food before he heads out to the gym. I sneak up to my room to try and nurse Lizzie up there. Eventually I hear the door close and thankfully I have the place to myself again. I calm down enough for Lizzie to latch and nurse. She goes right back to sleep and I'm so thankful she is such an easy baby.

When I get Lizzie situated I head back downstairs to figure out lunch. I make myself a quick sandwich and eat it before Chris decides to come home. I have a feeling once he does I won't be allowed to make anything.

I finish cleaning up the house after lunch and I hear Lizzie waking up. I want to give her a bath and possibly take a shower myself if I have time. I gather all her stuff and give her a fast bath. I'm about to get myself in the shower when the phone rings.

I run into my room and grab it knowing if it's Chris and I don't answer it will create a problem. Expecting his voice when I say hello, but instead I hear, "Hello is Margo there?"

I recognize the voice and say surprised, "This is... Oh my God Denise is that you?"

I am so excited when she laughs and says, "Yes, it is."

"How did you get my number?" I ask I haven't talked to her in forever. She found me in the hospital when I had Lizzie and before that we lost touch for years. I am so excited to talk to her.

"Your mom. I happened to be near your old house and I stopped in and she gave me your number. How are you? How is that sweet little daughter of yours?"

"She is amazing and cute and crawling" I start talking about Lizzie to bypass the questions about myself. "She sleeps through the night and honestly she is the easiest baby in the world. How are you what's new in your life?"

"Well, I have a new boyfriend and we are living together too." she says then adds, "The reason I'm calling is to see if you would want to go to a concert with me? It's a pretty awesome concert." I can't contain myself, so I ask who? And she says, "Whitney Houston."

"Holy shit, Are you serious?" I ask, "When and where is it?"

"It's in a week on Saturday. I know it's last minute, but my boyfriend now has to work, and he said to take whoever I want, and I thought of you." I know Chris is going to argue this and I don't care. This is one of my all-time favorite singers and there is no way I'm going to miss this.

"I'd love to go. Do you want to pick me up or just meet there?"

"I'll pick you up, we can go grab a bite to eat and then go, if that's okay with you?"

"Yes. That sounds so fun." I give her my address and add "I'm so excited. Thank you so much." I can't believe she thought of me for this.

I just finished that thought when she says "You were the first person I thought of. I know you love her as much as I do. Okay I need to run, I will pick you up in a week. Bye." I say bye and hang up so incredibly happy.

Chris still isn't home which I know isn't a good sign, my guess is, he is getting himself good and drunk. I don't even care. I jump in the shower and all I can think about is the concert and how fun it will be. I decide not to ask Chris to watch Lizzie. I'll call my mom and ask her, that way I won't worry about her. Now I need to figure out how to ask Chris.

I never hear Chris come home and thank God, he leaves me alone too. My guess is he was too drunk to care or even try. I get up before him and get Lizzie changed and while I'm nursing her he wakes up. "I can make you breakfast in a minute." I say, "She will be done soon." I'm trying to be nice after yesterday because I don't want to fight again this morning.

"Don't, I'm fine." He says, and I feel my stomach instantly tighten up. Great, he isn't going to let this go.

"I don't mind." I lie "And I can get it made so you have time to get ready for work." I wish he would stop glaring at me and accept that I'm trying.

"I said I'm fine" Then he adds surprising me, "I'm not going to work today."

All I can think to say is oh okay, and I head out to the kitchen anyways to make myself something to eat. I can't help feeling incredibly disappointed that he will be here today. I don't want to deal with his crap all day. I'm about to finish my eggs when he comes into the kitchen and says, "You might as well get used to me being here a while, I quit my job."

It's worse than I thought... he won't just be here today, he will be here every day. I know Instantly my face gives away my disappointment when he sarcastically says, "I'm glad to see you're so thrilled to spend more time with me."

I try to look as nice and non-confrontational as I can and say, "It's not that, I'm just surprised." but it doesn't help.

"Sure, now whatever plans you make behind my back have to be canceled."

"I don't make plans behind your back. I sit home all day and talk to no one, the only thing I do is take Lizzie for walks." I'm so annoyed he feels I have some sort of a secret life while he is at work.

"Sure, for all I know you meet up with some guy and fuck him while I'm busting my ass for this family." Oh, good grief, I don't want this to turn into a nasty fight.

"I'm sorry you feel that way, but I promise that's not the case. I'm happy you will be here." I turn to finish making my toast and dish up my food and try hard to look happy.

He finally leaves the room, so I eat my breakfast in peace, but the knot in my stomach is already there. I would love to eat just one meal without feeling as if I might throw up at any moment.

I go grab the clothes out of the dryer and start folding them. I can't help but feel angry he is going to be here all the time. I have nothing to hide, but I don't want him here. I feel so uptight and tense when he's around and the only time I feel relaxed is when he is at work. I wonder what happened, why would he quit? We have rent to pay, and now no money coming in. I know I can't go back to my parents' house either, not with Chris anyways, so now I'm worried about how we will pay for things. I know I need to ask him, and I'm dreading it.

Just then Chris comes back in the room and says, "I'm going to put an application in somewhere that I heard is hiring, I'll be back in a little bit."

"Okay" I say then add "Good luck. I hope you get the job." And I honestly mean it, which I think he can see it in my face.

He decides to play nice and come over and kiss me goodbye. "Thank you." he says, then adds "Love you." and he leaves.

I am not one to pray a lot. I kind of lost my faith somewhere along the way, but I am praying hard he gets whatever job it is. I have many reasons to want it, but mostly, I don't think I could spend every day all day with him. I also need to figure out how I'm going to tell him about the concert.

I busy myself most the day cleaning and fixing up the house. I want everything to look perfect when he comes home. I hope he gets the job too, maybe that will put him in a good mood.

For a change he comes home in a happy mood and bought me flowers. This is something he never does, and I am honestly flattered. I guess the saying all girls love flowers is true, I never get them and receiving them feels so wonderful.

"These are beautiful, thank you." I say then ask. "Did you get the job?" Hoping he will say yes since he bought flowers.

Instead he says "No, the guy that did the interview was a cock."

"Oh, I'm sorry, I guess I assumed because you got me flowers you got the job."

"No, can't I do something nice for you?" he asks and as he gets closer I realize he has been drinking. I can smell it on his breath, but he isn't yet to the point of being mean, I hope. I quickly say, "Of course you can and thank you so much. I'm truly sorry about the job." I try to show him I'm genuinely grateful and happy about the flowers.

"It's okay, I'll find something eventually, but in the meantime, we can spend a lot of time together as a family."

"Okay that sounds fun, maybe we can go to the zoo and fun stuff like that." I say getting excited to go do some fun things, but he shoots that down fast.

"We can't spend money right now so no, we can't do that."

"Oh, yeah that's true, I didn't think about that, but we can go to some parks and stuff like that and find fun free things to do." I say.

"Sure, those things sound fun, I have to go out tomorrow and put some applications in but maybe when I get back." He is being unusually nice, and I love when he's like this. I figure this is the best time to tell him about the concert Saturday. If I can catch him in a good mood, he will most likely tell me I can go, so it's now or never.

"Hey, so I haven't had a chance to tell you, but I got invited to go to a Whitney Houston concert on Saturday. My friend Denise invited me, and I told her I'd love to go."

His face instantly turns angry. "No. I'm not giving you money for that, I'm not working, and that's a luxury, not a necessity" he says.

"It won't cost anything she already has the tickets and she is driving so I won't have to worry about gas."

"I said no. You will want spending money for food or drinks and I'm not giving you any. Tell her I said no."

"Chris, I don't need money. I'm telling you I don't want money and I already told her I'm going."

"I don't care what you told her. You didn't ask me, and I have plans already, and I'm not babysitting Lizzie."

"First of all, it isn't babysitting your own child, second, I plan to ask my mom to, so you don't have to be bothered and third, did you ask me, if you, can go out? No? So then yes, I'm going." he walks up to me, so we are face to face and I'm standing my ground. I refuse to back down this time.

He laughs at me and says, "Okay sweetheart if that's what you want to believe, you believe it." and he walks away.

I let out a sigh of relief once he leaves the room and say a silent thank God that he didn't get mad. I know I should watch how I speak to him and not risk him getting mad, but I really want to go to this concert. Maybe now he will see I am willing to stand up to him and he will start allowing me to do more.

I go call my mom and ask her to babysit and she happily says yes. I knew unless she had plans, she would because she misses her so much. I feel bad that we haven't been over, but Chris has been adamant about not going. We share a car, so when he has it I'm stuck here, and I don't dare ask my mom to come here. I think if I did that, Chris would find a way to keep them from me longer. I figure right now it's best to let things cool down a bit, and go when and if, I can... to them.

Chapter 14

The rest of the week thankfully isn't too bad. Chris has left every day so far to supposedly put in applications at various places, but he always come home a little buzzed wreaking like beer. I keep my mouth shut and I thank God that he hasn't wanted sex.

Finally, Friday rolls around and I busy myself all day cleaning the house. I also during nap time, paint my nails nice and find a cute outfit to wear for the concert tomorrow. I'm so excited to get dressed up nice for a change and wear heels. Chris still doesn't let me when we go places together, so this is a rare chance I can.

I still haven't told Denise I don't have money to go to dinner, but I know she won't care. She's so easy going we can go get coffee and she will be happy. I have ten dollars I have kept hidden from Chris, so if we go grab something cheap I will be okay.

I found most nights when he comes home drunk, he has a lot of singles in his pants. Once he passes out, I take a couple, only a few so he won't notice, and I hide them, so I have a little money. I would have about five dollars more, but before I knew about the concert I took Lizzie for a walk and got myself a soda and snack. Chris doesn't let me drink pop or eat chips, so I ate them at the park we went to.

Tonight, Chris comes home beyond drunk. I am afraid he is going to be mean, but he is so drunk he barely gets his clothes off and passes out. Once again, I was able to grab a few extra dollars, and I found change in my purse, so I should be okay, for tomorrow to grab a bite somewhere.

I keep thinking one day I'll have a job and stop having to ask him for money. He never gives me any, yet he spends money all the time. I brought it up a while back and he said since he works, it's his money. He also said if I would listen to him better and clean more and take care of our house like he told me to, he would give me some, yet he still hasn't.

The next day I do everything I normally would do and try not to do anything to piss Chris off. He seems to be in a decent mood, so I start relaxing. I want to be sure everything looks perfect before I leave so he has no excuse to be mad.

I put Lizzie to bed for her nap, so I can get ready. I shower, and shave and once I get out I put lotion all over my body. I smell great, for a change and not like baby vomit. I love being a mom, but sometimes I feel I smell like baby shit all day. It feels good to get ready to go do something fun for a change.

I take my time fixing my hair and I put my makeup on and it looks nice. I decided tonight I'm even going to wear jewelry for a change. My outfit looks stylish and sexy, and I can see I have lost a few more pounds so everything fits good.

I pack Lizzies diaper bag and lay an outfit out for her so all I need to do is nurse her, grab some frozen breast milk, then change her and I'll be ready to go to my mom's. My mom has all the other stuff she will need like a bed, and toys.

Chris comes up only once right after my shower and makes a snide remark about how I never smell nice for him or look nice either. He stands there towering over me glaring while I sit on the floor doing my makeup. I do my best to ignore him and he finally leaves the room, all pouty.

Lizzie finally wakes up and I get her all dressed, her diaper changed and nurse her. She is such a sweet little baby, and thankfully so easy. I never have any trouble with her and she is such a joy.

I take her down already in her carrier to grab some frozen milk, and then I start taking stuff out to my car. Chris comes in from outside on our back patio and says. "Where do you think you are taking the car? I told you I have plans, and that car is in my name so, it's mine, not yours."

"I'm taking Lizzie to my moms, I already told you that I was asking her to watch her tonight."

"I told you, you are not going to any concert. I don't know why you think you are."

"Well I told you, I am." I say trying to be brave "I will be back soon and then you can have your car to go do what you want." I'm trying not to cry now, and I know he can see that.

"Don't push it, I said you're not taking the car, so don't even think about it."

"Fine, I'll have my mom come here and get her." I say, and he starts laughing and he turns and walks towards the kitchen.

"That's going to be hard to do when I take the phone with me." I see he is going to get the cordless phone, so he can leave with it. I realize I still have the keys in my hands for the car and he must not have noticed. I know I need to move super-fast if I'm going to pull this off.

As soon as he turns the corner into the kitchen I quickly go out the door. I run to my car and get Lizzy in the back seat. Her carrier snaps in easily to the base and I jump into the front and lock the doors.

Just as I start the ignition Chris comes running out and is yelling at me to stop. I start backing out and he grabs the passenger side door, but the door is locked, and he can't get it open. He starts beating on the side window and I am scared it's going to break, so I stop the car to tell him to stop it.

This gives him enough time to run to the front of the car. I know I will have to keep backing up to get away from him. Right when I start to back up though, he runs full speed up to the front of the car and jumps on the hood. I have no choice but to stop moving, because I don't want to hurt him.

I think he will get down now, but instead he starts kicking the front window. He is actually kicking the window in on me. It first starts to splinter and then the harder he kicks the more it starts breaking. I am so scared I start screaming, which then makes Lizzie start crying. I have tiny pieces of glass hitting me and I know it is also hitting Lizzie. The window doesn't break all the way, but little pieces of glass fly off it.

"Chris, stop it! Please stop it!" I am yelling over and over for him to stop "Please stop, you're hurting your own daughter!"

He stops kicking the window just long enough for Mark to get his hands on him and yank him off the car. I feel like I'm in a daze right now, but I know I need to get Lizzie and see if she is okay. I take the chance of him flipping out on me and I get out of the car. I hurry up and open the back door and grab Lizzie. She has little tiny pieces of glass on her.

At this point I'm more concerned with her than myself I use my bare hand to brush the glass off her clothes. I feel the glass cutting me, but I don't care. I also know it's all over myself and I need to go get these clothes off both of us.

I ignore Chris and his apologizing over and over. I feel like I'm walking in a fog, but I just move one foot in front of the other. I get up to our bedroom and I get the clothes off Lizzie. Once I'm done with her I strip my own clothes off. I throw on anything I can reach and take her into the bathroom to rinse her off. I try to make sure not to push any glass into her skin and I use the shower head to rinse her off good. I don't think any is in her skin and thankfully none of it cut her. I change her clothes and rinse my own arms off good.

I don't know what I'm thinking right now, but I go down stairs to confront him and he is still outside. I decide to stay down stairs and wait for him to come in, so I start nursing Lizzie. She is such a good girl, she eats a little bit, but mostly pacifies then falls right to sleep. I put her in her swing and go back upstairs to change my clothes again.

While sitting there I decide there is no way I'm letting him win. My friend will be here in about thirty minutes to pick me up and I am going to go to this concert. I have no way to let her know not to come, so I decide to go ahead and go. I'm so mad at Chris I think there is no way I'm letting him win this. I am going to this concert and he isn't going to stop me. Tonight, is the night I take a stand against him.

I quickly fix my makeup, put on another cute outfit, grab some higher heels than before, as a big fuck you to Chris, and head back down to wait. I'm hoping Chris is still outside and I'm happy to see he is. I wait patiently for Denise to come and after about ten minutes I see her pull in.

I hurry up, and grab my purse, then kiss Lizzie and tell her I love her. I walk out the door and look right at Chris, and say, "I guess your plans have changed tonight. Lizzie is fed and sleeping, I'll be home later." I get in the car and we drive away.

I instantly feel young, happy and free. Denise cranks up the music and we sing as loud as we can. After about fifteen minutes of belting out tunes, she turns the radio down and asks "So, where do you want to eat? I'm okay with pretty much anything." I know I've got to tell her I don't have much money, but I also know she won't care.

"I need to go somewhere where it isn't too expensive, Chris quit his job, so I only have about fifteen dollars." I say.

"Oh, I'm sorry to hear that. Money doesn't matter though this is my treat, so we can go anywhere we want." she says.

"Oh Denise, I couldn't. I don't mind paying for myself, but it just can't be a fancy place."

She shakes her head and says again. "No really, it's on me, my boyfriend makes good money and he wants to pay for this whole night, so we are going to let him." she smiles then says, "Is Mexican food still your favorite?"

I can't believe she remembers that about me. "Yes, it is, but I never get to eat it because Chris hates it." I say.

"Then it's settled Mexican and margaritas!" she shouts and cranks up the music again. I feel like crying because it's been so long since I got to let my hair down and have fun. I know I'll pay for it later when I get home, but for now I don't care. I start singing again with her at the top of my lungs until we reach the Mexican restaurant.

I'm thankful that I have been able to pump enough milk to last a few months if I need it, so I know I can safely drink and flush it out of my system. I would never drink if I had to nurse Lizzie tonight and I'm so happy I don't have to worry about that.

Dinner is wonderful, and I get a tiny buzz from my margarita. It's been so long since I drank, that all it took was one drink. I don't like getting drunk, but a little buzz is always fun.

We head over to the concert when we are done eating and Denise even buys me a concert t-shirt as a souvenir. The concert is amazing. She is such a fantastic performer and she even has her mom come up on stage to sing some beautiful gospel music. I cry, at how loving they are together, hoping I can have that kind of relationship with Lizzie when she's older.

After the concert, we decide to stretch the night out a little longer and go have more drinks. We aren't twenty-one yet, but both of us know we can still get drinks. Sure, enough within ten minutes we have a couple guys offering to buy us drinks and trying their best to hit on us. We play along and flirt back knowing there is no real interest on our part. After a few drinks, we ditch the guys and go to the dance floor and start dancing.

We are really enjoying ourselves, when this good-looking guy comes over and starts dancing by me then offers to buy me another drink. I say "Sure, but you have to buy my friend one too." smiling.

He smiles back and says "Sure, come on." We head up to the bar and he gets us both a drink and she disappears back to the dance floor. "Hi, I'm Matthew, or Matt" he says.

I shake his hand all giggly and say, "Margo, just Margo."

"I think you, Margo, are absolutely beautiful and I'd love to get to know you more. I don't think I've ever seen such beautiful blue eyes, I feel I could drown in them forever." I can't help smiling, this guy is so incredibly cute. I can't even believe he is talking to me, let alone complimenting me as if I'm the most beautiful girl he's ever met. I know I can't keep talking to him and I shouldn't feel any loyalty to Chris after earlier, but I'm not that girl. I would never step out on him even with everything he has done, I can't let go yet.

"Thank you. I appreciate it, but I have to tell you I have a boyfriend and a daughter." I can see that surprises him and I think he is trying to think of something polite to say to leave.

Instead, he says. "Not at all what I was expecting, you don't look like you had a baby. What if I say, there are no strings and we just spend one night together?"

I'm a little shocked by his bluntness and it makes me laugh. I have a big laugh, so it is probably louder than I meant, and people nearby look over, but I can't help it.

"Oh, well... while I appreciate the compliment... It's not going to happen." I realize as good looking as this guy is, this must be a regular thing for him. He uses his looks to get girls into bed. I can see why it works for him, he looks like he could model. Too bad he isn't genuine, and he resorts to that kind of fake behavior.

"Okay, but if you change your mind... I'll be around." He gets up and I head back to the dance floor. I find Denise and tell her about him and we laugh and decide we should probably get going. I see Matthew has moved on to the next girl and as we get close I hear him say, "I feel I could drown in them forever." I can see the girl is soaking up the attention, she looks about nineteen. I'm not sure if it's the mom in me, but I feel a sudden need to say something.

I walk over and smile, "Matthew? Hi. Remember me?" I can see he is nervous and thinking I'm going to say something about earlier.

"Yes of course I remember you, how are you?" He tries to play it off, but I can see he's also afraid I'm going to bring it up and call him out on it.

I smile bigger, flirting and say instead, "I just wanted to let you know you were right."

He smiles at me and flirts back, "Was I? Right about what?"

The poor girl asks, "Do you know her, is this your girlfriend?"

Before he can answer I say, "Oh no honey we only fucked once, but he was right genital warts are in fact contagious even with a condom. I caught your problem. My doctor said you must have a terrible case of it to have that happen to me like that. You were so right about that. I told my doctor how incredibly small your penis is, I mean like tiny..." I stress on that as I look at the poor girl, then finish saying, "I told him I didn't even know we had sex for sure and he said it doesn't have to be big, to carry a disease..." His jaw drops, and his shocked face is priceless, as I turn and walk away. I glanced back though to see the girl looking around trying to find any reason to get away.

I can't help laughing my ass off. I think guys like that are awful. Denise is laughing too, and she says that was quick thinking on my part. I don't know why I felt such a strong urge to do that, but it sure felt good. "I can't stand men that think it's okay to play with girls like that. It pisses me off and I knew I wanted to say something." I say as we get into her car and start heading back to my house.

"Denise, I can't thank you enough for the most wonderful night. It has been such a long time since I got out and had some fun, truly, thank you." I want to confide in her about everything, but I decide not to because I don't want to look dumb. I know I made this mess for myself and I have no one to blame but me. I also don't want to ruin this wonderful evening, even though it would be so nice to confess to someone. My biggest fear is people finding out how weak I really am, and that Chris does what he does to me.

Sooner than I want, we get to my house and I thank Denise again. I tell her I hope we can get together again soon. I know that won't happen, Chris will be sure it doesn't. I go around to her side of the car and she gets out and we hug. It takes everything in me not to cry my eyes out right then and there. I squeeze her a little longer than necessary and say good bye.

I watch her drive away and I know in the pit of my stomach, I will probably never see her again. My heart hurts so bad and by the time I get into our condo, I am crying. I know once Chris sees me crying it will start a fight, but I can't help it. I feel so incredibly lonely and sad this very moment.

I go upstairs as quietly as I can, so I don't wake up Lizzie or Chris. I get to our bedroom and I see they aren't there. I can't believe he took her and is still out this late. I'm hoping, maybe he somehow took her to my parents like he planned, but it's so late I can't call to ask. I'm hoping he doesn't have her out somewhere this late.

I change out of my clothes and wash my face and get ready for bed. The little buzz I had is gone, because now I'm worried about where Lizzie is. I pump my milk, so I can dump it out and get rid of the bad milk. I pull out the book I have been trying to read for a few months and start reading it to relax.

After a few chapters I realize I have been reading a long time, and look at the clock and see it's three am. I know Chris should be home by now, yet he still isn't. I have no idea where they could be, but now I'm getting scared something bad has happened. It's not like Chris to take her like this. Then my heart stops, and I feel a chill go down my spine. He took her. He always says he will take her from me. He took her.

I start frantically opening all the drawers in her dresser. Every drawer I open is empty. I go over to his dresser and see all his drawers are empty too. I run down the stairs and look in the freezer and all my frozen milk is gone. All of it. Gone. Enough to last at least a few months... He took her.

I run back upstairs and start panicking. I have no idea where he is, or who he could be with. I am praying he is at his mom's and she is safe with him. I am also praying he is feeding and changing her enough.

I feel so sick to my stomach and so incredibly stupid. I have no idea why I though a concert would be okay to go to or even worth this happening. I should have stayed home, he told me I wasn't allowed to go, I should have listened. I have no money, no car and no proof he shouldn't have her with him. We aren't married, there's no custody agreement and no child support order. He can take her out of the state, or even the country and I can't stop him.

I run to the bathroom and start throwing up. I'm hysterical now, crying my eyes out and vomiting. Mark finally hears me and comes out of his room to see what's going on. "He took her, he said he would take her and he took her." I say crying hysterically.

"Who? Who took her? Who is her? Who is he?" he is asking as I'm bawling my eyes out.

"Chris, he took Lizzie because I didn't listen, and he could be in France for all I know." He is helping me up off the floor in the bathroom and trying to get me to go in my room. I am struggling against him sobbing and babbling. I keep trying to make him hear me and understand what I'm saying. I think he finally gets tired of trying to be gentle and he scoops me up and carries me to my room like a baby.

"I'm sure he didn't leave the country, or even the state. Think about it, he has no car, no job and no money. Get some sleep, he will be back in the morning and you guys can figure this out. I roll over and cry and cry and cry. I can't sleep, all I can think about is what will happen to her and who will care for her.

I finally get up at six in the morning and go make coffee. I can't eat, so I sit by the phone and pray he will call me. I know by eight Lizzie will be up and hungry. I'm praying he thaws the milk the right way. He has never used frozen breastmilk and I'm so terrified he will microwave it and burn her.

By eight thirty I'm beside myself and out of desperation, I call my mom to see if by chance he took her there. "Hello?" my mom answers the phone.

"Hi mom, how are you?" I say hoping she will tell me Lizzie is doing good and ate breakfast already.

"I'm okay although, I'm disappointed that we didn't get to have Lizzie last night." Shit, she just confirmed she isn't there for sure.

"I know mom I'm so sorry," I apologize, and I'm about to explain when she says,

"It's okay, Chris called and said someone busted out windows in cars all around by you guys and broke your front windshield." So, he has his story ready to tell people, so no one asks questions.

"Yes, it was pretty scary." is all I think to say.

My mom continues to talk for a little bit about how she worries and thinks we should consider another area, a safer area. I can pretend to pay enough attention to not draw attention to the fact I'm crying on my end. I can get out a steady sentence about needing to change Lizzie and I hurry off the phone.

I am once again sobbing uncontrollably, when the phone rings. I grab it praying it is Chris, but not actually expecting it to be him. "Hello?" I get out somewhat steady.

"When does she eat lunch.?" Is what I hear. Oh my God it's Chris. I feel my heart start rapidly pounding in my chest.

"She eats every four hours, unless she gets crabby, then I feed her sooner. Where are you? When are you guys coming home?" I try to keep my voice steady, but I know he can tell I've been crying.

"None of your business and we aren't. I told you if you didn't listen to me I would take her from you and I have no intentions of giving her back. You might as well pack your shit and crawl back home to mommy and daddy."

"Chris, please don't do this. I promise I'll listen, please don't take her from me. What can I do to make you bring her back to me?"

"Nothing. I am done dealing with you and your stupidity. I gave you chance after chance to do the right thing and listen to me. It's too late, I'm done."

All I hear is silence, and I know he hung up the phone. I am numb. I feel this God-awful feeling of defeat. It is the darkest, saddest thing a human can feel. I can't even cry, and I feel as though I'm walking in a thick fog.

I feel as if I'm not even in my own body. I walk around the bedroom for a little bit, and touch things like her crib. I go down stairs and see her swing, and her blanket she was using, and I pick it up and hug it. I am soaking in her smell and by now, once again sobbing. I walk into the kitchen and grab a bottle of vodka that is Marks. I don't even care that he will get mad, I won't be here for him to get mad at. I start drinking it straight from the bottle, fast.

I have no idea how much time has passed, or how much I've consumed. I am drunk though, drunk enough to dull some of my pain. I walk upstairs and get a piece of paper, and I write a note to Chris and Lizzie.

Chris,
I know you will never believe this, but I loved you once. There was a time I would have taken a bullet for you if I needed to. Now, not so much. I have grown to hate you with a passion. You, have beaten me down for the last time. I cannot live life like this. I would rather die, than ever deal with you and your anger again. The only good thing you did in your life was give me Lizzie. Taking her from me is taking everything I have worth living for. So, go fuck yourself. You win. Goodbye.
No love, Margo.

Lizzie

My sweet, sweet Lizzie. Your dad will probably never give you this note. I will write it anyways, just in case. I love you with all my heart, but I can't do this anymore. Please know it isn't your fault. I hope you have a beautiful life, and somehow everything works out for you. I know you won't believe this, but I love you with all my heart. I will be with you always and forever…. I'm so sorry I failed you.
       Love you always,
         your mommy.

      I lay the papers on the nightstand, where I know someone will find them. I walk into the bathroom, determined to never feel this kind of pain again and take all the pills I can find. I have no idea what they are, but I don't care. I go into my room and lay down to let the pills start to work.

I lay there and close my eyes, wanting my last thoughts to be about Lizzie. I feel my heart breaking while thinking about my precious little girl. I think about her walking for the first time and talking. I think about her holding my hand to cross the street and looking up to me with her big blue eyes waiting to be told it's safe to cross. I think about her having her first kiss, her first heartbreak, her first prom and her wedding day. Then I think about the fact I wouldn't be there. For any of it. I instantly regret my want to die.

I get up off the bed and stumble my way to the bathroom. I shove my fingers down my throat and start to vomit. I do it over and over and over. I finally have nothing left to throw up. I walk back into my room and grab the notes and crumple them up and throw them in the garbage can. I go back to my bed, lay down and say a prayer that I got all the pills out of my system. The room is spinning, and I can no longer keep my eyes open, so I close them. My last thoughts are, I hope God lets me live.

Chapter 15

I thankfully wake up the next day. I'm not exactly sure what time it is, but I didn't care. The relief I feel, that I woke up is overwhelming. I want to shower and clean myself up and I know I'll need to call my parents to tell them I need to come home. The last thing I want though is for my mom to see me looking this bad. I get my clothes together and step into the hallway to go shower when I hear her.

"Lizzie?" I say kind of to myself, but out loud. I know I heard her. I would know her squeaks and noises anywhere. I run down the stairs as fast as I can, and she is right there. Sitting on the floor playing.

In what feels like slow motion, I run over to her and scoop her up in my arms. I am kissing her and crying and hugging her and laughing all at the same time. I don't even care that Chris took her. All I care about in that second, is holding my child again. I take her upstairs with me and I hold her and hug her and kiss her over and over. The feeling of love I have for her is pouring through my body. I can't stop crying, but this time from tears of joy.

Chris eventually comes in and stands there for a minute watching me with her, and he stares this uncomfortable stare he does. I don't know if I should look at him, ignore him or try to make conversation. I do know, if I decide the wrong thing it can set him off. Today, I just look at him quickly and go back to talking to Lizzie and playing patty cake with her.

He finally comes all the way into the room and sits down on the bed next to me. "I've decided to give you another chance to straighten up." He smiles and says, "I think I have an idea on how to make things better."

Right now, all I care is he said he isn't taking Lizzie away from me. I should be angry, but I want to make this work for Lizzie's sake. I want my family together and I will do almost anything to make that happen. I finally say "I want things to be better too, what are you thinking? Counseling?"

"No, I don't believe in that mumble jumble crap. I think we need to move and get our own place, just us, so Lizzie can have her own room. I think living here isn't good for us anymore." Well now I'm confused, he has no job. How does he expect us to do this?

"I think that sounds nice and all, but you don't even have a job." I say trying to not be too negative, so I don't ruin his decent mood.

"I know it won't happen overnight, but it's something I think we need to figure out how to do. I need to get a job and then I want to save money, so we can do this. Maybe we can even look at buying a house." I have no idea what got into him, but I am so happy he brought her back to me and is willing to give me another chance. I lay Lizzie down in her crib and I go throw myself in his arms and cry as he holds me.

"I want this so bad for us too. I want things to be okay." I say. He holds me and tells me he loves me and for the first time in I don't know how long, we make love. It isn't mean, there is no anger, just real love. All is forgiven by both of us.

After that things seem to go better, Chris goes when he can to put applications in at different places. He is relying on friends for rides, because the window is still broken on the car. Then my dad calls out of the blue and says he knows a place hiring and wants to know if Chris wants to go apply. My dad says he knows the owner well and will put in a good word for him.

Chris says yes, but the car might stop him from being able to work. My dad surprises us again and offers to have it fixed. I can see my parents are trying to help, and I am hoping Chris sees it too. If they could ever get along, life would be so much easier.

The next day my dad has our car towed to a place to fix the window, and he came and picked up Chris to go put in an application at that job. I am so happy to see my dad I started to cry. I play it off as being grateful about the car but seeing him makes me feel everything will be okay.

I make a nice dinner for Chris and make sure the house is super clean. I have Lizzie already bathed and fed, so when he comes home it can be like a date night. He gets home right when the roast is done, and he is so happy. He got the job.

He starts the following Monday and he comes home in a pretty good mood every day. I try my hardest to keep the house clean and have dinner ready every night for him. He is making good money and he says we should be able to save enough to move out in a few months. That thought is starting to grow on me, especially with how nice he is being lately. Twice he comes home and surprises me with flowers. He hasn't been drinking, so we laugh a lot and we are starting to enjoy our time together again.

I am in the middle of making dinner a couple months later, when I hear him come home early. I come out of the kitchen to see his hand all bandaged up. "Oh my gosh, what happened?" I ask, as I run over to him to see what happened.

"I cut my hand today at work. It's a pretty bad cut, I needed stitches." He says as I help him get his work boots off. "I'm so sorry. How long do you have to take off work?" I ask.

"Of course, all you care about is money." He says to me mad. I try to quickly stop this from turning into something it isn't.

"No, not at all. I'm worried about them firing you or something, because you love that job." I wish he would understand money means nothing to me. I want my family and I want us to be happy.

"Well they can't fire me, they have to find something for me to do there or they have to pay me to sit at home." he says, sounding a little nicer.

"Oh good, it wouldn't be fair to you if they fired you. I'm glad they can't do that." And I really mean it.

"I will need you to drive me every day because I need to be on pain pills and can't drive. So, you will have to get up and take me. You might want to go hang out at your mom's house because it doesn't make sense to drive there and back four times a day."

I can't believe it. He is telling me to go to my mom's house. I feel bad he is hurt but I'm super excited to get out of my house every day and have some freedom. I try hard to hide that though, so it doesn't trigger him to be mad.

I finish dinner and after we eat he takes a couple pain pills and within a half an hour he is out cold. I call my mom and she says it's fine to come over every day. I don't want to stay up late myself since we will leave so early, so I get Lizzie ready and we head off to bed too.

Spending my days with my mom has been great. We are having a nice time and we are enjoying Lizzie together. I think it works better for us to spend the day together but not live together. I feel almost as though our relationship is stronger than ever. A couple of times I want to bring up Chris's anger, but I also feel like that would be a betrayal to Chris.

He has been working so hard to try and get us in our own place, I don't want to rock the boat. I think If we can live completely on our own, he will feel happier. I was about to eat a late lunch when the phone rings. "Margo, it's for you, it's Chris." my mom says.

"Hello?" I say kind of surprised because he never calls me during the day.

"Surprised it's me? Why would your mom need to tell you it's me? Who else calls you there?" I instantly feel myself getting defensive.

"No one Chris, that's how people hand off phones to each other." I sigh a little irritated. "What's wrong?" I try that instead of telling him to go to hell and hanging up, like I want to.

"I'm not feeling well you need to come get me." he says.

"Okay, let me get Lizzie ready and I'll be on my way, or I can leave her here and we can come back for her? That would be the fastest way." I say.

"Are you that stupid?" Oh nice, he's name calling. "I just said I don't feel good, why would I want to go back to your parents' house and listen to your mom flap her jaw? Come get me and bring my kid."

I ignore the fact he called Lizzie his kid and I say "Okay, I have to get her ready and I'll be on my way." the whole time trying not to let my mom hear what's going on.

"You better hurry. Do not make me wait long." He demands before he hangs up. I have no idea how to let him know when I get there. I have never gone in, so I don't know how he will know I'm there. I guess I'll figure that out when I get there.

I hurry up and get Lizzie ready. I know she is ready to nurse, but If I take the time to do it he will get mad. I think she will be okay until I get him, and we get home. I hate that I always put his needs above hers, it doesn't feel right at all. I think about how I grew up seeing my dad do whatever it took to make us kids happy and I don't get the same from Chris for Lizzie. He will put his own wants or needs above hers all the time and it feels wrong.

I push that all to the back of my mind. I tell my mom I'm taking off, I hug her and head out. I quickly get Lizzie strapped into her car seat and I'm impressed with how fast I get out of the house. I try to hurry to his work, but I'm careful not to go too fast because I know if I get a ticket he will be livid. I make it to his work only twenty-five minutes after he calls, and that's not bad considering it's a twenty-minute drive.

Chris is standing outside, and I'm glad because I don't have to try to figure out how to find him. He opens the door and I'm about to say hi, when he says, "Jesus fucking Christ, I told, you to hurry and you made me stand there like an idiot."

"Chris, I left five minutes after you called, I can't help it takes twenty minutes to get here."

"That was longer than that, it was an hour." I start driving now and I try to ignore him because I'm trying to concentrate on pulling out of the drive, because there is a bad blind spot on the street for oncoming traffic. I get out and just get up to speed at fifty-five miles an hour when he says, "Pull over." I'm a little surprised so I ask, "Why what's wrong?"

"Don't ask me what is fucking wrong pull the fuck over." he is shouting. So, I slow down and I'm looking for a drive to pull into when he gets mad. "Fucking pull over are you stupid? Do you not understand the words? Pull. over. Pull. over." He yells even louder, "Pull Over! Do you fucking hear me now?" He is screaming at me now, so I think something is wrong, maybe with the car so I whip into a little utility drive off the road.

"Chris what's wrong? What is going on?" I ask and now I'm starting to cry because he's yelling, and I'm scared thinking the car is breaking. I think maybe he heard something I didn't hear.

"I need to go back to the shop, I forgot my pain pills." He says through gritted teeth

"Are you kidding me? You were yelling and acting crazy over pain pills?" I'm so mad at him. I can't believe he would act this way over pain pills. "I thought something was wrong, I was looking for a safe place to pull in and you were screaming at me."

"If you knew how to drive you would have pulled into any of the ten driveways we passed. I can't stand your driving." He is being so mean.

I finally can't take it anymore, I think all his yelling at me has finally gotten to me and I yell back at him, "You don't like my driving? I can't stand driving you. I hate the way you tell me how to drive and what I'm doing wrong the whole fucking time. If you don't like my driving, then you fucking drive. I'm done." I open my door to get out when suddenly I feel him yanking me back into the car by my hair. Out of reflex I reach up to grab his hand to stop him from pulling my hair and I don't realize I grab his hurt hand.

He yells "You fucking cunt." and the next thing I know he punches me in the back of the head and I fall face first on to the ground beside his car. I try to get up and just fall right back down. At some point I pass out. I wake up to him trying to lift me into the car. I help the best I can, so I am sitting on the edge of the passenger car seat, my legs still on the ground. I am about to pull my legs into the car when I feel the need to throw up.

I stay leaning out of the car, and throw up, the whole time terrified, he is going to hit me again. I am so dizzy I want to lay back and go to sleep, but I know if I tell him how awful I feel he is going to get angry again. I slowly pull my legs into the car and wait for him to close the door and start driving. All I can do is pray he doesn't hit me again and I also pray I don't throw up in his car.

I must have fallen asleep because I wake up and we are back home. My head is pounding, but I decide to not confront him about the whole thing. I don't think I could physically handle another hit like that. All I want to do is go in my room and lay down, but I know I need to nurse Lizzie first.

While I'm nursing Lizzie, Chris comes in and wants to talk. My head feels like it may burst, but I know I need to sit here and listen to him if I want to go to sleep. "If you would have listened and pulled right over that never would have happened." I don't want to talk, but I know if I pacify him and agree with him right from the start, he will get mad. It's a complicated balancing act I have yet to completely master with him, especially because his rules change daily.

"Chris, I was trying to find a safe place to pull in to, but you were yelling at me and I thought something was wrong with the car. I was just surprised it was all over your stupid pain pills."

"Watch it." He snaps. "I don't think I need to remind you not to talk to me like that." He is glaring at me, so I wait for him to finish. "I never would have had to do that if you wouldn't have grabbed my hand." Of course, this is all my fault.

"Chris, you were pulling my hair and it hurt, I didn't mean to grab your sore hand, it was a reflex."

"I wouldn't have pulled your hair if you weren't being a spoiled bitch." I know this is the point in this conversation where I'm expected to apologize. There is no way he will see himself as wrong, and I just want to go to sleep.

"I'm sorry, I didn't mean to do that. I guess I wasn't thinking." I say hoping he drops this.

"That's exactly your problem, you never think. Keep this shit up and I'll take Lizzie far away from you and find her a mom that can think with that thing we call a brain." Thankfully on that note, he leaves the room and I can get Lizzie to sleep so I can fall asleep too.

The next few weeks pass by smoothly and we never bring that day up again. It is just as well, I have no intentions of rehashing it over and over. It seems after every huge blow up there is a calm before the next one. He is out every day, again looking for a job. That's why he needed to leave, he was fired. He had never told me why they fired him, other than of course it wasn't his fault.

Once again, he comes home smelling like beer and some days he's unable to walk straight. I never say anything, and I let it go, it doesn't do any good to fight with him anyways because, he is always right. I also learned there is no point bringing up old stuff, it only makes him mad. He gets home today though in a great mood and says things are going to change for us. He surprises me with a bottle of wine and some steaks and says we will celebrate over dinner.

I have no idea what the news is, but it is nice to see him sober, and in a good mood. I cut up some veggies for a nice salad, and prep the steaks with salt, pepper and a little seasoning and I let it sit. I put the wine in the fridge to chill and about an hour later I cook the steaks. They turn out perfectly cooked with a fabulous sear on the outside and medium rare in the center. I know the seasoning is spot on and there is no way he can complain about the steaks being ruined or wasted.

We sit down to eat so I dish his food and open the wine and give us both a little. I already have some milk pumped for Lizzie again, so I know if I have a glass she will be okay. I wait for him to try his steak and see if he will acknowledge that it is good.

"This is delicious." He says and smiles at me then says, "I knew you had it in you to be a great wife someday." I am completely taken in by his compliment and I feel myself smiling back at him.

"Thank you, all I ever want to do is be a good mom and make you happy too." I say back. He keeps eating and smiling and saying things like how I make him so happy, how he can't wait to spend his life with me and one day he wants to get married. I'm two glasses of wine deep and feeling so heady and appreciated, he has won me back over.

I finally say, "So what exactly are we celebrating?" At this point he could almost tell me anything and I'd be happy about it.

"I found a job." He is beaming and I'm so happy for him, for us, that I feel myself smiling bigger than I was before.

"That's wonderful. Where is it and what will you be doing?" I ask.

"It is at an apartment complex, it's doing maintenance, and there's more." He says all smiles.

I wait and wait and finally ask laughing. "What is it? What more is there?"

He is laughing too and says, "I will be on call some nights after hours, but part of my pay is, we can live there free." I seriously can't believe my ears. We are going to move and have our own place? I can hear alarm bells going off in my head, but I push them away because he is so happy it makes me happy too.

I leap up out of my chair and climb onto his lap, straddling him on his chair and hug him. "For real? We are going to have our very own place? Just us three?" I'm so excited to make a home for him and show him how much I love him, I keep ignoring the gut feeling I have to say no.

"Yes, just the three of us, it has two bedrooms, so Lizzie can have her own room and it's pretty big. I saw the apartment today and it will be ready for us in two weeks." He says still smiling. He finishes his glass of wine and pours us both some more. I know tonight he will want to have sex and I won't try to stop him because he is being so good to me.

"Two weeks, I can get everything packed by then I promise." I say, then I start to kiss him, and he responds back to me. I press my body harder into his, grinding a little on him down there, letting him know how badly I want to make love. He deepens our kiss and I find myself responding with a passion I long since thought was gone. I know we will be heading up stairs soon and I can't wait to show him how much I love him.

He abruptly stops kissing me though, and says, "I have plans tonight we will have to do this another time." he lifts me up off him and gets up and walks away.

I feel so confused and sad. I say, "Where are you going?"

"Don't worry about it, I have another interview and I want to let them know in person I can't take the job."

I start to pout a little and I remember how that makes him mad, so I smile instead and say "Okay, I'll see you when you get home."

"Don't wait up, I don't know how long I'll be." He says as he walks out the door.

Once again, he makes me feel confused and alone, and tonight rejected. I never seem to get it right no matter how hard I try. I end up messing things up every day. I want this move to be perfect, and for us to make a nice home and a life together for our daughter. I pray this is the break we need to make it all happen. I completely ignore all the warning bells I have going off in my head.

Chapter 16

Moving day is finally here. I'm so excited and I can't wait to see our new place. I did what I promised, and I got everything all packed and ready to go. I was able to get most of it done by myself too.

After what feels like forever, we finally pull into the apartment complex and I'm so excited I can hardly sit still. I try to look all around, and I see as much as I can see. It's a pretty big complex which is nice because I can take Lizzie for walks in her stroller. There isn't a playground, because it's mostly older people here but that's okay, I can drive her or walk to one nearby.

Chris parks the moving truck and I park the car near him and I get Lizzie out of her car seat. I'm so excited that I'm bouncing up the steps to the second floor to wait for him to get the door unlocked. I can't believe my eyes when we walk in. The apartment is much bigger than I thought it would be and so pretty in side. I feel like we have won the lottery.

"Oh my God, Chris, this is absolutely beautiful and perfect." I can't stop smiling and looking at everything. There's so much closet space and the kitchen is nice and big. There are two bathrooms too, I never in a million years expected to have a bathroom attached to our bedroom.

This is going to be the change we need. All the struggles, all the fighting, it all lead us to here. We can now relax and enjoy life and our little girl. I don't think I have ever felt like things were ever going to be okay, until right now. Right now, everything is perfect.

The transition to our apartment has been great. The only problem is Lizzie still wants to sleep with us and I'm okay with it, Chris is not. I don't feel the need to make her sleep in her own room, especially being I'm still nursing her. Chris wants her out of our bed and so far, I've been able to avoid any fights about it.

The first few months fly by and Lizzie and I are getting into a nice routine. We get up, she nurses, she plays while I do laundry, she eats, we go for a walk, we come back, she nurses and plays, I clean up, she naps. Once she is napping I finally eat and relax and watch a little TV When she gets up she nurses, we go for another walk then we come home, and I make dinner. It's becoming a very nice routine.

Today was like every other day, until bedtime. Chris is insisting we put her in her own bed, in her own room. She is so upset she won't stop crying. I try to go in and he blocks the door and won't let me. I am forced to stand there listening to her cry and after 20 minutes I am in tears too, begging him to let me go check on her.

"Open that door and I promise you will regret it." he says and walks away from the door. I wait until he goes into the bathroom and I hurry up and go into her room and tell her it's okay, mommy loves her. I start to pat her back to get her to go to sleep when Chris comes in. I knew he would be mad, but I guess I thought things would be different now. I was wrong.

"I fucking told you not to come in here." He says as he grabs my arm and pulls me out of the room. He is tightly squeezing my arm, so I don't fight against him hoping maybe he will loosen his grip a little. He gets me into the hall and pushes me up against the wall. I hardly have the chance to let it sink in that he let go of my arm before he has me by the throat.

"When will you stop making me do this? When will you obey me, and stop acting like a spoiled brat?" I know I need to tread very carefully here so I say I'm sorry. "Sorry isn't enough anymore. I think you need to learn a little lesson." I am so afraid right now, that I start crying.

"No, I don't I will try harder, I promise. I feel so bad she is crying." I hear myself begging and I hate myself for it.

"I am so tired of you telling me you will listen to me and behave better, then you don't. Every time you disobey me it's like you're saying piss on you or as if you're spitting in my face." He has me by the arm again dragging me into the bathroom this time. I have no idea what he is planning but I'm terrified. I try to grab the door frame with my other hand to pull myself back out, but he yanks me hard and I stand no chance against his strength.

"Get undressed and get in the shower." He says as he turns the water on. I know better than to argue so I start taking my clothes off.

He does this thing where he can spit from under his tongue somehow. He has always thought it to be funny, and I think it's gross. As I'm undressing he keeps doing it and spitting on me. I try to ignore it, but after I take off all my clothes he keeps doing it. He is strong and holds me in place, so he can repeatedly spit in my face.

"Stop Chris, come on that's gross, please stop." I say over and over. "Chris, I'm not kidding stop it. I get it you think I was rude not listening to you, you can stop spitting on me." I try like crazy to get out of his grip.

He finally let's go of me and says to me "Get into the shower... now." I quickly touch the water to make sure for some reason he didn't have it hot and it's okay, so I step into the shower. "Start washing yourself." He says to me. I have no idea where he is going with any of this. I quickly grab the soap and lather up my body I get all soaped up. I start rinsing off when I see him start undressing himself, all I can think is great now he is going to expect sex. I feel sick to my stomach knowing what is going to come next.

I continue rinsing myself off, weary to turn my back to him so I only half turn and sure enough he steps into the shower. I brace myself for what is going to come, trying to tell myself just let it happen it won't be that bad.

I am wrong and didn't see this coming. Chris starts peeing on me, all over, anywhere he can make it hit. He is peeing on me. I am so stunned at first, I don't move. Once I realize what he is doing I try to get out of the shower, but he has me blocked in. The shower doors are impossible to open because I realize he's keeping it closed with his free hand. At this point he has gotten the pee as high as my chest. I feel so disgusting I start to cry and once again beg.

"Chris stop it, this is disgusting, please stop doing this." I try to keep my body under the water the best I can, so the pee will rinse right off, but I just want him to stop. "Chris, stop it." I yell at him and try to push my way past him, hoping if I do it quick and he isn't prepared I can get through. He grabs me and twists me, so my back side is facing his front side.

He has such a tight grip on my arms I know from experience I won't get out. He bends me over and presses down on my back, just below my neck and is pushing my face towards the floor. For a second, I think, is he going to try to fill the tub and drown me, but before I can let that thought run wild I feel him forcing himself inside me.

I feel like he is ripping me down there and he doesn't care as I scream out in pain. Once again, I'm not ready nor wanting this and add water to the mix down there and it's incredibly painful. I know better than to fight it, so I succumb to him and do my best to block him out while crying. This wasn't supposed to happen here, this was supposed to be a fresh start. I have no idea how to make it stop.

I wake up with a heavy heart knowing nothing is ever going to change with Chris. I think today when he goes to work, I will finally call my mom and ask to go home. It isn't at all where I wanted my life to go, but it is what I must do for Lizzie. I can't do this, I tried so hard to keep my family together. I will have to fight him in court to keep him from taking her from me. Staying here though, I keep putting her own well-being on the back burner, all out of fear.

I get up and go to the bathroom knowing I need to pretend to be normal until he leaves for work. I get myself together and head out to start coffee and breakfast. "Good morning." I say as I go over to start the coffee and realize he already did. "This smells good, thank you." I add and pour myself a cup.

"I was up so why not help out." he says smiling, and I feel uneasy because he is being too nice. I play along and smile back and go pull some eggs and stuff out of the fridge to make breakfast.

"You can make those for me, but not you." He says taking me a little off guard. "Today you will start your new diet. You are gaining weight and looking fat."

"Chris, I'm a hundred and thirty pounds, I hardly think I'm fat."

"You don't see all the fat shaking when I'm fucking you. I do and let me tell you, it isn't pretty. You're starting to look like your mom and that's disgusting." he smirks at me.

I'm embarrassed by him saying I look like my mom in the tone he used. I don't think my mom looks bad, but apparently, he does. I start cooking him some eggs and bacon and finally ask "Well what am I supposed to eat then?"

"You can have this." He says as he pulls out a box of cream of wheat out of the cabinet.

"That's for Lizzie though, she eats that every morning for her breakfast." I honestly hate cream of wheat and don't want to eat that. I know better than to argue so I start to make some for Lizzie and myself.

"I will have a list of approved things you can eat." He is saying and I'm half listening, all I keep thinking is as soon as he leaves I'm calling my mom. "Hey, are you listening to me?" he cuts into my thoughts.

I have to say, "I'm sorry I missed that I was thinking about the cream of wheat cooking." I have no idea what all I missed.

"I should have known you can't cook and listen at the same time. No surprise there you're too stupid to do two things at once." He is getting pissed, so I try to focus.

"I'm sorry Chris, what were you saying?" I turn the heat off, so I can listen.

"I said, I am going to keep you at about eight hundred calories a day or less if possible, until the fat gets off you. After that we will discuss what you will eat again." I seriously can't believe he is going to count my calories. I don't know how I will survive eating that little. I can't stay here, there is no way I can do this anymore.

"Don't try sneaking food either when I'm at work. I counted all the eggs, and the cheese slices and I know what else we have including the bread. You can eat a pack of ramen noodles for lunch and that's it." He starts to eat, and I go wake Lizzie, so she can have her breakfast too, so it doesn't get cold and gross.

The nerve of this man thinking he can tell me what I can and can't eat. I'm so pissed by the time I get in Lizzie's room I know without a doubt I'm leaving him today. I can't do this anymore and I refuse to be treated like a dog one day longer.

I march out to the kitchen to feed Lizzie and say goodbye to him, feeling strong and powerful. I get as far as the living room and I see him winding up the cord from the phone. He took the cord from the phone, then he walks into the bedroom and takes the actual cordless phone too.

"Just in case you think you're slick and want to call someone and bitch about the new rules." As he walks to the door, he smirks and says, "Hope you didn't have plans to leave." He closes the door and deadbolts it from the outside with the key.

I run over to my set of keys sitting on the kitchen table and sure enough my deadbolt key is gone. He took my key and locked me in this apartment. I'm trapped. I start panicking, what if there is a fire? What if I need to call for an ambulance? Why would he do this? Then I realize, he knew. He knew I was going to leave.

Chris does this every couple of days, for the next few months. He forces me in the shower and has sex with me, after first degrading me and urinating on me. Or if he chooses not to shower, he then finds it funny to be rough and to have sex with me while covering my face with a pillow or choking me or both. One of the times he was doing that with the pillow, then choking me, I almost passed out. Thank God, he stopped, and I was able to get air. I'm not sure if I would have suffocated or not, but it was incredibly scary.

He is letting me still only eat cream of wheat for breakfast and ramen noodle soup for lunch. Dinner so far, I have been allowed what he eats, and I try to save any leftovers I can, but he usually makes sure to eat it all. I find myself drinking a lot of milk, which I don't like but it makes me feel better after I drink it. I am lightheaded most of the day now, even cleaning up after Lizzie is exhausting.

I think about Lizzie's first birthday that just passed and how he wouldn't let me have a birthday party for her. I will never get that first birthday back, nor will I have pictures of her blowing out her first candle. I will never have a picture of cake all over her face saying first birthday on the back of it. She never got to open her very first birthday gift, something I can never duplicate. If Chris doesn't think it's necessary, then it isn't, and he didn't think it was necessary to celebrate it.

I feel so isolated and alone, weak and tired. I'm thankful she can now drink milk because I am producing less, and less milk and I am so drained from trying to nurse all the time. It's time to stop nursing for me. I have no idea how to stop him from treating me this way and at times I want to kill him. I know I could never do it, but there are nights I wish I was brave enough.

I try not to complain, doing so only aggravates him and makes him rougher and meaner. I don't dare cry in front of him or argue about anything at all. At night he allows me to talk to my mom, but he is right there so I can't even drop a hint that I need help. My mom is so busy running Brittany around and talking about her every time we are on the phone, she doesn't even realize I haven't been around.

Chris came home late last night, and thankfully was too drunk to try to have sex. He just let me know he is leaving again tonight and I will need to fend for myself for dinner. I know there isn't much food, so I decide to be brave and ask for some money.

"You can make what we have here." He says.

"Chris there isn't much food, and Lizzie is almost out of milk." I want to add because he drinks it knowing there isn't much left. He told me last week she can drink water as he poured the last glass for himself. I've never seen a dad act so selfish when it comes to their child and eating or drinking. I think how my father would have starved, so his kids and wife could eat first. "I don't mind walking down to the store to grab some stuff."

He is in a pretty decent mood and surprises me and says, "Fine I'll make a list, get only what's on it and that's it." I pretend to be serious and agree, when I want to shout that I finally get to leave the apartment.

Chris finishes getting ready and as always, I'm expected to tell him he looks nice, and handsome, when the reality is... I can't stand to look at him. I do my duty and lie as good as I can, and he finally goes to leave. "Chris, the list and some money?" He quickly writes some things down, hands me a ten-dollar bill and leaves.

Once I see him pull out of the drive I look at the list. He jotted down cheese slices, bread and milk. I see this is basically telling me to make grilled cheese. I look in the fridge and there isn't any butter, so I add that to the list.

I hurry up and get Lizzie changed into something nice and run into my room and change my clothes too. I decide to put a little makeup on since I haven't worn any in months. I remember I have some extra change in my purse, so I scrape it all together to get Lizzie a surprise ice cream cone.

Feeling the fresh air and sunshine hit my face makes me smile bigger and bigger as I walk. It feels so good to be outside and not locked in the apartment. I want to walk and walk and walk. I want to stay outside if possible until the sun goes down. I decide to get the ice cream cone first, and that way it can hold Lizzie over a little, so we can eat dinner later than normal.

I get to the ice cream stand and order her a baby cone and the lady asks, "Anything for you?" I asked how much a small cone was and I am short fifty cents, so I say no thank you, just the baby cone.

The lady smiles and came back with a baby cone for Lizzie and a small cone for me. "Ma'am thank you, but I don't have enough." I smile and try to give it back.

"It's on the house, don't worry about it." She says and pushes my hand back at me.

"Thank you so much, but I don't want to get you in trouble." I say.

"I don't think that is possible, I own this place and I think a little treat does us all some good." smiling she says, "Now stop arguing and go eat your cone before it melts and its wasted."

"Okay, Thank you so much." I say laughing and I go sit down at a bench to eat my cone and help Lizzie eat hers. The ice cream cone tastes so good I feel tears sting my eyes. It has been such a long time since I tasted something this good. I can't help but feel so grateful for the lady at the ice cream shop.

After a while I figure it is time to go to the store and get the food we need for dinner. I walk slowly trying to enjoy every second I can outside. I'm not sure when Chris will let me back out again. I know I should go use a payphone or something and call my parents, but I can't bring myself to do it. Admitting how bad things are is something I don't know how to do yet. I'm also deep down terrified he will take Lizzie from me and I'll never do anything to risk that. I will take any terrible thing he throws my way, to make sure I can keep her safe and with me.

I put the thought of a payphone out of my head not willing to risk losing her, and we head to the store to get the groceries I need. It doesn't take very long since I can't get much, and I find myself back at the apartment too fast. I decide to make the sandwiches and go eat outside with Lizzie picnic style. This will give us a little more outside time.

We have a wonderful time outside, but it is starting to get cool out, so I finally take her in. I give her a nice warm bath, and I hold her while she falls asleep. I don't get to do that anymore when Chris is home, so I enjoy doing it when he's gone. I put her in her bed and turn the T.V on to look for something to watch. After a while I get bored and go get ready for bed, I figure I might as well get some good sleep tonight.

Chapter 17

    I am sound asleep and startled awake by the bedroom door slamming into the wall. It takes me a second to realize what is going on. Chris is home, and he is drunk. I try to lay as still as I can hoping he would think I am still asleep and leave me alone. He stands there for a few minutes then finally walks back out to the other room.

    Just when I start to breath normal again, he comes back in the room. I think he is going to go in the bathroom, but he jerks the blankets off me and is yanking me off the bed. I try to catch my balance but between him yanking me off the bed and him being drunk I land hard on my knees on the floor. He jerks me up to a stand hurting my arm as he does it, making me yelp out in pain. "Shut the fuck up before you wake up Lizzie." he says to me then adds, "If you wake her up I swear to god I'll fuck you up."

I have no idea what the hell is going on, but I try to keep as quiet as I can by asking, "Chris what is wrong? Why are you so mad?" I try to think if there is any way he could know about the ice cream cone. I know I didn't have a receipt or use his money. So, unless he followed me there's no way he would know.

Oh no, would he do that? Would he follow me? He is dragging me like a rag doll into the living room. We get to the dining room table and he lets go of me and points to the money on the table. "What did I fucking tell you before I left?"

"I don't know, you told me a few things before you left." I say trying to regain my balance still.

"What did I say about the money and the food, are you that stupid you can't remember?"

"No, I remember, you told me to get only what was on the list and bring back the change. I did that, the change is all there with the receipt. I left it there, so you can see." I say hoping this will calm him down once he looks at it.

"Do you think I'm fucking stupid? Do you honestly think that about me?" He is getting too close to me, but I have nowhere to go without making it obvious he is scaring me.

"Of course not, I think you are incredibly smart and I love that about you." I try to be as believable as I can, I'm not good at lying.

He snatches me by the back of my neck and shoves my face two inches away from the receipt on the table and says, "Then read to me what you bought."

With tears falling on the table I look at the receipt and read "Bread, butter, cheese, milk."

"Did I have butter on the list? Did I say buy fucking butter? I'm pretty sure my list did not have butter."

"No, it didn't but I couldn't make grilled cheese without it and we were out." I say.

"Who the fuck said make grilled cheese?" he is so mad, and I can feel his fingers tightening on my neck. "You fucking fat cow, butter is nothing, but fat and you don't need it. Do you want to be a cow for the rest of your life?"

"I'm not fat Chris I've lost weight, none of my clothes fit me... look at me, I have lost weight." I say wishing he would let go of my neck.

He moves me away from the table and gives me a good shove. I fly across the room and land on my already rug burned knees from him dragging me. I fall onto my stomach, almost hitting my face on the ground. I don't even get a second to think before he is sitting on my butt pinning me to the floor. "I'll decide when you're not fat anymore." He says pushing my hips into the floor.

I try to move myself to get him off but now he has my hair and he stretches my head back, so he can say in my ear "Stop fucking moving." I stop moving praying he will loosen up on my hair, it feels like he is ripping it out of my head. It works he stops pulling my hair, but I feel him shift his weight on me, so he is laying on me, but not completely.

He starts pulling my underwear down and that's when I realize I'm only in a t-shirt and my underwear, and what he wants. "Chris stop, I don't want to do this." I try to roll him off me and take advantage of his shift change but it's no use. He instead uses my shift to get my underwear down to my knees which that backfires on me and won't let me use my legs to get him off. I start to panic and try harder to get him off me, begging.

"Chris this isn't okay, I said stop I don't want this, I said no." He leans onto my back with his chest making it impossible for me to move. I can feel him getting his pants down.

"Stop it get off me, no means no, get off me." I try again to move side to side and get him off me, but I can't make him move.

He grabs my hair again and says "When are you going to learn little girl? I own you, like a dog, you will sit when I say sit, stay when I say stay and not buy anything else when I say don't." He loosens his grip on my hair and says, "And If I want to fuck you I will fuck you, now be a good little dog and shut up." With that I feel him force his way into me. Once again, I give up the fight and cry knowing, there is nothing I can do to stop him.

When Chris finishes his assault on me, he gets up and leaves me there crying, and goes into the bathroom to shower. I get myself up off the floor and go into my bathroom to try to calm down. I change my clothes and climb into bed. Tomorrow when he isn't drunk I am telling him I'm leaving. I roll over pretending to sleep, praying when he comes out he leaves me alone.

I'm still awake scared, when he gets out of the shower, but I don't move at all. It works, I hear him start snoring shortly after he lays down. I eventually cry myself to sleep one more time, hating the life I live.

I wake up the next morning and the night before comes rushing back to me. I know today is the day to stand up to him. I don't know how but some way I will get through to him that I am leaving him. I get Lizzie out of her bed and go out and start her breakfast.

In the kitchen, on the counter is some money, Chris never leaves money out or lets me see what he spends it on. Chris must have forgotten he had it when he got so mad at me last night. Next to the money is a receipt, so I pick it up to see what it was for.

The receipt is for a strip club. I can't believe he would go to a place like that, he knows I wouldn't be okay with it. I start getting mad and l look at the money. There are a lot of singles sitting there and some fives and tens. Well screw him, he probably has no idea how much is there, so I quickly grab a ten, a few fives and some ones. I know I need to act quickly so I think fast, and I hurry up and shove the money into a coat sleeve in the closet.

A few minutes later Chris comes out and I don't say a word to him. I go about finishing mine and Lizzies breakfast and figure he can make his own. I sit down to eat with Lizzie and I hear him get the money, shove it in his pocket and go into our bedroom. I was right, he had no idea how much was there, or he would have said something right away. There is nothing Chris loves more than his money and letting me know it's not mine.

Chris comes back into the room and puts a piece of paper in front of me on the table. I glance over at it ready to ignore it and him when my heart stops. There sitting on the table is the letter I wrote him and the one to Lizzie, from the night I wanted to end it all. I thought I threw it away, and my face shows it. "Just in case you get any ideas about leaving, know this, I will take Lizzie from you and you will never see her again." I stare at him unable to wrap my head around it. "This here will show you are an unfit mother and no court in the world will let you raise or even be around her."

He grabs it off the table and puts it in his pocket and leaves. He doesn't lock the door, he doesn't need to, nor does he take the phone cord. I feel completely defeated and heartbroken that I put myself in this position. I was wrong, there is nothing in the world Chris loves more... than control.

I take Lizzie into the living room, turn on some cartoons for her and cry while holding her close to me. I have no choice, but to stay and take his shit. I won't let him take her from me. I feel somewhere in my past life I was terribly bad, and this is my punishment.

Every couple of nights, Chris goes out and comes home late and drunk. I wait until he starts snoring and once he's out cold, I go through his pockets. I can take a few dollars every night. I know he is going to the strip club and even though I don't like how he treats me, it still hurts. It hurts because he can't find it in his heart to love me and respect me. It also hurts that he won't let me get new shoes when mine have holes in them, but he pays girls to put their tits in his face. Above all, it hurts because I have no idea how many of these girls he is fucking.

The only good thing about him having the notes and letting me know it is he doesn't keep such a tight rein on me. I can go for walks again and occasionally he lets me take one of the cars to go to the store. Today was one of those days. My mom has Lizzie and I needed to go get her some clothes, so he gave me a little money to go to a few second-hand stores.

It was after the first store, that my crazy thought started to form in my head. With my heart pounding I pull into the parking lot praying none of his friends are here this early. I fix my make up and walk into the strip club. I have never been inside of one, so I had no idea what it would look like. It is pretty much what I thought, or pictured, darkly lit, and loud music in a blue cloud of cigarette smoke.

On the stage was a mostly naked girl sashaying her hips and moving sexy. There were other girls dancing by men, and others dancing together in little clusters of men. I take a seat at the bar, and try to blend in. I notice they keep their tops on and that is a little relief, at least their boobs aren't out in the open.

"You here for the try outs?" My thoughts are interrupted by a guy behind the bar. "You're late but go around the curtain over there and get ready you can get up next."

"Try outs?" I ask confused by what the guy is saying.

"Yes, the tryouts for the new dancer we are hiring?" He says looking me up and down.

"Oh, no I'm not, I'm uh... I'm with the girl up there now. You know, moral support." I have no idea why I say that, but It just comes out.

"Well that's a shame, you look like you would look good up there." He smiles, and I know he probably flirts with all the girls.

"Oh, well thank you but I've never done something like this." Then I add, "Not that I have anything against it." Just in case he thinks I'm judging it and he decides to throw me out.

"Well you should come out for our amateur night next Saturday night... winner takes home five hundred dollars." He says, "Plus any of the money made during their time up on the stage."

"What exactly would I have to do?" I ask not really thinking I would, but something makes me ask.

"All you need to do is fill out an application for it, show up, dance. And If you are the favorite, you win the money." He smiles then adds "Oh, and there is a twenty-dollar fee due on Saturday before you go on stage."

I hear myself saying "Okay, can I have an application?" He hands me one and before I can change my mind I fill it out. I get up to leave and say, "Thank you I'll see you then." and I head out to my car, thinking I'm crazy.

I must figure out how to pull this off, but I feel good doing something sneaky. If I won that money I could add it to my little travel soap dish I have hidden and eventually have enough money to get away from him. It will serve him right to come in there and see me up there. I hope I can pull it off though.

I hurry up and finish my shopping and head home planning what I need to do. First thing I need to do is figure out how to dance like that girl on the stage. I'm a good dancer, but I have never tried that kind of dancing. Luckily, I took dance for a while and I'm actually pretty good. I will need to practice when Lizzie takes her naps.

I spend the next week dancing every day as much as I can. I also practice at night when Chris goes out after Lizzie goes to bed. I use a mirror from my bedroom, so I can see what I look like, and I have to say I look pretty good. Next thing I need to do is figure out something to wear. That will be harder, but thankfully I have my stash of money I can pull money from. I know I can find what I need at the mall, I need to figure out how I can get there, or why. I am determined to pull this off and I am determined to win. I feel the old competitive me coming out and it feels great. I forgot what it was like to have something to look forward to.

A few days later I get a phone call from Angel telling me she is having her son's first birthday party in a little over a month. I know this can be the excuse I need to go to the mall. I hope Chris isn't a jerk about it.

"Chris, my cousin Angel is having a party for her son Gary next month and I heard the toy store in the mall is having a huge sale. Would you care if I went sometime this week to get him a gift?" I ask that night at dinner.

"Fine, get him a car or something, boys like cars." He hands me five dollars and gets up to go get ready to go out. I'm so glad he doesn't make a huge issue out of it and I can go tomorrow when he is at work. Now all I need do is figure out what to do with Lizzie on Saturday. I think I can get my mom to watch her, I'll have to tell Chris she's going there in a way that doesn't make him suspicious.

I head out to go to the mall first thing in the morning. I knew he wouldn't let me take the car and it's a long walk so I want to get an early start. Before I left I called my mom and basically had her think it was her idea to get Lizzie. I told her I had no gas money and if she wanted to, she could pick her up around seven o'clock. Chris always leaves by six to go eat with the guys so seven should be safe.

After thinking about it I decide not to even tell him. There is no reason he should know ahead of time and not telling him will hopefully insure I can get out. Telling him, I risk him saying no and then I won't be able to do this. I have everything planned except getting the other car keys. I'm worried I won't be able to figure out how to do that. We finally got a second car, but I'm not allowed to drive it and Chris never lets me take the other one either. There's only a few occasions where he allows me to take the old one, but for the newer one he takes the keys or hides them. I haven't been able to find the hiding spot yet for the keys. Worst case scenario I can take a bus, but I have no idea how to do that. If I need to though, I can learn fast.

    I finally get to the mall and find the store I need. I try a few sexy outfits on and finally decide on a simple black push up bra and a sexy black thong. I am ready to check out and the cashier lets me know the bras are buy one get one, so I quickly decide to go bolder and grab a red one too with another matching thong. Red can be a very hot color on me with my blonde hair and I want to stand out and look good.

I decide to treat Lizzie and myself to some food in the food court and I go all out. I grab some Chinese food for myself and French fries for her. I haven't eaten this kind of food in so long and it tastes so wonderful. I find myself shoveling the food in and I force myself slow down. I end up eating every bite I have on my plate. I feel a little sick and hope the walk back will make me feel better.

I hide my stuff in the bottom of the diaper bag and make sure to have the toy firetruck I got Gary easily visible in case I run into Chris before we get into the apartment. Thankfully he must be busy at work today. I don't see him, and I don't have to deal with him yet.

As soon as I get in the apartment I run and hide my stuff at the bottom of my dirty clothes basket. I don't think he will look there. I come out and get Lizzie situated and It dawns on me, I've never looked in his dirty clothes. What if he hides the keys there?

I run back into the bedroom and quickly grab his clothes and sure enough at the bottom of the basket are the keys to our other car. I shove the clothes back on them and run over to my basket and grab my stuff. I think quickly and go in the closet in the hallway and shove them behind all the blankets. I'm so glad I did that because he might look in my clothes.

I just get back in the living room and sit on the floor to play with Lizzie when I hear his key in the door. I take a few quick breaths to calm my breathing and my heart and smile happily when he comes in.

"Good you're back, it took you long enough. What did you get the little brat?" he always says such mean things.

"I decided to get him a fire truck and when you push the button on top it lights up and makes a siren noise." I say choosing to ignore the brat comment.

"Of course, you would, if you had your way you would be a firefighter fucking your way to the top." he says.

"Chris, I would never have done that. I wanted to be a firefighter since I was like ten, it was a silly dream, like my dream to write." I try to make him see I had other interests too.

"Oh, the writing thing again," He rolls his eyes. "I told you before you aren't smart enough for that. You didn't go to college for a reason because you can't do it, it takes someone with brains."

"Chris, I didn't go to college because I had Lizzie and chose to stay home and raise her. You do know I could go back to college, it isn't too late."

"Yes, it is. It would be a waste of time and money. It takes brains to go to college and you have none. Stop being dumb and talking about things that don't matter. You read books all day as if it will magically make your brain work. It won't." He is being so mean.

"I read books all day because I love to read. I love to pretend to be the character and really get into that imaginary place." I know he will never understand, because he can't read or write well.

"So, when the sluts in your book are fucking people you're pretending to fuck them? Nice, maybe I'll start pretending I'm fucking people too, I'll start with your sister." He says and slams the door as he leaves and heads back to work.

He doesn't get it, I live vicariously through the characters in my books. Not at all in a dirty way like he is portraying, but in an adventurous way that I couldn't ever do in real life. It's my way to see the world without seeing the world. I know I better make him a good dinner, so he will calm down, I go pull some chicken out and get busy.

Chapter 18

It's here, finally Saturday is here, and I feel like I'm going to be sick from my nerves. I try hard to keep it together. Chris is in a pretty good mood, probably because he is going out drinking with his friends. He has never asked if I ever want to go and I know now it's because he goes to the strip club. I hope tonight, he goes to the same one. When I put this plan into motion I never thought about if he would go to a different one. Now, I can't stop worrying about it.

Chris heads out on time, and my mom gets here about an hour later and gets Lizzie. I want to fix and curl my hair at home and I think I have just enough time to do it. This leaves me plenty of time to focus on my makeup once I get there. I really want to look sultry and sexy, and hot. I always look tired and rocking the "mom" look, so I want to completely shock Chris when I walk out on that stage.

I made sure the keys were still hidden and I grab money to pay for the entry. I also grab a little extra cash in case the car needs gas too. I finish my hair and it looks great. I quickly pack my little outfits I bought, and I head out.

Thank goodness, the car starts fine. I was worried he might disconnect the battery or do something I couldn't fix. I drive out of the garage and roll my window down so my curls will loosen and get a bit messy. I want a beachy surfer hair look, and I think the wind will give it the right mess that I need. It doesn't take long to get there and before I know it I am pulling in.

I get my stuff out of the car and walk in. I'm all smiles on the outside, but so nervous I feel I might throw up. I hurry up and go to the bartender to find out where I need to go and head to the back area where all the girls are.

A couple girls smile and say hi and are a lot friendlier than I expected. I'm not sure why but I thought they would all be bitchy and stuck up. I guess I pre-judged and stereotyped strippers based on my own insecurities.

There is one girl sitting behind a small desk and a little line in front of the desk, so I go over to her to register. I try to nonchalantly check out my competition and I realize there are a lot of pretty girls here. I am about to rethink it all when the girl behind the desk says, "Excuse me are you in line for amateur night or are you looking for someone?"

"Oh, I'm sorry, yes." I say then realize she has no idea what yes, I mean. "I'm here for amateur night, I'm sorry I'm nervous this is my first time doing this."

I smile, and she smiles back then yells, "Girls we have a virgin here." My whole face turns red and I want to bolt, but before I do, one of the other girls walks up to me and hands me a shot of something.

"Drink this, it will help keep you from running away, or throwing up." she smiles at me.

I quickly do the shot and feel the burn of it go down my throat. "Holy crap that was strong." I choke out.

"Yes, it is, it's Bacardi." The girl holding the bottle says.

"What is that?" I ask feeling silly I don't know, but I don't drink too often.

"It's rum, and this one is strong, one fifty-one. Trust me you will be feeling great." She says before she runs off with her bottle.

I turn back to the girl I was talking to before and say, "Thank you, I think I needed that."

She smiles and says "We all do, now if you need to get ready you can go in the next room. There are mirrors and changing rooms and lockers, use them. Trust no one with your stuff, it will disappear fast." I start heading that way when I hear her say. "And Margo, unless you watch it get pored don't drink anything anyone gives you." I smile and walk away wondering why.

In the back I see a bunch of girls scrambling to get ready together. I hear a few talking and figure out some are regular dancers here and some are like me doing the amateur night. The shot I did has kicked in and I'm feeling less nervous. I see the girl from the desk again that had the rum and I go over to ask her a question.

"Excuse me, I have a quick question." I say, and she smiles pours a shot and gives it to me. "Oh, no, I'm okay I wanted to ask if you know how this works now."

She hands me the shot anyways and says, "Trust me you still need this."

So, I throw the shot back and smile then say, "Now what?"

"Now you wait for them to introduce the new girls, like you. Did you give them a stage name or your real name?"

"My real name I didn't know I should have a stage name." I say embarrassed.

"It's okay, some girls don't, what is your name?" I tell her Margo and she says, "Okay I'll give you a stage name." She walks away, and a few minutes later comes back and says, "Now you will be known as Skye." I feel silly, but I thank her and the more I think about it the more I like it.

I go over to the curtain and peek out, I wasn't sure if I would be able to see Chris and his friends. Sure, enough he is here, with all his friends and some girls. The girls are not here dancing and one is sitting on his lap and he has his arms wrapped around her. I am so pissed off that I almost march out there and yank her off him. I take a second though and realize it's my pride that is hurt, honestly not the fact that he has a girl sitting on him.

I don't want to be with him. I truly don't ever want him to touch me again, so, I'm more upset he feels he can treat me like shit and do this stuff behind my back. All it does, is fuel my fire to win this money. When need be I can be incredibly competitive and today for me, this is a win only situation.

I go back over to the girl that has been helping me and finally say "I'm so sorry I never got your name?" She smiles and says that's okay, It's Amy, but I go by Jade here."

"Well thank you for all your help, I have another question. Do I pick a song or does the D.J?"

"On amateur night the DJ will pick your song, he likes to make you really squirm, so don't let him. Make sure you can get into it quickly and don't freeze." She starts to head out and says, "He will come back here in about five minutes to size you all up." And she goes out onto the stage.

I peek out the side of the curtain for a few minutes to see her dance and she is fantastic. I think I have a similar style and the crowd loves her. I notice Chris and his friends couldn't stop giving her money. I know I am going to have to be fantastic to win, so I step away from the stage to mentally prepare.

I am focusing on my own thoughts when I hear "Skye? Is there a freaking Skye here or did she chicken out and take off? Okay... also known as Margo?"

"I'm sorry." I speak up, and when I look up I'm startled to see an incredibly attractive guy talking to me. Good looking would be an understatement, this man is more like breathtaking. "That's me, I was mentally preparing" I blush, and I have no idea why I say that, but he smiles big. He walks over to stand in front of me, he's so close that I can feel the heat off his body.

"You a virgin?" He says, the innuendo he leaves hanging in the air has me blushing deeper. This guy is unbelievably good looking, he could easily be a model for a bodybuilding magazine. I can feel myself turning even more red as the heat reaches my cheeks. I'm terrified to speak because I'm not sure I'll remember how.

Finally, I swallow and hear myself answering. "No, I have a child, so I'm definitely not a virgin."

He laughs a little and says "I mean here doing this. Have you danced before?" I shake my head no as he circles me looking me up and down and when he gets behind me he smacks my ass. It isn't in a mean angry Chris way, but a hotter sexier way and I feel myself getting excited. I would never betray Chris, even though I hate him, so my turned-on feelings confuse me a little. When Chris is rough I want to curl up in a ball and die. This little smack on the ass though, from this guy, has me breathing hard and wanting more.

I hardly have time to process this when he steps even closer to me, grabs my hips and starts to dance, slowly, grinding, it's erotic. It feels as though there is an electric current running through my body. I start moving with him, grinding back and feeling tingles down there. I want him, I'm not sure if I want him to keep dancing or do more... but he lets go. He smiles, steps away, and says "Oh yes, you're a hot little number, I have the perfect song for you." He leans in and whispers "Don't blow it." Stressing on the word blow, then he winks and walks away. The way he says, "don't blow it" sends tingles straight to my groin, when Chris says it, I want to vomit.

I have no idea what that was. Deep down somewhere I know if I truly loved Chris, I wouldn't have felt that attracted to someone else. I calm down my breathing and try to push it out of my head, while trying to figure out what that guy meant and who he is. Jade walks over and asks, "What did Josh say to you?"

I told her, and she smiled and said "He thinks you could win this. He will pick you out a great song, it will be hot, so make sure you do it justice."

She starts to walk away and even though I'm a little buzzed I ask "Jade, could I have another shot?"

Jade goes and grabs me another shot, I do it quick and pray it kicks in, so I can relax a little more. I watch what seems like a hundred girls go out and come back. A few I can hear some good applause after, but nothing crazy, or what I would expect from a winner. I realize though maybe that's because I'm in the back and can't hear well.

I creep up closer to the stage to wait, there are only a few girls left so I sneak a peek at them when they go. They look nice, but they don't look like much competition with their lack of dancing skills. I pray when it's my turn, I don't choke. Chris is still there, and the girl is still hanging all over him. I can't wait to see his face. I can't wait to show him I know what he is doing.

Finally, I hear Josh say "Okay guys we have a real sweet treat for the last number. This hottie is going to light this stage on fire, let's get a little red light special before we go."

I know the song, I know what he is going to play, it's new, and sexy and I practiced with it a few times. I know exactly what I am going to do. I square my shoulders; the music starts playing and I walk right out and look straight at Chris and start dancing.

I see Chris open then close his mouth. I see his jaw start clenching, then I stop looking at him and I really get into the song. I strut my stuff all over the stage, then I go in for the kill. I go to the edge of the stage and crawl in front of Chris and his friends and snake my arms around Chris like I am flirting with him and I whisper, "I've seen you all night with your whore so now, you can watch me touch other guys and know I'll never willingly ever touch you again."

I back up from him and place my feet on the back of the chair of the man next to him, his friend. I lift my hips so down there, is inches from his face and move my hips up and down. The crowd of guys goes nuts. I put my legs down then ease myself off the stage, so I am straddling the guy. I move my hips and tease him over and over making sure to ever so lightly make contact to his groin with myself down there. I turn my back to him and bend down grab my ankles, sliding my hands up my legs on my way back up. I shimmy by butt back and forth then reach back and give it a smack.

I crawl back up on the stage and finish the dance. The music stops, and I hear Josh saying we have an obvious winner, and he says Skye. I am on cloud nine floating on the stage, thinking I don't think this is the kind of dancing my parents thought I'd put all those dance lessons to use for.

Josh puts on some upbeat hip hop music and grabs me on the stage and starts grinding on me. I feel myself dancing back with him and I glance over at Chris and he is pissed. I don't know if I have ever seen his face so red, and jaw so clenched. The girl he has been with all night is gone, and Chris is glaring at me and Josh. I'm so excited about winning the money I don't care. I let Josh turn me and grind into me from behind bending my body forward holding my hips as he continues to grind into me. I can feel from his pressure on me back there that he is just as turned on as I am. I am dancing with him as if we are alone and we are really heating it up. I feel his lips on my neck and hear him whisper in my ear how hot I am. I don't care that Chris is watching, I let him keep caressing my neck with his mouth. I've never been this turned on before... ever. It speaks volumes to me.

The crowd is loving the show and we dance for the entire song. Finally, Josh stops to go get the money to give to me. I smile, take a bow, looking directly at Chris and I bounce off the stage behind the curtain.

Jade is waiting for me and hugs me and tells me she knew Josh saw I would win. She said he has an eye for talent and I should consider doing this all the time. I thanked her then said, "I honestly have no desire to do this, I honestly did it because my daughters father comes here all the time, so I wanted to piss him off."

She laughs and says if I ever change my mind I could make good money dancing and to come back. I walk over and thank Josh for picking out a great song for me, and he hands me his number and says we should hang out sometime. I smile and put the number in my pocket knowing I'll never call him, but it was nice to get. I smile and head out to my car.

I see Chris's car is still there, but I don't wait to find him. I head home with the money and want to be sure I can hide it. I now realize Chris probably won't let me keep it, but I'm not sure he knows how much it was. I pry he isn't smart enough to ask around at the strip club. Chris likes to try to present himself as smart, when the reality of it is, he isn't. He's just mean. There's a big difference between being intelligent and forcing your physical power onto someone. He has that extremely confused.

I get home and split the money. I put half in my secret hiding place then the other half I leave in my purse. I don't want to give away my secret stash if he does end up insisting on the money.

I didn't think through to well what he might do when he gets home. I start to worry that I might have pissed him off too badly, especially that dance with Josh. He could come home and completely snap and beat the crap out of me. It's too late to leave again because I hear his key in the door, all I can do now is pray it's not that bad.

I wake up not sure last night even happened. I don't move, because I don't want to wake Chris yet, but I think about last night all over again. I was so surprised Chris wasn't angry when he came home.

All he said was, you looked nice tonight and he was impressed. He went in and took a shower and went to bed. I have no idea if the storm is going to come today or not. I know my mom will call about Lizzie soon, so I know I should get up. I try to slip out of the bed as softly as I can, so I don't wake him up.

I go out and make coffee and right when it's done my mom calls. She wants to keep Lizzie another night and I don't even say I have to ask Chris, I hurry and say okay. This way if for some reason he gets nuts today, she won't be here to see it.

Chris comes out right when I'm getting off the phone and I try not to let on I'm annoyed by it. I really wanted to drink my coffee in peace and not have to look at him. I get my coffee and go out in the living room and pick up my book, hoping I can ignore him by reading.

"Put the book down." He says after he grabs his own cup of coffee. I finish reading so I can end the paragraph and set the book down.

"Chris, I haven't even had my coffee yet, I don't feel like arguing this early in the morning" I sigh.

"I'm not planning to argue, if you talk to me, there will be no arguing." I know this isn't how it will go but I check my attitude in hopes I'm wrong.

"Okay, what would you like to talk about?" I ask.

"How much money did you win last night?" I knew he would eventually want the money.

Focusing on being careful with my coffee so he can't see I'm lying I say without falter, "Two hundred and fifty dollars, why?" Knowing he wants it.

"We have bills due, so if you're going to work and make money you need to help pay the bills." Oh, this is a different approach than what I was expecting.

"I wasn't working, and I have plans for that money." I say as confidently as I can.

"What plans do you think you have?" He snaps, and I know I need to tread lightly, like I thought it's all about the money and control. He could care less if I fucked another guy on that stage, if he got the money I made for it. It's so disheartening knowing I'm not at all cherished or loved.

"I was hoping you would be okay with me doing a little grocery shopping," I start then adding, "I will buy diet food for myself, but I'd like to stock up on some of Lizzie's favorite foods." I see him about to say no, so I add "Then I also wanted to be able to get you something for your birthday." Hoping he can't see once again I'm lying. His birthday is months away and I hope I'm gone by then.

He says instead, "Spend seventy-five on food and no more than seventy-five on me, I'll take the rest for bills." I can't believe he bought it, so I smile and say sure. I get up, so he knows the money is in my purse and go grab him his one hundred and give it to him. I hope now, he will have no reason to try to look for any other money. Thankfully like I thought, he wasn't smart enough to ask around. I know if he knew the real amount, he would have said something.

I ask if he wants some eggs and bacon and he says yes and surprises me and tells me to go ahead and make some for myself too. I'm so excited to eat something other than cream of wheat I find myself smiling. I turn my radio on, and make a fabulous breakfast with eggs, toast, bacon and I even have some pancake mix to make pancakes.

We eat a nice breakfast and while eating I tell him Lizzie is staying at my mom's again. He says, "That's good I have a surprise for you later." I am so surprised he isn't mad about last night that I find myself feeling excited about a surprise. "Make sure to fix your hair and makeup again, you looked nice last night." He says then adds "Be ready to leave by seven." He goes into our room, so I clear the dishes and right when I'm loading the dishwasher he says, "I'm going to work out with a friend, I'll be back later."

I don't even care where he is going but I say okay and get back to loading the dishes. I hid the leftover bacon from breakfast and one egg, and he didn't bother checking. I want to be sure I can eat a good lunch, but don't want to be obvious, so I ask, "Do you want me to have something ready for lunch, or should I only worry about dinner for you?" Keeping busy with the dishes I say, "I could make chicken salad sandwiches for you if you want."

"No, make the chicken legs and mashed potatoes for dinner. I'm eating lunch with my friend later and don't forget to be ready to leave by seven."

I nod, and start wiping the counters off and I say, "Have a good workout I'll see you in a bit."

After Chris leaves I turn my music up and dance all around the house happy. I run into the bedroom and find my hidden money and make sure it's still there. It is, and I sigh a sigh of relief. My biggest fear is him finding it.

I wait about an hour, and even though I just ate, I cook up the other egg, and toast some bread. I melt cheese on it and add the bacon and some mayo. I swear it is the best sandwich I've ever eaten. I go back in my bedroom and in an old purse I have hidden in my closet I pull out a snickers candy bar. I eat it incredibly slow to enjoy every bite. I'm learning to hide snacks throughout the house, and today I'm glad I did.

Feeling satisfied for the first time in a long time, I turn the tv on and watch a movie. After the movie I take a little nap, then get up and go shower so I can get ready. After I get out of the shower, I put the chicken in the oven and start fixing my hair and makeup. I can't help but wonder where he is taking me.

Chris gets home right when I start mashing the potatoes. It's perfect timing because the Chicken is done also. I decided to make some green beans too, and I'm hoping he doesn't get mad about it.

I dish his food and decide without asking to dish some for myself too. I set our plates down and go get some drinks for us, and he doesn't complain about the beans or my plate. He seems distracted and I am glad because I get to have another real meal tonight.

"So how was your day today?" I ask trying to make small talk.

"It was okay, I ran into an old friend from high school." He doesn't normally share these things with me, so I'm surprised he is.

"Why do you look like that's a bad thing? Is he a nice guy or someone you never wanted to run into?"

"He's cool, but I know if I hang out with him it will piss off Tim." He says referring to his one friend I can't stand. I think for a second knowing I'll need to answer carefully, because he knows I can't stand Tim.

"Does Tim have to know? Does this guy talk to him at all?" I ask.

"No, they don't talk at all, but if Tim finds out he's going to be beyond pissed."

"Then don't tell him, he shouldn't be able to decide who you hang out with."

Chris smiles and says, "You're right, fuck him. He won't ever know." He finishes eating and I clean up while he goes and takes a shower. For a change he talked to me tonight like I'm a real person. It felt nice to be able to eat the same dinner and talk like we are friends. Maybe something is changing with him after last night. Maybe seeing another guy thinking I'm hot did something.

We head out of the house around seven and he jumps on the highway. After driving for a long time, I ask him where we are going. He still won't tell me but has a cat ate the canary smile on his face. The farther away from home we get the more nervous I start to feel. I have never been on the highway this way that I can remember and if I have, never this far.

Finally, he gets off at an exit that I don't recognize, and we are in another city. It looks big, yet nice, not like in a bad part of town. I start to relax a little finally, thinking maybe he has found a new fun place to go hang out. I'm not great with surprises, so I'm about to ask again where we are when he pulls into a parking lot.

I look up at the sign and my heart sinks. It says "Glitter" then underneath "Girl. Girls. Girls. Bikini bar" He is bringing me to a strip club? Why would he think I want to come here? Does he think I'm into girls now and he wants that threesome he used to ask for all the time? My heart is pounding, and I try not to cry. I turn to him and say, "Why did you bring me here?"

"I thought you wanted a job to make some money? I figured this is about what you are worth, so I brought you here to work." I feel my jaw drop open. He honestly thinks I'm going to work here? Is he freaking crazy?

"Chris I'm not working here, there is no way I'm stripping for a living; besides I have nothing with me to wear."

"Yes, you do and yes you are." He pulls my bag out of the backseat, which I didn't see, and he puts it on my lap. It has the thongs and bras I bought in it. "Go inside and apply and you better get the job too. Don't mess this up, I'm telling you right now you need to start bringing in some money and this is how."

"Chris, I don't want to do this, I only did it the other night to show you I knew where you were going. I wanted you to see I could be just as hot as those girls you give our money to." I feel tears stinging my eyes, but I know if they start falling he will get more pissed, because my face will get puffy and red. "I wanted your attention and for you to think I could be that sexy, not that I wanted to do this for a job."

"Well you got my attention alright, and you made good money. It's time you contribute financially to our household, instead of sitting on your ass all day at home." I thought at dinner we were making headway, I should have known. He gets out of the car and walks around to my door and opens it. "Let's go, and don't think about making a scene." He grabs my arm and pulls me out of the car.

Chapter 19

      I walk with him inside the building and it is pretty much like the other strip club, dark, smoky and loud. I look around and try to see the lay out as we walk up to the bar area. A guy behind the bar asks if we want a drink, and Chris lets him know I'm here to apply for a dancing job. The guy looks me up and down and says, "Go upstairs and change, come down and dance and we will let you know if you have a job."

      I feel like such a piece of meat, but I head upstairs to change. I see a few girls up there, so I say hi and ask how long they have been dancing. I'm surprised when one of the girls says she is seventeen and been dancing since sixteen. I think how horrible and that grown men think it's okay to look at a child like that. I smile though and continue getting changed, not wanting to offend her.

      I'm changed and touching up my makeup when one of the girls came over to talk to me "Hi, you a new girl?" she asks, and I refrain from a smartass comment of, obviously.

I say instead, "Yes, have you worked here awhile?"

"Yeah three years. I'm what you would call a vet here, so don't fuck with my customers and I won't fuck with you." I think she has me taken as someone scared to stand up for myself.

I look her straight in the eye and say, "I'm not here to do anything other than make money, but If you think you scare me or you can intimidate me, we can take care of that right now." I step closer to stare her down.

She looks at me and then breaks into a huge grin "Girl I'm fucking with you, I'm Jasmine and I wanted to bust your balls a bit." She sticks her hand out to shake and adds, "You need a thick skin for this, I think you will be okay."

I relax a little and smile back grab her hand and say, "Okay, I'm Margo, but I'll go by Skye here." Then I ask her "Does anyone have any alcohol up here? I could use a shot or two, I'm kind of new to all this."

"Girl, we get our shit from customers, make them buy you a shot then pay upfront for a lap dance, you set the price not them. Men are cheap, so they will try to give you a buck a dance, don't let them get away with that shit."

"Oh my god, I have no idea what I'm doing. What do you mean lap dance and how do I get them to pay me?" I'm starting to feel overwhelmed.

"Hey, no biggie, shadow me when we go down and I'll show you. I like you, you have balls." I take that as a compliment and thank her and I'm about to follow her down when she says, "Where is your cover up?"

I have no idea what she means so I say, "I don't know what that is."

"Girl, you are green." She says then walks over to a pile of clothes on a chair and grabs a silky night robe. "Put this on to walk around down there, you don't want to give a free show, always make them want to pay to see you." She waits while I put it on and asks "Why are you here? What's your story? This doesn't seem like it's you."

I tie the robe close and say, "Honestly it's not, but my daughters father thinks I should and well, here we are now."

"Well doesn't he sound like a real nice guy, but more about that later. Follow me around and I'll show you the ropes."

"Oh, okay thank you." I say, and we head down stairs. "So, the guy at the bar said I need to dance and then he will let me know if I have a job, do I have to give him a lap dance?" I ask.

"Oh, God no" She laughs. There is a stage, he will have you dance up there and see how you do and unless you totally suck, you will be fine. We are very short on girls, so relax and you will be fine."

I'm so grateful for all her help. I start to relax, until we come around the corner and I see Chris there, getting a lap dance from one of the girls. I glare at him and he shrugs his shoulders in a, what was I supposed to say way. I ignore him and go up to the bartender. I have mixed feelings between thinking one day he will love and respect me, and anger knowing he won't.

"Hi, I'm ready." I say, and Jasmine says to him "Get this girl a shot, something strong to take the nerves away, on me." And she hands him some money.

"Jasmine thank you." I say then add "I owe you one." she smiles and heads over to the guy at the D.J booth.

A few seconds later she comes back and says, "I told him to play a good song, something to get the guys to have their eyes on you so JJ will see you're worth hiring."

"But you don't even know if I'm any good." I say then say, "And who's JJ?"

"You will be fine, and JJ is the bartender you were talking to. Nice of him to tell you his name huh? He's a prick but pretty harmless." She smiles, and I see her go ask a guy if he wants a lap dance.

A few seconds later I hear the D'J announcing me and the song, "I touch myself" comes on. I can't help but giggle as I get up on the stage. I think Jasmine and I might be good friends one day, because she knew exactly what I needed. I dance my ass off, and guys start crowding around the stage. I notice money being set down on the stage, and realize happily, I'm making money.

I can't tell if I'm excited about the money, the attention, or the possibility it could bring me freedom... but I start enjoying myself. The song ends, and I pick up the money, not wanting to count it. I fold it over and tuck it into my bra. I find my way back to the bar, and JJ says, "You're hired, if you want you can work the rest of the night."

I'm so excited, I bounce over to Chris out of breath and let him know I got the job and I can stay. I can't read him, so I have no idea if this is good or bad for me, but he says, "That's fine" and he starts drinking again and ignores me.

I run upstairs to change and secretly I want to count my money and see what I got already. I pull it out and I am shocked to see I already made fifty bucks. I only did one dance and I made that much money. I wonder how much I'll make by the end of the night. I hurry up and change, and I'm touching up my makeup when Jasmine comes back in.

"Girl you were hot, I knew I was right about you. Here use this too." She disappears over to her chair full of stuff and comes back with some garter belts. "This gives the guys a place to put the money so it's not on the stage floor. Every so often come up and get rid of the money so they don't think you are making too much. Buy a lock and use a locker."

"Thank you." I say incredibly grateful for all her help. To think, I always thought of strippers as bad people, yet she is one of the nicest people I have ever met. I go back down stairs and I'm immediately asked for a lap dance. I remember what Jasmine told me and I get the guy to buy a shot first, then I tell him it's ten dollars. I thought about saying five, but I figure there are a lot of guys in here maybe go high. It pays off, he puts ten dollars in the garter and I start dancing.

It's a little awkward at first, but I glance over, and I watch Jasmine and I see how she is doing it. I get into a groove and start dancing for a lot of guys. I stop having them buy me shots because frankly I don't like being drunk and I was getting a good buzz.

Every so often I get called to the stage and I put on a pretty good show there. I know Chris can see I'm making money, but I have no idea if he knows how much. I'm hoping I can figure out a way to hide some of it. If I can save some money, eventually I can get away from him and give Lizzie a better life.

I finish my last dance and I tell Chris I'll be back in a minute I'm going to change. I give Jasmine her robe and garter belt back, but she says, "Keep it, it looks great on you and I never wear it."

I say, "Thank you but I can give you some money for it."

She shakes her head back and forth then says, "No really keep it, I was most likely going to throw it in my closet and forget I ever had it."

I thank her again as I'm changing, trying to figure out where I can hide the money. If Chris thinks I'm lying, he will make me empty my pockets. I can't put it in my bag because I'm sure he will look in that too. If I tuck it in my bra and he decides he wants sex, I can't stop him, so he will find it there.

I try to hurry so he isn't mad, so while I'm thinking I start to count the money. I recount it twice thinking I counted wrong. Somehow tonight I made over five hundred dollars. I didn't even know that was possible. Holy cow, I don't think there is any way Chris would expect that. I took out half the money and I figure out where to put it. I shove it in my toothbrush holder and put all my makeup on it. I don't think he will look there for sure.

I head out and Chris is waiting for me, so I yell goodbye to anyone that is still there, and we head out to the car. I made sure to not make it look like I already counted the money, I kept it crumpled and messy. As soon as we get in the car he says, "Let me see the money." He doesn't even say I looked good or ask how I felt after doing it all night.

I grab my bag and start pulling all the money out, being sure to dump the whole bag on my lap then put all the makeup and my toothbrush holder back in. Him seeing me empty the bag should deter him from looking in it for more. I see him start counting the money, then he recounts it and I'm terrified he is expecting more.

He looks over at me and smiles a big smile and says, "Nice work." I feel I can relax a little and that I successfully pulled off hiding the rest of the money. I let him know they will call me with a schedule and I said I was available to work four days a week, if need be. "That's fine, just let me know ahead of time, so I don't make plans."

I'm confused by his response, so I ask, "What do you mean so you don't make plans?"

"What do you think I mean? So, I can drive you, are you really that dense?" He always finds a way somehow to fit in calling me a name. I feel myself instantly try to make myself smaller in my seat and not look in his direction.

I am too tired to argue, so I say, "I'm sorry I guess I am more tired than I realized." Hoping he will let it go.

"I'm not surprised, you're used to sitting on your ass all day watching TV doing nothing." Again, another dig at me, but I don't feed into it.

"I guess I should exercise a little more so I'm not so tired from now on." He looks over at me and does his smartass laugh. Thankfully the conversation bores him, and he turns the music up and I close my eyes and fall asleep.

The next week goes pretty well. Chris takes me to work, and on those days, we have my mom babysit Lizzie. I lie and tell her I found a waitressing job, and Chris is on call so if he needs to go fix something he can't have Lizzie. My mom doesn't mind, and everything is going very smooth.

I have been able to stash away extra money every night I work. I make sure to give Chris at least two hundred and eighty dollars a night and he seems to be satisfied with that. Anything over that I hide away, in my secret hiding place.

Tonight, though when I get to work I get pulled aside by JJ and he says my boyfriend can't be there. There is a rule about boyfriends and spouses, and I'm not sure how Chris will take this. I walk over to where he is sitting, and I tell him what JJ has said. He gets up and goes over to the bar. I see him having a conversation with JJ and he comes back and says, "Next time you work you can drive yourself." He goes back to his spot in the corner and sits down.

I thought for sure when we left he would tell me I can't go back, and I was kind of hoping he would. On one hand I love the money I have been stashing away, but on the other hand I miss Lizzie so much it hurts.

"Are you mad they won't let you be there?" I ask then add "What did he say to you?"

"He said they have had problems with boyfriends before starting fights. I told him I'm not like that I don't care, but he said it's the rule and if you want a job here, I can't come."

"Well, the nice thing about that is Lizzie can stay home then." I say feeling better that I won't be away from her so much.

"No, she can't." he says then adds, "I'm not babysitting every night, so you can go out and put your tits in a bunch of guys faces. I'm not sitting home by myself."

"Chris, that's rude, and you are the reason I am coming here. I can quit, I don't even like doing it. Besides you wouldn't be babysitting, you would be spending time with your daughter."

"No, she keeps going to your moms and that's enough, this conversation is done." he says, and I know better than to continue it any further.

One good thing about him driving me every night I work is, by the time we drive the forty-five minutes home he is too tired to want sex. I am very thankful, because I swear I never want him to touch me again. I haven't had to try to make up excuses to not have sex, he has pretty much passed out by the time I get out of the shower every night. I am nervous that will change now.

I start driving myself to work the next day. It is so nice, and I feel freer than I have in a very long time. I turn the radio up super loud and drive a little faster than I should. I feel like I did when I was a teenager and I had no real problems.

Work is thankfully busy tonight and I make fantastic money. I can hide over three hundred dollars and I'll still be able to give Chris his two hundred and eighty. I get home and I'm surprised to see he has a friend over. I've never met this guy, so I assume it's the guy his friend Tim doesn't like.

"Hi I'm Margo." I say when I come in to be polite.

Chris says, "He knows, he doesn't care. Go shower you stink like a bar." I feel my face turn red and I head into the bedroom to get a change of clothes feeling so embarrassed. I don't know why Chris always needs to make me feel like I'm gross. It is really starting to make me feel ugly and worthless.

I hear him say, "She always needs attention, she's so needy. That's the one thing I miss about Sheri. She wasn't like that." What a jerk. Why does he need to talk about his ex with this guy? I would never make someone feel the way Chris makes me feel, it isn't right.

I get into the shower wanting to relax and let my thoughts wonder. About fifteen minutes later I hear Chris come in and I say, "Chris I'm almost done I'll be out in a second."

"I didn't ask you what you are doing." He is so rude to just walk in here, but I learned not to lock the door. He informed me the one time I did that if I ever lock the door he will kick it in. He also let me know he will come in whenever he wants, even if I'm using the bathroom.

Chris yanks the sliding door open, and I see he is standing there with his pants pulled down with an erection. I don't have the energy to deal with this tonight, I try to think of something to say but before I can, he says "Get on your knees and suck it."

"Chris, there's no way I'm doing that, and I don't want to have sex, I'm not feeling well." I say hoping for once he will not force me to.

"I just told you what to do, what makes you think you can argue?" Before I have time to answer he grabs my hair and pulls my head towards his erection. There is no way I'm doing what he wants me to do. I make up my mind and I don't care if he kills me, if he sticks that thing in my mouth, I will bite it off.

"I'm not doing it Chris I swear to God I'm not."

He thinks he clever and starts rubbing my face all over it and I feel so sick to my stomach I fear I might throw up on him. I keep my jaw clenched, unless he breaks my teeth I'm not doing this.

After a minute I think he realizes he isn't going to get me to do it. I think I'm in the clear when he pulls my head away, but instead he moves my head away from him and pulls my hips in all in one swift movement. I have no time to try to get away before he is ramming his way into me, bent over like a dog.

I stand there numb, tears pouring down my face knowing if I don't get away from him this will happen for the rest of my life. He is saying mean things to me while he is pounding away at me like, I'm used up, and I'm a fat cow and I should be grateful he still even wants to fuck me. I tune him out and wait for him to finish.

Once he is done abusing me, he pulls his pants up and leaves me there crying. I hurry up and try to rinse him off me and quickly get dressed. I don't want him thinking he can come back and do it again.

I walk out of the bathroom and go to my bedroom and he is laying in the bed smirking. I'm so pissed, and so violated I finally don't care what he does to me. That's it, I am taking back my power to say no, and be heard.

I say, "I want you to know I hate you. I hate everything about you. That was rape. When a girl says no she means no, and you didn't care, you never care, you force yourself into me even when I say no."

I am grabbing my pillow to go sleep on the couch and he laughs, a shitty mean laugh, and says, "Prove it. Try to prove to someone you didn't want it. Good luck with that sweetheart. You are a fat ugly bitch, and no one will believe you."

"I don't care if anyone believes me, I know the truth and you are a pig. I can't stay here in this house with you, I can't stand you. I wish you were dead." I yell at him and I'm starting to feel crazy. I feel like at any moment I will lose my mind here. I feel he just for the last time pushed me over the edge.

"Leave, I don't care. I should throw your ass out now, and let you go live on the streets. You will never see Lizzie again and I will be sure they lock you up in a mental hospital."

He gets up and starts walking towards me. I turn to leave the room and he snatches my arm and yanks me backwards, so I am facing him.

"Do it. I.Dare.You. I want you to try to leave. I swear to you right now if you do, I will make the rest of your life hell. I will ruin any chance you have at seeing Lizzie and any chance you think you might have with any other guy. I have your notes proving you're unstable so please Margo. Do. It." He has such venom in his voice, I almost want to ask why. But I don't, I don't really care to know why he hates me so much.

He lets go of my arm and walks back over to the bed and lays down. I walk out to the living room sobbing. I know if I ever try to leave him, he will make good on his promises to ruin my life.

I toss and turn all night, and I am disgusted with my own thoughts. I keep pondering over and over, if there was a way I can kill him and not end up in prison. I think out elaborate plans and ways to make it look like an accident. I think about running away with Lizzie and hiding, changing our names and heading to Mexico, or Canada.

I finally find myself praying to a God I have long since stopped talking to. I have not had the best faith in God over the last few years, but I am praying for help. I was always told when you needed him the most, he could hear you, tonight I pray that is true. I know I could never actually take someone's life. I know I could never do that to Lizzie, But I need help and I have no one to turn to, so I decide to pray.

Chapter 20

The next morning, I wake up and pretend like nothing happened. I have a few days off, so I am going to pick Lizzie up from my mom. I miss her so much it hurts when she is gone, but I don't want her seeing the things her dad does.

I feel so confused on what is the best thing to do with her. I know she gets taken care of well from my parents, but I want her with me. She's my child, my whole world, and I want her home. I want to protect her from the violence and staying with my parents does that.

Chris doesn't make any problems for me this morning. He knows he won. He knows I won't risk not having Lizzie, so he doesn't even say a word to me about it. I plan to spend as much time as I can get away with, at my parents today.

Lizzie runs up to me and buries her head in my chest. I feel so much love for her radiating through my heart, I start crying as I'm hugging her. I can't stop the tears from pouring down my cheeks. My mom comes out and sees me crying and says, "Margo, is something wrong?"

I don't want to give anything away, so I keep my head bent down hugging Lizzie.

"No, not really I just miss her so much and I feel I'm missing so much time with her."

I finally pick her up and still hugging her carry her into the living room and hold her while I sit down. My mom tells me everything they have been doing, and how much fun Lizzie has had. They painted rocks, and baked cookies and made other fun crafts. It's so wonderful to see all the great stuff she gets to do while being here.

My mom and I are having a nice time, and enjoying our visit when Brittany comes in. I guess I wasn't in the mood to deal with her, so I tried ignoring her. I should have known that doesn't sit well with her. She always needs to be the center of attention no matter what.

"So, look who the cat dragged in. Decided to finally be a mom again?" she says.

"Brittany don't start your shit, I'm not in the mood." I say as she comes in and plants herself in a chair staring at me.

"Truth hurts? We didn't have Lizzie you did and that asshole boyfriend of yours, yet you ditch her on mom all the time."

My mom says in a warning tone "Brittany stop."

"Brittany I'm working, mom offered to help until I can get on a day shift, but you know nothing about real work." I say back.

"I would, but I can't get to auditions because mom is too busy being a mom again to your kid." Ah ha, this is the problem, Lizzie is taking people's attention away from her.

"Well last I looked you had a car and could drive yourself." I say.

"Bitch you know I'm not eighteen and need a parent to go, but you keep ditching your kid here. You probably don't even have a job. I bet all you do is follow that loser boyfriend around to make sure he isn't screwing other girls." She is being incredibly mean, and I feel this is out of nowhere, even for her.

"Brittany." My mom cuts in, "That's enough stop talking like that and stop saying things that aren't true."

"Aren't true? Which part? Her ditching her kid on you guys or her loser boyfriend trying to screw everyone?"

"Brittany that's it, go to your room. You are grounded and not doing anything for the rest of the month." My mom yells at her.

She gets up and I think she is about to listen to my mom and go to her room when she turns to me and says, "I bet it kills you that your boyfriend always wanted to fuck me. Why don't you ask him about the night he tried to make me do it?"

"What the fuck are you talking about?" I ask then add, "You think every guy on the planet wants you and when they don't you make up stupid stories to make them look bad." By now I'm making my way closer to her, all I want to do is put my fist through her face.

"No, your boyfriend tried to force me to have sex and the only thing that stopped him was me saying I would bite his dick off." She is so close, I lunge at her.

I tackle her by the waste and body slam her onto the ground as I say, "You're nothing but a fucking liar. You're a little slut that thinks all guys should want you. My guy didn't, so now you have to make up lies."

"I'm not lying, he wanted to fuck me, and I kept saying you are my sister and pregnant and he kept trying to force his tongue down my throat. I tried to fight him off, but he was too strong."

I have her pinned down and I hear her enough to stop myself from hitting her for a second and ask, "I was pregnant?" I'm starting to put it together as to when. "When was this? Where did this happen?"

"The night he took me to the mall, he got us beer and I was getting drunk, and he tried it that night." She is crying now, and I'm still pissed, but more at myself. "He took me to some deserted area off the main road and tried to fuck me."

Oh my god, that's where he forced himself on me in the dirt and I thought it was out of passion. I remember the spot very clearly. I had a terrible feeling that something happened that night, but I brushed it off. My gut had told me all along those two going to the mall together was a bad idea.

I get up off her and I'm trying to wrap my head around it all when I hear my mom say, "You were only fifteen, he was twenty or twenty-one, we need to press charges."

At this I start to panic... he has the notes. "Wait a second, that's Lizzie's father, think what this will do to her."

"I am not right now thinking about that. I am thinking about my own child and how I allowed this man in my home." My mom is pissed.

"Mom, we don't even know if she is telling the truth, she lies about everything." I say, I am so surprised by this all I can only think to defend him.

"I'm not lying, ask him. Better yet, bring him here and ask him in front of me. You will see he did it." Brittany is adamant that I confront Chris here.

Instead, I pick up the phone and call him. I think part of me is terrified to see him face to face and ask these questions. I think deep down I know that if I do, he could turn his anger on me.

He answers, "Hello?"

"Chris it's me, I'm at my mom's house and something is happening." I say.

"What's wrong? Is Lizzie okay?" he says, and I can hear real concern in his voice.

"She's fine, Chris, Brittany is saying you tried to force her to have sex with you." I blurt it out.

There is silence for a second then he laughs and says, "Is she now? Well she's lying, she wanted to fool around, and I told her no. My guess is her pride is hurt and she is mad." I knew she was lying.

"Okay, well she is insisting you come here and confront her face to face. Will you come?"

"No, I won't" he says then adds, "Tell that little girl I have a real job, and I'm not risking it, so she can have attention."

"Chris, I need to know, did this happen? Did you try to have sex with her?"

"I told you once no." I can hear his tone changing "Get Lizzie and come home now. You are done going there."

"Chris, I don't want to." I know if I go home it could get bad. "I need to stay and figure this out."

"Get Lizzie and come home, or I swear to god I am taking those notes you wrote to the police station and coming to get her." Crap. I knew he would get mad, but now I need to figure out how to leave, and fast.

"Okay, I'll be home soon." I say and hang up the phone. I turn towards my mom and say, "Chris said she is full of shit, she was the one that tried to do stuff with him and he told her no, now she's mad." I try to sound confident when I say it, and not at all like I doubt him. I need to get out of here and hurry home before he uses those notes.

"I need to go, this is bullshit, and I'm not feeding into her drama." I go get Lizzie and start heading out.

"Margo, we need to talk about this." My mom says.

"No, we don't. Maybe you need to get her," I point to Brittany "some mental help."

I hurry up and get out the door and slam it closed. I have no idea what to think. In my head I'm so torn, between wanting to believe my sister and wanting to believe Chris for Lizzie's sake. On one hand, Brittany is a drama starter, she likes to have attention all the time. I know for a fact she can twist things to make herself look good and her target terrible. I also know, for a fact, Chris takes what sex he wants and thinks it's okay.

I always thought he assumes I owe him. I'm his girlfriend, we live together so I owe him sex whenever he wants it. Would he really force another girl too? Could he be that vicious? Did I put my sister in a terrible situation and not even know it?

All I can do is see what he says. The more I think about it, the more I realize I should have confronted him face to face to see his reaction. I gave him time to compose himself and frankly I'll probably never know now.

When I get home, Chris is sitting on the couch reading a magazine. I get Lizzie some toys to play with and I sit on the other side of the couch to talk. Before I can say anything, he says "Brittany is a liar, and the fact you even thought she was telling the truth pisses me off." Well, I guess we are getting right into it.

"You have to understand, it sounds pretty real. I remember that night, I didn't want you going with her. I begged you to stay home, yet you insisted on going. Now, no one will believe you so either way, my family will take her side." I say.

"Well fuck them, we don't need them for anything and they don't need to have anything to do with Lizzie. Your whole family is nuts, just like you."

"That was mean." I say, "Why do you have to always call me names?"

"It's true, your whole family is nutty. I should take Lizzie and run and keep her as far away from you all as I can." Once again, I feel that deep fear he will make good on his words. Right now, I desperately need to convince him I believe him. I can't risk having him take her from me. I also know I'll search day and night to find those notes. If I can ever find them, I can finally leave him.

"I never said I believed her, I said my family will. I have no idea what happened that night so why don't you tell me." I am pretty sure anything he says will make her look like a liar. I honestly don't care, I want him to think I care about his side of it, but I don't.

"That little slut asked if I'd buy her some beer. I said fine, so I got her some and she was getting drunk. She then tried to grab my cock and I told her don't, then she shoved her hand down my pants before I could stop her." I find this incredibly hard to believe, I know his strength and I know hers. She is weaker than I am, and there is no way she could force anything on him. I sit there though and listen to him lie.

"She climbed over onto my lap and was trying to shove her tongue down my throat. I lifted her off me and told her I was taking her home. That's it. She's pissed I said no, that's all this is." He sits there with his eyes boring into me looking for any doubt.

"Fine, whatever. I have no idea what I'm supposed to do now about my family." Is all I say.

"Screw them, we don't need their shit."

"Chris, they watch Lizzie, so I can go to work, so does this mean I have to quit?" Part of me is praying he says yes.

"No, I'll adjust my night on call hours around your schedule, and Lizzie can hang out with me."

Wow, this is a change. He's willing to watch her, I'm kind of shocked. I leave the conversation at that and get up to go do some laundry. This gives me time to think about everything. I honestly think my sister is telling the truth. There is no way I can say anything, or I risk losing Lizzie. I'm forced to make the decision to no matter what back Chris up, and not risk losing my daughter. Once again, I feel my heart completely breaking.

I feel awful my sister had to go through that. I feel guilty that somehow, I couldn't protect her. Right now, though, I can barely keep my own head above water, and doing that means keeping my daughters above water. I have no choice but to play along with Chris and pretend to believe him.

The next few days nothing else is said about it. My mom tries to call and leaves messages on my answering machine, but Chris said I'm not allowed to call her back. I feel more isolated than ever, yet there is nothing I can do about it.

I go back to work and even though my heart isn't in it, I make enough money to not piss Chris off. Slowly though throughout the week I make less and less, in fact I haven't made any extra money over "Chris's take". Tonight, I'm not feeling well, so I make very little money. I don't even realize exactly how little until I leave and there's nothing I can do about it.

I didn't expect the reaction I get from Chris when I only hand him ninety dollars the next afternoon. He starts with nasty shitty comments about being too ugly to make money, then moves into being too fat and gross. By that evening and about six beers later he turns nasty. Thankfully Lizzie is already in bed for the night.

"What are you doing snorting coke up your nose?" he says then "Or are you out fucking someone and not bothering to dance anymore?"

"Chris calm down, I haven't felt well, and it's been slow at work. I think if I was doing coke, you would be able to tell."

"Well you have lost more weight and that's the first sign of doing coke." He obviously forgot hours ago he was calling me fat and gross.

"I've lost weight because you have me on a ridiculous diet and I am physically active most nights dancing." I can't believe his way of thinking.

"Most nights? What is that supposed to mean? What are you doing on the nights you aren't dancing?" he is starting to move closer. "You slipped up honey, I just caught your ass in a huge lie." he says. "So, who are you fucking? It sure isn't me."

"Stop it, I'm talking about the nights I'm here at home with you and Lizzie, I don't dance the nights I'm at home. It's been slow, but the girls say that happens occasionally." I can't believe he is acting like this.

"Right, you think somehow you are paying me back for what your sister said? I will not be with a slut that does coke." I try to back away from him, but he closes in on me quicker than I can get away.

He gets his hands on my sleeve of my coat and whips me to the ground. The next thing I feel is his boot hitting me in the side. He has never kicked me before, so it isn't something I'm expecting. His boots are work boots, they have steel tips in them and I am now gasping for air.

I ball myself up getting prepared for another kick, trying to protect my head, when the door buzzer goes off. I have no idea who is here, but I'm so grateful because he stops. Chris walks over to the window and looks out and says, "My friend is here, we are going out, you can lay there on the floor like the dog you are and think about what you have done."

He leaves, and for the first time in a long time he deadbolts me in. I lay on the floor for what feels like forever crying. I finally get up and go check to be sure Lizzie is still asleep. I stand by her crib, crying and praying. I need a way out. I can't raise my daughter in a home where one day she will see that and think it's okay. I pull her out of her bed and hold her, just standing there rocking her back and forth. I need to figure a way out. I kiss her and put her back to bed, thankful she could sleep through an earthquake.

My ribs hurt, I have trouble bending and breathing in a full breath. I'm guessing they are bruised, but I don't want to look and see. All I want to do is search the house from top to bottom for those damn notes.

I start in my bedroom, thinking for sure they would be in there somewhere. I'm careful to not misplace anything or rumple his clothes. I search every space I can think of in his dresser and on it. I move into his closet next being very careful looking through his boxes of stuff he has still packed.

Nothing. I find nothing.

I move into the hallway and start searching one closet at a time. I am careful to listen for the door to be unlocked, ready with an excuse. There is no way I can let him know what I'm looking for, so I am being very thorough yet careful.

The next room is the bathroom, it's small and I don't expect it to be in there, but I will still look. I am sore by now, but I need to keep looking. I hear the door buzzer, and I jump about a mile. I look out the window and I see Chris's friend Tim. I know he doesn't want Tim knowing he is hanging out with Trevor. I also know I can't tell him he has locked me in either.

I open the window and yell down "Hey Tim, how's it going? Chris isn't here."

"Oh, where is he?" He yells back, and I want to say none of your business but instead I say, "He went to his moms for a bit and still isn't home."

"Interesting, I drove by there already and he isn't there. Are you sure? Is he hanging out with anyone else?"

Wow, he's incredibly rude and honestly a bit disturbed to think he can dictate who Chris hangs out with but I say, "As far as I know they were going to dinner and I'm not sure what else, but I can tell him to call you when he gets back."

"Fine, let him know I've been looking for him and I need to talk to him."

"Okay, I will. Have a good night." I say and close the window.

I can't help but wonder what the heck that was all about. Tim was acting weird and seemed pissed off at Chris for something. I put my search on hold, my side is hurting badly, and I don't know if Chris will be home soon. I'd rather not have him catch me looking through anything.

I cut up an apple and get some peanut butter to dip it in and just start a movie on the VCR when I hear him unlocking the door. There is no way to hide the food and I'm hoping it being somewhat healthy he won't say anything.

I'm surprised when he walks in with Trevor. I'm in a t-shirt and underwear, under a blanket, but I have no pants on. I was doing laundry earlier and my stuff is still in the dryer in the laundry room down the hall. Being dead bolted in, I had no way to go get it out once he left.

"Oh, hi, I didn't know you guys were going to come hang out here." I say and try to keep my tone surprised yet not as if I'm hiding anything. I have nothing to hide except my half naked ass, but the way Chris is acting lately who knows what he will think.

"We came to lift weights a bit, feel free to watch." Chris says, he sounds a bit off, but I assume he has been drinking more.

"Well I need to tell you something." I say and motion for him to come here with my finger. He looks a little surprised and interested at the same time. I realize too late he thinks I'm flirting with him. He gets too close for my liking and half lays across me to put his ear by my mouth.

"I don't have pants on, I'm in only my underwear." I whisper in his ear.

He smirks and reaches under my blanket and starts trying to stick his fingers in down there, while his friend is right there across the room.

I push his hand away and try to not make my face look as disgusted as I feel, and I say "Um, your friend is here." He isn't getting it "I can't get up or go anywhere because I have no pants on." I see the lightbulb finally go off in his head. He seems different, not drunk and if I didn't know better on something.

"Oh, okay, wrap the blanket around yourself and go get pants on." I'm surprised he is being nice about it, so I quickly get up and do that.

I come out a few seconds later and I hear the door buzzer again. "Chris, I forgot to tell you Tim stopped by looking for you."

Chris turns around and yells at me, "Why the fuck didn't you tell me sooner? What the fuck did you say to him?"

"Nothing. I told him you went to your moms and you guys went out to dinner. You just got here, and I needed to go get dressed."

"Bull shit, why is he back here then? What did you tell him? Are you trying to fuck me over?" I have no idea what he is talking about and I have no idea why it matters.

"That's all I said I swear, why? Why is he so mad?"

"What do you mean mad? Why would he be mad? What the fuck did you say?" I'm surprised he's talking to me like this in front of Trevor. Usually he keeps his calm in front of other people.

"I told you what I said, I don't understand what the problem is? I take it Tim doesn't like Trevor? Who cares? He isn't your boss or parent."

"Just forget it" he says and goes over to the window and opens it like I did earlier.

"Hey, Tim what's up?" He sounds like a completely different person talking to Tim. Scared. He is kissing his butt which surprises me.

"Who are you out with tonight?" Tim has a lot of balls acting like that.

"I went to my mom's" Chris says.

"Bullshit do you think I'm stupid? Tell Trevor to come out." Tim yells up

"Dude, Trevor isn't here."

"Yes, he is, that's his car, are you doing Roids?" He must point to the right car because Chris swears under his breath. I don't know what that other part means. Who is Roids? Is that some girl they know?

"Okay, he's here, and no it's not what you think."

"Chris, you better get your ass down here and explain."

Chris turns from the window glaring at me. "So much for not saying anything, I swear to god, if I find out you did you are dead."

"I didn't I swear." I say as he goes outside to talk to Tim.

Chris comes back in about a half hour later and tells Trevor to go ahead and leave. "I told him you stopped by only to let me know you were leaving town and won't be around."

"Alright, thanks and I think we need to cool hanging out for a bit."

"Yeah, I agree, we can meet up in a few weeks and square up when this blows over."

Trevor leaves, and Chris tells me he's leaving to go meet up with Tim. I have no idea what all of that is about, but I hope this was the end of it. Tim is as unstable and scary as Chris and twice his size.

I am awakened by Chris slamming our bedroom door into the wall, it takes a second for me to even know if it's day or night still. I quickly realize it's still dark out so nighttime. I once again think at first, it's because he is drunk, but see it's because he is pissed off. I look over at the clock and realize he has been gone for hours, it's now four thirty in the morning.

He is leaning over me fists clenched and he snatches the blankets off me. "Why the fuck did you tell Tim I was out with Trevor?"

I instantly have my guard up scared. "I didn't. I don't know what he said to you, but I swear I didn't say anything. I swear."

"Bullshit, I know you did, he tried to cover for you, but I know you told him."

I sit up trying to get up off the bed when he pushes me back down and sits on top of me pinning me in place.

"I fucking told you to never say anything about Trevor to anyone, how else did Tim know his car?"

"I don't know but I swear to you on Lizzie's life I didn't say anything." I barely get the sentence out when he smacks me across the face.

"You little fucking liar. Do you think for one second, I can believe a whore like you? Do you want me to go to jail? Bitch if I do, I promise you will be locked up in a mental ward for sure."

I pull my hand up to my cheek which is hurting and throbbing. "Jail?" Then I hear myself say, "Chris, that hurt, you didn't have to hit me as hard as you can."

He starts laughing and says, "Oh sweetheart that wasn't as hard as I can, this is…" and bam, before I could get out of the way he hit me so hard everything goes black.

Chapter 21

I have no idea how long I was out. I am trying to sit up and I realize I can't see out of my right eye. I also can't seem to sit up and I feel like my head weighs a hundred pounds. Chris is standing over me crying saying he's sorry, but I can't remember why.

It starts coming back to me and I feel panicked. What if he does it again? I don't know if I'd survive it. I find strength to get up off the bed and I just make it to the bathroom when I start vomiting. I'm so dizzy I can hardly keep my head over the toilet bowl. I'm crying and throwing up and wishing to die. The thought hits me like a ton of bricks that once again I would rather be dead, than live like this. It's such a sad heartbreaking thought for any mom to have, but I constantly have this thought that death would be better than this.

Only minutes pass, but it feels like hours. My head is hurting, my face is hurting, and I can't seem to stop throwing up. As I'm bent over the toilet I realize this is my fate. If I stay with this man, I will forever live like this. I realize also that as bad as this night is, I know it will get worse. He will kill me, or I will kill him. I know I can't do this anymore.

I finally stop throwing up and I get up to go back into the bedroom to lay down. Out of habit I guess, I look at myself in the mirror and instantly wish I hadn't. My face on the left side from the first hit, is black and blue. The right side, wasn't something I ever expected to see of my own reflection. Not only is it black and blue with a gross purple color, my eye is completely closed shut. This would explain why I can't see. I forced my eye open and let out a cry. Where my eye should have been white, was completely red. I can't keep my eye open long, but I can still see from it, I guess that is a plus.

I feel myself about to get sick again and fall back onto the floor in front of the toilet thankfully again in time. The whole time Chris is standing there, and I can hear him saying things like, he's so sorry and he wouldn't act that way if he didn't love me. If only I would listen to him like he's been saying, or I make him so angry and if he didn't love me he wouldn't care. I try to block him out, but when I get back in bed he is right there.

"Please talk to me," he is saying "Margo I'm sorry talk to me, please... I promise It will never happen again."

"Chris, I can't talk, my jaw hurts, my head hurts, and I want to go to sleep."

"No, you shouldn't sleep you might have a concussion." He scares me by saying that.

"Maybe I should go to the hospital, aren't those dangerous?" I try to get up, but he stops me.

"No. I'll watch you and take care of you, we don't have to go to the hospital."

"Chris, I think I should go get looked at. My jaw is hurting badly and so is my head, I've never felt like this before." I want to go to the hospital, praying they will keep me and I can figure out a plan to leave him.

"We can't, Lizzie is asleep and who would watch her? It's not good to take her to the hospital this late. If you feel bad still in the morning I will take you then." He makes sense. I don't want to drag her out of bed this late and honestly, I just want to sleep now.

"Okay, I need to rest a second." I close my eyes and try not to replay in my mind what happened.

I wake up screaming sometime in the middle of the night. I can't tell if it was all a dream or if it truly happened at first. Chris wakes up and pulls me close to him. I snuggle into him and start to feel cozy and safe, when he says, "I'm so sorry Margo." I tense up realizing I shouldn't ever feel safe in his arms. It was not a dream.

I try to sleep, but with his arms around me I feel I need to be alert. He could finish me off if he wanted to and tell people anything. No one would know the truth, because I hide it from everyone. No one knows what he does to me and if he kills me, no one would know to speak up about it.

I sleep terribly, and, in the morning, I feel like my head is going to split in half. When I look in the bathroom mirror again, my face looks worse than I thought. I start to cry and once again feel like I may throw up. I make it to the toilet, but nothing comes up. I know I need to go ask Chris to take me to the hospital, but I'm scared to do it.

When I walk into the living room, I see he already has Lizzie up and is feeding her. I take this as a good sign that he wants to go ahead and get me checked out.

"After she is done eating are we going to head to the hospital?" I ask, realizing I sound drunk. My jaw hurts so bad and my cheeks are so swollen I can't talk right. Lizzie looks at me like I grew a second head and it dawns on me she doesn't recognize me.

Chris interrupts my thoughts saying "No, I think you are fine now. I don't think it's necessary to go to the hospital now."

"Chris I'm not okay, my jaw hurts so bad I can barely use it, my head feels like it's going to split open and I can't talk right." I try to reason with him.

"Put ice on it and take some Tylenol. I don't want to drag Lizzie to the hospital and if we go, they will ask questions and I don't want to deal with that."

"I'll tell them I fell. I don't have to say what happened, but I think I should go get looked at."

"I fucking said no." he is raising his voice and I flinch "Don't act like I do this all the time, stop acting scared." He yells at me. I see him getting red in the face and his vein in his forehead is starting to really stand out. He starts clenching his jaw and I can see he is working up to exploding.

I know I have only about a minute to squash this and keep him from coming at me, so I pick up Lizzie. I pray he won't attack me with her in my arms. "Okay, I guess if you think it's best not to go then I can try to take it easy here." I say and go sit down with Lizzie on my lap.

I do my best to play with her and pretend I'm not in a lot of pain. He eventually stops staring at me and goes in the kitchen to clean up from their breakfast. He surprises me and comes out with some toast and coffee for me. I don't want anything to eat, but I smile the best I can and say, "Thank you, I appreciate that."

"Obviously you can't work for a little bit, tell them the car broke so maybe you won't lose your job." I haven't even thought about that, but I realize he is right. I need to call because I was supposed to go in tomorrow tonight.

"Okay, I'll call a bit later, I don't think they are even open right now."

"And you need to stay inside. I'll get food when it runs low, but people can't be seeing you like this or they will assume it was me." It takes everything in me not to say, well…

"Okay, but does that mean I can't take Lizzie for walks?"

"Are you really that fucking stupid? What did I just say?"

"You said I can't go to the grocery store." I reply hoping that was right.

"No, you apparently have no brains or can't hear, I said, you need to stay inside. That means, STAY THE FUCK IN THE APARTMENT." he is shouting again.

"Alright, don't yell. I have a terrible headache, so I can't think right now, I'm not trying to be difficult or upset you." I say, keeping my tone apologetic, knowing if I blame myself he should calm down.

"Just stay inside and don't answer the phone, you sound like shit." I want to say yes, because of what you did to me, but I keep my mouth shut. There are so many things I want to say to him, like if he puts his hands on me one more time I will kill him. I truly feel it in my heart I might finally kill him.

I know if I did I would end up in prison, but he wouldn't hurt me ever again. I don't want my daughter raised by anyone else, but it wouldn't be him. If I killed him, he could never take her away from me. I know none of this is rational, but at this point, I honestly don't feel I have other choices. It's me or him.

Chris finally leaves, thankfully he still feels he should go do his own thing. My head and body hurt, my ribs still hurt from him kicking me, but I am determined to look for those notes. I will from this point forward utilize any alone time I have to look. I realize quickly though I'll have to wait another day, I can't take the pain.

Today I resume looking, I tear apart my entire kitchen. I look in the last two closets and I come up short. I feel so defeated I start to cry. There must be a place I'm missing. I try to think, if I were hiding something where would I hide it. I feel I have looked in every place I would stick something.

I give up the search and make Lizzie Lunch, I want to nap with her and try to rest. I am so exhausted I fall asleep as soon as we lay down. I wake up to the phone ringing and I hear the answering machine pick up and it's my mom.

"Margo, we need to talk. Please call me or dad back. We need to talk to you and figure this all out." I wait for her to hang up, and I hit the delete button.

I can't talk to my parents right now. I know If I get on the phone with them, I will start to cry, and they will know something is wrong. I need to find those notes, before I can deal with them. I need that threat over my head gone, his power to take my daughter needs to be gone. Once that happens, then I will ask for help. I pray I can stay alive, or I don't kill him before I find them.

I slowly start to heal. The color on my face is slightly better, my bad eye has gone down and in the last few weeks I have been able to keep Chris calm. My biggest fear is him doing that again and permanently messing my face up. I don't let my brain wander too far in the direction of how he could have killed me. It's too hard to think about that fact.

I have used the excuse I'm afraid he will roll over and accidentally elbow me in the face, to sleep on the couch. He doesn't create an issue over it because, I made sure to say I know he would feel awful if it happened. I made it seem like I was looking out for him and his feelings.

Every night when he goes to bed, I wait to hear him start to snore. I get up and grab the biggest kitchen knife we have, and I stuff it in between the couch cushions. I don't know if I could ever actually use it, but if he tries to hurt me again, I will have it. I always quickly hide it in the morning so there is no chance Lizzie can find it, but also so Chris can't. I think if he did, I have a good excuse prepared, that I'm afraid of burglars, but I don't want to risk it.

I am eating lunch, Lizzie is in bed and the phone rings. I finally decide to answer it, thinking it is my mom again. "Hello?" I say.

"Hi, is Margo there?" it's a man's voice. It sounds familiar, but I can't place it.

"Um, this is." I say sounding weary.

"Hey, how are you? It's Jason, I work with you."

It took me a second, before I realize who it was "Oh, hi, how are you?"

"I'm good, I'm actually filling in doing the schedule for the next few weeks and wanted to know if you would be coming back?" Just then Chris walks in, so I held up my finger for him to hang on.

"Jason can you hold on for a second?" I put my hand over the mouthpiece of the phone and say to Chris, "It's my work, they want me to come back this week or I might not have a job, what should I say?"

He comes closer and looks at my face, "You can put heavy makeup on and probably cover this up, tell him you can come back."

"Jason, I'm sorry about that, and yes, I'll be able to come back this week."

"Okay great I'll put you down Monday, Tuesday, Thursday Friday and Saturday."

"Okay that will be great thank you." I hang up the phone and tell Chris the days I'll be working.

"Good, it's about time you stop sitting around here moping and feeling sorry for yourself." I can't even comprehend him saying that. The reason I don't leave is because he won't let me out of the house. I don't respond though, I feel he is looking for a reason to fight with me.

I switch the subject and let him know I'll have dinner ready by six and he says fine and that Trevor will be here for dinner. I try not to look surprised, but I thought he wasn't hanging out with him. I don't say anything, but I feel there is something shady about them hanging out and Tim not liking it.

Trevor gets here right when Dinner is ready, so it is perfect timing for all the food to still be hot. I dish up Chris's plate and offer to dish Trevor's too. After I set his down I go and dish my own and Chris says, "Hey moose, are you really going to eat all of that?"

I look at my plate, I have one chicken leg on it a scoop of mashed potatoes and a scoop of corn. To me it doesn't even look like much. If I lived at home still I would probably eat double this. I say, "I was planning to why?"

"Well I guess if you want to be a cow for the rest of your life then you should." Then he starts mooing at me. He is honestly sitting there mooing at me like a cow. The worst part is he is doing in front of his friend. I put the mashed potatoes back and sit down to eat my chicken and corn.

I try to half listen to their conversation so if need be, I can answer anything politely if addressed. Luckily, they don't care to involve me in it too much. Trevor does though, ask about my face and before I can respond Chris makes up some story of me falling or something.

I try to tone the guys out while they work out and pretend to read my book. Occasionally, though they will talk in hushed tones. I can't make it out and I know it can't be anything good. Once they are done working out, they leave. This seems to be the new norm and I'm okay with it. This gives me the time every night to search for the notes.

The next night I get back to work. I was sort of looking forward to it, but once there I have no desire to dance. I know I have money hidden and I can give Chris some of it to make up for not dancing tonight. I was going to go change when Jason saw me and called me over to him.

"Hey welcome... Oh my god what happened to your face?" Oh no I wasn't planning to see anyone until I covered it all up.

"Oh, this, I um, I fell and well I tripped, and I guess being klutzy I hit my head pretty hard." I think I covered it up pretty good. He stands there with his mouth hanging open. I'm so embarrassed I mumble that I need to go get ready.

I hurry up and get changed and try to cover my face up the best I can. I can still see some of the bruising but it's darker downstairs than up here in the dressing room. I hope dark enough to avoid more questions or stares.

I head down and look around and it's unusually empty. I go take a seat at the bar and Jason comes over, so I order a shot. I never drink and drive, I learned quickly that the "shots" any guy buys for us are poured from a vodka bottle filled with water if we request vodka. It's the only way to make our drink quotas and not end up completely drunk. Some of the girls will take random other shots and on the sly spit them back in their beer bottles, I don't think I can do it. I don't feel talented enough, so I always ask for "vodka" and get the fake stuff.

"You want a real shot?" he asks.

"For a change, yes I do." I say then ask, "Why is it so slow tonight?"

"I'm not sure but hopefully for you girls it will pick up later."

"Yeah, or I'm screwed." I say before I realize what I say.

"Why, what's wrong?" he is staring at me and I feel myself turning red.

"Nothing, I need to make money that's all." I lie and drink my shot, so I can look away.

"So, what actually happened to your face?" he is being pushy.

"I told you I fell." I say.

He walks out from behind the bar and comes over to stand right by me. "That's bullshit, and you know it."

I say "No, really it's the truth, I'm very klutzy." then add "Oh, it's my turn on the stage." I quickly walk away wanting to be anywhere but there.

I get up on the stage and the music starts. I slowly take my robe off and I'm dancing to an empty room. I see Jason come over and sit in front of where I'm dancing. I go over and ask him "Do you need me again?"

"No, there's no one here so I figured you could dance for me." He reaches up and sticks some money in my garter belt. I don't pay much attention and just keep dancing. It's kind of weird and awkward, I'm still sore, but I needed to get out of my house. The song finally ends, so I put my robe back on and go back to the bar to sit.

Jason comes over and sits by me." So, he hits you, doesn't he?" he says.

"I don't know what you're talking about." I say.

As soon as I say that he swings his arm super-fast towards me and not thinking I flinched so bad I almost fall. I stare at him like a deer in headlights and he says, "Yeah, I thought so, you need to leave him."

I tear up, and I'm shaking. I finally say, "I can't. He told me if I try he will make my life hell. I have a daughter and he will take her from me."

"He can't take your daughter from you, he would have to prove you are a terrible mom and I doubt you are."

"He can prove I'm mentally unstable." Now I have tears falling.

He hands me a napkin and says, "How can he prove that?"

"I did something incredibly stupid and I put it on paper, and he has it. He told me if I leave him, he will take my daughter from me and I will never see her again."

"Have you looked for the paper?" Are you sure he even has it?" I smile a sad smile, I know he is only trying to help, but it makes me feel like one more person looks at me like I'm dumb.

Full out crying now, ugly face crying, I say, "Yes, I have looked I have spent months tearing through our apartment looking. I have looked in every single place I can think of. I looked in every closet, even the bathrooms. I have no idea where it could be."

Jason pours me another shot and says, "Here this will help." I take the shot and wipe my face.

"I'm sorry, I didn't mean to cry like that. I know I need to leave and until I find those, I'm stuck there." I put my face in my hands and add "This, here tonight, won't help. If it doesn't pick up and I don't make money, I'm fucked."

"What do you mean? Does he make you do this?" Jason asks.

"In a way, I guess I could say no, but then, well... you know." I say and point to my face.

"What an asshole. How much does he expect you to make tonight?"

"At least two hundred dollars, Last time I worked I only made ninety. Let's just say the bruises on my ribs are from that."

"That son of a bitch. What kind of a man hits a girl?" I can see the sincerity in his eyes.

"Not a man, a monster and that was from a kick while wearing steel toed work boots." I can see it registering in his face and he's shocked.

"Fuck that paper and fucking leave, let him try to take you to court, I bet he would lose." he says.

"I have a question; do you have kids?" He shakes his head no, "If you did," I say "You would know why I could never do that. I can't risk him taking her from me. It's not a bet I'm willing to place or lose on."

"There has to be a way for you to leave." I can see he is genuinely concerned. It feels good to finally talk to another person about it all.

"Once I find those papers, I won't even give it a second thought. I'll be out of there.

Jason reaches into his pocket and pulls some money out. He hands me two hundred dollars and says "Here take this, I don't need it. I make good money here and I work another job."

"Oh, my God no." I say, "There is no way I can take this, I can't even promise to pay you back, I appreciate it but no." I know I have my stash of money, but that is my save my daughter money and I can't use it.

"Yes, please there is no way I can go home and sleep and think he is doing that again."

"Okay, but I promise when it picks up again I will pay you back. I really appreciate it, I couldn't face all the accusations again tonight. I'm too tired and frankly, I don't have the energy to defend myself."

"What accusations?"

"He says mean things like I must be snorting coke and that's where the money goes. Oh, another good one is I must be fucking someone, and that's why I'm not making money."

"What a dirt bag. He is saying that stuff and creating a stereotype against dancers to make you feel he will use that against you."

"I never thought of it that way, because honestly I don't think he'd actually care if I was doing that. He cheats on me, I know he does. I honestly don't care to say anything because if it keeps him away from me, I'm better off."

"That's no way to live."

"I know, but for now it's easier to let it all go, and in return he leaves me alone."

"I hope you can find what you're looking for and soon."

"Me too and Jason, thank you. Thank you for the money and thank you for the talk."

"You're welcome, I could tell from the start you are different, you don't fit in here. I don't mean that in a bad way, you're just too classy for this."

"Thank you, you are very sweet. I don't think that's a fair statement to these other girls, they work hard here" I say.

"You're right, I didn't mean it like that I meant it as a compliment to you not a slam at them." He says back.

"Okay good, well I'm up." I smile, and I go dance my turn. The night stays slow, but we don't get any more time to talk.

The next few weeks when I work, if I don't at least have at least two hundred dollars to go home with Jason helps me out. I know I shouldn't take the money, but he insists. I have tried to pay him back finally with the money I have stashed away, but he won't take it. I know eventually I will have to insist, but for now, it keeps me safe.

Every time I come in he will ask if I found the notes, and every time I shake my head no. I keep hoping one day I can walk in and say I found them, I found them. He helps me think of new places to look, and he has his friend the D.J. even helping. They come up with some unusually funny places to look but I humor them every time.

Chapter 22

This weekend is my cousin's son's birthday party. I'm super excited to go, but my eye is still slightly black and blue and the white still has red in it. I know what I'm going to say, but I'm nervous to go and for anyone to guess the truth. To top it off, Chris is insisting on going. I know I'm going to be uncomfortable, but I can't tell him no.

I think at the last minute to say my sister is going and so are my parents. I know it's a risk that he may tell me I can't go, but I'm hoping he won't. My hope is he will stay home but tell me to go. He tells me there's no way he is going if that skank is going to be there. I tell him I'm sorry, I just found out and I'm so upset because I wanted him to go too. I do my best to convince him I'm so disappointed.

I decide the day of the party to seriously underdress and not do my hair or makeup. I don't want him having any reason to start a fight and tell me I can't go. I act mopey and pretend it's because he isn't going. He buys into it and finally says "Take Lizzie by yourself and try to have a good time. Lizzie should be around other kids a bit. I think she will have fun." My gamble thankfully paid off.

I agree with him and tell him I'll try, and I appreciate him understanding that I still should go. I told him I have no idea how long the party will be going on and he said that's okay, he is going to go out with Tim. I tell him something like, cool have fun I'll see you later. I try the best I can to not look overly happy as I head out the door.

As soon as I pull out of the driveway I feel such a flood of joy rush through my body. I turn the music up, roll the windows down a bit and sing at the top of my lungs. Lizzie is in her car seat happy, she loves music too. She is so cute trying to sing with me and dancing in her car seat. I feel the happiest I have felt in such a long time.

The party is so incredibly amazing. Little Gary is the most adorable little boy I've ever seen. It is so great seeing Angel, I can't stop smiling and laughing. A few people have made comments about my eye, but no one pushes the issue. My parents aren't there, which I am grateful for that. Had they been here, I may have told them everything.

I stay after everyone else leaves and Angel and I have a fantastic time talking and visiting. It has been such a long time since I've sat down and talked to another girl. I even bum a few cigarettes from her and knowing it would piss Chris off makes me enjoy them more than normal. We watch the kids play and I love seeing that. I hope somehow, someway they can grow up and be close to each other.

I finally get going, I know I can't push it and stay too late. Even though Chris says he won't be home, I can't trust that he won't be setting me up. I know If I come home too late I will be in trouble.

I make sure to buy some gum, so he won't know I was smoking. I can blame the smell on my clothes and hair on everyone else. I also decided to buy some cheap wine. I have no idea why, but it just seems like a sneaky fun thing to do.

When we get home, I am relieved to see Chris isn't home. I give Lizzie a bath and get her ready for bed. Once she falls asleep I open the wine and start a movie. I am about halfway through the movie when the phone starts ringing. I run to grab it, not wanting it to wake up Lizzie.

"Hello?" I ask.

"Hey Margo, it's Jason, can you talk?"

"Hi, yes I can he isn't home." I say as I pour myself some more wine.

"I wanted to check in with you and see how things are going." He is so nice.

"It's going okay, I still haven't found anything but I'm not giving up."

"Well I thought of some other places." he says, "Look in his books."

I laugh, "Chris doesn't have books, I don't even think he can read well. He has magazines, but I'm pretty sure he only looks at the pictures." I say still laughing.

"Oh, well maybe look in those? Also, my friend said look behind pictures, remove the cardboard and look behind it, and lastly for tonight, look in his Cd's. Take the covers out and see if it's tucked into them, maybe if there is a thick one it might be in that?"

"Oh, that's great." I say, "I appreciate your help thank you so much, I will let you know..." The door flings open and Chris is standing there, seeing at me on the phone, smiling and I see instantly, he's pissed.

"Who are you talking to and thanking?" I freeze. I have nothing to hide other than looking for those notes and getting help to do it. I know my friendship with Jason is only that, friends, but I somehow know I look guilty. I'm shocked more than anything, but I know Chris will read it as guilt.

Jason whispers, "Tell him work, I got you extra days."

"It's work, I was able to pick up some extra days and I was saying thank you."

He walks over and snatches the phone out of my hand. "Who is this?"

I hear Jason say "Jason, I was telling Margo I can add her to a few shifts if she wants them."

"Don't call here again." he says and slams the phone down. He looks at me and says "I knew it, you're a fucking slut. Is that the guy you have been fucking?"

"No, I swear to God, I swear on Lizzie." I cry.

He flings his hands across our counter clearing all the clean dishes off it and a bunch of them break on the floor by me.

"Chris, please listen to me. He was calling about work."

"Bullshit, I heard you laughing down the hall." Oh my god, I knew it, he has the wrong idea.

"No, I mean yes, I laughed but it was about one of the girls at work, she was being hit on by some gross old man. He was wasting time telling me about it while he was figuring out the days. That's it." I lie.

"And this?" He says picking up the wine bottle. "This was what? You just sitting at home getting drunk alone not flirting with some other guy on the phone?"

"My cousin gave me the wine, she said she wouldn't drink it and knew I liked wine, I had no idea he..." He whips the wine across the room breaking that too.

I'm barefoot, I need to somehow get out of the kitchen across the glass, the phone keeps ringing, but I don't even try to answer it. I finally think fuck it and walk across the broken glass hoping it doesn't cut me up too bad. I try to get away from him, but he grabs me and throws me halfway across the room.

I land hard on my butt, but on the couch, by the time I have my bearings, he is on me pinning me down in typical Chris fashion. Straddling me, sitting on top of my legs. I don't have the knife yet; the knife isn't in the couch. All I can think is I should have put the knife in the couch.

"If you even think I will let you leave, you are so wrong." He is putting all his weight on me, pinning me down. "You belong to me, I own you. Do you understand that? I bought you, I paid for your house, your clothes, your shoes, the toilet paper you wipe your ass with. I own you. The only way you leave is in a body bag, or when I'm done with you. Do you understand?"

I know he's telling the truth. There is no way, he ever lets me leave. He is going to force me to kill him before he kills me. I wish I had that damn knife stashed already. I know tonight, right here, right now, I would do it.

He switches gear and starts trying to kiss me. I cannot believe he would even think I would be okay with that. I try to turn my head away from him and he is pushing his body harder down on me. I keep turning my face side to side, and he grabs my face with both his hands. He is trying to keep my face still, but I won't stop. He finally pins my face to the side and I think he is giving up, but instead I feel him biting my cheek.

I'm in shock for a second but I can somehow buck him up hard enough to make him lose his grip on my cheek. It throws us off balance a little bit we fall back onto the couch, him on top of me laying now. I quickly pull my legs open and bend them to try to kick him with my heel in the back. I land one good kick, but he's quick, and strong. He grabs both my legs and has them pinned up by my head. I'm stuck. My ribs still hurt, and I can't get the strength I need to push him off without them hurting more. The pain is incredibly intense.

I realize quickly I have no leverage to get free. I have no way to fight him off and I know he knows it. All I can think now is that he is going to start hitting me or kicking me again. Right when I feel I can't breathe enough anymore, and I might die from the pressure he is putting on me, the door buzzer starts buzzing. I know he doesn't want to answer it. I don't think he would have either, but he doesn't have to. Within seconds of the buzzing there is fierce pounding on our door and I hear "You need to open your door right now, this is the police."

He lets go of me and says, "You better pray they don't take me from here because I will take Lizzie by morning."

I try to straighten myself up, before he opens the door and lets them in.

"We had a call about a domestic disturbance." The police officer says as he walks in. I see him looking around the room at the mess. I see him looking at me on the couch looking small. I see his body shift quickly to put himself between Chris and me. I hear him say "Take him out in the hall and handcuff him." I start to cry.

The officer comes over to me and I can't stop crying. He grabs a blanket and wraps it around me, but I can't stop shivering. I can't talk, I just cry.

"Ma'am we need to know what happened here." I can see he wants to help me. He has the kindest eyes I've ever seen, but I can't tell him.

"I can't help you if you don't tell me what happened." he is kneeling, so he doesn't tower over me. I'm sure it isn't comfortable, but he continues to stay by my side kneeling by me. "Do you need an ambulance?"

I shake my head no, I don't think I do and I don't want to draw attention to myself. I see him looking at my face. I know he can see the old bruises, and I think the bite marks. I can't make the words come out.

The other officer calls him over by the door just inside of it. I hear him say "According to him, she has been drinking and she got a little jealous he was out with friends."

The officer that was with me says "I don't buy it, she has old bruising on her face."

"But will she talk at all?" the other one says.

"I don't think so, she's either in shock or scared. It looks like she has a new bite mark on her cheek too."

"Jesus Christ, why do these women always protect these men." I can hear the frustration from the other officer.

"I don't know, they usually have some leverage, it's a power trip. Here's the thing, if she doesn't talk we have to leave him here." The kind eyes officer says.

"Damn it, okay," says the blunter officer. "I'll bring him back in, I hope we don't find her dead one day." and he leaves to go get Chris.

The officer with the kind eyes comes back over to me and says, "Listen honey, I know you are scared, but please, if you want him arrested you need to tell me what happened."

I finally look at him and say, "I can't, but thank you... my daughter, I don't know what I would do."

"I can take you to a woman's shelter, or if you have family you could call them. The shelters help you get back on your feet. They are very helpful, and they will make sure he can't find you."

I have come full circle, back to the offer of help through a woman's shelter. "I appreciate your kindness, but I can't." I say.

I see the sadness in his eyes. I know he is frustrated with me. He reaches in his pocket and pulls out a little card. "Please hide this, if you need help call this number anytime." I see the card is for a domestic abuse hotline. I get up and go quickly put it in the vase on the bookshelf.

I walk over to the officer and say, "Thank you so much for caring." I give him a hug and go back to the couch.

Seconds later Chris comes back in, and I see the officer quickly wipe tears from his eyes. He turns to Chris and says. "I can't prove what happened here tonight, but I know what happened. If we ever come back here on a domestic call again, you will be arrested." They start to head to the door and he turns around and says, "I'll be back some time tomorrow, if there is so much as a hair out of place on her, I'm arresting you. And ma'am who ever Jason is, he is a pretty good friend, I think he stopped something terrible from happening here tonight. I'll see you tomorrow." he stares at Chris for a few seconds, then they leave.

I am terrified Chris will say fuck it and hurt me. I sit there waiting for him to do something. Instead he walks into the kitchen and starts cleaning up the glass. A few minutes later he comes out and sits by me on the couch.

"I'm sorry that happened. I wish it didn't. I wish you wouldn't make me so mad and push my buttons. I wish I didn't love you this much. I know if I didn't love you like this, I wouldn't do this. Maybe I should try not to love you anymore.

He lays his head in my lap, and cries like a child. I have never hated someone the way I hate him. His tears do nothing for me. I have no feelings for this man other than hate. I sit still and let him cry, numb to it, it's too late for me to feel anything different.

He finally decides he has showed me enough remorse and says he is going to bed. I say okay, I want to shower I'll see him in the morning. He doesn't make a big deal out of it, so I wait a little bit. Sure, enough I hear him start to snore, I sneak into the hall and grab a blanket and go to the kitchen and grab the knife.

I head out to the couch, I stash my knife and lay down to sleep. As I'm lying there trying to fall asleep I pray. I pray that tomorrow is the day I find those letters. I pray tomorrow I can end this nightmare. I pray If not for me, please for my daughter. I finally fall asleep, dreaming of a better life.

True to his word, the officer with the kind eye shows up the next day to check on me. He says his name is officer Jenkins. I shake his hand and thank him. Chris is there, but he's rude and won't even look at the officer, he pretends he isn't there. I walk him out and to his car, after he made a point of saying he will pop in on me from time to time.

"I want to tell you I'm not dumb, I know what I need to do. I don't plan on staying much longer, I just have to situate myself." I say quietly.

He is silent for a couple seconds before saying, "I'm proud of you for knowing that, but promise not to wait too long. It will happen again, and I can't really pop in much. I could get in trouble for harassment if he presses the issue."

"I promise I will leave, I have to take care of a couple things to be sure my daughter will be okay."

"If you can or think of it, can you drop by once you leave or send me word somehow? I want you to know I care that you get out of this situation." He is such a sweet man and reminds me of my father, and I tell him that.

"If you were my daughter and this was happening I'm not sure I could stay true to my badge," then he adds with a shy smile, "off the record."

"My dad doesn't know, I'm afraid if he did he might end up in prison… off the record." I smile at him and we are at his car. "Thank you again so much." I say and give him a hug.

"Stay safe sweetheart." he says, and I watch him leave.

I walk back up to my apartment with a weird heavy feeling in my heart. I hope I didn't lie to him and I can one day get out. I have some places I would like to look for the notes, but Chris isn't leaving. I am starting to feel like they will never be found. I also have a fear, they aren't even in this apartment anymore.

Chris stays close by for the rest of the day. The next morning, he surprises me by waking me before he leaves, I thought for a minute he was going to be nice. Instead he says "I will never forgive you for what happened the other night. If they fire me, I'm taking Lizzie and using those notes, and I'm throwing you out on the street."

He walks out of the room, and he slams the door a few seconds later. I know I won't be able to fall back to sleep, so I get up and I figure I'll drink some coffee and start my search. I walk into the kitchen and automatically look at the phone, thinking I should call Jason and let I'm know I'm okay. I notice he took the phone cord, I don't know why I'm surprised, but I am.

I slowly with a sick feeling in my stomach, walk over to the door and try it, It's deadbolted. I look for my keys, and they are gone. I stand there, numb, wanting to cry, but not being able to. I know I should feel mad, or upset, something, but I feel absolutely nothing.

I finally make my cup of coffee and go in the living room to watch some morning news. I don't want to wake Lizzie, so I figure I'll put my search on hold and take some time to myself. I turn the T.V on, and nothing happens. I try a couple times then look behind it to see if it got unplugged and the cord is gone. He took the cord to the T.V too. Our T.V is incredibly old, and I never knew the cord could be completely removed, but it can, and he did.

What kind of person does that? Then I laugh, out loud, thinking what kind of person does any of the stuff he does. I don't know why this surprises me or makes me so mad. I'm madder about this than I am the phone cord. I feel it's one more way for him to try to control every aspect of my life.

I still don't want to wake Lizzie on accident, so I think about reading my book, when I look over and see all his magazines. I doubt he would, but what if he hid the notes in one of those? I know I need to be very careful looking. I can't let him catch me, or know I was looking at them, because I am not allowed to touch them.

I slowly take one out and shake it to see if anything falls out. I knew it wouldn't be that easy, but I can't help but feel disappointed when nothing falls. I tell myself not to be silly, and I move to the next one carefully putting back the last one. I do this tedious task, for an hour. I find nothing.

Lizzie starts to fuss, so I quickly look over the magazines good and it doesn't look like I ever touched them. I know once she is up, I might forget to check, and he could come home at any time to check on me.

I get Lizzie, and I am making her breakfast, when sure enough I hear him unlocking the door. I decide to say nothing about the T.V or the door. I don't want to give him the satisfaction of knowing I'm upset. I pretend to be busy with Lizzie and breakfast, while he gets another cup of coffee.

"I hope you weren't planning on going anywhere today." He says to me.

"No, I figure, I'll hang here today and get some cleaning done." I lie, not feeding into his bullshit.

"Good because you're not going anywhere for a long time." He is standing by me as if he is my father.

"Oh, is that so, dad?" I say bitchy "Am I grounded now again?" Fuck him and the fact he thinks he can tell me what to do.

"Little girl, don't fuck with me, I swear to god, cop or no cop I'll make you regret it." He slams his cup down in the sink and leaves, once again locking me in.

I give the middle finger to the door, I know he can't see it, but it makes me feel better. Lizzie is done eating, so I put her down and make myself some breakfast. I'm surprised he left me any coffee and food today.

After I eat, I want to start looking for the notes again. I set Lizzie up to color, knowing it will keep her busy awhile, coloring is her favorite thing to do. I head into the bedroom and want to look behind some of the picture frames we have in there. I need to be careful but figure I can tell him I bumped one over cleaning if need be.

I finish looking in my room, so I move back into the living room. I quickly look through those, and once again I come up short, I have tried just about everywhere I can think of to try. The last place I have left, is his Cd's. I really don't think he would hide them in there because he knows how much I love music, and I might borrow a Cd.

I start looking through the Cd cases, he has a lot of Cd's to look through. I luckily happen to hear the door downstairs close, and I quickly stash them back, when I hear the key in our lock. Not having the T.V on, I think just saved me from getting caught. I quickly run into the bathroom.

I can feel my heart beating out of my chest, I need to calm it. I quickly pull my pants down and sit down on the toilet. I take as many big calming breaths as I can before I hear "Margo?" and then the door flings open. I use this to my advantage.

"Oh, my gosh Chris, you scared me half to death." I place my hand on my heart very dramatically.

"What are you doing?" he says, and it takes everything in me not to be sarcastic.

"About to pee, why? What's wrong?" I try to act concerned.

"Nothing is wrong why is the door closed?" Is he seriously asking me this? I don't know what world he grew up in, but I want to say, closing the bathroom door is proper.

I say instead, "Oh, I guess habit, I close it all the time during the day I think."

"Well when you're done get out here and make me lunch, I don't have a lot of time." and he walks away leaving the door open. I can't believe the way he is acting, knowing the police could show up again. It really makes me realize how he doesn't respect them, nor fear any type of consequences for his actions.

I finish up in the bathroom, and head out to make him his lunch. I give him his sandwich, and some chips. He says, "You don't ever fucking listen, do you?" I have no idea what he is talking about, so I just look at him.

"Don't stand there with that stupid look on your face, you know I like my bread toasted." He only told me once to toast his bread, normally I never toast it. Today he is being a jerk, but I walk over and grab his sandwich to go make him a new one.

"You think I'm made of money? Are you planning to waste that?" he is raising his voice.

"No, I'm not, I'll eat it and make you one with toasted bread." I say.

"No, you can have soup, bring it back, I'll fucking eat it." he snaps at me. I'm so tired of this. My life feels so worthless and the energy it takes to not "instigate" anything with him is exhausting. I give him back the sandwich and go heat myself some ramen noodle soup for the millionth time.

Thankfully when he is finished eating, he doesn't stick around. He leaves his mess for me to clean and I don't care. I want him to hurry up and get out, so I can start my search again. He kisses Lizzie goodbye and locks us in once again.

I immediately go back to the Cd's and start my search. After a couple minutes, I sit back and think wait, what Cd, would I never in a million years barrow? So, I started looking at the titles, not opening the ones I would borrow.

I start with a few that I know I would never listen to, and they are empty. I am wondering if I should start back where I left off before, when I open a case for the B-52's. I hate their one song, "Love shack", so I avoid this band at all cost. Chris knows this because he purposely plays it to aggravate me. I see a piece of yellow legal paper sticking out from in the middle of where the CD cover is.

With shaking hands, I slowly slide it out of the case and open it. It's there. It falls out into my hands and without opening them, yet I know they are my notes. I do open them though to be sure both are together, and sure enough they are both in there. Both, I can't believe it, his and Lizzie's are together. I quickly put them away. I can't risk him knowing I know where they are. I put everything back how I found it.

I'm so happy I sit down on the couch with Lizzie in my arms and I hold her close and I cry. I whisper to her over and over "We will be okay, I promise, now we will be okay."

Now, it's all about waiting for the right opportunity to get rid of the notes and leave. I pray to god, he was too cocky to make copies. I don't think he would be smart enough to do that. I think he thinks he outwitted me and there was no reason to. He never once threw it in my face to worry about, so I feel It's safe to bet, he didn't.

I wait patiently all the next week for any chance to make a run for it. Chris has been diligent in locking me in, taking the phone cord, the extra phone, and even the TV cord. It's his way of showing total power over me, by not letting me watch TV. I honestly don't mind though, I'd rather read and play with Lizzie anyways.

He goes out every night and locks us in then too. He is sure to takes everything else with him when he goes. I have my emergency money ready to grab at a moment's notice and a laundry basket with clothes for Lizzie. I only pack one extra outfit for me in it, unfolded. I can't pack a lot or fold it, or he will notice it sitting there. Right now, he assumes it laundry I need to fold and put away.

Finally, over a week after finding the notes, I get my chance.

Chapter 23

The door buzzer buzzes Saturday morning and Chris looks out the window. He glares at me and says, "It's my boss, keep your mouth shut."

I have no idea what he thought I would say, but I wasn't going to broadcast he's an asshole.

His boss comes up to our apartment, which he has never done before. Chris invites him it and he says, "We have a problem down in the boiler room, I need all hands-on deck."

"Okay, I'll be there in a minute." Chris says I know by his response he's trying to get him to leave.

"I need you to come quickly now, I'm sorry if this ruins any weekend plans you have but I need you to hurry." His boss says.

Chris has no choice, but to put his work boots on and leave everything. There is no way he can grab the phone cord or the cordless phone and not explain why he is taking it.

I need info so acting concerned I say, "I hope it nothing serious?"

"Me too, I'm hoping to have it under control within the hour." His boss says.

Chris looks up at me glaring and to keep him from being suspicious I add "Be careful, boiler rooms make me nervous. It's not dangerous is it?"

"No ma'am, it shouldn't be dangerous, just heavy work." His boss says.

"Oh, good, that's a relief, I'll see you in a bit then." I say to Chris and start getting stuff out to make Lizzie her breakfast. I am praying my hands aren't shaking. I'm so close to getting my shot to get out of here.

Chris walks over to me and hugs me and leans in to look like he's being loving and kissing my cheek and says, "Do not leave this apartment, or I will deal with you when I get home and you won't like it."

"Chris, I have no money to do anything and even if I did, I have nowhere to go." I whisper back.

He pauses in front of the phone because his boss steps out into the hallway. He unplugs the part from the wall, but right when he's about to unplug the part from the receiver, his boss sticks his head back in. "Chris, we need to hurry so we aren't stuck here all day."

He has no choice but to leave it. I see he is pissed, but there's nothing he can do. I make sure to follow them to the door and hold it open while they are leaving. I position myself to stand in the open doorway, making it impossible for him to close the door. Now he can't deadbolt me in, not with his boss standing right there. If he tried it would be too obvious, so he's stuck having to leave without it.

I peek out the window, careful not to be seen if he were to look back. As soon as I see him out of the apartment building, I grab the phone and dial my mom. I pray to God this is a day she is home and not out running Brittany around. I stand by the window waiting for her to answer in case he comes back. "Hello?" I hear her say.

I don't know what it is about hearing your mother's voice when you are hurt or scared, but I instantly start crying.

"Hello?" she says again and I'm afraid she will hang up thinking it's a prank call.

"Mom..." I can't get anything else out.

"Margo? Is something wrong? Is Lizzie okay?"

"Mom..." I take a huge gulp of air and say, "Mom I need you to come and get me, I have no car seat, and I can't explain, but I need you to not ask questions and come right away. If dad is there can you bring him?" I say.

"Okay, Margo, is Lizzie okay? And dad isn't here should I have him come home from work?" she asks.

"No!" I yell I don't mean to yell, I just need her to hear me. "Mom I don't know how long he will be gone and if he comes back he won't let us leave." I cry.

"I'm on my way and don't worry about him, he doesn't scare me. I'll handle him." she says as she hangs up the phone.

It takes about thirty minutes to get from my parents' house to my apartment. I run to the Cd's realizing I should have checked for them first. With shaking hands, I find the Cd case I hurry and open it. I pull the cover out and they are there. I grab them, put the case back and run into my room and grab the money and laundry basket.

I shove the notes in my back pocket, I don't have time to do anything else. I know I won't make the mistake of throwing them away here. I look at the clock it's only been five minutes. I decide to hurry and feed Lizzie. I don't want her being hungry and upset when we leave.

I keep looking out the window, while Lizzie feeds herself some Cheerios. I am so afraid he will get here before my mom that I am shaking. My mom says she will handle him but what if she can't, what if I'm forced to stay here? I start pacing now in front of the big picture window. I know I will see her if she pulls in from this spot, and I don't want to waste a minute by missing her pull in. I know time is of the essence right now.

I leave the window to run in and grab a few more of Lizzie's outfits and realize I almost forgot her favorite blanket. I quickly add them to my heaping laundry basket. I know for myself, I'm going to have nothing. The thought makes me cry, but I try to think how much more I'm going to have once I leave. I tell myself it's all replaceable, I will have my freedom and no amount of clothes are worth more.

I see my mom pull in only twenty minutes later, she must have flown here. It almost feels like a dream, the kind where you are in slow motion trying to move fast, but you can't. I feel like it takes twenty more minutes for her to get out of her car and get to the door. I don't wait for her to press the buzzer, I buzz the door as soon as she gets to it.

I open the door and hand her Lizzie. "Mom, here hurry and put her in the car." I say.

She doesn't ask anything she just takes Lizzie from me to go put her in the car. I grab the diaper bag that I stuffed with diapers, lotions, baby wipes and baby shampoo. I throw it over my shoulder, grab the laundry basket, and take a quick look around at what was my prison. I walk to the door, and I walk out.

I hurry up throw my stuff in the car and get into the back seat by Lizzie. My mom backs out of her spot and we start to leave when I see him. I see him come walking around the bend, and he knows. He knows from my mom's face, I left him. I see it all register in his own face when I see the anger. I know he will go to get those notes, and I know what he will find. Nothing. He has nothing, he has no notes, no daughter, no me, no control. He has no more power over me.

I keep myself together long enough to ask my mom to please go to the police station. She doesn't say anything but nods her head, and a few minutes later she pulls in. "I won't be long but need to do something really fast."

I walk in, not sure if he is on shift today, but thinking I need to at least leave a note. I walk up to the little window, and there is a woman sitting behind a bulletproof glass window. She looks up and says, "Can I help you?"

"Um, yes, is Officer Jenkins by chance in today?" I ask.

"As a matter of fact, yes, he is. Let me go grab him for you." she says.

She disappears through a door and comes back a few minutes later. She smiles and says, "He will be out in a minute."

I take a seat and a few minutes later I hear the lady say, "She's out there I haven't done a pat down yet." then she says, "Miss?" I stand up, nervous because I have never been patted down. I have nothing to hide, it just makes me nervous.

As soon as I walk up to the window, he smiles and says, "She's okay."

He comes through the door and I run right up to him and hug him. "I did it, I left, I am free." I say crying. I don't know why, but this man touched me so deeply, by showing how much he cared for a stranger. "Thank you, truly thank you so much for all your compassion and not judging me. I wanted you to know I left. My mom is out in the car and taking me and my daughter home with her and my dad." I let go of him and see he has tears in his eyes.

"You're very welcome, and I'm so proud of you. I do what I do, to help people just like you." He gives me another hug, the steps back and says "It will be hard, he will try to get you back, he will beg. Don't do it. He will apologize and promise to change. He won't. No matter how lonely you feel or how hard it gets, don't go back. Remember your very worst night with him, and never forget it. Do not go back for one tiny happy memory he will dig up and remind you about, and guilt you over." I see something in his face, I dare to ask.

"Have you been where I am?" I find it hard to believe a strong man like him could have ever been in my situation, but I hear it can happen. This doesn't only happen to woman.

"Yes, but as a child. My father beat my mom to death. She went back. We left, and she went back on promises of change. They never change. I became a cop, because I never want men like my father getting away with what he did to my mom, my sister and myself."

His admission shakes me to the core. I knew that night, knew in my heart he was different than any other officer that could have shown up on my doorstep.

"We ran to a battered women's and children's shelter. They took great care of us and they were helping her get skills to get a job. She made the mistake of meeting with him and he charmed his way back into our lives, two weeks later, she was dead."

My heart breaks for him and his sister, I give him another hug and say "I won't go back. I never want to be like your mom and die like that. I won't do that to my daughter. I need to raise my daughter and let her see I can succeed and we are not victims anymore. It ends today. I never want my daughter to look at me and say, 'This has happened to me too'. I never want her to go through something like this because it's all she knows. I want to find the right man and show her the right example of how to be treated." I smile at him, and we say our goodbyes.

I go out to the car, to my mom. I am still crying, and I get in the car this time up front with her. I lean over and hug her, sobbing. She hugs me tight while I cry for a bit, then I finally wipe my tears and say, "Mom, I know you want to know what happened and I promise to tell you later. For now, though, can we go home?"

"Yes." she says, "It's time for you and Lizzie to come home." and she starts heading to my childhood home. My home once again.

Driving home, to my parents' house, I have a lot of time to think. When I walked out that door, there were a few things about how I saw life, that I know have changed forever. Without fail, the sun does come up. Even on my darkest days the sun came up. No man will ever make me feel life isn't worth living or influence my emotions about my life. I feel in my heart, God is real, and he heard the prayers I said. I will never let a man put his hands on me or control me again. I know without a doubt I need to talk to Brittany and fix things. Even as annoying as she is, she is my baby sister and she too was a powerless victim. Deep down I always knew in my heart she was right. She was hurt, and I failed her because I chose my daughter over her. I hope one day she can understand why and forgive me. I know because of that, I will keep my daughter safe no matter what it takes from this day forward. Lastly, and most importantly, I will never be a victim to domestic violence again. His power over me is gone.

I am free…

So, I thought…

Tracey Haynick is a domestic abuse survivor. As a survivor she wanted to write a story about the subject and shed some light on what goes on behind closed doors. After talking to many survivors, she found they all had the same thing in common; they didn't recognize the first of many initial signs. If just one person can be helped by this book to recognize the signs of abuse and get out, her book was a success to her...

Tracey Haynick is a daughter, a wife, a mother, a survivor.

One last thing…

If you enjoyed this book I would appreciate if you would post a review on Amazon. Your support will really make a difference and I read each review personally to help me make this book even better.

Thanks again for your support.

Made in the USA
Middletown, DE
21 October 2018